An excerpt from *Rancher Under the Mistletoe* by Joanne Rock

"I'm ready to head out."

Clay made no move to gather her supplies. But then neither did Hope. The awareness in the air had grown so dense, it seemed to hold her feet in place.

"Are you sure about that?" His low voice stroked along her senses.

"I'm only sure of one thing, actually."

"I'm listening," he assured her. Encouraging her. His eyes roamed over her in a way that felt like a touch.

"I. Um. What I'm sure of is that I couldn't have gotten through tonight without you. So, thank you."

She clung tight to the lie with both hands, knowing if they stood this close for much longer, she would lose all resolve and launch herself at him.

But after a tense three-heartbeat pause, Clayton nodded. Backed up a step. Exhaled hard.

"You would have been just fine on your own. But I'm glad I was here anyway."

An excerpt from *One Night with a Cowboy* by Tanya Michaels

"So you aren't a paying customer?"

"No," Mia answered. Didn't he believe her?

"I'm one of the hands on the drive. What do you think that makes us?" Jace mused. "Coworkers?"

"I'm not sure it makes us anything."

"Well." His grin was mischievous. "Not yet, anyway."

"Are you flirting with me?" It was an awkward question, but Mia believed in forthrightness, more than ever since Drew's betrayal.

"When I'm flirting, you won't have to ask. But if you'd rather I don't, now's a good time to say so."

Did she want him to flirt with her? Yes.

No, you're here as a professional. She opened her mouth to politely remind him of that, but instead heard herself say, "Too soon to tell. I reserve the right to say no later."

"Noted. But fair warning—I'll do my best to make you want to say yes."

USA TODAY BESTSELLING AUTHOR

JOANNE ROCK
&
TANYA MICHAELS

RANCHER UNDER THE MISTLETOE
&
ONE NIGHT WITH A COWBOY

HARLEQUIN®
DESIRE™

Recycling programs for this product may not exist in your area.

ISBN-13: 978-1-335-45788-2

Rancher Under the Mistletoe & One Night with a Cowboy

Copyright © 2023 by Harlequin Enterprises ULC

Rancher Under the Mistletoe
Copyright © 2023 by Joanne Rock

One Night with a Cowboy
Copyright © 2023 by Tanya Michna

For questions and comments about the quality of this book, please contact us at CustomerService@Harlequin.com.

Harlequin Enterprises ULC
22 Adelaide St. West, 41st Floor
Toronto, Ontario M5H 4E3, Canada
www.Harlequin.com

Printed in U.S.A.

CONTENTS

USA TODAY bestselling author **Joanne Rock** credits her decision to write romance to a book she picked up during a flight delay that engrossed her so thoroughly, she didn't mind at all when her flight was delayed two more times. Giving her readers the chance to escape into another world has motivated her to write over one hundred books for a variety of Harlequin series.

Books by Joanne Rock

Harlequin Desire

Return to Catamount

Rocky Mountain Rivals
One Colorado Night
A Colorado Claim

Kingsland Ranch

Rodeo Rebel
The Rancher's Plus-One
Alaskan Blackout
Rancher Under the Mistletoe

Visit the Author Profile page
at Harlequin.com for more titles.

You can also find Joanne Rock on Facebook,
along with other Harlequin Desire authors,
at Facebook.com/HarlequinDesireAuthors!

Dear Reader,

Trouble is brewing at Kingsland Ranch when the first person prodigal son Clayton Reynolds sees in Silent Spring is Hope Alvarez, the woman he walked out on three years ago. He doesn't plan to stick around Montana beyond the six weeks he's promised to his half brothers, but seeing how often his veterinarian ex-girlfriend is at the ranch makes him all the more determined to leave after Christmas.

As for Hope, she's got every reason to dislike the holidays, and Clayton's presence in Silent Spring only makes the season tougher for her. Until the rugged wildlife biologist shows up at some of her calls to help with difficult animal cases. How can she not admire a man who knows how to rehome a wolf pack? Soon, she's remembering all the reasons they were so good together.

It's an unforgettable December for Hope and Clayton. Except neither of them can forget that Christmas is just around the corner and Clay's time in Montana is quickly coming to an end. Will they find their way back to each other before the wilds of Alaska call him home? Join me for a romance to remember and visit me at joannerock.com to learn more about all my series for Harlequin Desire!

Happy reading,

Joanne Rock

RANCHER UNDER THE MISTLETOE

Joanne Rock

For my youngest son, Maxim, an independent thinker with serious grit and fortitude.

Thank you for inspiring me to achieve my goals.

One

Hope Alvarez scrubbed her hands in the utility sink at the Kingsland Ranch foaling barn, very ready to leave this workday behind her.

Turning the water on full blast, she rinsed off the grime as she calculated the pieces of equipment she still needed to collect from the birthing stall so she could pack up quickly. As a relatively new veterinarian, Hope would have normally enjoyed the sense of victory gained from guiding a first-time foaling mare through a high-risk delivery. The colt had given them all a scare when he'd first struggled to breathe, but he'd rallied quickly without even needing to be intubated.

Professionally speaking, it had been a good day. A great day, even.

Personally, however? Spending time in the place where she'd both fallen in love *and* gotten her heart broken sucked ass. It didn't matter that the object of her one-time affections no longer lived at Kingsland Ranch and hadn't since he'd left town without a word to her. Didn't matter that Clayton Reynolds wanted to break up with her so much that he had moved off the grid to a remote part of Alaska to avoid her.

How was that for taking ghosting to a new level?

Just being here, in the same barn where she'd once waited out a thunderstorm with Clay by slow dancing between the stalls, was wrecking her head.

"Hope." A male voice rumbled from behind, alerting her that the owner of her four-legged patients had followed her. "You can't imagine how much your work here today has meant to us."

Steeling herself for facing Levi Kingsley, Clayton's half brother who didn't resemble him physically yet shared so many of his mannerisms it was uncanny, Hope shut off the water before turning around. Levi had inherited the darker coloring of his Creole mother while Clayton had the same light brown hair and leaf-green eyes as their father, Duke Kingsley. Yet both Levi and Clay—born just months apart to different mothers—shared a way of dominating a room just by being in it. The focused gaze and squared-shoulder body language that quietly communicated they were in charge without ever being aggressive.

"I'm glad I could be here," she assured Levi while

she dried off, uncomfortable with extra praise for performing tasks that were clearly in her job description. "I'll stop by tomorrow to check on the new dam and her baby. Until then, my assistant, Cassandra, will be on-site keeping an eye on things."

Because even though Hope felt sure the new colt would be fine, she'd made arrangements for her assistant to remain at Kingsland for the next few hours to monitor the foal's feeding. Hope refused to linger in this barn, where that slow dance during a rainstorm had led to an unforgettable encounter in the hayloft.

Now, she moved to retrieve her workbag so she could pack up her equipment. Levi followed her as she located her flashlight and twine near the tack room, the place where Clayton had twirled her under his strong arm during their long-ago dance.

"You saved the life of an extremely valuable mare—" Levi began.

"I would have treated a backyard pet just as carefully," Hope pointed out, mindful that every animal she worked on deserved 100 percent of her focus and skill, not just the million-dollar breeding horses.

"Of course," Levi acknowledged diplomatically as he handed her a box of exam gloves just outside the birthing stall. "But considering that your help was worth a small fortune to us today, my brother and I would like to pay you something more in line with that value. How about a stake in the colt? It's sure to be a champion considering the bloodlines."

"That's kind of you, Levi, but I definitely don't need any more than what my office will bill you." Even though she was desperate to leave—the pillar near the birthing stall was the same pillar Clay had pushed her up against to kiss her breathless—Hope paused to pack the collected veterinary tools back into her bag in a way that would allow her to easily find them all again. Organization did not come naturally to her, but she forced herself to follow careful protocols in the work realm.

She was about to reenter the foaling area to retrieve the last of her gear when Gavin Kingsley emerged from it, holding her scissors and a roll of tail wrap.

Gavin—like Clayton—was a half brother to Levi and Quinton Kingsley. But unlike Clay, he'd been gifted with the Kingsley name since his mother had been briefly married to their father. Gavin was a former rodeo star turned horse breeder, and he'd recently married Hope's high school friend Lauryn. Absurdly, Hope's other close pal from childhood, Kendra Davies, had just moved in with Levi Kingsley. So there was little escape from Kingsley men in Hope's life, even when she wasn't actively paying house calls to Kingsland Ranch.

At least neither of Hope's friends knew about her relationship with Clay, or how he'd trounced her heart. Lauryn had been completely embroiled in her horse rescue that summer, while Kendra had been working at a public relations agency in Denver at the time. Kendra might have suspected there was more to her relationship with Clay, but she hadn't pushed.

Gavin frowned at her now, nudging the brim of his Stetson higher with his thumb. "Hope, there must be a way you could put some additional capital to use at the new veterinary clinic—"

She was already shaking her head as she took the last of her things and zipped up her canvas bag.

"Honestly, I'm doing fine," she assured them, uncomfortable with accepting a monetary gift. Doubly uncomfortable taking funds from Clay's family. What if he found out somehow? She'd heard the Kingsley men had been searching for him in Alaska. Apparently they wanted to share their inheritance with him since their father had left both Gavin and Clay out of his will. Hope had been bracing herself for Clayton's potential reappearance. And she had to admit the tension was taking its toll.

For now, she redirected his brother's largesse. "I'm hosting a holiday gala before Christmas as a fundraiser for a new large animal clinic. The best way to help me is by attending."

And bringing a slew of their well-to-do friends. As long as those guests didn't include Clayton Reynolds, she'd be fine. Or so she hoped. The holidays were a rough time of year for her ever since her mother's death on Christmas Eve nine years before. Hope's decision to host a fundraiser this year had been an effort to distract herself during that time, but it had the distressing side effect of forcing her to think about seasonal themes, music and decor weeks before she'd normally be faced with all that relentless good.

Ignoring the hurt of old wounds, she shoved the last of her supplies into her bag and zipped up the compartments while the Kingsley men frowned at her. Levi's phone buzzed at the same time one of the ranch hands entered the barn and called to Gavin. Sensing her chance for a quick exit, Hope backed up a few steps, heading for the side door closest to where she'd parked her truck. She grabbed her coat off a hook near the door but didn't bother to put it on. After the close confines of the stall, she would welcome the cool air.

"Cass will call me if there are any problems with the colt," she assured Levi and Gavin. "And I'll check in tomorrow either way." Lifting her hand in a wave, Hope shouldered open the sliding door.

Stepping out into the chilly November morning, she raked her fingers through her dark hair and pulled free the elastic tie that had kept the long strands out of the way while she'd coaxed the mare through delivery. She couldn't wait for a hot shower and breakfast after the long hours with the first-time dam. Gavin's call that the mare was going into labor had come shortly after midnight. While overseeing a foal's birth was easily within the wheelhouse of the Kingsland staffers—Gavin included—this horse had some high-risk factors that had warranted her presence.

Opening one of the custom aluminum side panels

she'd had installed on her pickup, Hope stuffed her duffel into its proper compartment and locked the box again. She walked around to the driver's side of her truck and slipped her arms into the sleeves of the oilcloth coat she wore for her work. Now that she'd had a chance to cool off, the dampness in the air was quickly seeping into her clothes and making her shiver. She had just pulled the zipper all the way up when she heard the rumble of tires over gravel nearby.

Turning, she spotted a gray SUV that didn't look like a work vehicle. Too sporty, for one thing, with chrome add-ons that served no practical purpose. Too clean for another. Even Hope's truck was covered in dirt and dust, a by-product of driving into fields to tend animals in their grazing pastures or on locations where they'd been injured.

Those thoughts had just circled through her mind and started to reformulate into a logical conclusion that the driver might be an outsider when Hope caught a clear view of the person through the windshield.

The sight sucked the air from her lungs.

Stunned and breathless, she reached a hand out for something to steady her. Her fingers clenched the grab bar, locking around the cold metal in case her knees gave way. Because the face behind the wheel of that shiny SUV was one she hadn't laid eyes on in three years.

Not since he'd vanished from her life without a freaking word.

Clayton Reynolds had come home.

Caught without an easy escape, Hope knew she had no choice but to brazen out this meeting. She'd have to ignore the old anger about his disappearing act. Swallow the resentment about how he'd treated her and pretend the wounds he'd inflicted didn't still flare up from time to time. Because obviously a man as cold and callous as Clayton Reynolds didn't deserve to see how he'd crushed her.

Digging her heels in, she braced herself to face him. Get this meeting over with. Shove it behind her.

And then put Clayton in her rearview mirror for good.

Fate had a twisted sense of humor.

Clayton could only shake his head at the timing of his arrival in Silent Spring, Montana, that couldn't have been worse. Because what were the odds that he'd not only come back to Kingsland Ranch to face the family who'd disowned him three years ago, but that he'd also have to confront the woman who'd delivered her own knife to his back?

Maybe Fate wasn't just twisted. Today, she seemed downright sadistic.

He slowed his rented SUV as he neared Kingsland Ranch's biggest barn, recognizing he couldn't just drive past Hope Alvarez standing beside her pickup as a few snow flurries began to fall. They'd made eye contact. She knew that Clay had noticed her. To continue on his way to the Kingsland Ranch main

house after he'd spotted her would be pure coward-
ice. But damn, he'd not been prepared for the sen-
sory overload of seeing her again.

Fat white snowflakes swirled around her pretty
face and shiny black hair, her bulky lavender-colored
jacket not doing a damned thing to hide her generous curves. She was petite, but her powerhouse
presence made him forget that until he had her underneath him...

Something that wouldn't happen again. No matter
that she looked like an R-rated Snow White with her
pink cheeks and rosebud lips pursed into a frown.
Just looking at her brought back a visceral reminder
of her citrus and cinnamon scent.

Steering the luxury SUV into the space beside a
sleek burgundy-colored work truck with her name
stenciled in black on the door, Clayton told himself
to keep things light. Say hello and move on. He was
only in town through Christmas because he'd told
Quinton Kingsley he would at least listen to what
his half brothers had to say. After that, Clay would
return to Alaska where he belonged. His work in
wildlife biology suited his solitary nature well. Even
when he'd been living off-grid, he'd been able to develop a research project on the impact of the shifting tundra ecology on North Slope species. Work he
would continue in the New Year.

For now, however, he shut off the engine on the
SUV and stepped out of the vehicle. Even before he
turned to face her, he could feel the weight of Hope

Alvarez's dark-eyed stare. Briefly, the old hungers stirred, his body reacting to her nearness the way it always had. Then he tamped down the heat with a reminder of how things had ended between them after a ten-week affair.

"Hello, Hope." The gravelly pitch of his voice was low and intimate.

Not nearly as careless as he would have preferred. But then, he'd never been a man with a talent for game playing and artifice. He locked gazes with her over the hood of the SUV as he walked around it.

Moving closer.

"Clayton." She folded her arms across and assessed him coolly.

So different from his other, happier memories of her, when she'd had her head thrown back, gasping his name while he sent her over the edge. How many times had those visions kept him warm on a cold night in the Arctic tundra?

"I'm here to meet with my brothers." He'd never been a man of many words, yet it seemed important to stress the point that he'd returned for family reasons—not to bother her. He recalled all too well that she hadn't ever wanted to see him again. She'd been very clear about that. "I'm going to be working with them through Christmas."

"Levi and Gavin are both in the foaling shed." Hope pursed her lips, as if weighing how much to say. Or maybe she simply regretted having to speak to him any more than necessary. "One of their mares had a rough delivery last night."

"Is she okay now?" His gaze flicked toward the freshly painted gray barn. Oversize pine wreaths hung on the sliding doors, the bows of their red ribbons fluttering lightly in the breeze.

He recalled when a back corner of the structure had been overhauled for pregnant mares, keeping them out of the general population as they got closer to foaling. Hell, he'd helped install the extra padding in the birthing stall with his own two hands. Clay had always been more comfortable actively involved on the ranch than hanging out with his father, who preferred to bark orders into the phone from his home office. Clay's inclinations had continued in his wildlife work, where he took the jobs that involved tracking wolf packs or tagging a struggling reindeer herd over the administrative tasks. Although since moving to the North Slope and going off-grid, he was more apt to study Arctic foxes and polar bears.

"The dam is doing well. The colt needed some intervention at first but now he seems—" Her attention shifted to a spot behind his shoulder. "Uh-oh."

"What is it?" Turning, Clayton glimpsed Levi and Gavin Kingsley striding side by side down the short incline from the barn. He hadn't seen Levi in three years since he'd left Silent Spring. Clay hadn't spent time with Gavin in far longer than that. The last he knew, Gavin had been a rodeo star who resented their father as much as Clay always had. There'd been a time when he and Gavin had been close, bonding over their shared status as the "lesser" sons Duke Kingsley distanced himself from. Duke had never had much use for either of them, finally omitting them from his will altogether.

Clayton had made peace with that fact since he hadn't much use for his father either. Then Quinton Kingsley had doggedly tracked Clay to his home in Galbraith Lake on Alaska's North Slope. After a very rough start to that conversation when he'd learned that Quinton had fathered a baby with Clay's stepsister, McKenna, Clay had listened to Quinton's request that the four brothers divide the Kingsley legacy evenly between them. Well, evenly aside from the fact that Quinton also wanted to abdicate his shares in Kingsland Ranch to Clay. Clayton hadn't agreed to any of it, but he had promised to spend some time with his half siblings to work out a compromise.

But only until the end of the year.

"I should have already gotten underway," Hope muttered, reaching for the door handle on her pickup.

"Wait a minute." Clayton palmed the door reflexively, unwilling to watch her leave when he'd purposely stopped here to get this first meeting behind them. "Since we're both going to be in Silent Spring for the next few weeks, maybe we should figure out how we can…" Avoid each other? He hated to be flat-out rude. But he also guessed she didn't want to run into him any more than necessary. "…minimize chance encounters."

She sucked in a breath before huffing it out again in a white cloud between them. She gave him a tight smile.

"Trust me, I'll make every effort to stay out of your way—"

The rest of her clipped words were drowned out by a hearty greeting from Levi. "Clayton. Welcome home, brother."

Handshakes that turned into slightly awkward, back-slapping hugs were exchanged with his siblings, with Hope watching them from her wary dark eyes. Clayton felt plenty of misgivings himself, unsure where he really stood with his half brothers. He hoped the next five weeks would give him the lay of the land. And he sure as hell wished that he would be able to do his fact gathering about the Kingsleys without the distraction of having Hope around.

Levi's gaze hopped from the rented SUV to Clay's wrinkled travel clothes. "We didn't know when to expect you or we would have prepped a better welcome." Then, Levi's focus returned to Hope. "Although we were pretty busy this morning with a foaling mare. Hope saved a colt that wasn't breathing. It was touch and go for a while."

"Just doing my job." Hope managed a half smile, but Clayton could see that she was antsy to be underway.

Interestingly, she seemed even more uncomfortable with the praise from his brother than she'd been at seeing Clay again. He remembered that about her.

She'd never been one to seek a spotlight, preferring to work in the background. They'd shared that in common, and he'd been drawn to her quiet work ethic.

Before Hope could bolt, Gavin thumbed the brim of his Stetson higher and turned toward her. "Hope, as soon as you walked out of the barn, Levi thought of the perfect way for us to thank you for rescuing Jewel's colt."

She shook her head, dark hair swishing against the jacket she wore over a long-sleeved black tee. "That's really not necessary—"

Levi cut in, clearly committed to rewarding the savior of the ranch's newest quarter horse. "Kingsland Ranch will donation match whatever funds you raise at the Christmas gala for your new veterinarian offices."

Christmas gala? Clayton wouldn't have pictured Hope—always so focused on her efforts in the field and the health of her animal patients—organizing a glitzy fundraiser. But then again, her commitment to the causes she cared about might be enough to drive her to great lengths. Even putting together the kind of event she wouldn't normally attend herself.

"Donation match?" There was interest in her voice. She tugged the hem of her jacket, settling the quilted down fabric more firmly around her curvy hips as the snow flurries picked up speed.

Gavin nodded. "Kingsland will contribute the same amount you raise, dollar for dollar, to support the new large animal clinic. Advertising that ahead of time should help bring in some more attendees." His gaze flicked over to Clayton. "Assuming, of course, Clay agrees with us. He's an equal stakeholder now."

Technically, Clay hadn't signed the paperwork the family's attorney had drawn up for him. But he wasn't prepared to get into those details now. He felt the weight of Hope's attention on him. Unwelcome, but still so damned arousing.

"A large animal clinic would be a welcome asset in Silent Spring." He had no intention of crossing Hope while he was in town, so he wasn't about to gainsay his brothers in this. "And Kingsland would directly benefit since it's the biggest ranch in the state."

Hope peered at him through the falling snow for a beat after he finished speaking. Weighing his words? But then she nodded once, as if she'd made a decision as she turned toward his brothers once more.

"In that case, I accept. Thank you—um, all—for the generous gift." Reaching for the door handle on her truck, she pasted a smile on her face—one that Clay recognized was purely for show and not even a close facsimile of her real grin. "And now, I really do need to get going and check on some other patients."

"Of course." Gavin rushed to play the gentleman and take the door from her, a gesture that—in spite of everything that had gone wrong between Clay and Hope—might have made Clay bristle if he'd thought Gavin was hitting on her. But he'd heard that Gavin had tied the knot with the town sheriff's daughter a few weeks ago. Even so, the more space between Hope and Gavin, the better for Clay's peace of mind. "Let us know if there's anything you need from us in advance for the fundraiser. Clayton would be a good contact for that since he's our resident animal expert."

"I don't think—" Hope began.

"That's not really true," Clayton said at the same time.

Both of them had rushed to respond so quickly that Gavin and Levi exchanged a look.

"That is," Clay continued, glancing at Hope framed in the partially open truck door, "I'm no more of an expert than either of you when it comes to domestic animals."

"Good one." Gavin rolled his eyes as he clapped Clay on the shoulder. "Don't let him fool you, Hope. Clayton played a key role in developing a large animal research station on the Seward Peninsula."

Guessing that arguing further would only raise eyebrows, Clay ground his teeth to refrain from reminding Gavin the needs of wild reindeer and caribou were a far cry from cattle and horses.

"I'd forgotten about that," Hope mused aloud, her tone still sounding reluctant. "Maybe we can talk more when I check on Jewel and the new colt tomorrow."

Surprised at the suggestion they spend time together, Clay's gaze flew to hers. Something in her eyes related the opposite of her words, however. As if she was giving him fair warning of her presence on the ranch so he could steer clear.

And damn it, Clayton couldn't deny the rush of disappointment he had no business feeling. Hadn't he wanted to keep his distance from the woman who'd chosen to end things with him by letter instead of telling him to his face?

Recommitting to the plan to avoid Hope Alvarez, Clayton nodded and gave a fake smile of his own. "Sounds good. We can talk then."

He was vaguely aware of the goodbyes said all around after that. He heard Hope's engine fire to life before she pulled away from Kingsland Ranch. And somehow, he managed to agree to a meal with his half brothers so they could discuss possible next steps with the legacy Duke Kingsley had left behind.

But through it all, Clayton could only think about the extra warmth in his veins after seeing Hope again. He shouldn't have a damned thing to do with the woman after the way she'd treated him. Yet the simmering need inside him told him very differently.

Three years hadn't made a dent in his attraction to Hope. And the five weeks stretching out in front of him may as well have been five years when he thought about how tough it would be to resist the lure of a woman who drew him like no other.

Two

As she parked her truck outside of the big gray barn at Kingsland Ranch the next day, Hope took deep, calming breaths, reminding herself she had a mission to get her through the visit. A solid three-point plan she'd come up with over a rushed breakfast following a sleepless, frustrating night, with dreams full of Clay. She gathered her vet bag and hopped down from the pickup, grateful the snow hadn't stuck from the day before. Hopefully she still had a few weeks where she could work in the field without the added obstacle of snowpack. But not even the good weather could distract her from the irritating knowledge that her brain could still indulge hot fantasies of a man who'd ended things between them without a word.

How could she have spent half the night having sexy dreams, and the other half berating herself for thinking about a guy who had no business taking up mental real estate? So in addition to being cranky and sleep-deprived as she tugged open one of the barn's sliding double doors, Hope feared her chances of running into Clayton here again were excellent. At least she had the three-point plan to keep her on track.

Get in and get out.

The quicker the better.

Minimize interaction with Clayton Reynolds.

Somewhat soothed by the reminder of the strategy, Hope breathed in the scent of fresh hay and horse as she stepped from the cold outside and into the relative dimness of the barn compared to the bright Montana sunshine outside. She didn't anticipate any problems with Jewel or the new colt this morning. Her assistant had messaged her shortly before dawn to give her an update on the pair, and she'd said they were both doing well.

Still, Hope preferred to see both animals with her own eyes after the eventful delivery.

The stall door was partially open, giving her a split second of warning that someone was already in the space partitioned off from the rest of the barn. Through the sliver of daylight visible from inside the enclosure, she could see a pair of square shoulders testing the seams of a blue-and-gray-checked flannel shirt. The owner of those shoulders leaned down to stroke a colt's soft brown coat with large, gentle hands.

Hope didn't need to see the face attached to that broad back. Her rapidly beating heart and quickened breathing told her exactly who was inside the stall.

Perhaps she made a sound of some kind, because the next instant, Clayton was swiveling around to face the door. Green eyes finding hers immediately, vibrant even in the dim lighting. Her hands clenched into fists inside her coat pocket.

"Hope." His deep voice smoked through her, warming her insides when it should do just the opposite.

Get in and get out.

Clinging to the three-point plan like a talisman, Hope pushed the stall door open the rest of the way so she could step inside. She steeled herself against the draw of his charisma that threatened to rekindle midnight fantasies.

"How is Jewel?" she asked brusquely, moving into position alongside Clayton as if he were any other concerned ranch hand and not someone who used to set her blood on fire.

Used to, she reminded herself.

"Dam and foal are both behaving normally from what I can see." Straightening where he stood, Clay backed up a step to give her more room. "Your assistant said the colt fed shortly before she left, and when I entered the stall a few minutes ago, the foal was at the udder again."

"You spoke with Cassandra?" Hope stroked Jewel's neck, settling the mare before examining her. Some dams could be overprotective of a new foal, and Hope had learned at an early age not to piss off a new mother of any species.

She was surprised to learn that Clayton had talked to Hope's assistant. He must have been in the barn late into the night, or else he'd risen before dawn.

"I did." Something about his clipped answer made her glance away from the mare to gauge his expression. He rubbed the back of his neck, his face troubled. "I had no luck sleeping last night so I checked in with all of the animals. Cassandra was the only human I ran into at three in the morning."

An unwelcome flash of jealousy—one she definitely should not be feeling—had her struggling to remember the three-point plan. The quicker the better, right? But she wouldn't rush an exam on an animal that deserved her undivided attention.

"Travel days can disrupt a sleep schedule," she observed quietly as she ran her hands along Jewel's sides, assessing.

There was nothing unusual to note. Yesterday she'd run a test on the new mother's colostrum and the results had been good there too. Now, she moved on to examining her colt, the long-legged wobbler who'd given everyone such a scare the day before when he'd failed to breathe on his own.

Clay shuffled over another step, changing places with her so that he could distract the mare while Hope checked the colt's heart rate. Clay was good like that, and she remembered that he'd been well versed in animal behavior long before he'd gone for a wildlife biology degree.

Unbidden, old memories surfaced. Back to the days before they'd had an affair. Clayton used to visit Kingsland Ranch for a couple of weeks every summer. But she hadn't taken notice of him until the year she was eighteen and she'd entered a couple of the sheep she'd raised in contests at the county fair. One of her rams had taken top honors that year, and Clay had been a judge. With a nine-year age difference between them, she understood why he hadn't paid much attention to her beyond complimenting her work with the ram. But she'd developed a major crush, and she hadn't been surprised to learn of his interest in wildlife biology given his obvious emotional intelligence with animals.

"Not sure the insomnia is travel related," Clay said dryly as he stroked Jewel's face, keeping the dam turned toward him, his easy way with animals as appealing as ever. "It may have more to do with Levi twisting my arm into taking on ranch manager duties while I'm in town."

"Seriously?" Hope couldn't hide her surprise, even though additional conversation with Clay went against every part of the three-point plan. "Why would he do that when he knows you're only here temporarily? Wouldn't it require weeks or months just to learn the job?"

If he took offense at her interest in having him leave Silent Spring again, he didn't show it.

"I formally trained for the ranch manager position three years ago," he reminded her, the flatness of his voice hinting that there was zero fondness for that time in his life.

The same time they'd been having a relationship.

Her stomach clenched uneasily as she stood, her exam complete.

"I'd forgotten about that." She'd been so over the moon about being with Clayton after secretly crushing on him for years that she hadn't been as dialed in to what was going on in the rest of his world. A symptom of her youth, perhaps, or believing herself to be in love for the first time. "You never had the chance to do the job you'd invested in."

Because of his haste to end things with her?

Or because of his argument with Duke Kingsley, which she'd heard about secondhand but had never had a direct account of since Clay left town right afterward?

"That's correct." Clay shifted away from the animals to lean a shoulder into one wall of the wide stall. "My half brothers seem to think I'll change my mind about accepting a portion of the Kingsland legacy if I spend more time here."

The whole town knew the way the Kingsley patriarch had slighted two of his four sons in his will. Duke hadn't been a beloved figure in Silent Spring to begin with. Then his stock had gone down still more when it became public knowledge that he'd dumped coal ash illegally on one of his properties, committing a serious environmental crime.

But three of Duke's sons had banded together to clean up the toxic damage—both the literal and the social kind. Now it seemed they wished to bring Duke's fourth son back into the fold.

"Levi and Gavin want you to stay?" she mused aloud, trying not to panic at the prospect of Clay moving back into her hometown.

He gave a mirthless laugh. "Yes, but you don't need to worry about that happening. I've already told them being ranch manager here won't change my mind."

If she were another kind of woman—daring and bold like her friend Kendra, for instance—maybe she would have seized the conversational opening to ask him why he'd left the first time. To challenge him for answers about their shared past. But she wasn't Kendra. Hope's emotions ran deep, and she only shared them with people she trusted. If she opened the lid on her feelings now to question him, Clay was sure to see how deeply his leaving had cut her. Her pride was having none of that.

"And yet you accepted the position?" Realizing she was clutching her stethoscope like a lifeline, she willed her fingers to let go. Her hands to fall at her sides.

Clay shrugged, lifting one big shoulder in a careless gesture that didn't match an expression that seemed more uncertain. Torn, even.

"I'd like to think I did it to give Levi a break. He's

newly in love, and I figured taking some of the ranch manager duties off his shoulders would give him more free time to help Kendra settle into the main house. And besides—" he pushed away from the stall doorframe and took a step closer to her "—how else am I going to fill my time for the next five weeks?"

Her heart thumped harder as she imagined ways to spend that time. Impossible ways, obviously. But that didn't stop the slideshow of possibilities from scrolling across her brain until her blood warmed and her cheeks heated.

"That's very selfless of you," she said finally, tugging off the stethoscope and returning it to her duffel just for something to do to distract herself. She didn't care to think about Clayton's good side any more than she wanted to contemplate his proximity.

Shouldering the strap of her bag, she moved toward the door to leave before realizing Clay stood in her path. And, it seemed, had no intention of stepping aside.

This close to him, she feared he would sense her fluster, the old attraction simmering no matter how much she wanted to stuff it down. The silence felt heavy between them, the only sound a soft snuffle from the colt and the swish of Jewel's tail.

"We should talk about the fundraiser before you leave," he said finally, his green eyes cool and calm. Businesslike even.

She wanted to match his aloofness, but her throat was so dry from the sudden onslaught of desire that she had to swallow twice before she could even answer him.

"There's no need. I appreciate you supporting your brothers' offer to match the donations I raise at the event, but I am handling the event on my own." This close to him, even in the subdued lighting of the barn, she could see the subtle streaks of blue in his green eyes. The shadow along his jaw where he hadn't yet shaved today.

Now, he huffed out a laugh, his eyes twinkling with amusement. "How well I know that there isn't anything Hope Alvarez can't do on her own. That being said, you are aware that Levi and Gavin hoped we could play a bigger role in your gala, if only to assure you raise the funds you need for the new clinic."

Frowning, she ignored his slight about her independence to focus on the last bit since she didn't want to upset her relationship with Levi and Gavin. "You misunderstand. They only offered the funds as a way to thank me for saving the colt."

Jewel snorted, tossing her head and stamping a hoof as her foal tried to feed.

Clayton nodded toward the door in a silent demand they speak outside the stall. No doubt he'd read Jewel's cues the same way she had—the new mother preferred some quiet time to feed her foal. Or maybe the mare sensed the tension between them and felt protective of her newborn. Following Clay's lead, she exited the stall, and he pulled the door shut behind them, latching it into place to secure the animals.

The rest of the barn was still quiet, the structure utilized mostly for grain storage. The cattle were housed in a different facility, far from the main house. She continued to follow Clay farther from the stall, her gaze roaming more freely over him since his back was turned. She'd forgotten the impact of his physical presence. The breadth of him. The strength. Even now, his muscles were apparent every time he moved, the fabric stretching tighter over his thighs as he strode. He paused by a stack of hay bales near the double doors that led outside, where he turned to face her.

Had he caught her staring?

She flushed uncomfortably and straightened the handle of her bag, smoothing the nylon and tightening a buckle while she waited for him to speak.

"You should know that Levi Kingsley, of all people, is always looking out for Kingsland's best interests." Clay folded his arms in a way that showed off the worn leather strap of a watch she remembered his mother had given him. She recalled how much he admired the woman who'd raised him, a woman who hadn't let Duke Kingsley's abandonment dim her sunny outlook on life.

Clay had a decidedly less positive view of his father. And from his words about Levi, she had to wonder if that skepticism extended to his half brothers. In the past, she'd thought they'd all gotten along. But then again, Clay had never remained in Silent

Spring for more than a few weeks at a time, except for that last visit three years ago.

"I disagree. I think Levi is extraordinarily generous. He personally toured environmental fairs all over the country to show support for those causes in the wake of your father's coal ash dumping debacle." She'd followed the goodwill publicity tour each day, partly because Kendra had organized the whole thing in her job as a crisis PR manager, but also because the fate of Kingsland Ranch mattered to the health of her veterinary practice.

Clay raised an eyebrow as he absently toed one of the hay bales into better alignment with the rest of the stack. "But he was in hot water with the environmental groups in the first place, so his efforts were very much designed to bolster the ranch." Perhaps he heard her swift intake of breath because he rushed to add, "I'm not saying my brother isn't a good guy. But as a savvy CEO, he's usually working more than one angle. In this case, he's definitely trying to speed the growth of your practice so that it benefits the Kingsland herds."

Hearing him spell it out so bluntly, Hope could see his point. Of course that was Levi's goal. He needed that clinic as much—perhaps more—as Hope did. But she felt more than a little chagrined to realize how easily Clay had read the dynamics of the situation that she'd been too close to recognize. Worse? Clay had known Hope was oblivious about the bigger issue at stake because even after all this time, he still knew her well.

The idea chafed.

Swallowing her pride because of her professional connection to Kingsland, she tried to set aside the knot of conflicting feelings for the man to figure out her next move.

"So what do you suggest I do with that information now that I understand what's at stake here?" She considered herself a better vet than a businessperson, but as the owner of a small practice, she had no choice but to be both things. "How do you suggest I give Kingsland a 'bigger role' in the Christmas gala?"

As it was, the event was already draining her. She worked long days at her new practice. Now, she spent most evenings engaged in event-planning tasks related to the gala. Having to sort through donors' personal agendas on top of it all was more than she could handle. Especially when the Christmas-themed everything had brought more emotional weight— and old grief—than she'd counted on. Even now, here inside the barn, small green wreaths hung on the cast-iron light fixtures that flanked the double doors. Holiday touches were everywhere.

"That question was half of what kept me awake for so long last night," he admitted as he scraped a hand roughly over his jaw.

"Seriously? It doesn't need to be a concern of yours." She couldn't imagine why her small business would keep him awake, but it rankled that she'd been having sex dreams about him while he'd been concerned over the financials of a new vet clinic in Silent Spring. "You said yourself you're not going to accept a share of your father's legacy."

He leveled another look at her. A different look that hinted at more than just impatience with her lack of understanding. His slow, thorough perusal of her awakened her body everywhere his eyes grazed.

"Just because I'm not accepting a physical share doesn't mean that I want to throw my brothers' offering in their faces," he said slowly, his words so disconnected with the hot chemistry sizzling between them that for a moment she was too confused to follow. "I'm here to make peace with them. To settle things after the abrupt way I left town three years ago."

The reminder of his disappearance helped her to refocus. Hadn't she told herself she would not linger around him today for this very reason? She needed to cut ties with their past.

"But what does that have to do with you being awake half the night?" She didn't mean to be dense. But the twitchy way Clay made her feel definitely distracted her.

"I was wrestling with the fact that, in order to make my brothers happy, I'd need to do something that you're not going to like." He rose from the hay bale to stand close to her. Not too close. But near enough to make her heart pound harder.

"Such as?"

"Such as work with you on the Christmas gala

to make it a success, the way Gavin suggested yesterday."

Hope blinked, waiting for his words to make sense.

But they didn't. Because she remembered how Clay had dodged doing anything of the kind when Gavin had mentioned Clay's experience in bringing an animal research station to the Seward Peninsula the day before. Hadn't Clay been as reluctant to work with her as she'd been with him?

Shaking her head, she wanted to brush past him and walk out the barn door. "You don't want that any more than I do."

"On the contrary, I want what's best for Kingsland Ranch." His low voice was calibrated to the same tone and pitch he would use with a nervous mare. "And I want to do a good job here for the next five weeks so I can leave Silent Spring knowing that I did my best to make peace with my half brothers."

She wanted to fling his soothing tone and his reasonable words back in his face. To ask him if he'd been concerned with making peace when he'd left her three years ago with no explanation. No call.

But damn it, she would not lose her cool now. Especially not when there was an excellent chance she'd be seeing way too much of him in the weeks ahead. Blowing out a frustrated breath, she forced her mouth into something resembling a smile. Or possibly she just bared her teeth at him.

"Fine. I'd be more than happy to let you take over licking the stamps on the invitations," she said in the most even tone she could manage when her skin prickled with irritation. Frustration. Something bordering on anger. "I usually work on the gala after I finish my rounds. How about we meet tomorrow at Red Barn Roasters?"

She referenced a popular local coffee shop, hoping the public setting would keep her thoughts focused and her emotions at bay. No matter how she felt about this man, she wouldn't allow it to interfere with maintaining a good relationship with an important client. Clayton wouldn't be in town for long, but Kingsland Ranch was a fixture of this community. They weren't going anywhere.

"That sounds good to me," he agreed easily, as if the conversation was a walk in the park for him. As if seeing her didn't affect him one way or another. "Why don't you text me when you're heading over and I'll meet you there?"

She took a deep breath, reminding herself that he couldn't be quite as impartial as he seemed. Hadn't he admitted earlier that the idea of seeing her more had been part of the reason he hadn't slept the night before? Better that than for her to continue believing she'd meant nothing to him. That their parting hadn't cost him in some small way.

"Fine." She refrained from asking if he still had her cell phone number. For months she'd wondered if he'd blocked her number since her texts had gone unanswered. The memory brought with it a fresh wave of pain that was her cue to get going. She wouldn't allow him to see any sign of wounds he'd left behind when he'd ghosted her. "I'll see you then."

Brushing past him, Hope shoved open the oversize barn door before he could help her with it. Then, charging to her truck, she saved her string of epithets until she was alone behind the wheel, the driver's side door firmly closed behind her.

What had she just agreed to?

Remembering point three of her morning's strategy made her laugh bitterly.

Minimize interaction with Clayton Reynolds.

The idea mocked her now. How often would she have to come in contact with him over the next five weeks now that he was going to work with her on the Christmas gala?

Turning over the truck engine, Hope told herself it was time for a new strategy.

Three

When Hope still hadn't messaged him by six o'clock the next afternoon, Clayton drove to Levi's bar, the Stockyard, to pass the time. Hope had dominated Clay's thoughts all day long, distracting him when he should have been reviewing data on optimizing the ranch's food stores. Now that he'd given up work for the afternoon, he only had to wait for her to text him.

He was curious about the business that Levi had bought after creating his own liquor brand, Gargoyle Kings. But the other reason he found himself here was more self-serving. Because Clay found it tough to spend much time around the main house at Kingsland Ranch where Levi kept his office.

The same office where Clay had once—briefly—

worked with his father when he'd made the effort to become a part of the Kingsley family.

Shaking off the memories of that ill-fated summer and the argument that had severed his relationship with his old man for good, Clayton pulled open the pub's heavy glass door. Warm air scented with chicken wings greeted him along with the twang of a steel guitar. The place was already busy with a happy hour crowd. Groups congregated near the mahogany bar and at the scattered high-top tables, but even more people thronged around the pool table, dartboards and country music duo singing in the back of the room. Two tall Christmas trees flanked a jukebox along the far wall, the boughs strung with white lights and silver bells. A big ball of mistletoe hung over the small dance floor and saddle-back seats gave the place throwback vibes. The woman singing switched from a Loretta Lynn standard to a smoky lo-fi tune with ease, the musical range never overpowering the clamor of happy hour conversations.

"Back here, brother," a familiar male voice called through the din.

Turning from where he'd been observing a fierce darts competition, Clayton spied Levi at the far end of the bar, close to a cash register and a door that most likely led to the kitchen. Dressed in a gray suit and black tee, Levi somehow appeared at home here amid the more casual crowd even as he sat by himself on one of the saddle barstools.

Edging through the crowd, Clay made his way

over to his brother. He checked his phone once, even though he knew his ringer was on from the last time he'd checked. Did Hope work into the evening every day? Stuffing the phone into the back pocket of his jeans, he wondered if she would try to find reasons not to meet him. He'd recognized that she was not pleased at his suggestion they work together on her Christmas gala. But he'd been honest about his reason for pushing the agenda. He could be an asset to her as she worked to set up the new clinic. And that clinic would benefit Kingsland.

Offering his brothers that much would be a way to ease some of the guilt he was bound to feel when he left Montana at the end of the year.

"Nice place you have here." Clay greeted his brother with a clap on the back while Levi waved over a server. "It helps me understand why you don't mind handing over some of the ranching responsibilities."

"You deserve the ranch manager position, pure and simple," Levi argued as a young guy dressed in a white polo with the Stockyard logo appeared in front of them, pen and paper in hand. "What can we get you to drink?"

"Club soda for me," Clayton told the server before turning back to his brother. "I'm waiting to hear from Hope Alvarez so we can discuss the animal clinic to-night."

"I appreciate you taking that on." Levi gestured to the saddle beside his, newly vacant as a party of two moved toward an open table. "Have a seat and tell me what you think of the Stockyard as a bar owner yourself."

Clayton shook his head at the mention of the Cyclone Shack, a rough and tumble place in Dutch Harbor, Alaska. "My name might still be on the deed of the Cyclone Shack, but McKenna's been running the show ever since she took it over eighteen months ago."

His stepsister had arrived in Alaska after a world of problems of her own back then. It had been Clay's pleasure to give her a place to land, and she'd been a natural running the business. Her presence in his life, taking over the tavern and a small tour business he'd been running, had made it easy for him to pursue other things once the news had reached him that Duke Kingsley had died. In the back of his mind, Clay had known his brothers would come looking for him. That the past would have to be dealt with.

But he'd put it off for as long as possible, going off-grid to do research work in Galbraith Lake for the past year. He hadn't been ready to face his father's final words to him. Still wasn't. And that was undoubtedly the other reason he'd decided to work with Hope on her animal clinic fundraiser. The woman had the power to direct all his focus toward her.

"I'm anxious to meet McKenna." Levi finished his drink—a glass of ice water, if Clayton had to guess—and gave Clay a level gaze. "I never imagined that Quinton might go to Alaska and not return, but he's a different man since he met your stepsister."

Clayton's fingers curled into a fist beneath the

bar as he recalled the last time he'd met Levi's full-blooded brother face-to-face.

"I would hope he's transformed into someone who will be a good father," he muttered darkly, his protective feelings for McKenna still strong no matter that she'd fallen in love with Quint.

"I'm certain he will be," Levi assured him while the guitarist slid into a country version of a holiday tune. "Once he and McKenna arrive in town for the holidays, we can finally begin hammering out the logistics of Dad's estate."

Clay's gut clenched hard at the thought of more uncomfortable conversations. He swiveled on his seat to watch the dance floor lights change to red and green, a disco ball effect swirling on the couples who continued two-stepping.

At the same time, his cell phone vibrated in his pocket. When he found himself rushing to answer, he told himself it was only because the interruption saved him from talking about the inheritance he could not accept. Not that he'd been looking forward to seeing Hope all day long.

As her digits filled the screen and a rush of desire heated his blood, however, Clayton knew he was lying to himself. Excusing himself to take her call, he stood and hit the button to answer. Even as he did, he wondered if she would try to back out of the meeting. He'd been expecting a text, after all, not a call.

"Hello, Hope." Head down to focus fully on the conversation, Clay walked toward the back corner of the building where someone had propped open a rear door a couple of inches to allow a cooling breeze into the crowded establishment. "How's your day shaping up?"

"Not well, unfortunately." She spoke with clipped efficiency. "I won't be able to keep our appointment tonight."

Something in her tone put him immediately on alert.

"What's wrong?" His shoulders went tense, concern for her overriding everything else. He understood firsthand the potential danger of working with large animals. "Are you all right?"

"*I'm* fine, but Sarge McMasters's wife just phoned to say there was a wolf attack at their farm. One of the calves needs medical attention." Hope might sound calm to someone who didn't know her well, but Clay could tell she was upset.

And while he felt bad for the McMasterses, he was also relieved that Hope was okay. In fact, the degree of his relief—like a physical weight off his chest—seemed out of proportion for a woman he hadn't seen in years.

But as quickly as that thought came to him, he shuffled it aside to focus on what she'd shared. No doubt the McMasterses were beside themselves. The well-respected older couple still ran a small dairy operation the last time Clay had been in Silent Spring. Sarge, a local veteran, had been a 4-H leader for decades.

"Did she say if the wolf is still active?" Turning from the back door, Clay signaled to Levi that he needed to leave, pointing toward the exit. He respected that Hope was a capable woman, but Clay hated to think about her working on an injured animal with a predator lurking nearby in the dark. "Was this the work of just one wolf or a pack?"

"I don't have a lot of details because Letitia was pretty broken up." In the background of the call, Clay could hear road noise along with Hope's GPS offering directions. "Apparently Sarge's dog, Buster, interrupted the attack. Sarge heard him barking and discovered the Texas heeler standing guard over the calf at the edge of their northern grazing pasture. Anyway, I'm almost there now, so I'll have to reschedule our meeting."

Clayton was already in the parking lot of the Stockyard. The sun had set while he'd been indoors, and the temperature had dropped a few degrees. Flurries stirred in the crisp air. He hit the unlock button on his key fob and climbed into the rented SUV, trying to visualize the closest road to the McMasterses' northern pasture.

"Of course. I'll meet you on-site and see if Sarge needs a hand securing the herd." Clay had plenty of experience with wolf packs. Moreover, he'd always liked Sarge, a guy quick to take in all outsiders and loners who showed up at his 4-H meetings. There'd been plenty of summers when Sarge had made Clay feel welcome in Silent Spring, even when

Duke Kingsley had been less than enthused to see his son.

"You'd really do that?" Hope sounded surprised, making him wonder exactly how poorly his character rated in her mind.

Dismissing the irritation as he secured his phone to the holder on the dashboard, Clay started the vehicle. "I'm already on my way. You said the north pasture?"

Now he understood why she was using her GPS. Because no matter that Hope knew Silent Spring like the back of her hand having grown up here, the property lines of farms and ranches weren't necessarily well marked.

"That's right. Look for a dirt turnoff just past Vaughn Road on the left. And—" She hesitated before adding in a rush, "Thanks, Clay."

Some of his earlier irritation faded at the relief in her voice. Perhaps she'd been more nervous than she'd let on about this incident.

Which made it all the more urgent to be by her side.

"No problem. I'll see you shortly." He shifted into a higher gear as he hit the main road.

Eager to lend a hand to a neighbor, of course. Not flying like a bat out of hell to protect a woman he had no business wanting.

The calf's cries were pitiful as Hope finished her initial exam of the animal. The injuries were extensive. The owners were emotional. And quite frankly, the work environment sucked, as it was past sunset in a cold field with the flurries turning to a steady snow.

Hope told herself to get a grip though, reminding herself this was what she'd trained for, circumstances be damned. With a ring of concerned gazes on her while she worked, she used her flashlight to check the baby heifer's eyes and to locate all the lacerations left by claws and teeth. Sarge and his wife, Letitia, hovered closer and closer, the couple flanked by their young ranch hand and Sarge's dog, Buster, who'd interrupted the wolf's strike.

In Hope's arms, the little calf twisted and bucked against her as she worked, but she didn't want to administer sedation until she was sure she didn't need to move the poor creature to a sterile operating room.

She did her best to calm the animal—Petal—but she was still frightened from the trauma of the wolf attack. Having a throng of worried humans fretting audibly around her wasn't helping. Something Clay would surely recognize and address as soon as he arrived. She held tight to that thought as she continued to assess the damage, applying pressure to the worst of Petal's injuries.

"Letitia, would you grab the light kit out of my truck bed?" Hope understood how much animal owners wanted to help, to do whatever they could to save lives that were precious to them. Providing Mrs. McMasters with a concrete task would not only give the woman something else to focus on, it would benefit Petal to have a more subdued environment.

"And Sarge, why don't you and TJ roll out the blanket on top of my bag next to Petal? You can help me move her on it so I can care for her."

While the others fulfilled their tasks, Hope managed to irrigate a couple of the worst wounds, assuring herself that the calf could be treated in the field. She'd handled bites before, but never anything this severe. And it didn't help that, as she swiped away a patch of drying blood from around the calf's neck, she spotted a jaunty Christmas jingle bell on a red rope collar in place of a traditional cowbell.

For an instant, the holiday memento squeezed the breath from her, reminding her of a long-ago Christmas when she'd spent the holiday in the deepest grief she'd ever known. But as she breathed past that thought, Hope was left with the more important reminder that Petal's jingle bell marked the animal as a beloved pet as much as she was a means of making a living. Hope couldn't afford to fail her or the people who loved her.

Just as Letitia returned with the battery-operated lamp, a set of headlights wheeled over them briefly, the hum of an engine a welcome sound in addition to the calf's plaintive wails.

Clayton.

Relief rushed through her along with a warm tangle of other things Hope didn't care to analyze. All she knew in that moment was that she was grateful for his presence no matter their past history.

"I hope you don't mind that I told Clayton Reynolds he could stop by," Hope announced to her patient's owner as she eased Petal sideways toward the blanket. TJ and Sarge edged the fabric beneath the calf. "He's had a lot of experience with wolves and might have some ideas for how to better protect the herd."

"I expect a hunting party will clean up this problem quickly enough," Letitia retorted as she switched on the field lamp, flooding light over Petal's wounded shoulder and limbs. "We'll flush them out first thing tomorrow morning."

Hope knew better than to argue and supply information about local wolf preserves since it wasn't her land or her livestock. Thankfully, Clayton chose that moment to step into the circle around the injured animal.

"Hello, Sarge." Clay greeted his former 4-H leader in a subdued voice, but his low-key manner didn't diminish the warm embrace he received from both of the McMasterses.

Hope took full advantage of their momentary distraction to finish cleaning the calf and administer a local anesthetic. In her peripheral vision, she noted the way Clay lured the group farther from where she worked. His low voice was barely audible as he spoke to the McMasterses, his tone somehow perfectly calibrated to settle nerves and offer guidance. Having him here, quietly helping her, lured a memory of their shared past from the recesses of her mind while she selected the debridement devices she'd require once Petal's sedative kicked in. The summer she and Clayton had dated, she'd been between clinical rotations in her next-to-last year of veterinarian school. She'd been in Silent Spring on an externship, assisting at a small animal clinic. On a free weekend, Clayton had taken her hiking in the nearby Madison Range. They'd come across an older man tussling with a golden eagle who had a fishing hook embedded in its beak. Although the guy was attempting to help the bird, he had only managed to infuriate the predator.

Then, just like now, Clay had somehow relieved the stranger of his duty so that Clay could wrap the eagle in a more comfortable hold with his flannel shirt, hooding the creature's eyes to settle it.

With Clay's help managing the bird, Hope had been able to remove the fishing hook with a multi-use tool she'd carried in her pocket. Together they'd freed the creature without further injury to it, or to either of them.

A happy memory of Clay she hadn't thought about in a long time.

Now, with those old visions scrolling through her mind, she'd managed to work methodically, cleaning off more of Petal's wounds and applying temporary pressure dressings to the worst of them. By the time Clay stepped closer to her, she was ready to begin debriding the deepest laceration as soon as her watch told her Petal's sedative had reached full potency.

"Need anything from me?" he asked softly, keeping a respectful distance from her patient who now lay on her side, her head propped to keep her airway clear.

Hope glanced over at him, his handsome face cast in stark shadows from the bright lamp spotlighting the calf. That he chose to be here at all, in a Montana grazing pasture in the dark when most people were sitting down to an evening meal, said a lot about his character. But the thing about Clay was he truly did *choose* it. Hope knew for a fact he hadn't shown up for her sake since he'd made it clear long ago that he was moving on without her. Clay was here tonight, weathering the drop in temperature and increasing snowfall, because he had an innate care for animals, the same way she did.

When more old memories threatened to rob her of her focus, she cleared her throat and returned her attention to the important task at hand.

"Keeping the McMasterses occupied is great, actually." She made an adjustment to the field lamp and then sanitized her hands again. "This next phase requires concentration and a steady hand, so I can't have interruptions, no matter how well-meaning."

"Got it." He nodded once, his green gaze appearing to take in the gravity of the situation as he looked over the bovine patient. "I'll set some relocation traps with Sarge, and Letitia will head back to the main barn to prepare a recovery stall for the calf."

"An excellent plan." Hope peered into the darkness just beyond the ring of light where she'd set up her triage station. "You feel confident the wolves won't come back?"

A shiver ran through her at the idea. She wasn't the wildlife expert that Clay was, and she didn't know much about wolf behavior. But she didn't relish the idea of fending off a pack if they decided to return for the meal they hadn't finished the first go-round.

"The best way to prevent it from coming back is for us to find him first," he explained grimly. Then he gestured to the young ranch hand standing near Hope's truck. "TJ will stay here with you to keep you and Petal safe. The kid seems like he can keep a clear head in a crisis, but if you need me, have him shoot a text and I can be right back here."

"That all sounds good," she agreed quickly as her watch beeped with an alert that it was time to begin the next phase of her work. "Thanks, Clay."

"Of course." Straightening to stand, Clay met her gaze in the lamplight, his look steady as he told her, "Petal's lucky to be in your hands."

His confidence warmed her.

As a vet, she placed her faith in years of training and let that guide her, day in and day out. She had confidence of her own. But she couldn't deny the way Clay's certainty bolstered her as she faced a difficult set of procedures on a beloved creature under less than ideal conditions.

Tonight, she allowed herself to soak up someone's faith in her, letting Clay's words ground her and settle her nerves as she began the work of saving a life.

Four

By the time Clayton finished checking the fence around the McMasterses' pasture and setting some modified leghold traps in case the wolves returned, Hope had finished caring for Petal. Apparently she and TJ had been able to relocate the wounded calf to the isolated barn stall Letitia had set up for the patient. While Clay had been on the phone with a friend from the local fish and wildlife agency earlier, Hope had texted a photo of the calf sleeping peacefully with the help of a sedative. There'd been a blanket folded under the animal's head for a pillow, and a second blanket tucked around her body while the freshly bandaged limbs peeked out from the covering.

The image made him smile now as he tramped through the fresh snowfall toward the barn. Sarge had returned to the house an hour before him, so Clay made this walk alone. The simple white farmhouse he'd passed a couple of minutes before had been dark within, but as Clay approached the barn he could see a single lamp shining. Hope's truck was parked next to the structure, the cargo bed pulled close to the doors and the tailgate still down from when they'd moved the calf.

Tucking his phone in the front pocket of his canvas jacket, Clay edged around the pickup to push open the barn door slider. Inside, the lack of wind and snow warmed him even though the structure probably wasn't heated. Most Montana ranches relied on insulators like hay and bedding to keep animals warm in the cold temperatures. As long as they had shelter, that was usually enough unless the animals were very young or old.

As Clay walked toward a partition in the back near the only overhead lamp still illuminated, he could hear a feminine, musical hum. Not wishing to catch Hope by surprise in an unguarded moment, he called to her from the middle of the barn.

"Am I allowed to check on the patient?"

The humming halted. A scuffling noise sounded from within the closed stall.

"Clay, I didn't expect you." Hope's voice sounded before the low stall door opened. "Come on in."

The section must have been used for goats or

sheep in the past, the fencing the right size for those animals. But no doubt it would keep a recovering calf safe too.

As he stepped inside the enclosure with walls on three sides and the low partition on the other, Clay noted the portable space heater plugged in near where Hope must have been sitting. There was a blanket spread over fresh hay with her phone and a granola bar wrapper in the middle of it.

Petal lay in the same position she'd been sleeping in when Hope had snapped the picture, the baby heifer snuffling lightly in her sleep.

"How are you doing?" he asked, his gaze shifting to Hope. Her hair had been coiled around a pencil, the dark mass sliding slightly off-center as she walked toward the space heater to turn it down. She'd changed out of the green twill coveralls and rubber boots she'd been wearing before. Now, in the warmer barn, she wore a clean set of blue scrubs and a long gray sweater, although a stethoscope still hung around her neck. Her discarded coat lay by her duffel in a corner of the stall. "You must be beat."

"I'm doing fine, actually." A half smile pulled at her lips as she peered up at him. "It's amazing how thoroughly a patient's good outcome can beat back fatigue."

"You think she'll recover then? A couple of those wounds looked really deep." He knew how serious a leg wound could be for an animal who would probably weigh eight hundred pounds in less than a year's time.

"Infection is always a possibility," she admitted, casting a glance over her shoulder at the black-and-white calf. "But I'm pleased with how the wounds have responded to debridement. I did everything in my power to make sure she heals. Now I can only monitor her and cross my fingers that her immune system takes care of the rest."

Her selfless commitment to her patient spoke volumes about her. He admired her intense work ethic as much as the soft touch she had with her patients, as well as their owners. But who kept an eye on her? Who would prevent her from working herself to exhaustion in a county in desperate need of skilled vets around its most remote areas?

"Including sleeping in the barn?" He shook his head, concerned for her since she'd already had a long day even before Petal's injury. "What happened to 'Doctor, heal thyself'?"

"I won't stay much longer. I just wanted to check her vitals one more time to make sure she comes out of the sedative without any problems." Glancing down at her digital watch, she seemed to note the time but didn't make a move to check Petal's vital signs yet. "How about you? Any luck with the wolf?"

Keen dark eyes locked on him as she lowered herself to sit on a nearby hay bale and pointed out another one in an invitation for him to do the same. He didn't have a chance of refusing, the old camaraderie they shared as warm and vibrant as ever. He'd always enjoyed talking to her. Even when he'd first become aware of her that summer he'd voted her ram best in show along with two other judges, when she'd been just eighteen years old and not even on his radar, Clay had recognized the thoughtful care she used with her animals. She'd been extraordinarily educated about breeding and raising sheep, her knowledge outstripping competition that had been involved in the business for decades.

In the ensuing summers that their paths had crossed—often at 4-H events where he'd helped Sarge with various projects, or at the local rodeo when he'd support Gavin's bull riding—Clay had watched her transform from precocious teen to formidable vet student. Still, he'd kept his distance since he'd been well aware of their age difference. Right up until the summer she'd propositioned him at a town picnic and bonfire following a fishing derby. A night he'd never forget.

"We saw signs of a den, but no sightings," Clay confessed, grateful for the distraction, something else to think of other than the memory of being with her that fateful summer. "Not that I really expected to. The wolf population has come back strong because they're highly adaptable, cagey creatures."

Hope frowned as she repositioned the pencil holding her hair in place. "I was really hoping you could trap and relocate it before Letitia has the chance to take out the whole pack. She was distraught tonight."

Clay tried not to notice the way her raised arms caused her breasts to strain against the blue cotton top, her curves every bit as mouthwatering as he remembered.

"I'll try again at sunrise," he assured her, a plan already in place for collaring the pack and rehoming them. "I set a few modified leghold traps—"

"Meaning they won't injure what they catch?" Her dark eyebrows knit together in obvious concern.

No doubt she'd witnessed wounds from incidental catches. Domestic dogs or deer could be seriously injured that way. Ranch life was more nuanced than most people realized, and thoughtful land management required commitment and compassion. While he wasn't staying in Montana, Clay still felt a connection to the land where he'd spent so many summers. He wanted to make good decisions for Kingsland in the weeks that he was responsible for the acreage.

"That's the idea." Plenty of poachers weren't concerned with the suffering of their intended prey or accidental catches. But skilled huntsmen took more care. "I'll check the traps first thing in the morning. If we don't have anything, I can find them from a helicopter and use tranquilizer darts to relocate them."

"Really? You could do that?" She glanced at her watch again, clearly keeping track of Petal's next check.

Outside, a gust of wind howled around the barn, rattling a loose piece of sheet metal somewhere on the roof. Clay could feel remnants of the cold air seep through the building, stirring the sweet scent of fresh hay.

"I've tagged Arctic wolves that way before." He'd ended up using his degree in far different ways than he'd originally planned when he believed he would one day step into a role at Kingsland Ranch. And he didn't regret his decision to move for a moment. He loved his Alaskan home, felt a peace there. "And I already messaged a buddy of mine in the game office here who said he could get the tranquilizer equipment to go with me tomorrow since it's a two-person operation."

She reached behind her to retrieve her black anorak and slid her arms into the sleeves. Her lips quirked. "Arctic wolves? I'll bet life is a lot different for you in the tundra."

For a moment, he had the urge to share stories of his work up there with her. She, of all people, would understand the beauty of it as well as the unique challenges the environment presented for his kind of research. Plus, it was an easy time for confidences, the quiet of the barn and the exhaustion of the evening kicking in. Hope peered at him expectantly, her dark eyes stirring all the old hungers for her.

But then he recalled that he would have never retreated that far north if not for the whole debacle with his family and—truth be told—with her. With an effort, he quashed the impulse to share more.

"It is very different," he settled for saying, dragging his gaze away from her. When his attention fell on the calf, he noticed the big brown eyes were slowly blinking. "Looks like someone's waking up."

Immediately, Hope was on her feet, hurrying over to the patient to stroke the animal's face and neck. To soothe her and examine her at the same time.

It was a pleasure to watch Hope in action now that she'd completed the education she'd worked so hard to earn. A moment later though, he found his thoughts once more straying back to that summer she'd propositioned him.

The summer she'd cornered him away from the flickering bonfire and whispered in his ear highly suggestive ideas about how they could spend the rest of the evening. He hadn't allowed himself to think about that night, the way she'd commanded his attention, in a long time. Yet now that he was back in Silent Spring, the memories returned more often. Especially tonight when their guards were down and it felt like they were on the same page again. If only for a little while.

"How are you feeling, sweet girl?" Hope crooned as the animal shook her head enough to make the jingle bell on her neck ring.

The optimistic holiday sound felt like an encouraging omen for recovery. There was warm intelligence in Petal's eyes as she gave an experimental lick to Hope's wrist. Clearly the baby cow understood who to thank for saving her.

Hope's compassion and skill still drew him in as much as the spark that leaped between them. Clayton rose to pace around the stall in a futile attempt to think about something else. Something besides the way Hope had fit perfectly against him. How she could surprise him with her passionate ways when she maintained such an outward cool composure.

Now, tugging off her stethoscope after checking Petal's vital signs, Hope rose to her feet. "I think it's safe to leave her for a little while. TJ has his alarm set to check on her in an hour from now. He'll call if there are any changes."

Clay quit pacing, his eyes finding hers in the dim stall. She still clutched the stethoscope in one hand while she withdrew the pencil from her topknot, releasing a tumble of dark hair around her shoulders.

He knew in his gut that she'd acted out of comfort and not from a desire to tempt him. But the sight of her taking her hair down felt intimate. Sexy. Downright provocative. Especially when he'd been battling attraction to her ever since he'd retuned to Montana.

"That's good then," he said finally, realizing he was staring and that he'd been silent for too long. "Let me help carry out your things so you can get home and get some sleep."

Although he already knew he wouldn't be sleeping.

His reward when he got home would be a cold shower. Or twelve. It might require that many to bring down the fever raging in his blood right now.

Was it possible to catch fire from a man's gaze?

Hope felt the slow burn crawl over her skin as Clayton stared back at her, a hand's reach away. Awareness filled the air between them, weighing on her. Tempting her. The night seemed to have stripped away her defenses, with Clay's kindness and capability overshadowing old pains from the past. He'd done so much good tonight. For her. For his friend Sarge. For healthy ecological balance. And all of it had been on a volunteer basis since he could have been at home sleeping right now. Instead, he was by her side after a rough call, caring for her patient's safety as much as she did. And it was tough to scavenge up the old hurt and animosity at him for leaving town three years ago.

While the silence thickened between them—a quiet space filled with a desire she wouldn't voice— Hope struggled to recall what he'd just said. Something about helping her bring her things to the truck.

"That's not necessary," she assured him, afraid that spending another minute in his presence could send the last of her resolve up in flame. "I've got everything together. I just need to fold the blanket and I'm ready to head out."

Clay made no move to gather her supplies. But then, neither did she. The awareness in the air had grown so dense, it seemed to hold her feet in place, not letting her move. The temperature in the barn continued climbing, even though she'd turned down her portable heater.

Overhead, the single barn lamp buzzed with an electronic hum while Petal's breathing settled back into an even, snuffling rhythm. Hope's heartbeat raced, clamoring louder until it drowned out everything else.

"Are you sure about that?" His low voice stroked along her senses, making her suck in a breath and hold it.

One eyebrow lifted in question as he took a step closer to her. Almost as if he'd read her mind and could easily interpret the hot thoughts that circled her brain and teased her body. She caught a hint of his scent, a woodsy aftershave that intensified her memories. Her need to taste him again.

"I'm only sure of one thing, actually," she surprised herself by saying, the words tumbling free without her permission.

Kiss me.

At least she'd managed to lock down the rest of the sentence.

Another step brought him near enough to inhale the breath he'd exhaled, a comingling of air that felt like a precursor to something far more carnal.

"I'm listening," he assured her. Encouraging her. His eyes roamed her in a way that felt like a touch.

It was all she could do not to tilt her face up toward his in silent demand for his mouth on hers.

"I… Um…" What was she doing? He'd been back in Silent Spring for mere days and already she was practically dizzy from wanting him. Seriously. She was like a spellbound creature, waiting for the brush of his lips that would breathe new, sensual life into her. "What I'm sure of, is that I couldn't have gotten through tonight without you. So, thank you."

She clung tight to the lie with both hands, knowing if they stood this close for much longer, she would lose all resolve and launch herself at him. Fix her mouth on his and drag her tongue along his lower lip. Remind herself of his taste. Remind *him* how hot they were together.

But after a tense, three-heartbeat pause, Clayton nodded. Backed up a step. Exhaled hard.

"You would have been just fine on your own." He scooped up the blanket she'd used for a seat and folded it neatly before shouldering her heavy work duffel like it weighed nothing. "But I'm glad I was here anyway."

Spurred to action by his movements, Hope unplugged her space heater and wrapped the cord around the handle to transport it. Her pulse still raced and her body still throbbed with unanswered need. But that was by her choice, right? She'd resisted the magnetic draw. Her feet were moving.

She'd be in her truck and on her way home in no time.

Rushing now, she unlocked the stall door and hurried through the barn, Clay close at her heels with the rest of her things. Leaving the barn light on for TJ, she closed the main doors behind them as they exited the building into the chilly night air. The snow had stopped, leaving the ground dusted with a fresh coating of white. The moon had risen while she'd been indoors with Petal, the sky clearing. Shivering at the cold wind that lifted her hair from her neck and fanned her scrubs against her body, she fumbled with her key fob to unlock the truck cab.

"Do you want your bag in the back, or up front with you?" Clay asked, solicitous as always.

"I'll put it in the cab," she managed over a shivering breath, gesturing to the passenger seat as she pulled open the driver's side door.

While he loaded the blanket and her bag, she tucked the portable heater into its proper locked bay over the cargo bed. By the time she'd closed the tailgate and made sure all of the other metal storage boxes were locked, Clay had finished stowing her other gear.

He walked around to the back of the vehicle now, holding her long wool sweater by the shoulders. "You should put this on before you freeze out here."

A different kind of shiver went through her at the thought of standing close enough to him for him to help her into her sweater. It was a testament to how on edge she was that she almost refused.

But the temperature had dropped significantly while she'd been in the barn and her teeth were chattering so even she could hear them. No chance of rogue attraction ratcheting up the heat out here.

"Good idea. Thank you," she murmured instead, turning her back to him so she could slip the first arm in one sleeve.

Even before the warmth of the wool settled around her, Clay's broad shoulders blocked the wind, his chest so close to her back that she absorbed his body heat by proxy. He stood that near to her.

If she leaned back even an inch, she'd be in his arms.

The idea made her jittery. She fumbled to push her fingers through the second sleeve, her hand grazing his thigh in the process. She went still at the brief touch, her palm closing around itself to hold the tactile memory.

Behind her, Clay reached for the fabric belt that wrapped the cardigan in place. She sucked in a breath to tell him that wasn't necessary. But his hands were surer than hers, deftly tying the two ends together, while his strong arms flexed and shifted around her.

Her mouth went dry.

Every touch that she'd experienced since he'd left town three years ago paled in comparison to this. Every other kiss had been forgettable next to his. Sure, she'd dated since then. But she might as well have experienced a three-year dry spell by the way her knees wanted to buckle at just this small contact. His jaw bent close to her head. His arms lingered around her a moment longer than strictly necessary.

And she couldn't hold out a second longer against the draw of this man.

Turning in his arms, she faced him. Her heart knocked against her ribs in a bid to get closer still, and she accommodated it, arching her back so that her breasts molded to his chest.

There was no denying this thing between them. Not tonight at least. Not right now.

Tilting her face up to his, Hope gave in to the need that had been chasing her for days. She laid a hand on his chest, her nails lightly scoring the flannel of his shirt as she met his gaze in the moonlight. The look he gave her scorched her insides.

But it was nothing compared to the feel of his lips on hers when finally—finally—the kiss she'd been craving made her forget everything else.

Five

Clay hadn't been expecting a kiss. Not even when he'd recognized the smoldering heat in Hope's eyes tonight.

For as long as he'd known this woman, she'd been a quiet dynamo. She pursued her goals with a tenacity and focus that most people only dreamed about. She'd put herself through vet school in just seven years thanks to preparation that had started in high school. Hell, she'd pursued *him* the same way despite his good intentions regarding their age difference, making it plain that she wanted him.

Making it impossible to refuse her when he wanted her too.

Now, he'd been counting on that strength of purpose of hers to maintain the status quo of their relationship, assuming she'd hold him at a distance while he was in Silent Spring. Because while he might have enjoyed seeing those hot looks she sent his way tonight—proof that he wasn't alone in that simmering attraction—he sure as hell never thought Hope would act on it.

So yeah, this kiss knocked him on his heels.

He'd had zero time to mentally prepare for the onslaught of Hope Alvarez at full throttle. The showstopping curves no pair of unisex scrubs could ever disguise pressing up against him. The unveiling of her personal, passionate side that he'd guess not many people had ever seen. The committed way she threw herself into everything she did. From the kiss that held nothing back to the telltale sound she made in the back of her throat, a soft, feminine demand for more that was damned near his undoing.

Her fingers scrabbled up his chest like a climber looking for a hold. Her thighs shifted restlessly. And her breasts… He didn't dare think about the way her soft flesh molded to him, the tight points making his mouth water for a thorough taste. Right now, it was all he could do to weather the storm of this kiss without laying her down across the front seat of her truck and sinking himself inside her.

Because after the way things ended between them three years before, he couldn't possibly be reading this situation correctly. Except, with her teeth lightly testing his lower lip, her tongue tangling around his, how else could he interpret the kiss?

For one more mind-drugging moment, he allowed himself to revel in the pleasure of having her back in his arms. He raked his hands up and down her sides, fitting her even more tightly to him. Even through the layer of heavy wool, she responded to his touch, her hips tilting forward. The last of his blood surged south, effectively starving his brain of oxygen and rational thought.

That truck seat suddenly sounded like a viable option...

"Oh, God, Clay, I'm sorry," Hope said on a breathy gasp, pulling away.

Cold doused him, but not quickly enough to revive logic and reason. He waited for his mental faculties to return, his body on fire for her in spite of the chilling splash of reality. She leaned against the side of her truck, her fingers tracing along her forehead. The door to the vehicle remained open, yawning out a slice of light from the dome fixture.

"You're sorry," he repeated slowly, trying to make sense of what had just happened. "For what? The kiss? Or for putting an end to it just when—"

What? Things were about to get interesting? When they had been about to make bad decisions together? When they were ready to take what they both obviously still wanted? He didn't finish the question since he didn't know how to without spurring a discussion he wasn't ready to have while functioning on stupe-fied brain cells.

Her dark gaze crashed into his, her expression anguished mixed with a hint of annoyance.

An emotional blend that he totally identified with right now.

Hope scraped her fingers through her dark hair, a huff of air leaving her lips in a white cloud thanks to the cold. "Sorry to act on old feelings after the way things ended between us last time."

He nodded, mulling over the answer that didn't tell him a whole hell of a lot. And he couldn't help wondering why her answer was so important.

"Is it such a crime then?" he asked, wanting clarification on the point. His pulse thumped fast, his body very aware of every place where hers had come in contact with his. "Acting on those feelings when the attraction is still very much alive and well?"

Nearby, a rustle of weeds in the brush interrupted, reminding him they weren't really alone on the McMasterses' land. The ranch hand, TJ, could be arriving soon to check on Petal. Until then, there were night creatures out looking for a meal. For all Clay knew, the wolves could be lurking nearby. And he'd been honestly considering a quickie on Hope's truck seat. That told him all he needed to know about how much she affected him.

"It's obviously not a crime," she snapped, yanking her sweater tighter around her body in a way that made her curves all the more visible. "Just a very bad idea after the way you left town without a word to me. Not even the decency of telling me you wanted to end things."

The accusation rolled over him, her perspective so skewed from his own it would be laughable if Hope's eyes didn't burn with fire and resentment.

"You're serious," he realized, shaking his head in disbelief that she could indict him for leaving Silent Spring three years ago. "Even though *you* told *me* in no uncertain terms you wanted me out of your life for good."

He couldn't think about those final days in Montana without a visceral reaction, and his gut knotted even now. There'd been the breakup with Hope, for one thing. But before that, there'd been the complete annihilation of his relationship with his father. That bond had always been precarious, but Clay had worked hard to overcome his disappointments with his father enough to spend more time at Kingsland Ranch that summer. He'd thought he could be a better, more forgiving man. And he'd believed Duke when he'd said they would focus on working together as opposed to pretending a familial connection they'd never mastered.

In the end, Duke had resorted to his old, demeaning ways, gouging into the sore places from Clay's past and reminding him why Duke had always found his son lacking. Clay was so lost in that memory that it took him a moment to notice Hope's furrowed brow. Her pursed lips. A moment later, she seemed to draw a steadying breath, her shoulders straightening.

"I have no idea what you mean," she said flatly, her arms still hugging her midsection while the night breeze ruffled her dark hair. "I never had the chance to speak to you before you left."

She plucked a stray strand of hair from her eyelashes, tucking it behind one ear while she stared up at him curiously. Her expression—without guile and seemingly in earnest—made something shift uneasily inside him. Could he have misread the way things had ended between them?

"You didn't need to speak to me," he reminded her, the night eerily quiet around them, the fresh snow dampening the usual night sounds of rustling branches or scurrying animals in the underbrush. "The letter you left me said you needed to move on."

It's time for me to let you go...

The line had been seared into his brain. She'd used mortifyingly gentle language to skewer and gut their fledgling relationship. Her note had been out of left field and completely unexpected when things had been going so well between them. They were like-minded in many ways—prizing hard work, shunning emotional drama. They shared common interests in their efforts to protect animals. And the heat between them had been blistering.

So yeah, the message she'd written had blindsided him at a time when he was already raw from his father's betrayal. She'd left the paper propped on her kitchen table where he couldn't miss it. They'd gotten into a Friday night habit of him stopping by her house, using the key she'd given him and making her dinner. Then, they'd eat together when she'd finished her workday at the externship. That Friday, however, he'd found a note saying things were over.

"I didn't—" she began, her voice high and breathless. "I never—" She paced away from him, her boots soundless through the soft layer of fresh snow.

Then, stopping at the end of her truck bed, she pivoted to face him. Her eyes were wide. Shocked? Dismayed? Clay didn't understand her reaction. Why would she deny it three years after the fact? They'd both moved on.

She clutched at the lapels on her sweater, twisting the fabric in one hand as she whispered, "Oh, my God. The letter."

Frustration arrowed through him.

"What gives, Hope?" He crossed his arms, forcing himself to stand still and have this out with her even though he didn't appreciate the false surprise. "It's done with now. I'm not exactly crying in my beer about it."

The arrow seemed to find its mark. Straightening, she let go of her sweater and walked toward her truck cab, only pausing when she lifted the first boot onto the running board.

"I'm glad." Her smile was stiff. Fake. "Because that letter wasn't meant for you."

Stunned, he could only watch as she settled into

the driver's seat and yanked on her safety belt. He wanted to know what the hell she meant. Had he misread everything all this time?

But it was long past midnight, and he could see the weariness etched in her features beneath the anger. Frustration.

There was no shortage of those emotions to go around, which was why he shouldn't try to stop her from leaving. And yet, how could he sleep tonight with everything he'd thought about their relationship turned upside down?

He leaned into the still-open truck door, one hand on the window and the other on the roof of the vehicle. "So if you weren't breaking up with me, who were you trying to let go?"

Not in a million years would he have envisioned a woman like Hope Alvarez two-timing him. Something was off here. Some piece of the puzzle was missing.

His body was strung tense as a bow. He drummed his fingers on the metal roof for an outlet. Clay watched Hope's shadowed profile as she bit her lip, her eyes blinking fast before she faced him.

"You remember me telling you how my mom died on a Christmas Eve nine years ago?" Her voice rasped with emotion.

The change of subject almost gave him whiplash, but he wasn't about to gripe when Hope was thinking about a tragedy from her past.

Clearing his throat as he attempted to recall everything he knew about her mom's death, Clay nodded.

"Of course. She had a car accident on the way to pick you up while you were a student at Montana State."

"That's right." Hope nodded, her fingertips tracing the outline of the steering wheel as she stared out the front windshield. She appeared lost in thought. "Mom wasn't alone, though. She was a passenger in my boyfriend's vehicle. The plan was for us to all spend Christmas together since his parents were on vacation."

A sense of foreboding brushed along his senses, swirling around him like a rogue wind. He recalled the kid had died as well, hit by a logging truck that slid on an icy patch of highway.

"I do remember that now," he admitted, sliding his hand off the truck roof to lay a comforting touch on her shoulder. They'd talked about the accident only once, but she'd told him that holidays continued to be tough for her even back then—six years after the fact. "I can't imagine how awful that must have been for you."

Hope turned shining dark eyes toward him. "It really was. I went to counseling and grief therapy to come to terms with it. Not just the bereavement, but the guilt. And one of the tools the therapist suggested was penning a letter to the deceased—"

The foreboding that had been building in the back of Clayton's brain exploded. Missing puzzle pieces fell into place. The past reordered itself in a way he'd never, ever imagined.

He was reeling.

He wasn't even aware that he'd backed away a step until he swiped a hand over his face and reopened his eyes, seeing the new distance between them.

"The letter I read that day was to him." It wasn't a question. Because it all made perfect sense.

The gentle language that had infuriated him because he read it as though she thought she needed to protect his feelings.

The calls she'd made to his phone. He'd been so upset and angry that he'd blocked her after she'd rang him a couple of times. He hadn't the slightest idea how often she'd tried to reach him after that.

"Yeah, it was." Hope stared at him for a long moment before reaching for her door handle. "Until you mentioned the note, I hadn't even recalled that I'd been working on the letter that day. I'd written it sort of spur of the moment because it felt like I was finally ready to put that part of my life behind me—" Her lips quirked before she gave a bitter laugh. "But like you said, that part of our lives is done with now. No sense crying in our beer."

Had he said that? No one had ever accused him of being overly sensitive, that was for sure. But even for him, that sounded callous.

Clay knew this conversation was far from over. Yet there wasn't any more to be said tonight when they were both dealing with enough revelations to knock them sideways. Clearly, what they'd shared back then hadn't been as special as he'd once believed if their connection could be broken so easily. Had that note been his excuse for ending things when he was already itching to get out of town after the fight with his dad?

He didn't want to think he'd ever been that shallow. That self-serving. But he didn't know what to believe right now. So he didn't protest when Hope pulled the truck door closed and backed away from the barn, her tires kicking up a little snow as they spun before finding traction.

He'd been spinning his own wheels for three years, hadn't he? Misreading Hope. Leaving town without a word. Cutting her out of his life like she'd never been there.

As the sound of her truck engine faded into the distance, Clay lifted his face up to the moon, recalling why he was more at home in Alaska's northern tundra. He was better with wildlife than relationships. The sooner he left Silent Spring, the better.

If only he didn't have the memory of Hope's kiss still burning in the back of his brain. Even now, despite everything that had just happened between them, his blood still simmered with the unfulfilled longing that kiss had triggered. His body hadn't gotten the message that they wouldn't be repeating the lip-lock. But that didn't mean he would stop thinking about how much he craved another taste.

One week later, as Hope parked her truck in front of the Stockyard, she had to admit her usual MO for overcoming problems was proving futile.

She'd worked herself to exhaustion for days in an effort to stop thinking about Clayton and the stupid, star-crossed moment that had derailed their relationship. She began her days at dawn and never allowed herself to come up for air, so that by the time she lay down after midnight her body was too weary to ache for things she couldn't have. Except she ached all the time anyhow.

For the relationship she'd thought she'd had with Clayton. For the man she'd thought he'd been. But even if he'd never seen that letter she'd written— one never intended for him—how long would they have lasted? He hadn't even asked her about the note. Hadn't spoken to her. He'd just left town. Blocked her. Ghosted her.

Things would have never worked between them. She wasn't good at wading through the emotional stuff. But him? He didn't even acknowledge it, apparently. He'd read that letter, assumed the worst and vanished on her. Even now, when she'd told him that the note hadn't been meant for him, Clay had clammed up. Shut down. It hadn't even made a difference, it seemed.

And that hurt after the kiss they'd shared. Because even though she'd initiated it, he'd definitely participated. But she was tired of those thoughts circling endlessly around her brain.

So when she'd finished visiting her patients for the day, Hope had texted her girlfriends to invite them out for happy hour at the Stockyard. Which was how she found herself wearing a red cocktail dress and sky-high heels at six o'clock on a Thursday, teetering across a snow-dusted parking lot and clutching her wool wrap as she approached the doors to the bar. She needed the perspective of friends.

She'd almost reached the glass entrance when a familiar feminine voice called to her from behind.

"Hey, sexy mama, looking good!" The greeting was followed up with a wolf whistle, and by the time Hope turned to find her friends, she saw Kendra and Lauryn piling out of Kendra's sleek new BMW sedan.

Laughing at their catcalls, Hope pirouetted to model her dress, careful not to slip as she opened her cape, peep show style. "I figured I might as well go big or go home."

And okay, maybe she'd thought there was a small chance she would run into Clayton tonight since the Stockyard was his brother's bar. She wasn't pursuing Clay, *obviously*, but she also didn't want to look like she was crying in her proverbial beer.

Damn the man, anyway, for getting under her skin with his kisses and then reminding her all the ways they couldn't possibly work.

"I like it," Kendra announced, her eyes moving over Hope approvingly as she stabbed the lock button on her key fob. "Two thumbs up."

With her long blond waves and willowy figure, Kendra turned heads wherever she went. Tonight, the public relations expert wore black jeans with red heels and a satiny red blouse that tied at her waist, the ribbons trailing down one thigh. An open moto jacket was thrown over her shoulders as she hurried toward Hope.

Beside her, Lauryn wore a forest green wrap dress with a feathery, festive ruffle at the hem. A chocolate-brown trench coat kept the elements at bay, and her knee-high boots matched the coat. Her brown hair was in a low braid that rested on one shoulder, a green ribbon threaded through it.

"You both look gorgeous," Hope said as she held the door open for them. "I'm glad we could get together before the holidays."

She was proud of these women who made a difference in their communities. Lauryn, for rescuing horses and turning her small operation into an equine therapy center. Kendra, for saving Kingsland Ranch from negative publicity that had threatened to derail the good works the Kingsley brothers wanted to do with the wealth left to them by their father. Kendra had turned the publicity tide, focusing national attention on environmental causes.

Minutes later, they were seated at a high-top table in a back corner with a good view of the dance floor. In fact, a young server hurried over to wipe down the table for them and take a drink order even though the place was packed, premium service Hope suspected was tied to the fact that Kendra was wearing an engagement ring from the bar's owner, Levi.

Her heart ached a little to see how happy both of her friends were in their new love relationships. She was thrilled for them both. Truly. But she wondered why deep romantic connections eluded her.

They'd barely hung their coats and settled in for a catch-up when the waiter returned with their bucket of beers, all Gargoyle Kings brand, which was the label Kendra had dreamed up with her father and now ran jointly with Levi. While the server set them up with chilled glasses, Hope took a moment to peer around the festive happy hour.

A huge ball of mistletoe hung low over the dance floor, and couples two-stepping past often made a point of dipping beneath it for a kiss. There was no band yet, just music from the jukebox, a tune that was something both Christmassy and country. In fact, the whole bar had taken country Christmas to heart, with wreaths hung on everything from the neon moon near the dance floor to the huge set of Texas longhorns above the bar.

What she didn't see, however, was Clayton Reynolds. A fact that should have been a relief since she didn't know what more there was to say between them. Yet she couldn't deny a hint of disappointment too.

She'd gone to the trouble of wearing a pretty revenge dress. She at least wanted the satisfaction of having him see her in it.

Her thoughts had gone fully dark when Lauryn's teasing voice called her back from the edge of the resentful-frustrated place where she'd sat all week long.

"Hope, are you with us?" Lauryn asked, waving her fingers close to Hope's nose as if she was an unresponsive patient on the exam table.

Sitting up straighter on her stool, she pulled her chilled glass full of beer closer to her.

"I'm one hundred percent with you. Sorry for spacing out." She lifted her glass to her lips and was about to take a drink when Lauryn stopped her with a hand on her wrist.

"Wait! We were trying to make a toast before the first sip. I was just saying how great it is to have you both back in town." Lauryn had lived in Silent Spring ever since Sheriff Hamilton and his wife had adopted her as a girl—maybe thirteen or so, Hope guessed. She'd been a year ahead of Lauryn in high school and they hadn't run in the same circles.

But their love of animals had made their paths cross later in 4-H, and Hope had visited the rescue many times to help her friend with her horses.

"I couldn't agree more," Hope admitted, raising the glass as gratitude washed over her to have friends who would answer the call when she needed distraction from her problems. "I'm super grateful to claim you both as friends. Cheers to us, ladies."

Clinking their glasses together, they took their first sips and Hope felt some of her tension ease. She was glad she'd worn the red dress, whether or not she had an audience. It felt good to be out, to tend her social needs for a change.

Kendra leveled a narrow look at her across the table

as she set her glass down. "Okay, now that we've dispensed with the niceties, we're both dying to know." She exchanged a glance with Lauryn while a welcome rush of cold air wafted through the warm bar. "What prompted the last-minute request for a girls' night?"

Debating how much to say, she picked at the label on her beer with an unpolished fingernail. She'd dressed up tonight, but not even her fancy outings made her veer from her commitment to short, easy nails in her line of work.

"I needed an escape from my own thoughts," she confessed with a shrug, not sure she was ready to relate the particulars yet, especially since they were both closely connected to the Kingsley family now.

"Personal thoughts? Work thoughts?" Lauryn prompted, leaning sideways to bump shoulders with Hope. "We can't help if we don't know."

My boyfriend ghosted me after reading a note I wrote to someone else as a therapy exercise. Also, he doesn't seem to have any regrets about it.

Yeah, she wasn't saying any of that.

"Christmas can be tough for me," she said finally. And even though it was true enough, she cringed inside a little at using the old grief to deflect from this latest wound. "So I like keeping busy—"

Her words were interrupted by a man's voice across the table.

"Sorry to interrupt, ladies." Levi and Gavin Kingsley appeared out of nowhere, each gravitating to the sides of the women they loved. It was Levi who spoke though. Gavin had already buried his lips against Lauryn's neck. "We saw you sitting over here and wanted to at least say hello."

Hope's heart beat faster.

Not because of the arrival of Levi or Gavin. Not because she envied the affection those men lavished on her friends.

But because, two steps behind his half brothers, Clayton Reynolds had entered her field of vision.

And no matter how much she'd told herself for days on end that it didn't matter that he hadn't reached out to her to talk about the revelations of last week, she felt the magnetic pull of the man as surely as if they'd just slid into bed together.

From the fiery look in his green eyes, she suspected he was feeling it too.

"Will you both excuse me for a sec?" Hope asked her friends as she retrieved her bag, refusing to acknowledge Clayton. Reminding herself she wouldn't be the one to make another overture toward him. "I'm just going to hit the ladies' room."

Slipping off her chair, she tilted her chin high even as everything inside her shouted that she was a coward for running. She turned her back on Clayton and walked away.

Six

Regret fired through him at Hope's retreat.

Because of him.

He didn't want to ruin her night with her girl-friends. She deserved a fun, festive evening consider-ing how hard she worked. She looked stunning in her flame-red dress, a body-hugging number that made it impossible for him to look away. He watched as male heads turned when she walked past, a phenom-enon that made him want to gouge out other men's eyes. The fiery possessiveness of that thought told him how much she still affected him. Since when was he a jealous man? Only Hope could elicit that kind of fierce protectiveness.

His feet were following her across the bar before

he'd even considered what he'd say to her. Or why. He still didn't know what to think about how they'd split three years ago. The news that she hadn't meant to end things with him had floored him. Maybe if he were a better man, he'd continue to give her some breathing room tonight while they both came to terms with what had happened between them. Yet she drew him like a magnet.

"Hope, please wait," he called to her just as she'd reached the alcove that housed doors for the bathrooms and an employees-only area.

She paused by a life-size painted sculpture of a cowboy leaning against the wall, his Stetson tilted down to cover his face. Some overzealous decorator had laid a pine wreath around the hat, filling the alcove with the scent of fresh-cut balsam.

"Hello, Clayton." Hope pasted on a too-polite smile that revealed nothing.

Like their conversation a week ago hadn't meant anything.

His gut tensed. The backs of his shoulders knotted.

"Are you avoiding me?" He kept his voice low, mindful of the bar patrons laughing and talking behind him.

Now and then, people passed into or out of the alcove, and he didn't want anyone overhearing a private conversation.

"Avoidance?" She shook her head and gave a bitter laugh. "That's your approach, Clay, not mine."

Up close, he could see the subtle shimmer of eye

shadow along her brow bone. The dusting of pink on her cheeks. They were unusual for her, and he could count on one hand the times he'd seen her wear makeup. She didn't need it, and yet the presence of those feminine touches told him tonight was a special evening for her. And he'd wrecked it.

"Yet you're the one hightailing it out of here the moment I walk into the place." He didn't wish to argue with her, so he didn't have the slightest clue why he was picking a fight. Swiping a weary hand over his face, he reminded himself how many times he'd wanted to talk to her during the past week. How many times it had required all of his willpower not to text her. "Sorry. That was uncalled for."

The blasé expression she'd been wearing melted away, revealing confusion in her eyes.

"You aren't entirely wrong though," she admitted, her lips quirking on one side. "I wasn't in any hurry to rehash what happened the other night." She hesitated before adding, "I assumed you weren't either, since you've been careful to steer clear of me all week."

His reasons were more nuanced than that. But where could he begin picking through all the thoughts he'd had the last seven days since learning the truth about their breakup?

He was about to answer when someone ran into him, an elbow catching him in the abdomen before he could right the swaying woman headed toward the bathrooms. Turning back to Hope, he said, "You know, the dance floor might be a better place to talk."

One dark eyebrow rose before Hope peered around his shoulder to assess the small space in front of a guitarist who was just setting up her equipment for a performance. For now, the sound system still pumped in music from a popular country Christmas album.

"All right, I'm game," she agreed, her dark eyes glinting in the swirl of red and green lights overhead.

Desire punched through him so fast he had to concede that he'd probably issued the invitation just so he could have his hands on her again. As avoidance schemes went, his was an epic fail.

Now, taking her hand in his, he led her through the crowd to the floor currently occupied by just one other couple. The older pair twirled around in perfect harmony, their eyes only for one another. As Clayton pulled Hope toward him, banding one arm around her waist, he felt the deluge of old memories.

Lowering his head to speak closer to her ear, he confided, "Would you believe the last time I danced was three years ago in that barn with you?"

He could feel a tremor of response ripple through her even though her expression remained neutral.

"Sadly, that was my last dance too." Her fingers played absently over the fabric of his flannel shirt, a touch that ratcheted up his awareness of her every movement.

He told himself not to read between the lines of her comment. Just because she hadn't taken a turn around the planked floor with anyone else since their breakup didn't mean she hadn't been involved in other relationships.

He hadn't even thought to ask her about her dating status these days. "You aren't seeing anyone else now? Haven't seen anyone else? Since us?"

Her brow furrowed, annoyance scrawled over her features as she looked up sharply. "Do you honestly think I would have kissed you the other night if I was seeing someone?"

"You're right. Of course not." He shook his head, regretting the caveman thinking that seemed to prevail whenever he was around this woman. He also noticed she didn't answer his other questions, and he wasn't quite sure what to make of that. "I know you better than that. And for what it's worth, I wasn't exactly avoiding you this week. Just trying to give you some room to decide where things stood between us."

He'd thought about her nonstop. Relived that kiss thousands of times. Even now, just seeing her lips painted a lush shade of red made him recall the taste of her. The hungry way her mouth had moved over his, like she had missed the feel of him as much as he'd missed her.

"You weren't avoiding me?" she asked on a laugh. "Your SUV was spitting gravel in your wake on the one day when our paths almost crossed at Sarge's farm."

The music changed to a more upbeat tune as the guitarist began her set list, but Clay never altered his slow two-step around the floor. Neither did she. He and Hope might be at odds in other ways, but their bodies moved together as one, their steps fluid and easy, remembering each other's rhythm.

"I remember the day you're talking about." He had been in a rush, but not for the reason she thought. "I was late getting to a meeting with the local head of the parks and wildlife department. They needed additional proofs of my qualifications to transport the wolves, and I didn't want to mess up the process after I'd gotten Sarge and Letitia to agree we could relocate them."

He had more than enough paperwork and certification behind him, but there had been red tape and slowdowns, the bureaucratic hoops to jump through anytime he got involved with government agencies.

Hope seemed to relent the point, some of the tension in her spine relaxing. It took all his willpower not to shift his palm on the small of her back, to massage away the rest of the anxiety with his fingers.

"Thank you for doing that." Her eyes shone with that approving gleam that had almost been his undoing a week ago. "I've seen enough trapping injuries to appreciate a humanitarian approach to relocating wolves."

He'd seen those injuries too, especially when trappers didn't bother to check their traps on a regular basis. All the more reason to do his job.

"I feel confident we got the whole pack. Sarge hasn't seen any more signs of activity." Clayton noticed the dance floor getting more crowded as happy hour kicked into high gear. He told himself that was why he tucked Hope fractionally closer, why he was edging her nearer to the outskirts of the crush where the world was more private. "But back to my original question. Since you're not avoiding me, and I'm not avoiding you either, can we set up a time to meet about your Christmas gala?"

Their original date got canceled the evening Petal was injured. He hadn't forgotten about that. Because no matter how much his brain told him it was a bad idea to revisit a relationship that had failed so hard the first go-round, Clay couldn't deny the irresistible draw between them whenever he saw Hope.

Every. Single. Time.

Did she have any real choice?

Hope's need to maintain a good relationship with Kingsland Ranch for the sake of her client base hadn't changed since the first time she'd agreed to a meeting with Clay. But considering the way her breathing went shallow and her heart raced just being in his arms again, she recognized that the more time they spent together, the higher the chances that she would end up right back where they'd been three years ago. In bed together having hot sex, for one thing. Which, taken by itself, wasn't necessarily a bad idea. But she knew herself well enough to know that sleeping together again would have an emotional fallout. Especially at this time of year when the holidays were fraught with complicated feelings.

Even now, her body hummed with pleasure at the feel of his big palm curving around her hip to hold her in place. Her fingers strayed lower on his chest, splaying wide to touch more of him.

"We can meet," she agreed, her blood heating in anticipation even though she already knew she was going to add caveats. Public places only, for instance, since crowds around them would help keep things platonic. And they needed to stay work focused. No more straying into conversations about their past that wouldn't resolve anything.

Before she could spell that out, however, the guitarist finished her song, the crowd around them pausing to applaud. They did the same, and for an unwise moment, she mourned the loss of Clay's touch while they both clapped.

At the same time, the musician leaned near her microphone to speak. "Thank you. And, in the spirit of Christmas, don't forget to steer your partner toward our dance floor mistletoe tonight."

Everyone peered up to find the bundle of greenery.

Hope didn't have far to look since it was directly over their heads.

She wasn't sure if the crowd was reacting to the fact that the guitarist had pointed out the holiday symbol or to the realization that a couple already stood beneath it. Either way, the bar patrons erupted in whistles and cheers, clearly expecting the first public kiss of the evening.

Hope appreciated the noise, actually. It distracted her from the pang that went through her at the thought of how long that last bundle of mistletoe had lingered in her house during the months following her mom's death.

Thankfully, Clay's gaze found hers, and the heat in his eyes dragged her out of those dark thoughts. In fact, the smoldering look was so potent it sent a shiver of anticipation through her. From the cacophony of shouts and people egging them on to kiss, Hope heard her friends' voices—Lauryn and Kendra—clear and distinct from the rest.

"Go for it, sexy mama!" Kendra hollered. While Lauryn's higher pitch called, "Show them how it's done, Hope!"

In spite of herself—and in spite of the sadness that had surrounded her holidays for so long—Hope laughed.

"Guess there's no getting out of it," she said softly, lifting up on her toes while she steadied herself with one hand on Clay's shoulder.

But she didn't have far to arch because a moment later, Clay lifted her up at the same time his mouth crashed down on hers, kissing her like a man on a mission.

The whole place erupted. At least, she thought that's what happened. It was tough to hear over the rush of blood to her ears, her heart pounding so loudly she practically rattled from the vibration. The heat, the warmth of his body, enveloped her,

as his arms wrapped around her so they touched...
everywhere.

A moment later, the guitarist launched into a new
song. Clay broke the kiss but didn't let her go. Her
lips tingled where his mouth had touched hers. The
applause died away, and life in the bar seemed to go
on around them while they remained together, arms
still banded about one another.

People began dancing again. And yet Hope hadn't
peeled herself off of Clay. Or was the problem that
he hadn't returned her to her feet?

"I should get back to my friends," she said weakly,
wriggling in a way that only made her hyperaware
of Clay's every muscle.

Her emotions were in as much of a tangle as her
nerve endings. And those were short-circuiting all
over the place.

"Right. Sorry." Clay lowered her to the floor with
delectable slowness, heightening the pleasure already
coursing through her. His gaze sizzled over her already sensitized skin. Then, clearing his throat, he
said in a low voice, "But we still need to set a time
to meet."

Her heart skipped a beat at the idea of being alone
with him. Look how fast just a kiss had gotten out of
control—both times their lips had met.

"Maybe it's not wise." She edged backward, off the
dance floor to stay out of the way of couples twirl-
ing past them.

"Didn't we agree we weren't going to avoid one

another?" He shoved an impatient hand through his short hair. "I'd like to talk to you about what kind of vet facility you'd like. I did a lot of research on high-tech equipment for another animal center that may be beneficial for you."

She blinked at the abrupt change of topic.

Was that really what they would discuss when they got together? She didn't doubt his experience in that arena. But how could he go from that scorching kiss to discussing vet equipment? She wanted to look into his eyes, scan for a hint of his intentions, but he was already leading her through the crowd to return her to her table. Which was probably just as well since she'd lost her ability to read him anyway. Or else her attraction to him was making her see what she wanted to see where he was concerned. And that wasn't a good idea in light of the way they'd misread one another in the past.

Although she hadn't imagined that fiery kiss. The whole freaking bar had witnessed it.

Surely her friends would give her some objective advice. They might champion mistletoe kisses in the spirit of the season, but once she explained the history between her and Clay, they would surely see things differently.

Clay tucked her close to dodge a raucous pool game where a winner jumped around with his cue like she'd just clinched the World Cup. Hope gripped Clay's hand tighter when a server lifted a full tray of bright red cosmopolitan drinks over her head. A moment afterward, they arrived at the table where Levi and Gavin were still shoulder to shoulder with their significant others.

All four sets of eyes turned toward them with varying degrees of speculative interest.

Kendra kept the moment from feeling awkward, however, by lifting her beer glass in their direction. "Cheers to you for breaking in the mistletoe."

Laughing, Lauryn raised her glass and Hope did the same as she slid into her seat.

As she took a sip of the frothy IPA, Clay bent to speak into her ear. "I have some free time tomorrow. Text me when you finish work."

Her throat went dry as every cell in her body swooned appreciatively at that deep voice rumbling against her ear.

She could only nod, not trusting her own voice to reply in anything other than a breathless squeak. Cheeks hot along with the rest of her, she peered across the high-top table at her friends, noticing them watching her interaction with Clay with rapt interest.

At some point Gavin and Levi had drifted away, leaving just the three friends again, their bucket of beers a centerpiece on the table.

"Sooo," Lauryn began, her braid falling forward as she leaned closer. "I feel like the sexual attraction is so thick right now, there's still a force field of it kind of resonating around you."

Her friend was right, but it wasn't something Hope intended to advertise. Especially when she hadn't a clue how she wanted to proceed. So she shook her head. "It's not like that."

But her friends paid her no mind.

Instead, Kendra nodded, pointing her finger at Lauryn. "Oh, my God, you nailed it. That kiss was like a nuclear event and she's still radiating."

Behind them, another couple must have danced under the mistletoe, because there was more shouting and clanging of glasses before a big eruption of *oohs* and *aahs* along with a few cheers.

Ignoring the kissing to focus on the conversation, Hope covered her eyes. Her friends weren't stupid. She might as well confess. "Ladies, I don't want to radiate. There's too much history between Clay and me."

Lauryn gasped. "I knew it. From that summer three years ago, right? I was busy with the rescue that year, but I always thought there was something between you."

"We never took it public," Hope admitted. Although even as she said it, she wondered why. Had she felt something was off between them? Or was it a case of not really committing even then? "And it was only for ten weeks, but at that time it felt—real."

Kendra reached across the table to squeeze Hope's wrist, her silver bangles clanking lightly over the wood. "Levi told me that summer ended really badly for Clayton after the big fight with Duke."

Lauryn bit her lip before adding, "Gavin said no one but Clay really knows what the fight was about.

But it must have been bad to drive him to the most remote parts of Alaska for three years."

Both women looked at her expectantly.

"I—" Hope began, before snapping her jaw shut again. All this time, she'd believed that Clay had wanted to get away from her. Only last week had she discovered that he believed she wanted to break up with him. But was there much more to his disappearance than that?

"I should ask him about it," she said finally, realizing that she'd taken a wrongheaded approach to her attraction to Clayton. Maybe she'd been too focused on her own needs when she could have given more consideration to his.

"I know Gavin really wishes he would stay in Silent Spring," Lauryn added. "Maybe this time he will."

Was that even a real possibility? Hope took another long sip of her drink to hide the bolt of panic the idea gave her. It was easier for her to focus on his departure, a definite end to the confusing feelings he stirred inside her.

Kendra must have seen her face, however, since she patted Hope's shoulder, her bracelets jingling as she said, "Don't let that freak you out. You're a strong, smart woman, and you're in charge of your feelings and what happens next with Clay."

Hope peered from Kendra to Lauryn—who nodded in earnest agreement—and back again. The vote of confidence felt good. The endorsement of her friends whose opinions she respected. Some of the tension sighed out of her before Lauryn added, "Besides, you can always shut things down and walk away if it's not right for you." Readjusting the bow on her green hair ribbon, Lauryn made it sound simple.

Easy.

And it gave Hope an idea. Just in case these heated encounters with Clay really did lead to more intimacy. *She* could be the one to end things this time if things got too difficult. No need to wait around for more heartbreak.

Hope felt the new realization settle into place. "I appreciate the pep talk. And the assurance that I can call the shots so I don't get hurt again." But before she dismissed a relationship that hadn't even begun, she really did want to hear more from Clayton about his view of their shared past. That summer he'd left. "But I also think I've been content to paint Clay as the villain in our breakup for so long that I might not have looked beyond my own disillusionment to appreciate what he was dealing with back then."

Kendra set her empty glass on the table and then shoved aside the silver bucket of drinks so there was nothing between them. "We don't want you to get hurt either. But sometimes relationships can be worth the risk."

Since when was she the kind of woman who played it safe? She'd never seen herself that way. Hadn't she been the one to move her relationship with Clay out of the friend zone in the first place?

But before Hope could argue the point, Lauryn

added, "Personally, I would gamble for the sake of that kind of radiation."

Hope didn't agree or disagree, telling them she'd think about it.

But inside, she already knew she had the advice she'd been seeking. She would see Clayton again, of course. This time, she would ask him directly about the summer they'd split. He'd gotten to hear her side of things, but he still hadn't told her his. It was high time she got some answers.

And, worst-case scenario and she got in over her head again? She'd be the one to walk away.

Seven

Gritty-eyed after another sleepless night, Clayton stepped out the back door of the house allotted for Kingsland's ranch manager and breathed in the cold morning air. Before Clay's arrival in Montana, the place where he was now staying had been mostly vacant over the past year. His brothers had hired occasional help, but mostly they'd been taking turns filling the role left open after Duke Kingsley's demanding ways had sent the previous manager packing.

Clay knew enough family lore to recall the four-bedroom, one-story stone home where he'd been staying these past weeks had been the original main house back when his grandparents ran the operation. Clay's mother had lived in Silent Spring as a teen when her

father worked as a ranch hand at Kingsland. Dena
Reynolds had never shared Clay's bitterness over
her relationship with Duke, so she'd gladly shared
the story of their brief courtship. Followed by Duke
walking away when he found out she was expecting.

And that was followed by Dena learning Duke got
engaged later that month to his also-pregnant girl-
friend, Adele Boudreux. Clayton had been born just
two months before his half brother, Levi Kingsley.
While Levi had been the privileged, acknowledged
"firstborn," Clay had never been publicly claimed.
While he didn't give a rip about that for himself, it
still made him furious that Duke had slighted Clay's
mom that way. He'd offered her support money in
exchange for a nondisclosure agreement, although
Duke's wife had gotten wind of Clay anyhow and had
insisted Duke bring Clay to Kingsland each summer.
He'd hated leaving his friends for the summer. And
he'd really hated the tears in his mother's eyes every
time he boarded the plane for the mandatory visit.

Clay had gotten along with his stepmom, Adele,
well enough, but she'd died in a trampling accident
when he was nine years old. After that, summers
at Kingsland only got worse, until that final unbearable one that coincided with his own mother's
death from a heart defect. To honor her warmhearted,
forgiving spirit, he'd tried to make peace with his
father that year, to no avail. Cementing Clay's dislike of the place.

Now, walking across the snow-dusted grass of the

side lawn toward a detached garage that held farm equipment and his rented SUV, Clay tugged on a pair of leather work gloves as he wondered if he'd hear from Hope this morning. She'd messaged him two days prior to say the event venue in Bozeman where she'd planned to hold her Christmas gala was having staffing issues. Apparently, she had needed to contact them before she could meet with him.

Fair enough.

Even making allowances for her busy work schedule, he expected to hear from her today. So when he heard a vehicle turning onto the ranch access road closest to his house, he couldn't deny a surge of anticipation that it might be her. He slowed his steps as he circled the equipment garage to a small barn on the property. Gavin had been keeping one of the more unpredictable stallions at the barn to separate him from the rest of the quarter horses and acclimate him to more handling. Clay had taken charge of the animal, Moondancer, due to proximity. His first order of business this morning was to turn out the horse.

But as the sound of tires crunching over gravel grew louder, Clay paused outside the low gray barn to keep a watchful eye on the road. The vehicle that appeared wasn't the hoped-for burgundy-colored truck, however. Clay didn't recognize the newer-model silver pickup.

He damned well recognized the woman in the passenger seat, however. His stepsister, McKenna, was already rolling down the window to call to him.

"Guess who's here?" she shouted, her red ponytail sliding forward as she waved. "The Alaska coalition is ready to crash your holidays."

A grin split his face at her antics. His stepsister, McKenna, was eight years younger than him and an absolute pistol. She ran a bar in Dutch Harbor by herself and took tourists out on guided tours of the Aleutian Islands for extra income. He'd never met anyone so self-sufficient. The fact that she'd been his biggest champion and the most loyal person he knew made her one of his very favorite people.

Clayton returned her wave as the pickup pulled into the driveway near the equipment garage. Now he could see Quinton Kingsley in the driver's seat. The father of the baby McKenna was already carrying. Clay reminded himself he'd given Quinton his blessing—well, sort of, after punching him—and that the guy made McKenna happy. That's what mattered most, right?

For her sake, he would keep the peace with Quinton. While McKenna wasn't a blood relative, Clay loved her like the sister he'd never had.

Already McKenna was flinging herself from the vehicle. She jogged toward him in jeans and boots, her open jacket not even zipped over her white fisherman's sweater. A leather thong around her neck was decorated with a single silver jingle bell. There was no sign of her pregnancy yet under her baggy sweater, but she was only a few months along.

"Did we surprise you?" She threw her arms around

Clay, and he lifted her off the ground to spin her—carefully—in a circle before setting her back down on the snow-covered grass. "Quinton thought it would be better that way."

He forced his lips into a smile as Quinton drew near, his black duster and Stetson well suited for the ranch even though the guy ran a tech firm out of Sunnyvale, California. Or at least, he used to run it out of there. Quint was giving Alaskan life a try since meeting McKenna.

"Hello, brother," Quint greeted him, rubbing his jaw in an obvious callback to their last meeting. "I come in peace."

Clay reached to shake his hand. "Me too. I'm in Silent Spring for all the right reasons thanks to you."

When Quinton had found Clay in Galbraith Lake the month before, Clay hadn't been in any hurry to return to Montana. But his half brother had helped him see maybe the time for peacemaking had arrived for real now that Duke Kingsley had died. After all, Clay's conflict had always been with his dad. He just hadn't been sure how his brothers would view his presence after the angry way he'd left town, especially considering Clay had been left out of the will.

"That's welcome news." Quinton nodded his satisfaction as he turned to take in the old ranch home, one arm wrapping around McKenna's waist when she tucked close to him. "And it's good to see you in the ranch manager house. It should have been yours three years ago along with everything else Duke promised you. Kingsland would benefit from your guidance."

Refusing to create false expectations about his presence here, Clay reminded him, "Thanks for the vote of confidence, but this is all very temporary. I'll be heading back home after Christmas."

Something important for him to keep in mind as he waited for Hope's call. No matter how much their kisses filled his dreams, he needed to remember he wasn't staying in Silent Spring. It wouldn't be fair to act on the attraction she stirred, let alone the feelings he feared might go along with them. He wouldn't risk a repeat of their messy breakup when he left.

And make no mistake, he intended to leave this place.

"I hope you'll at least keep an open mind," Quinton cautioned him. "For now, I don't mean to interrupt your work. We just wanted to say hi before we let Levi and Gavin know we're in town."

McKenna beamed at Clay as she winked. "That's all my doing, you know. You're the most important brother as far as I'm concerned."

In that moment, her staunch devotion reminded him so much of his mother it choked him up for a second. McKenna hadn't been Dena Reynolds's biological child, but orphaned McKenna had looked up to her stepmother, emulating her in many ways, including her sunny optimism and her loyalty to the people she cared about.

Clearing his throat, Clay reached to give her ponytail a tug before answering. "That's because you're good people, Kenna. I'm happy we'll be together this Christmas."

While they said their goodbyes and Clay's visitors headed back to their pickup, Clay was surprised to realize that he hadn't just been saying that about Christmas. He hadn't spent time with family during the holidays in many years. He regretted not being there for his mother's last Christmas, even though he'd had no way of knowing it would be his final opportunity to celebrate the season with her.

No one ever knew, did they?

As he pulled open the door to the small barn and made his way past the first few empty stalls to greet Moondancer, Clayton figured that was all the more reason to feel good about the time he was spending in Silent Spring. He would smooth things over with Levi, Quinton and Gavin. Explain why he didn't want any part of Duke Kingsley's legacy and hope they understood well enough for him to leave town on good terms.

Because in the end, Clay wasn't staying.

And when he saw Hope next time, he owed it to them both to make that clear.

The Christmas gala was falling apart.

Seated in a cramped office at the back of the building that served temporarily as her clinic, Hope stared at her cell phone in disbelief. She'd just finished up her workday half an hour ago and had turned her attention to working on the fundraiser. Business at the clinic had been slow all day because of inclement weather, a surprise snowfall that had made the roads by turns slushy and icy with the temperature hovering right around freezing.

Little did Hope know her phone call to the swanky hotel and ballroom where she planned to hold the gala would result in a fresh disaster. She'd mailed out invitations for the event a month ago. Yet the venue had just informed her that—despite the signed contract she had with them—they could not host her Holiday Top Hat and Tails Gala.

Pressing her fingers to one temple as she stared out the window at the whiteout, Hope couldn't hold back a sense of defeat. There had been more problems behind the scenes at the event hall than just staffing issues, the way the venue director had suggested a week ago. The place was suffering the fallout of a messy divorce between its married partner owners. One of the wives had absconded with the keys and the books after draining the business account. The wife who remained in town had given up hope for a speedy resolution to the drama, canceling all bookings through the end of the year.

Hope could take legal action, of course. But that wouldn't provide a place for her to hold a black-tie gala for two hundred people. And how would she afford to hire a lawyer anyhow? Setting her phone on the metal desk she'd purchased used, she left her office full of makeshift furnishings to return to the clinic area, where she'd funneled all available funds toward the best possible equipment for her patients. It still wasn't enough, hence the fundraiser. But she was proud of what she'd built here in a structure that was a renovated barn on the property where she'd grown up.

"Hey, boss, I was just leaving." Her assistant, Cassandra, stood on the mat near the front door, winding a green-and-red plaid scarf around her neck. "Did you need me for anything?"

At six feet tall, Cassandra was a strong, capable woman who proved a tremendous asset not only because of her empathy toward animals and their owners, but also for knowledge of the area since she'd grown up in foster homes around western Montana. She'd returned to the area recently to pursue her certification as a veterinary technician. And because she'd fallen for local rancher Emilio Medina, who lived close to Kingsland. Cassandra's height, pale hair and bright blue eyes gave her the appearance of a Viking shield maiden. The quilted puffer jacket she wore and fur-trimmed boots only enhanced the impression.

"No thanks," Hope demurred, waving her out the wreath-trimmed door with a gesture. She'd leaned on Cassandra often enough over the past couple of weeks. Hope had no intention of keeping her after hours for the sake of a fundraising dilemma. Especially when Cass had done her a favor by coming in on a Sunday in the first place. "You should head out before the snow gets any deeper."

"If you're sure?" Cassandra gave her a searching glance, but Hope only nodded. As her assistant reached for the door handle, however, she paused as her mitten brushed the jingle bells looped over the knob. "I left your messages on my desk. Clayton Reynolds checked in while you were in with your last patient."

Hope didn't miss the sly interest in the other woman's voice or the gleam of amusement in her eyes. No doubt she'd heard about the very public kiss Hope and Clay had shared under the mistletoe at the Stockyard the other night. Seemingly half the town had been in the bar to see it, based on how many people had mentioned it to her since then. And those residents who hadn't been in the bar seemed to have heard about it.

While Hope and Cassandra were friends in addition to colleagues, Hope wasn't about to satisfy the other woman's curiosity.

Even if her own was piqued. She and Clay hadn't spoken outside of a couple text messages since their mistletoe kiss three nights ago. She was definitely overdue to speak to him about the gala. Every day she put it off a little longer, hoping she would magically wake up one morning and not feel the tug of attraction for him.

"I'll get in touch with him," Hope promised, slipping past the office Christmas tree behind the reception counter to avoid Cassandra's knowing gaze. Butterflies were already flitting around her stomach at the thought of hearing his voice, of seeing him again. Finally, the discussion she'd planned was in reach of happening. "Drive safe," she added, busying herself with looking through a patient file drawer to defer further conversation.

When the door closed behind Cassandra, leaving a small whirl of fresh snow on the reindeer front mat, Hope sank into the vacated chair at the check-in desk. She had a fresh crisis on her hands with the holiday gala, and she still needed to feed her animals before she could return home for the day. There were currently no animals boarding at her practice, but Hope continued to maintain a small flock of Corriedale sheep on her own property. Normally, after work and tending her animals, she looked forward to her free evenings. After her relentless pursuit of her veterinarian degree, a goal she'd thrown herself into all the more after her mom's death, Hope had enjoyed occasionally pausing to savor the good that had come out of her efforts, not just for the animals she so deeply cared about, but also for their people. Whether it was easing the arthritis of a family's beloved retriever, or overseeing a high-risk birth, she was glad to make a difference in the community.

But somehow her professional victories didn't fulfill her quite as much as they had before Clayton's arrival in town. He invaded her thoughts, hijacking her peaceful contentment with the status quo and making her evenings alone feel a little…empty.

Now, she picked up the pink message paper left in

the center of a black desk blotter where Cassandra sat during the day. Clay's contact details were penned in a careful hand, and Hope stabbed the numbers into the landline, thinking the faster she got the call over with the better. Because while she'd be damned if she avoided him, she also didn't want to place too much importance on their next meeting.

Even if she hadn't confronted him about his side of their breakup three years ago. Even if the kiss they'd shared in front of half of Silent Spring replayed in her mind on an hourly basis.

By the time he answered after one ring, Hope's heart was pounding.

"Hello?" The timbre of his voice made her shiver.

She licked her lips before speaking, realizing his caller ID would only show the name of the practice, and not her in particular.

"Clay, it's me," she began, speaking too quickly because she was all aflutter at the idea of seeing him again. As if she was still the eighteen-year-old who had been sort of besotted with him when he handed her first prize for one of her rams at the county fair.

How could an attraction last for so long? Men had come and gone in her life, in no way leaving her brokenhearted, yet her fascination with this one remained.

"Hope, I've got an emergency on my hands." He sounded tense, something she hadn't picked up on when he first answered the call.

"What's wrong?" Immediately on alert, she rose

to her feet then paced out from behind the reception desk.

"A stray mare is out by one of the Kingsland stallions." His words were clipped. There was a lot of movement in the background, like Clay was running or something. A horse whinnied, long and loud. "A young stud who has been a troublemaker before. He's already injured himself trying to jump the fence."

Guilt stabbed through her that she'd been slow to return his call, wanting any discussion to be in person, which couldn't happen until she'd finished her workday. She had one hand on her coat while she pinned the phone to her shoulder to keep talking as she picked up her keys with the other.

"I'm getting in the truck right now. I had no idea you called about an injury—"

"I didn't," he rushed to say, an engine starting in the background. "I just got home myself and called Gavin to help me rope the mare before Moondancer gets any more out of control. But I can see the horse is already bleeding at the right shoulder, so if you can come too—"

"Of course." She locked the door to the clinic behind her before getting behind the wheel. Grateful to have the vehicle outfitted with everything she could potentially need, she turned the key in the ignition and blasted the heat. "I'm at the office, but I'll be there as soon as I can."

"The roads are icy, Hope. Be careful." His words were almost lost in another loud whinny that sounded in the background, almost a squeal. It sounded aggressive. Or scared, perhaps.

Involuntarily, Hope found herself pressing harder on the gas in spite of Clay's word of caution. Tires spit gravel.

"I'll be fine," she protested, hating to think of the kinds of injuries that could happen to anyone who got between an aggressive twelve-hundred-pound stud and the target of their interest. "You're the one who needs to be careful. You know a young stallion can be unpredictable at best when—"

"I'm going after the mare," he assured her, gentling his voice a fraction. "Getting her out of here is my first objective so Moondancer calms down enough for you to take a look at him."

A truck door slammed on the other end of the call, and she guessed that Clayton had reached wherever it was he'd been driving to. Closer to the stallion's pen, she suspected, since the horse noises grew louder. Snorts and squeals.

Her trepidation grew.

But before she could say anything else, Clay spoke again.

"I've got to try to catch this horse, Hope." He was breathing hard. Probably trying to run closer to the mare, or maybe swinging a rope to catch her. "I need to hang up, but we're at the barn near the ranch manager's house on the Kingsland property. Do you recall where that is?"

She remembered the Kingsland Ranch like the

back of her hand thanks to the ten weeks she'd dated
Clay, plus plenty of professional calls since then.
But she'd never driven there in such a hurry as she
did now, picturing Clayton getting between the riled
animals.

"I'm on my way."

Eight

Of the two agitated animals, Clayton had gambled that it would be easier to calm the mare first. He'd brought a rope from the barn, prepared to secure the dappled gray, but when he'd cautiously slid from the SUV to analyze the situation, the loose horse's prancing and pawing warned him he would be foolish to approach by himself.

Waiting beside the vehicle for his brother to arrive, Clay flexed his fingers and tried to breathe out the tension in his muscles as he kept watch on the animals. He knew how well horses picked up on anxiety in the people around them, so he needed to be calm and relaxed when he approached the overwrought pair. He hadn't been at Kingsland when his stepmother had been trampled by a horse while trying to separate Quinton from a rearing animal, but he'd felt the trauma her death had left on the Kingsley family. She'd been an excellent horsewoman too, so Clay didn't deceive himself for a moment that he could fare any better with an agitated animal. He only hoped the stallion didn't further injure himself with a fretful mare dancing just out of reach.

A hope dwindling fast with the gray lady horse posturing in a way that signaled she was in heat.

Thankfully, a pair of headlights cut through the night gloom at the same time, the sound of an engine muffled by the fresh snowfall. It had to be Gavin since his half brother's spread, Broken Spur Ranch, was next door to Kingsland, both properties built along the Madison River.

At the sight of Gavin's four-wheeled ATV trundling easily over the soft snow, some of Clay's tension eased. Of Duke Kingsley's four sons, Gavin outstripped them all in horsemanship, a fact supported by his decorated rodeo career as well as his efforts to spearhead the new breeding program at Kingsland.

"Thanks for waiting for me," Gavin called out as he switched off the four-wheeler and hopped off the machine. "I'm glad to see the time in Alaska hasn't eroded your horse sense."

Clay couldn't read his brother's expression in the moonlight, though he could see well enough to recognize Gavin was unfastening a bucket of grain from the back of the ATV.

Was that a hint of bitterness in his voice?

A loud whinny split the air, speeding Gavin's movements.

"I prefer to think of it as animal sense," Clay explained as Gavin joined him, the grain bucket in his hand. "And it applies to other creatures besides horses. I wouldn't approach a polar bear solo either."

His words got a light laugh from his sibling, which had been Clay's hope. For the horse separation to go well, they *both* needed to be calm and relaxed. Even now, the stallion reared, his frustration evident.

"Fair enough," Gavin admitted, passing Clayton the bucket of grain he'd brought as incentive. "Do you want to do the talking and offer Ms. Hot to Trot some feed while I get the rope around her?"

"Sure thing." Pail in hand, Clay approached the mare from one direction while Gavin circled to her other side, making sure to remain in her field of vision so as not to startle her. "Once you have her," Clay called in a calm voice, "I can manage Moondancer. Hope should be here any minute to look at that shoulder wound."

"Good deal," Gavin answered as he strode closer to the gray. "Text me afterward to let me know what she thinks of the cut. It looks bad."

They both knew how important a stallion's shoulder was for effective breeding. No wonder Gavin had sounded tense when he arrived. The stud program he was building depended on a handful of animals with sought-after bloodlines, Moondancer included.

"Will do," Clay said in a softer tone as he neared the mare, extending the bucket toward her so she could smell the contents. He didn't see a brand on the animal's left side, but perhaps Gavin would find one on the right. In a quieter voice, he crooned to the gray. "Hey, pretty lady, we're going to help you back home, okay?"

The mare emitted a snort and a snuffle, a white cloud huffing into the cold night air as she lifted her head to study Clay. In the second of quiet that followed, Clay could hear the approach of another vehicle. He didn't turn toward the source of the sound, but in his peripheral vision, he could see the arc of headlights through the night sky.

Hope.

Before he could consider the rush of anticipation the realization brought, a rope looped around the mare's neck in a quick, clean maneuver. The rodeo champ's roping skills were still sharp.

"Well done, brother," Clay praised him as he rewarded the mare with some of the feed. He stroked her neck and breathed a sigh of relief as Gavin slipped a simple rope bridle over her head.

Nearby, the rumble of a truck engine grew louder, the headlights landing directly on them for a moment before the driver killed them along with the engine. She'd parked near Clay's SUV at the other end of the pasture where the snow had been at least partially plowed.

"Thanks, but I'd wager you could have roped her

in your sleep," Gavin answered as he tugged the mare away from Moondancer's pasture fence. He peered at Clay over the horse's muzzle. "You think I've forgotten who taught me how to rope in the first place?"

Memories sideswiped him of a long-ago summer. Seven-year-old Gavin had been as much a Kingsley outcast as Clay had been since Duke divorced Gav's mother after a five-year marriage. Only it had been tougher for Gavin to accept that since the first five years of his life he'd been living full-time at Kingsland, an accepted son. After the divorce, he'd been relegated to summers too, and the scars from that slight had later manifested into a massive chip on his shoulder.

But that summer when Gavin had been seven, Clayton had taken it upon himself to be the kid's friend. He'd taught him every roping trick he'd known since Gavin had been keen to impress his ranching family. Back then, the youngster hadn't yet learned that no amount of talent or effort would alter the way Duke Kingsley viewed his outsider sons.

"I'm surprised you remember that," Clayton admitted, wondering how he'd allowed himself to view his brothers as the enemy these last three years when there'd been a time they'd all been friends. Especially him and Gavin.

Gavin scoffed as he continued to stroke the mare's nose. "A kid doesn't forget his early heroes."

Before Clay could absorb that comment, Hope joined them, already wearing her rubber boots and

work overalls. Her dark hair was caught in an un-
even knot at the back of her head, held by a pencil.
Even in the dim light of the moon, Clay could see
her cheeks were flushed, her expression worried.

Still, the sight of her sent a welcome rush through
him, and it wasn't just about the hot chemistry. There
was also a whole lot of gratitude that she was here
with her skill set and empathy.

"I got here as soon as I could. How is he doing?"
Her gaze darted from the stallion prancing around
the enclosure to the newly settled mare. Then, ever
so briefly, to Clay, as if she wanted to check him over
too. "You were able to separate them okay?"

Reflexively, her hand went to the mare's neck while
she spoke, stroking and soothing. Hope was so good
with animals. Deeply intuitive about their needs or
distress.

That she'd been worried about him too stirred old
feelings to life, emotions he didn't want to remember
since they'd only ended in heartache for both of them.

Gavin cleared his throat after an awkward pause,
making Clay realize he'd been lost in thought when
he should have answered her. Now, Gavin shifted
the mare to his side, turning her slightly.

"She's got a brand from a spread a few miles away."
He pointed to the simple outline of the interlocking
*D*s that symbolized the Dusty Diamond Ranch while
snow flurries melted on the mare's back. "I'll take her
out of here and give the owner a call so Clay can settle
Moondancer enough for you to tend him."

Right. Because that was the job he'd agreed to when he came to Kingsland for a five-week stint. He was supposed to be managing the ranch and helping the animals in his care, not thinking about how Hope's touch would feel.

"I'm on it." Turning on his heel, Clay headed toward the stallion's pasture, aware of Hope's presence behind him every step of the way.

"I'm going to use a longer-acting sedative since that wound looks like it might take a while to stitch," Hope observed, her breathing fast, puffing into the air as she hurried to keep pace through the soft snow. "It will take about ten minutes to kick in once I get close enough to give the dose."

"You don't need to administer it in an IV?" He'd been present at enough medical procedures to know some drugs needed to be given in a vein, an approach that required an animal to remain still.

Some vets sedated first, then utilized a heavier tranquilizer drug.

"I'll start with a dose in the muscle. We'll know more once we clean him up, but the way he's moving around is an encouraging sign." As they reached the pasture gate, she paused beside him while he fished in his pocket for the baby carrots he'd brought.

"I'll see if I can distract him long enough for you to inject him." Clay knew the animal needed to be calm and still, so he took his time letting the horse smell the food first, hoping it would help the stallion settle down.

"I've got some homemade treats he might like too." Bending to dig in her workbag, she emerged with a couple of lumpy-looking cookies in a silicone bag. "There are oats, apples and carrots in these."

The big white creature stretched his neck over the fence toward Hope's bag, clearly having homed in on the scent. He still danced from foot to foot, his tail swishing fast, but he seemed to be settling. The woman was like an animal magician, pulling new tricks from her sack.

"You make these in all your free time?" he asked as she passed the bag to him.

Hope laughed, a welcome sound after the stress of the night. She was already prepping the needle and sterilizing a site. Clay stroked the horse's neck, reminding himself to focus on the job they needed to do rather than the way Hope's eyes shone in the moonlight, her dark hair sliding forward over the brown parka she wore over her overalls.

"I've been known to do a little stress cooking now and then," she admitted, resting one hand on the stallion's side while Clay fed him the lumpy cookie. "And lucky for me, the animals never complain about the aesthetics of what I make."

She was so quick about administering the shot, the horse didn't flinch as he munched the treat. Clay even managed to get a bitless bridle on him so at least he would have an easier time leading the animal.

"Moondancer seems to approve." Clay wondered about the stress of her job. In his short time in Silent

Spring, she'd worked a lot of nights in addition to the days she put in at the clinic and on-site around the region. "And considering all the professional expertise you've offered Kingsland recently, I'm going to insist on helping you with your fundraiser. Even if it means hiring out a third party for you to accept a hand."

Her gaze shot to his. Considering the offer? He suspected she hadn't rescheduled a meeting about the gala because of the chemistry between them. Time spent together lately seemed to end with their mouths fused and their hearts racing.

His mouth went dry at those memories.

Would tonight end the same way?

Hope stared up into Clay's eyes, a few flurries still floating between them even though the worst of the snow seemed to have passed. She'd been in a panic on the way to the ranch, something that rarely happened in her professional life, and it had been because she feared something happening to the man standing next to her.

Ever since he'd returned to Silent Spring, she'd told herself she didn't want anything to do with him. He'd hurt her, therefore she wouldn't let him near her again. But all the directives from her brain felt meaningless in the face of her emotions when it came to Clay. At the end of the day, he made her feel things in a way no one else ever had, and she couldn't just turn that off because it was inconvenient.

"It's not that I don't want to work with you," she said finally, realizing she'd been staring at him for too long. She returned the used needle to a sharps container in her bag before shouldering the duffel. She had a job to do first and foremost. "Would you see if you can coax him closer to the barn so I have better lighting?"

They didn't have much longer before the horse would be difficult to move. She wanted Moondancer near a stall so they could secure him after the procedure.

In the meantime? Maybe she could use her work time to ask Clay the questions that had been circling her mind for days. She followed the horse and the man toward the barn, her boots heavy with the weight of snow and the task before her. Not stitching the stallion, which she could do quickly once she got him cleaned up. But discussing the past with Clayton.

"How's this?" After entering the enclosure, Clay guided the stallion along the wall of the barn, taking advantage of an exterior light on the building. "That way he's got support on one side if he grows wobbly."

"Here is fine," she murmured, surreptitiously moving her stethoscope over the animal. "He's already slowing down. I think it's safe for me to enter the enclosure now, don't you?"

At Clay's nod, Hope shimmied between the fence rails before reaching back for her bag. Minutes later, she had a work station set up around the animal. Clay held the horse on one side to ensure the creature's safety while sedated. Hope cleaned the wound methodically before setting up the tools she would need to stitch the gash.

All the while, she was very aware of Clay's proximity and how well they were working together. Especially after the scare she'd had earlier, the adrenaline rush of fear for him. The aftermath of those feelings left her nerves raw and her pulse a little shaky.

"I got some bad news from my event venue in Bozeman today," she said finally, needing to fill the silence before she did something foolish like admit she'd been thinking about him nonstop for days. "They canceled my contract and said they won't be able to hold the event."

"Isn't that what a contract is for?" He peered over the horse's lowered neck to meet her eyes. Though they stood outdoors, the barn blocked the wind and the temperature hovered just above freezing. "How can they do that?"

"No clue, but there's no way I can resolve the issue in the dwindling amount of time left. I need to think of something fast since the invitations already went out." She set aside the tools she'd used to clean the wound and sterilized her hands to prepare for stitching.

The cut was deep, but at least it wasn't jagged. She'd have an easy enough time closing the wound.

"Have the event at Kingsland," Clay offered, his

gaze still on her as she worked. The sedated horse's nose was almost on the ground in a five-point stance, so they could see one another well enough even on opposite sides of Moondancer's head. "You can use the Thoroughbred show arena Duke built before his death. Have you seen that space? It looks more like a museum than a place to show off animals."

Hope paused as she readied the needle. "I've been in there," she recalled aloud, her brain working fast to calculate the logistics of switching venues, barely daring to hope it would work. "Lauryn held her Studs for Sale bachelor auction there last spring, actually. It worked really well as an event space."

Kneeling in front of the horse to reach the shoulder wound more comfortably, she went to work sewing the flesh, relieved at Clay's thoughtful offer. Would it be bad business to hold the event on a client's property? It didn't strike her as unethical. And did it even matter when the Kingsley brothers had wanted to donation match in the first place? It would be public knowledge that the largest ranch in Montana was supporting the gala.

And a huge weight off her shoulders to have it taken care of with the event just weeks away.

"There you go. I'm texting Levi right now to make sure we're clear for the date." A moment later, Clayton chuckled softly to himself. "Studs for Sale. I look forward to hassling Gavin about that one."

Hope unspooled more surgical thread, her needle

moving faster now that the worst of the gash was closed. Relief washed through her to have the matter of the venue settled.

"Thank you, Clay, for making this easier for me. I was pretty stressed about the cancellation." She heaved out a sigh, a wave of fatigue catching up with her as the worries of the day abated. Clay was unharmed. Her event would go on. Although as those concerns diminished, another one floated to the surface of her thoughts. "I've been meaning to ask you about something else."

From the other side of the animal, Clay said, "Go ahead. And Levi already gave us the green light on using the show arena. Why don't you and I go over the details tomorrow?"

Would he even want to help her with the gala after she put him in the hot seat about their past? But it bugged her that he'd never really reacted to the news that she hadn't tried to break up with him. That he'd essentially ghosted her for no reason.

"I'd like that." After the breakneck pace of her workweek and the snafu in planning her event, she could admit she needed help. Tying off the last stitch, she set aside her tools then placed a clean dressing over the cut. "We can take him to his stall now and get him comfortable before he comes around."

She peeled off her gloves as she rose to her feet. Clay was already leading the stallion through the open half door at the back of the barn. Once they had the animal secured in a stall, they returned to her work station where Clay helped her gather her tools.

Her gaze strayed to his broad shoulders as he lifted her bag for her.

"So what else did you want to discuss?" he asked, leaning a shoulder against the barn wall. His tall form cast a long shadow over her.

Leave it to the Alaska resident to be perfectly comfortable conducting a conversation in the night air. Temperatures in the thirties were probably mild for him.

Although Hope felt warm enough too. From working? Or from the way Clay's nearness always made her blood simmer?

Tugging a bottle of scented hand sanitizer from her pocket, she coated her hands before putting on a pair of lined leather gloves.

"I've been thinking back to that night at the McMasters ranch when I told you the note you read three years ago wasn't meant for you." Folding her arms, she leaned against the barn near him, mirroring his posture. "You didn't say much about it at the time."

Clay's eyebrows shot up. "You took off right after dropping that bombshell, so I didn't really have time to get my head around it."

"And now?" she prompted him, telling herself to keep her eyes on his and not indulge her desire to look her fill.

Just being this close to him again, talking about what they'd shared, made her heart beat faster. Her defenses were nonexistent after the adrenaline let-down from the tense drive over here.

He gave a wry twist of his lips. "Are you asking if I have regrets? Because I can assure you even before that, I regretted the way I took off without talking to you. It says a lot about where I was in my life that I could be such a self-centered ass."

Her lips felt dry. She tried to swallow, the old emotions clogging her throat. His admission didn't change the past, but the words were a small balm for a deep wound, and she was glad of them.

"I tried to contact you after you left." She didn't know what possessed her to reveal still more of her hurt. She'd left teary voice mail messages at first. Later messages were cold. Angry.

He shook his head, taking a step nearer. "I never got any messages. I blocked your number before I even got on the plane, thinking it would be easier that way."

Knowing he hadn't heard those messages and chosen to ignore them was a little less painful than the alternative.

Besides, having his big body this close to hers made her temperature spike. What had she hoped to accomplish by asking him about the past? She'd wanted answers from him, and now that she had them, she felt slightly mollified. Yet the bottom line was that he'd left town and they hadn't spoken until his return three years later. No discussion tonight would change that.

Although the brush of his knuckles along her cheek sure made her wish things were different. If only for a night. Her pulse sped faster, blood heating, desire tripping over her nerve endings in a way that made every part of her feel more alive. No one else had ever affected her the way this man always had.

"I'm sure it was." She licked her lips, levering herself away from the wall where she'd been leaning. If she remained here any longer, she'd end up kissing him again. Already, the draw between them was pulling her closer. "I should get going. It's been a long day—"

Clay's hands bracketed her waist, steadying her. His forehead tipped forward, leaning against hers. For a moment they just breathed one another in. A shiver spun through her at the feel of his warmth. His strength. Hunger for him—for his touch, his kiss—had her edging closer.

The moment felt full of tantalizing possibilities.

"Stay with me, Hope." The words were as silky and persuasive as anything he'd said to the horses earlier, his voice rumbling through her. And Hope guessed those words were even more effective on her because she found herself lifting her arms to twine around his neck.

Her fingers scrabbled against the stiff collar of his heavy jacket. Restless. Seeking. A sigh shuddered through her.

After the hellish day she'd had, the scare that something could happen to this big, indomitable man who'd made such an impression on her, Hope gave the only possible answer to his request.

"Yes. Please."

Nine

With the certainty of Hope's voice echoing in his ears, Clay wasted no time leading her back to the ranch manager's house. The draw between them had been crowding out everything else in his mind since his arrival in Montana. Now, at last, they would give in to the heat and attraction, explore this chemistry that drove him to distraction every single day.

They were silent and focused as they walked through fresh snowfall past a stretch of the four-rail fence wrapped with white lights, the posts decorated with small wreaths. They headed past the back door of the main house where another, bigger wreath framed a leaded window. He tried not to walk too fast, not wanting her to slip as they followed the vague outline of the flagstone path under the blanket of white. Yet every cell in his being urged him on, hungry for another taste of Hope.

"I still need to wash up," she reminded him as his boots hit the stone steps that led to a wraparound veranda. She was already unzipping her parka and shoving it off her shoulders. "I'll leave my overalls out here."

It took a long moment for him to drag his eyes away from her as she shimmied out of the rubberized overalls she wore, revealing a red sweater and faded jeans tucked into her boots. Her movements were quick and efficient as she slid the wide-legged overalls right over her boots. No doubt she'd repeated that same action many times over the years.

For him the sequence was far from ordinary, however. He was already imagining what it would be like to undress the rest of her. To bare the body he'd once spent weeks getting to know intimately. When she'd finished stripping off the work attire, she slung the coat and overalls onto a wrought iron patio chair that had been dragged up against the stone wall of the house, probably to keep it out of the elements when the house had been left vacant.

Seeing her lay aside the clothes spurred Clay to drag his eyes away from her to push open the back door that led into the mudroom. "There's a bathroom downstairs." He held the door for her and then pointed to the left. Thankfully, he'd left the lights on, so her way was illuminated. "Just off this hallway."

"I'll just be a minute," she said with a nod.

He breathed in a hint of her fragrance as she passed him, and it took all of his restraint not to pull her closer so he could taste her everywhere until he located the source of that scent. Instead, he slipped off his boots and hung his coat while she disappeared down the corridor. His heart jackhammered so that it was all he could hear while he washed his hands and face over the farmhouse-style sink in the large, old-fashioned kitchen. There was a turn-of-the-century fireplace built into one wall, the exposed brickwork almost the same color as the heavy wooden rafters. Clayton forced himself to look at that as he toweled off, needing to think about anything else besides the shower water clicking on in the other room. He could hear the tankless heater flip on, the water rumbling through pipes, and the thought of Hope naked under his roof was killing him.

He wanted her so badly it hurt. She was a fever in his blood, especially now that a night together was inevitable.

Think about something else. The last thing he wanted was to rush this opportunity with her.

Clay unbuttoned the flannel he'd layered over a T-shirt and laid the garment over a kitchen chair. He had a few memories of his grandfather sitting at the head of the massive table in the middle of the room, his chair pushed back close to the fireplace to enjoy the warmth of a blaze. Then, the kitchen had been filled with the scents of home. Bread baking. A slow-cooked, savory dinner simmering on the stove all day. Clay had avoided the kitchen since he'd moved into the old house, unwilling to remember the happier moments at Kingsland.

Now, however, he could push aside those thoughts easily enough when he heard a door open nearby. Soft footsteps padded along the oak planks of the floor as Hope retraced her steps.

To him.

Anticipation fired impossibly hotter, the scent of his soap drifting on a humid wave from the open bathroom door. When he turned, he found her standing barefoot on the simple braid runner in the hallway, her hair clipped into a twist at the back of her head, as if to keep it from getting wet when she'd showered. A pair of tiny horseshoe earrings glinted in her lobes. But the bulk of his attention remained glued to her body. Where she wore nothing except a thick gray towel she'd wrapped around her petite, curvy frame.

Clay rubbed a hand along his chest where his heart beat wildly. "I hope you know when you look like that, you run the risk of sending me into cardiac arrest."

A smile curved her lips. Or at least, he could hear the smile in her voice when she spoke because he hadn't fully succeeded in pulling his gaze from her pinup curves. "Is that right?" She cocked a hip, striking a pose that every woman who'd grown up with Instagram seemed to know was guaranteed to make men drool. "Good thing I make house calls."

He met her eyes then, fully focused on the moment. On her.

"You're sure about this?" He closed the distance between them, wanting to be certain she had no second thoughts. Desire scorched his veins while he waited for her answer, every nerve ending alive.

An old-fashioned pendulum wall clock ticked loudly in the momentary silence. And he feared she would opt out. The possibility of losing this night with her raked him with regret.

Then she smiled. Thank heaven, she smiled.

"Would I be standing in your kitchen in nothing but terry cloth right now if I had any doubts about what I want?" She looped her arms around his neck, fitting her body to his like a missing puzzle piece.

Yes.

Clay gripped her hips to pull her closer still, needing to feel every inch of her against him. All around him. The tension that had been threading through his muscles eased now that he knew there would be no turning back. Another kind of tension quickly took its place, an imperative need to remind her how good they were together.

"Then we want the same thing," he growled in a low voice as he dipped his head to kiss her.

Her mouth molded to his as she sighed into him, her lips parting on contact. Would the rest of her open to him as sweetly? The thought sent the kiss into overdrive as he explored her with his tongue, remembering all the things that Hope liked best. Her hips pushed forward, and he leaned her back over one arm, wanting more. He couldn't get enough of her, from her cinnamon flavor to a hint of light perfume that clung to her hair despite the shower. Having the fragrance of his soap layered over that more delicate scent was just flat-out sexy.

It was almost as much of a turn-on as the soft sounds she made in her throat while he splayed one hand on her back, feeling the delicate curve of her spine through the thick towel. The swell of her breasts flattened against his chest, the fabric she'd tucked there coming loose so the towel slid lower.

He felt his restraint slipping right along with it.

Unable to wait another second, he broke the kiss only to sweep her off her feet and cradle her in his arms. He didn't waste a second striding toward his bedroom.

Maybe another woman would have put up a mild objection to being carried, or at least claimed she was capable of walking to the bedroom on her own. But Hope didn't dream of protesting the unique thrill of being swung up into this strong man's arms and held protectively against his chest.

But that was Clayton Reynolds—he was the stuff fantasies were made of.

And she needed this, needed him, needed the blissful distraction he offered. She yearned for positive memories to edge out the negative, even if only for a few hours.

She allowed herself a moment to savor the feel of his shoulder under her palm, the medical professional inside her as mesmerized as her womanly instincts. She traced the impressive anterior deltoid. Caressed the pectoralis major that women would weep over and other men would envy.

Enthralled by his body, Hope barely noticed when they left the well-lit hallway for the dimmer bedroom until her toes lightly brushed the doorframe. Then, seeing the sprawling mattress that was so big it had to be a California king, a shiver trembled through her.

"Is it too cool in here for you?" he asked, slowing his step as he reached the edge of the bed dressed in simple white and taupe linens. A green-and-red plaid quilt lay folded at the bottom of the bed, a nod to the holidays. "I can turn on the fireplace."

He was already walking in another direction, toward the built-in fireplace so he could punch a wall switch with one elbow while still clutching her in his arms. A blaze leaped in the gas hearth, filling the room with an orange glow. The evergreen boughs laid on the mantle released their fragrant scent as the room warmed.

"I'm not cold." Reaching to touch his face, she stroked her fingers over his bristly jaw before cupping his chin to turn him toward her. "The shivers I'm having are the kind only you can fix."

His eyes raked over her in a way that made her toes curl, a mixture of fierce hunger tempered by more gentlemanly restraint. Like he might devour her whole, but he'd be sure she enjoyed every minute of it. An ache spread between her thighs.

"In that case, I'm bringing you to my bed now." His pace was faster now. Urgent. "A place you've already visited plenty of times in my imagination ever since I found you in my driveway my first day back in town."

Part of her wanted to know all about that, to quiz him on every interaction they'd had in his thoughts. But she was too keyed up to indulge her sensual curiosity that way. Especially when they could have more than just the fantasy of one another tonight.

Depositing her carefully in the center of the bed, Clay straightened to stare down at her. The towel that had been clinging to her as he'd carried her had fallen away on the landing, the terry cloth now pinned beneath her, the ends she'd tucked so carefully between her breasts fallen to the wayside. She knew her curves were extra—they'd made the puberty years a daunting time, and to this day they made clothes tricky to fit. Yet she didn't mind the attention Clay lavished on her body now, his eyes fastened to her while his hands flexed at his sides. Almost as if he was thinking about putting them all over her.

"You don't have to settle for just imagining me anymore," she reminded him, hardly recognizing the husky drawl of her voice.

But then, the anticipation had ratcheted up beyond

her breaking point. She'd felt a sensual hunger like nothing she'd ever experienced before. She *needed* this. Needed him.

Still, when he reached for the hem of his T-shirt and raked it up and over his head, she gasped at the ripple of muscles on muscles in the burnished glow of firelight. He looked hewn from granite, the rows of internal oblique muscles and external oblique muscles making her mouth go dry and her thoughts scatter like dust. She wasn't sure if she wanted to trace each ridge and line with her finger or her tongue. Preferably both.

But a moment later, he was flicking open his jeans. Not to take off, apparently, since he left the denim on his hips. When he adjusted himself a moment later, she suspected he'd just wanted to give himself more room. That realization had her elbowing up to a sitting position and scooting to the edge of the bed so she could kiss him just above the black cotton fabric of his boxers.

The low groan of approval that hissed between his teeth only fueled her desire. She licked along the warm skin while his fingers sifted through her hair, holding her in place. And that too was hot as hell because it told her how much she was getting to him. This intense, quiet man who didn't reveal much of himself was trusting her with his needs.

So she gave in to the urge to trace her fingers along his abs, letting one hand explore the texture of him while the other raked aside the boxers so she could taste him. She licked and savored, sucked and slid over the hard length of him until he hauled her up by her shoulders.

Their eyes met in the firelight, both of them panting. Both a little dazed. At least, that's how she felt, and she was pretty sure she recognized the unfocused glaze of his eyes as someone who was enjoying himself.

"Why did you stop me?" She ran her fingers over her lips that trembled a little.

She was so keyed up. Anxious, but in a good way. Anticipating. Her whole body humming with pleasure and they'd only just begun.

He blinked away the dazed look to really see her. He cupped her face in his strong hands. "Because you were driving me too close to the edge with that sweet mouth. And when we find release for the first time tonight, it's going to be together."

His thumbs caressed her cheekbones. Who knew that could be such a turn-on? She got gooseflesh everywhere, her eyelids falling half-shut as he treated her face like a sacred object.

"I can accept that," she agreed, smoothing her hands up his arms and over his biceps toward his shoulders. "As long as I can kiss you more later."

His low growl rumbled his chest until he tilted her face up and kissed her. And kissed her.

No part of her mouth went untouched. No square inch unexplored. He took his time with her until she practically vibrated from wanting him. She gripped his shoulders harder, willing him closer even though they were practically fused. And yet he must have gotten the message because at last he pushed her back on the bed, following her down to the mattress with his big, hard body. Wedging his strong thigh between hers.

Pleasure rippled through her at the feel of him there, the flexing of his muscle through his jeans giving her an intense, erotic thrill. A pleasure intensified when he lowered his mouth to her breast and tongued circles around one taut nipple.

"Clay." She murmured his name helplessly, lost in an overload of sensations she hadn't experienced in…three years.

She pushed away the thought, unwilling to let anything rob her of this moment with a man who was like her own private orgasm whisperer. The tension between her hips was already close to breaking and he hadn't even been inside her yet.

"I've got you," he crooned in her ear, his breath a harsh whisper. "I'm going to take care of you."

When she scrabbled at his jeans with her fingers, wanting to help take them off, Clayton rose from the bed and shucked the rest of his clothes. He produced a condom from a nightstand drawer and rolled the protection into place. Hope barely had time to admire him in profile before he was back on the bed with her.

Not that she was complaining. Having him touch her was even better than looking her fill. She loved the weight of him on top of her as he stretched out over her, even though his elbows bracketed her shoulders to keep his upper body raised. He parted her legs with one knee, making room for himself while her heartbeat went wild.

As much as she wanted to simply enjoy the physical intimacy, she couldn't resist the temptation to trail her fingers along his stubbled jaw as she stared up into his green eyes.

For the space of one breath, and then another, their gazes locked. Asked questions neither of them were ready to answer. When he edged his way inside her, taking his time, Hope was only too glad to shove aside the emotions stirring to life behind the scenes. This was a night for pleasure. Something they both deserved.

Something they were skilled at giving each other.

A fact she remembered vividly once he was seated fully inside her. She couldn't hold back the cry of pleasure as she squeezed his hips with her thighs, wanting to hold him right *there*.

Clay's voice in her ear was a low reverberation that hummed over her senses. "You sure you want to do that?" He nipped her earlobe before adding, "You might like it even more if I move."

To illustrate his point, he slid back slowly as if to withdraw, making her whimper at the loss. Then, he thrust his hips forward again, plunging deeper inside her. The sensation was nothing short of exquisite.

She let her thighs go slack.

"Yes. That. More." The words tumbled out in a disjointed series as she closed her eyes to luxuriate in the incredible things he did to her body.

He gave her exactly what she craved. For long minutes they relearned one another's rhythms, found new erogenous zones. He lifted one of her legs, hooking it around his arm as he drove deeper inside her, and she nearly came from just that. She stroked her fingernails lightly down his chest, making a shudder run through him.

Being with him was everything she remembered and so much more. By the time she rolled him onto his back to take a turn being in charge, she had staved off release at least three different times. Now, sitting up with her hair fallen from the knot she'd put it in earlier, the tousled locks spilling over her bare shoulders, she felt wild. Free.

She'd missed these sensations.

Missed him, a contrary part of her brain piped up before she shut it down fast. Nothing was going to spoil this amazing connection tonight.

"You look damned good sitting there." Clay's fingers sank deeper into her hips while she shifted her knees on the soft duvet.

"I'm glad because I'm determined to make you feel as incredible as you make me feel." She moved experimentally, loving the way his mouth fell open, his eyes fluttering closed.

Splaying her palms over the heat and strength of

his broad chest, she steadied herself to repeat the movement. Again and again.

His body tensed beneath her, muscles rippling, tendons in his neck flexing as she moved faster. When he gripped her hips to slow her down, she made to protest, but before she could speak, he flipped her onto her back again.

"Remember what I said?" His words were a warm breath on her cheek before he reached between their bodies to stroke her clit. "When we go that first time, we go together."

She couldn't have answered if she tried. All sensation centered around his touch. He knew her so well. Knew what she wanted even when she didn't. Because a moment later, she couldn't fight the release that shattered over her. Couldn't have said that she was incapable of waiting since the orgasm pummeled her, seemingly involving every muscle in the lower half of her body.

But then, maybe the pulsing of her body set off his, because seconds afterward, his hoarse shout mingled with her cries as he found his finish. Her satisfaction doubled, her feminine muscles still fluttering with happy aftershocks. When he was done, he slumped to her right side on the bed, tucking her against his chest.

As she inhaled his warm scent, so sated and comfortable, she told herself not to question what they'd just done. It had been blissfully good, and for right now that was enough. The morning would be soon enough for recriminations. For her to shore up her defenses against a man who would only leave her again.

Clayton had a whole life in Alaska that he had no intention of leaving. It hadn't escaped her attention that when she asked him how he felt about mistaking the letter she'd written as a way to break things off with him, Clay hadn't said he regretted leaving her. Only that he regretted not speaking to her before he departed.

A telling stance on the past.

One that made the writing on the wall very clear about their future apart. So for now, Hope adjusted Clay's pillow beneath her head and took this time for what it was—a one-off that gave them both temporary pleasure and closure on the past.

This time around, she'd already decided she would be the one to walk away if things got too complicated. She might give Clay her body, but she knew better than to let him anywhere near her heart.

Ten

Still reeling from sex that had knocked him flat, Clayton threaded his fingers through Hope's dark hair, stroking the silky strands over and over. Their connection took his breath away. Hell, *she* stole his breath. And now he had no idea what happened next, so he just kept combing his fingers through her hair. Soothing her or himself? He could feel the tension in her body returning as the minutes ticked past, and he regretted that she couldn't simply relax and enjoy lying by his side.

Yet he understood why.

They'd come together in a moment of fire and need, ignoring all the history between them. The discussions about their past had been abbreviated. Brusque.

He'd oversimplified his answer to her question about whether he had regrets over leaving Montana. He'd shortchanged the conversation because memories from that time in his life were painful. And not just because of Hope.

He owed her a better explanation of what had happened that summer. So while he reached behind her on the nightstand to find the remote for the fireplace, he tried to formulate what to say. He'd never been much for sharing things about himself, a tendency that had grown all the more ingrained during his years in Alaska. Especially in Galbraith Lake where he'd taken isolation to new levels, seeing no one else for weeks on end.

"I should tell you something," he began as he used the remote to dial down the height of the flames in the grate now that the chill had left the room.

After the effort he'd had to expend in the Arctic just to stay warm—whole days of chopping wood and dragging it back to his shelter to manually feed the firebox—the remote-controlled heat seemed all the more decadent.

"That sounds ominous." Hope slid the pillow out from under her head to re-fluff then sank into the white goose down again, her expression wary.

He dragged the green-and-red plaid throw up from the foot of the bed to cover them before setting aside the remote.

"I didn't mean for it to be." Clay noticed she'd repositioned herself in a way that inserted a little more space between them. He was running out of time to explain himself. "It just occurred to me that I owe you a lot better explanation of what happened before I left Silent Spring the last time."

She hugged the blanket closer, still looking as though she might be ready to run. He hoped that wasn't the case. Their chemistry had been even better than he'd recalled from three years ago. And those days had been hot enough to sear themselves permanently into his memories. He hated the idea of sending her running now, but he owed her a better explanation of how it had all shaken down.

"I'm listening." She shifted to lie on her side again, facing him. Knee brushing his lightly.

The feel of her body reminded him that it would be so much easier to forget about the difficult conversation and lose himself in her all over again. But he'd passed that point now. There would be no turning back.

"The whole town seems to know that I had a blowup with Duke that last day." Clayton hadn't talked about it with his brothers, but they'd referenced it since he'd been back in town. Apparently Sheriff Hamilton had overheard some of the altercation, and that had come out when Gavin and Lauryn began seeing one another.

Unfortunately, Clayton had thrown Gav under the bus during the argument, claiming the two of them would "get even" with their father when they destroyed his legacy. Not his finest moment. It hadn't inspired the sheriff's confidence in Gavin, apparently, and Clayton regretted damaging his brother's reputation when he'd only been spouting off.

"Yet no one knows quite why you argued," Hope prodded him gently, moving closer again, her legs shifting under the blanket and stirring a hint of her fragrance. "Although anyone who spent time around your father knew his character well enough to suspect any dispute was likely his doing and not yours."

He wasn't sure he deserved her kindness and loyalty, but he appreciated hearing it just the same. For a moment, he stared into the silent, steady flames of the gas fireplace while his thoughts returned to that day in his father's office at Kingsland Ranch.

"I had been working my tail off to be a better man. To make some kind of peace with Dad since my mother had died earlier that year and it meant something to her that I try to get to know him."

Hope's cool fingers slid over his wrist. Squeezed. "I can imagine the importance that would have placed on your relationship with Duke."

"I wanted to do right by my mother's memory." She'd had a tough life, and just when Clayton had reached a point where he could make things easier for her, she'd slipped away. "So I put up with Duke in his dark moods when it was more amusing for him to berate my efforts at Kingsland than to give me the tools I needed for success."

That was putting it mildly. Duke had insisted on signing off on all ranch purchases himself, making it impossible for Clay to conduct day-to-day business without involving him. Then, instead of simply green-lighting expenditures or contracts Clay negotiated, Duke would try to haggle for lower prices or complain about the terms, chasing away good contacts and tanking deals.

"I remember something like that had happened the day we waited out the rainstorm in the barn." Hope threaded her fingers through his, fitting their hands together. "You said Duke had refused to sell some yearlings for a price you'd already verbally agreed to."

He'd forgotten he'd shared that with her. He'd been beside himself that day, furious at being undermined and having his word rendered worthless. That had been the beginning of the end.

"It only got worse after that episode." He'd shut out a lot of his memories of that last dispute, but he forced himself to remember now. For Hope's sake. "I waited until I'd cooled down enough to tell him I couldn't work with someone who thwarted me at every turn. That ticked him off, and he began a tirade about my shortcomings, suggesting he wouldn't have to step in if I knew what I was doing."

Coming from anyone else, Clayton could have mentally separated himself from accusations that were completely unfounded. But back then, the words still had some power to hurt since he'd really wanted to heal the relationship in honor of his mom's memory.

"You obviously knew that wasn't true." Hope's fingers brushed the backs of his knuckles, her touch as gentle as her words. "I wonder what made Duke such a bitter, miserable man when he had so much."

"The death of his first wife," Clayton answered without hesitation. He'd gleaned as much from the ugliness that Duke had spewed during his final meltdown with Clay. "He didn't have a great moral compass to begin with, but I think Adele's death made him resent anyone who wasn't as unhappy as him. Except for Quint and Levi—they got a pass because they were Adele's sons."

"You think so?" Her fingers stilled as she tilted her face to see his better.

Turning his attention from the fire, he met her dark eyes.

"I know so." Since the information had been obtained in a painful way, however, he was hardly pleased to share it. "That much became clear when he accused me of being like my money-grabbing—" clearing his throat, he couldn't bring himself to repeat the words verbatim "—mother. Duke intimated my mom tried to sabotage his relationship with Adele by 'getting herself' pregnant."

He'd lost it then. Not physically, of course, since he'd never strike the man his mother had genuinely cared for. But his temper had run hot enough to say words he'd regret afterward—like threatening to destroy everything Duke had built.

"No wonder you wanted to leave town," Hope

murmured, tipping her head to rest on his shoulder. "And how sad that he alienated everyone who might have filled the void his wife left."

Her viewpoint intrigued him since that hadn't occurred to him no matter how many times he'd tried to put the incident into perspective over the years.

"Afterward, I was ashamed to have behaved in a way that would have disappointed Mom." He hadn't wanted to share the story with Hope at the time, even though he'd headed over to her place that night. Where he'd found the note he thought she'd left for him. "Especially when my whole point in coming here was to honor her memory."

Levering up on one elbow, Hope looked down into his face. "Her death was so fresh then. You were probably much harder on yourself than you deserved."

The simple wisdom of Hope's understanding words put some of the old bitterness to rest. No doubt she could relate to the way a beloved parent's unexpected passing could amplify a lot of emotions.

"Thank you for that." Clay stroked a lock of dark hair that cast her face in shadow, tucking it behind one ear. "I retreated to Alaska to put distance between me and Duke. And to forget about how completely I'd failed my mom."

Her lips quirked into a sad, wry smile. "And, possibly, to retreat from anyone who might have put the incident into context for you."

She remained very still, stiff almost, until he wrapped an arm around her shoulders and settled her beside him. His mind reeled with the possibility she'd mentioned as he avoided her dark, insightful eyes. Had it been easier for him to leave Hope—to take the out the letter had given him—so that he didn't have to talk about what happened with Duke? So he could hang on to his anger and resentment about the falling out?

So the relationship would have a convenient end?

The idea that she might have a point did not sit well with him. Because it meant that he could no longer sell himself the fiction that Hope had wanted him gone. He'd have to face the fact that maybe he'd been the one to tank the relationship all along.

Walking slowly, Hope carried a fifteen-foot ladder over to the bare Douglas fir Christmas tree in a corner of the Kingsland Ranch Thoroughbred show arena. The ladder wasn't heavy, just super awkward. If it started tipping one way, she'd fall over for sure.

Why hadn't she waited for Clayton to help her?

Oh, right. She was too stubborn by half and wasn't sure she was ready to face him after the awkward days that had passed since they slept together.

Since he'd not only reintroduced her to the best sex of her life, but he'd also revealed something more significant about himself than she'd been privy to before—that his departure from Silent Spring had far more to do with his father than her. Although he hadn't spelled it out for her, she understood that he'd used the letter she'd written as a convenient excuse to leave without a word to her.

She was glad for the clarity. Because knowing that only confirmed they hadn't been right for one another. And yet she'd caved to their attraction again, making the aftermath of their night together all the more awkward. She guessed he felt the same way, judging by how they'd both retreated to their own corners the next day. When they'd said goodbye in the morning, he'd promised to make all the arrangements for her to use Kingsland Ranch to host the Christmas gala.

Which he'd done. By text.

More proof that he thought their night together had been a mistake. He was happy to help her, but he didn't plan to get tangled up emotionally. No doubt she would only wither from that kind of inattention and lack of communication. He was a man content to be alone.

For her part, she'd assured him she would recheck Moondancer throughout the week while the stallion quarter horse healed. Which she'd also done. Timing her arrivals for when she'd had a good idea he was occupied elsewhere. Something that hadn't been tough to do since he'd been texting her regular updates on his progress with using the show arena, often adding a line about his activity for the day. That he was at the coffee shop or leaving the ranch to meet with a prospective cattle buyer.

Now, setting the ladder down so that it rested on

an exposed rafter beam holding up the twenty-foot ceiling, Hope congratulated herself on successfully relocating it even as she vowed she wouldn't risk moving the thing alone again. She didn't appreciate when people took unnecessary risks with their animals that ended up causing injuries. So she ought to heed her own advice and not take unwise risks of her own.

Now, to start decorating the tree, a task that always brought mixed feelings for her as she recalled how much her mom had loved the holidays.

Hope was digging into a storage bin of multicolored lights when a woman's voice called from the far side of the otherwise empty arena.

"Hello? Anyone here?"

Hope couldn't place the voice, low and husky for a woman, with a slight northern lilt to the words. Maybe a ranch hand she hadn't met before? Ranch workers often came and went with the seasons, especially the ones who contributed the unskilled labor. Young people inclined to ranch life sometimes traveled the country that way, signing on for anywhere that needed helping hands and a strong back for a season.

"I'm in the show space," Hope called, straightening from the bin with a neatly wrapped length of lights in hand. "Near the tree."

Maybe Clayton had asked one of the ranch hands to assist her tonight. He had planned to meet her here after 6:00 p.m. to decorate the Douglas fir he'd cut three days ago, and Hope had figured she'd get a head start to minimize the awkwardness of prolonged time together. Or, more likely, to avoid the irresistible draw of their attraction before she did something foolish like develop feelings for him again.

Still, it was only five o'clock.

A moment later, a tall redhead dressed in black jeans and boots with a crimson sweater and black puffer vest strode into the show arena, her long pony-tail resting on one shoulder as she let out a low, appreciative whistle.

"Well, these Kingsley men sure don't spare any expense do they?" the woman observed aloud as she gazed around at the pale wood walls and matching rafters. "Their horses live well."

She trailed a gloved hand over a handrail near the rows of seating surrounding a pristine dirt floor that had been covered with a temporary platform for the Christmas gala.

"You're right about that," Hope answered, forgetting about the lights in her curiosity about the newcomer whose comments weren't the sort of thing a new ranch hand would make. "Can I help you?"

Amusement lit the woman's deep blue eyes. "Heck no. If you're Hope Alvarez, then I'm here to help you." She took a step closer and thrust out her right hand. "I'm McKenna Reynolds, Clay's sister."

Sister? Hope did a double take as she shook the woman's hand. Before she could say anything, however, Mckenna shook her head and laughed.

"Stepsister, technically," she corrected herself as she straightened with a shrug. She had a casual air that suggested an easygoing nature. The kind of woman who would be easy to befriend. "No blood relation. It drives Quinton wild when I call Clay my brother since that makes it sound like Quint and I have some sort of seriously twisted relationship going on. But I love Clay like a brother just the same."

Hope smiled warily. She couldn't recall ever being so charmed while simultaneously feeling certain she'd just received a subtle warning. Clay had a champion in this woman.

"Well, it's nice to meet you, McKenna. Clay mentioned you were in town for the holidays. Welcome to Silent Spring." Hope tried to recall the things Clay had told her about his stepsister over the years. When they'd been seeing one another three years ago, he'd said McKenna worked somewhere on the west coast. As a hotel concierge, she remembered.

But since then, the woman had moved to Dutch Harbor, Alaska, to take over the bar Clayton had bought before he moved to Galbraith Lake. That part she knew from conversations with Lauryn and Kendra, since Levi and Gavin had invested time and money in the search for Clayton so they could divide the inheritance from Duke. An inheritance Clay didn't want any more than he wanted to stay in Silent Spring.

"Thank you." McKenna pointed to the open bin of lights and ornaments before sliding off her puffer vest and tossing it over a nearby arena seat. "But don't let me slow you down. Can I give you a hand with decorating? Clay mentioned you had a lot to do to get the space ready for your fundraiser."

Was that all Clay had said about her? Hope wondered how much McKenna knew about their relationship.

"I'm grateful for the help, thank you." Hope tried to keep up with the woman who was already plugging in an end of the light strand and working out logistics of passing the reel back and forth so they could circle the tree faster. McKenna Reynolds wasted no time. And considering Hope liked to get things done efficiently too, that was saying something. "And I hear congratulations are in order for you and Quinton. The whole family is thrilled about your baby news."

"Thank you. I'm relieved Clayton came around to accepting Quinton and I being together," McKenna admitted, pausing to tuck the lights deeper between the branches of the fir. "It seems like he's finally realized the Kingsleys aren't the enemy. Now that his dad is gone, I'm hoping he'll improve his relationship with Quinton and his other half brothers."

"He deserves a strong family." As she said it, Hope realized how fiercely she believed that. "After all the grief his father caused him, and then losing his mom—" Realizing what she was saying and the relationship that McKenna shared with Clay's mom, she peered around the tree at the other woman. "I know you were close with Dena Reynolds. I'm sorry for your loss."

McKenna's blue eyes were bright with emotion as she nodded. "She helped me understand that you can forge your family with love. That it didn't have to be about the people who share your genes."

"She sounds like a wise lady," Hope offered gently, dragging a step stool toward McKenna so they could finish lighting the top of the tree.

"She was. And I've tried reminding Clay that was her way of thinking, but he still blames himself for not working things out with Duke before his father's death." Climbing the step stool, McKenna went quiet for a moment before adding, "Clayton will do anything for the people he cares about, but he never gives himself a pass."

The idea resounded through Hope, bringing her past with Clayton into even sharper focus. Clay hadn't just been angry the day he'd left Silent Spring. He'd felt like he'd failed his mom. He'd said as much when he'd talked about that last day, but until McKenna underscored the point, Hope hadn't fully appreciated how upset he'd been. How defeated. For the first time since his return to Silent Spring, she fully relinquished the old hurt, truly forgiving him for shutting her out when he'd been reeling with his own pain.

Hope climbed her own ladder to finish stringing the multicolored globes.

"He's a good man," she admitted over a throat

gone tight with emotion. Because now that she really understood him, she had no defenses left. No way of telling herself she shouldn't care about him.

Just like that, the emotions flooded in, her old feelings for him resurrecting. Redoubling. It was a good thing he was leaving after the Christmas gala or she might fall for him all over again. This time, she would be the one to make the break. To ensure he didn't feel some false sense of obligation to remain in Silent Spring when he was happiest at his true home.

In Alaska.

Besides, Hope had enough experience with abandonment to not want a repeat. Her mom's Christmas Eve death along with Hope's boyfriend had been devastating, but she'd moved on. Six years later, however, Clay's departure without a word—never even answering her texts—had stirred up the old grief. She refused to put herself through that kind of hell again.

Before McKenna could say any more about her stepbrother, the exterior door opened with a rush of wind and a bang.

The sexy rumble of a male baritone filled the room.

"I'm here and I'm ready to work," Clayton called from the entrance.

From her vantage point on the ladder, Hope could see him dressed in jeans and a gray-and-red flannel, his long-legged stance covering the space in no time. Her pulse accelerated, heart beating wildly. She had it bad for this man, didn't she? Despite all the precautions she'd taken to not fall for him. But she wasn't taking any chances in the romance department this go-round. Not after the way he'd hurt her last time. When the Christmas fundraiser gala was over, she was going to be the one to end their relationship.

It would hurt less if she was the one calling the shots. She would be able to return to her own life afterward without the worries and regrets that had plagued her long after his previous departure.

Until then, however, she would enjoy their connection for what it was. Hot, intense and deliciously physical.

Eleven

Seeing McKenna and Hope working side by side to decorate the Christmas tree made Clay's chest go tight. An instrumental holiday tune played softly from an overhead speaker while the women wrapped branches with miniature lights. He couldn't help but think how much his mom would have enjoyed this. Not just having McKenna and Clay together for the holiday season, but seeing him and Hope working together. He hated that his mother hadn't gotten the opportunity to enjoy this moment. Dena Reynolds had never met Hope in person, but she'd nudged him in her direction once when Clay mentioned her.

She's a perfect fit for you, his mom had said once when Clayton showed her a photo of Hope with her prize-winning sheep. It had been a few years after he'd awarded her the county fair prize and Hope had been collecting a much bigger honor at a national show.

Clay had written off the comment at the time, explaining that Hope was too young for him. That she was studying to be a veterinarian and that her work kept her busy all the time.

Like I said, a perfect fit for you with the shared love of animals and a relentless work ethic, his mother had pressed, though Clayton had barely listened at the time. Still, he'd recalled those words when he'd dated Hope in the months after his mom's passing. Maybe that had been one of the things that drew him to her. Yet he'd never felt truly worthy of this vibrant woman who thrived on social connection and building a sense of community around her. Clay had been a loner his whole life, an outsider even in his own family. The scars of his father's dismissal may have healed, but Clay had never shaken the tendency to retreat from the world when shit hit the fan. Hope deserved better than that. It shamed him to think how he'd cut off all connection with her three years ago, never even receiving her unhappy calls and texts.

"Well, if you're here to work, you should be the one up on this stepladder and not your preggers sister," McKenna admonished him, descending with an athletic grace that belied her condition. Of course, McKenna could keep her footing on a boat tossed around by the worst conditions the Bering Sea had to offer, so it was no wonder a three-step stool was hardly putting her in danger. "Help Hope with the last of the lights while I find the tree topper."

"Aye, Captain," he said dryly, shaking off the old memories to focus on the moment. He would make the most of his remaining time in Silent Spring so he could return home with memories to keep him warm.

His eyes went to Hope as she climbed a few rungs higher on the much bigger ladder she'd been working from, and he automatically clocked the rubberized feet to be sure they were well secured. She wore a pair of black leggings that hugged her curves and a green T-shirt that read Santa, I Tried, with a graphic of a puppy surrounded by shredded paper.

The familiar hunger he experienced around her was even stronger now after being together a week ago. He'd done his damnedest to give her space since then, sensing her wariness in the aftermath of their passionate encounter and the deeply frank conversation that had followed. But with the gala around the corner, his need to help her overshadowed any urge to give her some breathing room.

Besides, he'd be leaving Montana soon. If they couldn't excise this heat between them before that, how would he move forward alone? The idea made him tense, pulling the back of his neck tight. Yet Hope deserved someone who would be a strong partner for her. Someone who wouldn't need to disappear to the wilds of Alaska's remote North Slope when life turned complicated.

"Hello, Hope," he called to her from the floor. "I don't suppose you'd let me take over on the ladder work?"

She peered at him from above, the scent of pine strong as she wove lights through the branches.

"Actually, I'd be delighted to have you finish the top." She balanced the reel of green wire on a rung. "I've got a lot of other decorating to start, and I'm honestly not a fan of heights."

He moved to hold the ladder as she climbed down. He'd done so on instinct, to keep her safe. But the position put him in close proximity to the backs of her thighs. Her curvy ass.

The surge of desire was bad enough without Hope's quick intake of breath as she descended between his arms. The smoldering look she shot him over her shoulder had him calculating the fastest way to slake the thirst for both of them. For that matter, if his sister hadn't been in the room...

But she was, so that didn't bear thinking about. Clamping his teeth on his tongue in an effort to battle back the need to touch Hope, Clayton scaled the rungs in record time. Now wasn't the time to think about taking Hope back to his place.

Or enjoying every single minute of his time left in Silent Spring.

Maybe it was the sexual hunger that made him work at double speed. As if he could stamp out the ache for her if he completed enough manual labor. But within another hour, the show arena was decorated from floor to ceiling. White lights wrapped the rafters. Balsam boughs draped the windows and wound around the railing that circled the arena, with red bows fastened at six-foot intervals. The area of the floor that Hope had designated for dancing was surrounded by four-foot spruces in pewter pots, the needle tips sprayed silver and white to look like snow.

Clayton's gaze swiveled to Hope where she knelt near the podium to plug in the lighted garland she'd draped over the lectern. She drew his eye far more than the decorations, even though the place had been fully transformed in the last sixty minutes.

His throat went dry just watching Hope flip her hair over her shoulder, her back arching as she reached behind the podium to thread an extension cord to a hidden outlet.

While he contemplated the sexy picture she made, a hand lowered into his vision, fingers waggling in a bid for attention.

"Distracted much?" McKenna asked him in a quiet voice as she lowered her palm. Under her other arm, she carried a roll of silver tulle she'd used to wrap around the arena posts.

"Not at all," he lied through his teeth as he turned to glare at her. "Just admiring the results of our decorating efforts."

"That's not all you were admiring," she teased in the singsong way only a sister could get away with.

"If you stop scowling at me, I just might make myself scarce so you can put the moves on her."

On the other side of the arena, Hope stood before gathering her scissors and zip ties to walk toward them. Even now, knowing McKenna took it all in, Clayton couldn't tear his eyes from Hope.

"Deal," he agreed under his breath. "Remind me to sell you my half of the Cyclone Shack for a bargain basement price."

McKenna gave his arm a light punch. "Hasn't anyone ever told you to never negotiate while preoccupied?" In a louder voice, she called to Hope, "I need to take off to meet Quinton for dinner, but I think your event space looks pretty rocking now."

Spinning on the heels of her black trainers, Hope pivoted to take in the view of the holiday decorations. "It does look great, thanks to both of you." She turned back to McKenna to smile warmly. "I really appreciated the extra hands. It was great meeting you."

"You too, Hope. I'm looking forward to the gala." McKenna grinned as she looked back and forth between them, then winked at her brother. "Have a good evening, you two."

Yeah, subtlety had never been McKenna's style. Clayton had to laugh as his stepsister bounded toward the exit.

"It's great seeing her so happy." He recalled how devastated she'd been when she first arrived in Alaska less than two years prior, after an ex-boyfriend posted a revenge porn video of her online. "A month ago,

I would have never pictured myself saying this, but she's like a new woman since Quinton came into her life."

"Or maybe it's motherhood that agrees with her," Hope said as she set down her scissors and the bundle of zip ties on a speaker beside the dance floor. Nearby, empty storage bins were neatly stacked to be returned to her truck now that most of the decorations had been used. "She's definitely got that maternal glow."

Clayton's glance swung toward her, and he wondered if it was coincidence that Hope didn't believe romance was enough to inspire fulfillment and joy. Did she feel that way because of him?

He wanted to ask her. Learn more about this woman who still affected him on every level even after three years apart. But as often happened around her, his tendency to test out conversations in his mind before speaking backfired. Because while he was mulling over just the right words in his mind, she cocked a fist on her hip and looked him up and down with frank feminine appraisal.

"So was it just my imagination, or were you sexing me up with your eyes for the last hour?"

Hope watched Clayton from under her lashes, telling herself she could savor the heat and chemistry they shared without getting burned again. She had a plan for weathering his time in Silent Spring with her heart intact, and she would execute it. Unlike three years ago, now she was in the driver's seat, and she had no false expectations about what was happening between them. No illusions that Clayton wanted more than *this*.

The red-hot, sizzling draw that crackled between them right now. That was worth indulging again even if their emotional connection would never work. She understood that now.

And there was something so rewarding about watching Clayton's quiet, impassive facade burn away beneath the torch of sexual attraction. He might embrace the cold and frozen life of the Arctic, but with her, he craved the heat.

"Not your imagination," he admitted, his voice pure gravel as he stalked closer, green eyes darkening. His hands lifted to reach for her even before he closed the gap between them.

Building anticipation for his touch.

By the time his palms landed on her waist, his fingers splayed wide on her back, a shiver shuddered through her at the contact. She bit her lip for a moment to stifle the hum of pleasure that curled its way up her throat at just that simplest of touches.

"The steamy looks have got me pretty revved up." She walked her fingers up his broad chest, marveling at the solid wall of muscle. "I'm wondering what you're going to do about that?"

His nostrils flared, his grip on her waist tightening a fraction and then relaxing again. Tighten. Relax.

Almost as if he battled for control of himself. The very idea sent a thrill shooting through her.

"I might just back you up against the nearest wall to sink myself into you if you keep teasing me this way," he warned her on a low growl. "And I won't give a damn about all the evergreen garlands you just went to so much work to hang."

Oh, she liked that.

Pleasure bloomed inside her along with a rush of heat between her thighs. She was almost tempted to test him.

"Then maybe we should find somewhere more private," she suggested instead, suspecting he'd regret wrecking her decorations far more than she would. "Your place is closer than mine."

"I've got a better idea." Relinquishing his hold on her waist, he took her by the hand and charged toward the back of the building at a fast clip.

They passed the Christmas tree and rounded the makeshift dance floor, the scent of a fresh-cut fir filling the air.

Hope hurried to keep up, especially since his long legs made his stride much bigger than hers. Her heart skipped a beat when he led her into a shadowed corridor with a sign marked Private at the end.

"Are we going to christen a supply closet?" she asked, already envisioning herself pinned up against the metal shelving, purring her satisfaction while Clay buried himself inside her.

The idea earned a wry laugh before Clayton

reached into his flannel pocket and extracted a single key. But he didn't use it to unlock the door. Not yet. Instead, he turned to face her, backing her into one wall as he bracketed her head with his hands.

"Why am I not surprised that would be okay with you?" His breath fanned over her face before he lowered his mouth to her neck for a greedy kiss, sucking and licking.

She was so aroused and sensitive, she felt a phantom double of the kiss between her legs. Her breasts beaded, the nipples drawing impossibly tight. Aching.

"I just want you," she confessed on a breathless whisper, her arms winding around his neck to hold him closer. "It doesn't matter where we are."

He edged back to study her in the dimly lit hall, his green eyes searching hers while she wondered what had made him pause. But then he was lifting her off the ground, scooping her up with one arm beneath her butt. Tightening her hold on his neck, she wound her legs around his hips so he could carry her.

While he fit the key into the lock, Hope rained kisses along his granite jaw and hot neck. She tousled his thick hair and arched her back so that her breasts rubbed against him. Teasing? Maybe a little. Mostly, she was just so hungry for the heat and connection they shared.

They hadn't touched one another in a week and that had been tough enough. Then, working with him on the decorations for an hour—being in the same room and not being able to touch—had driven her appetites to unbearable levels.

When he pushed his way inside the door marked Private, Hope dragged her attention away from Clay just enough to take note of the fact that they were in a large, modern office space cast in shadow thanks to the lowered blinds and recent sunset. Clayton reached for a light switch, however, and flipped on an overhead fixture before dimming it halfway. Hope could see a garland-draped fireplace built into a slate accent wall and two gray sectional sofas that faced one another, a low cocktail table between them, its surface half-covered with a binder open to pages that featured photos of horses.

On the other side of the room there were the traditional desk and opposing chairs. Bookshelves holding silver-framed photographs and tomes about breeding. Yet Hope's gaze kept returning to the armless sofas while Clayton locked the door behind them and tossed the key onto the cocktail table.

"No one will bother us here," he promised, setting her on her feet.

For a long moment, they stared into one another's eyes, the weight of wanting each other hanging between them. And, possibly, more than that.

Refusing to acknowledge anything beyond the physical, however, Hope shoved aside the thought and laid her hand over his chest. Felt the rapid-fire beating of his heart.

"In that case, you should finish what you started

out there," she urged, smoothing her palm down his chest to rest on his abs briefly before descending lower still. "Do you think you can deliver on all the promises you made with the combustible looks you gave me?"

Clay reached for the hem of her shirt, lifting it up enough for his hands to cup her ass through the thin fabric of her cotton leggings, pulling her into him.

"You don't have enough time for me to do all the things I want to do with you," he fired back, lifting her up so the vee of her thighs rested over the heavy erection pressing the fly of his jeans. "In less than twelve hours from now, you'll be out the door to rescue the animal world when I'm only just getting started."

His words stirred her as much as his touch, and she was already so keyed up she wanted to rip off all her clothes. He'd positioned her sex right over the hard length of him in a way that titillated, making her body short-circuit with the need for release. For him. But then, his words were powerful seduction too. A part of her didn't want to believe him about how much time he could spend working her into a fevered frenzy. But she remembered from past experience, that summer when they'd spent whole days in bed after whole nights of loving each other, that this man wasn't exaggerating his passionate appetites. Or his capacity to pay attention to her…

But thinking about that too made her confused, taking the focus away from the physical.

"You let me worry about when I have to leave," she insisted, fingers moving to the buttons on his flannel. Working them awkwardly as she pressed a kiss to his lips. Then another. "Right now, we have all night long."

"I'll take whatever I can get." Levering back to look at her while still holding her in his arms, he walked them toward the nearest couch before lowering her onto the dark gray cushions. "As much as you'll give me."

Beneath the surface of passion, her emotions churned. Hungry and wanting like the rest of her. She ignored them to pull her T-shirt over her head, delighting when his eyes fastened on the swells of her breasts in her white lace bra.

"Take all you need," she whispered.

And then there was no more need for words. He kissed her thoroughly. Touched her through her clothes until her leggings were as damp as her panties. Only then did he peel off the rest of her clothes. He produced a condom from somewhere as he undressed, laying it on the table briefly while she watched the play of light and shadow over his impressive body.

Then, the condom packet was ripped open and the protection rolled into place. Hope's vision narrowed to Clayton and what they were about to do. Anticipation crowded out everything else, her body on fire for him. She wanted this—craved him—like nothing and no one else.

Reaching for him, she pulled his body down to hers on the couch, arching toward him at the same time. His *ahh* and her *ooh* mingled in a harmony that mimicked the perfect sync of their bodies moving together as one. His thrusts absorbed by her hips. Her cries captured in his mouth.

It was great sex, yes.

But a little part of her brain told her that it was also so much more than that. She'd been running so hard and fast from her emotions, ready to lose herself in the physical, only to find her feelings here too. And they were raw. Open. Vulnerable.

Just like the rest of her.

So it didn't surprise her when her orgasm hit her hard and fast, pummeling her with a sweet eroticism that had her panting Clay's name and holding on to him for dear life. She wasn't surprised either when her feminine muscles coaxed his release, his thighs flexing and hips punching deeper as his finish claimed him.

But the fact that transcendent sex had shaken her out of her own stubborn insistence that she could enjoy something purely physical with this man? That stunned her. Left her reeling and gasping every bit as much as the orgasm.

Tipping her head to his chest, Hope listened to the erratic vibrations of Clay's heart, wishing she hadn't just discovered that she was in serious danger of repeating the worst mistake of her past—blindly falling for someone who wouldn't think twice about walking away from her.

When Clay shifted on the sofa to lie with her cradled in his arms, her eyes burned from the recognition of a tenderness she'd secretly never stopped craving. A love that always hovered just beyond her reach.

She could tell herself all day long she was capable of indulging in sex without getting tangled up by the emotions that came with it. But she now knew, with this man it simply wasn't possible for her. So no matter how perfect they were together, there would be no repeating what they'd just shared.

The Christmas gala and their parting couldn't come soon enough. Once more, the holidays would be a season of saying goodbye.

At least this time, she was prepared.

Twelve

Parking his rented SUV in front of the Kingsland Ranch main house, Clayton stepped out onto the snow-covered driveway an hour before Hope's Christmas fundraiser was due to begin. No doubt the pavement had been plowed less than an hour ago, since the snow was lighter here than everywhere else, but the western Montana weather was showing its unpredictable nature tonight, swapping from sleet to snow and back again, making conditions hazardous. Clay just hoped it didn't diminish the turnout for Hope's gala after all her hard work.

She'd been busy with work and preparing for the gala since he'd seen her last, but he hadn't forgotten the intensity of what they'd shared in the office of the Thoroughbred show arena. It had been a night he would never forget, even though a sense of gathering doom had dogged him afterward, and yet he couldn't quite pinpoint why. Because he was leaving her again? He'd known all along he wasn't the right kind of guy for her. She deserved someone at her side who would embrace the kind of life she led—as full of animal owners as it was of animals. Someone who didn't require frequent escapes to the ends of the earth for the quiet reflection that had always been Clay's sanity saver. Not when she held a job that tethered her here.

Now, climbing the steps to the familiar facade that had been the setting for his life's unhappiest dramas, Clayton could hear a jazz-fueled rendition of a Christmas standard cranked to a healthy volume indoors. Levi had invited his brothers to congregate here before the fundraiser for reasons that weren't entirely clear to Clay. Uneasiness crept through him as he lifted the wrought iron knocker he hadn't touched in three years. Maybe this meeting and the unfinished family business was the source of the trepidation that had hounded him for days. Clay recognized that his brothers hoped he'd change his mind about the inheritance they wished to share with him. But while Clay had enjoyed his time in Montana doing the work he'd once believed would be his life's purpose, and he was grateful to have patched up some of the family bonds with his half siblings, he couldn't imagine giving up the freedom that came with living on his own terms in the Alaskan wilderness.

Although ever since the last night with Hope, he'd found himself wondering what she would think of a life like that at his side. Not that he would ask her to give up what she'd carved out here, a thriving veterinarian practice she wanted to grow and expand, starting with tonight's fundraiser. But he also wondered what she would think of seeing her first Arctic fox in the wild, or walking the wide-open tundra under the green splendor of the northern lights. He couldn't help but think she would enjoy the challenges of that formidable terrain, and he could imagine her caring for the creatures who called it home.

Just then, the front door opened wide, emitting the scents of mulled spices and evergreen as Levi's fiancée, Kendra Davies, stood in the entryway. She wore an emerald strapless gown with a diamond necklace in the shape of a snowflake. Her long blond waves spilled over her shoulders, and her fingers were painted white and ice blue with crystal chips in another snowflake motif. Objectively, he knew she was a stunning woman. But for Clay, no one held a candle to Hope and her unadorned beauty.

"Merry almost Christmas," Kendra greeted him, a glass of dark wine in a clear crystal goblet in her hand. "Don't you look handsome in a tuxedo?" she said admiringly, her blue eyes raking over him. "We're having mulled wine if that works for you? Levi wanted to have a quick toast before we head over to Hope's fundraiser."

"Wine is fine, and Merry almost Christmas to you

too. You look beautiful, Kendra." Clayton had met her on a handful of occasions over the years, most notably when her PR firm had coordinated an animal wellness event for the local cooperative extension as part of the agency's public outreach. At the time, Clay had been volunteering at an animal shelter during a summer visit to Kingsland, and the shelter had been an outlet for him when his father got to be too much.

Remembering that made him wonder if the shadow his father cast had tainted all his memories of Silent Spring. How much had Clay missed out on by allowing his dad to live rent-free in Clay's mind?

"Thank you." Kendra inclined her head before she ducked into the kitchen. "Everyone is in the family room, and I know they're excited to see you. I'll be right in with your wine."

Standing in the foyer of the house he'd been in every year of his life but the last three, Clayton almost didn't recognize the place. Oh, the layout was just the same, but the dark and forbidding vibe of his youth was long gone. There'd been a time when everything in the home was off-limits, from the mahogany wainscoting that had been custom-made and couldn't be brushed up against for fear of scratching, to the glass models of every significant horse Duke Kingsley had ever owned. Duke never missed an opportunity to flaunt his wealth, and he never missed the chance to tell his sons how grateful they ought to feel to him for allowing his offspring to coexist on his massive estate.

Even temporary summer residents like Clayton needed to acknowledge their privilege and good fortune at being born to Duke Kingsley. The ominous storm of Clay's thoughts was scattered a moment later when someone shouted his name.

"Hey, brother, in here," Levi called from a space Duke used to call a parlor, but which now opened up to the living area and French doors that led to the back porch. The stuffy furniture no one was allowed to sit on was gone, replaced with gray leather sectional pieces drawn around the old stone fireplace. A wood fire blazed in the hearth. "We've been waiting for you so we can make a family toast."

Curious, Clayton walked deeper into the room as all eyes turned his way. Someone turned the music down so that it played softly in the background now. McKenna stood closest to him, dressed in a simple sheath gown of white, her red hair her only accessory. She gravitated toward him now, taking his arm so they could walk together toward the fireplace where Levi, Gavin and Quinton all stood dressed in black tuxedos.

Before Clayton reached them, Kendra entered with a full glass of wine and handed it to him. Lauryn materialized from another corner, dressed in a fire-red mermaid gown with ruffles at the hem.

"A family toast?" Clay asked warily as he took the crystal goblet from Kendra. "Is this some kind of Kingsley tradition I didn't know about?"

Gavin let out a wry laugh while Levi shook his

head and answered, "Not at all. We're trying to build new traditions around here to stamp out the crap from the past."

Quinton leaned forward with his glass raised. "Welcome to Kingsley 2.0."

"You really think that's possible?" Clay asked, shaking his head, recalling the smug, mean-spirited way Duke had talked about Clay's mom to him the last time they ever spoke. "After the old man pitted us against each other all our lives, and even more so in the will, trying to wreck our heads right to the bitter end?"

"We don't have to forgive him. We only have to forget him," Gavin suggested in a way only Gavin could, since Duke's youngest son had borne as much of their father's scorn as Clayton had. "And we have the chance to do something positive with his legacy, something constructive."

For a moment, the crackling of the fire and the holiday jazz were the only sounds while Clayton thought that over. His grip tightened on the stem of his glass.

"You all have my blessing for whatever you want to do with Duke's legacy. But as for me, I still want no part of it." The money had been his father's weapon. The symbol of his power.

McKenna's fingers tightened on his arm, giving him gentle and silent support while the rest of the room absorbed the words.

Levi spoke first. "That's understandable. As long

as you know you're still a part of this family, Clay. Because that's something you can't walk away from."

Across the group, Clay met his brother's gaze, seeing his sincerity. And, yeah, his love. There was a bond here that Clayton felt, even after all the times he'd left this house hurt and angry in the past. His brothers weren't a part of that.

Quinton cleared his throat before adding, "Or, if you try to walk away, you already know we'll meet you in the most godforsaken corners of the earth to drag you back home once in a while."

Clayton felt the smile tug at his lips a moment before he laughed out loud. He appreciated the levity in a night that had already gotten emotional, and he hadn't even seen Hope yet. The sense of foreboding still hung heavy around him despite this meeting with his siblings that had gone better than he could have hoped for. He'd had to disappoint them, and yet they'd understood why he didn't want to be a part of the Kingsland Ranch legacy.

Yet he didn't really feel lighter. Maybe all along the growing wariness this week had to do with saying goodbye to Hope after the gala. His chest tightened again, his smile fading. Still, he raised his glass to his brothers as they stood in front of the fireplace.

Kendra and Lauryn joined them, and Lauryn handed McKenna a glass of nonalcoholic wine. Six sets of eyes watched him. His family, he realized.

"I'd like to propose a toast," Clay started, the words suddenly there for him now that he needed them. Now that he felt a greater confidence that these people were in his corner. "To each and every person in this room, for setting an example of what a real family is all about."

"To found families," Lauryn echoed on the other side of the circle as she stood beside Gavin. The scratchy sound of her tearful voice reminded Clayton that she'd been adopted after years in foster homes.

She understood about forging connections with people you claimed for yourself.

"Cheers." Levi seconded the toast, and as one, they each lifted their glasses high.

And drank to the bond between them that had nothing to do with blood and everything to do with choice.

Someone turned the music up, and then there was more laughter while Gavin tried to show them a holiday version of a line dance he'd learned in his years on the rodeo circuit. Clayton enjoyed the moment, feeling a simple kinship like what he'd always had with McKenna. Was it real? Would it last?

Clayton believed that it could. That everyone gathered under this roof wanted to strengthen their family bond and be better people. Something he could get behind. Which made him wonder if there was any need to leave right after Christmas after all. Sure, he wanted to return to Alaska, the place he considered his real home.

Yet was there a rush to go now, when things were going well at the ranch? When he and Hope had found an exciting connection again? He knew he wasn't the right man for her forever. But would she consider a few more weeks together to savor the incredible connection they had?

The possibility tantalized him. Now more than ever, he looked forward to heading over to Hope's Christmas gala. Because the only thing that would make the evening better for him would be to see Hope's face. To hold her. Touch her. Kiss her.

Maybe then he'd shake this feeling of trepidation, like everything he'd fought for these last five weeks was coming to an end.

Nerves strung tight at being in high social mode all evening long, Hope greeted Sarge and Letitia Mc-Masters as the fundraiser kicked into high gear. The waitstaff was passing hors d'oeuvres and refilling glasses while the live band played an upbeat version of "Blue Christmas." Guests posed for photos in front of the green screen where they could digitally impose an image of their pet or livestock in the background, a popular activity that netted some extra funds for the veterinary equipment she needed. Hope had been circulating among the crowd for over an hour in her formfitting tulle and lace black gown, and so far, the evening was going exactly as it should. Yet Hope feared she wasn't doing enough. Kendra was great at this kind of thing—hosting events and making small talk were like breathing to her public relations expert friend. But for Hope, the nonstop smiling and greeting people was tiring.

Maybe that's why she'd chosen to work with animals over people. An hour into the event and guests were still arriving, citing the slippery road conditions for their delay. Clayton and his brothers were here, at least, having shown up as a group shortly after the start time. She and Clayton had greeted one another, but Hope had quickly excused herself, citing a need to make the rounds and personally thank everyone in attendance.

She could feel his eyes on her now, however, her extra senses tingling just like any wild animal's. That deep-seated primeval awareness of being watched made the hair at the back of her neck stand up.

Alerting her to danger.

Because no matter that the predator in the Thoroughbred show arena wore a tuxedo and looked like her hottest fantasy, Clayton Reynolds possessed the power to wound her. A reality she'd become keenly aware of the last time they'd slept together and she'd realized she had feelings for him. Still.

She only hoped she had the emotional fortitude for the clean break the situation demanded. He was leaving Silent Spring. She would return to the life she'd built here without him. End of story.

Hope Alvarez had never shied away from doing hard things. Tonight would be no different. She just wished he didn't look quite so brutally handsome in his black tuxedo jacket, custom-tailored to his broad, athletic shoulders.

He walked toward her now, an extra drink in his hand, and it was all she could do to focus on what the McMasterses were saying to her.

"Petal is running around on that leg like she'd never been injured," Letitia explained, her simple black dress the kind of staple every northern woman had in her closet for dress-up occasions. But with her hair pinned up and a pair of diamond sparklers in her ears, the woman revealed an elegance all her own. "We can't thank you enough for all you did, Hope, not just to heal her, but to calm us all down on a night I was so upset I was shaking."

"I'm just glad I could help," Hope told her honestly, remembering her fears for the little calf that night.

Clayton arrived at her side just then, passing her a glass of water, which she appreciated even more than champagne. How had he known? She smiled her thanks as Clayton smoothly greeted Sarge and Letitia before he added, "Hope's ability to help local animals will be even more formidable once she has the equipment her practice needs for more advanced fieldwork."

The note of pride in his voice caught her off guard as he referenced the short presentation she'd given half an hour ago on the kinds of equipment she hoped to purchase with the funds raised that evening. His confidence in her touched her. Why did he have to be so charming tonight, making it even tougher to end things between them?

"That's why we're here," Sarge assured him, dressed in a dark blue suit with his thinning hair slicked back. He shoved his hands in his pockets and rocked on his heels while the band swapped to a country Christmas tune that drew even more guests to the dance floor. "Dragging animals around to be treated three hours from home only adds to the trauma and fear when they don't feel well in the first place. Services like this are good for our livestock communities."

A moment later the older couple excused themselves, leaving Hope alone with Clayton for the first time all evening. She took a grateful sip of her water even though her heart began beating faster at the realization of what needed to happen next. How had they reached this point again already? Just three years ago, she'd vowed never again to lose her heart that same painful way as she had with Clay the first time. Having him disappear from her life with no chance to talk about why had been too reminiscent of her mom's death. And her boyfriend's.

They were simply there one moment and then gone. No goodbye. No final words. Just...vanished from the world, leaving a gaping hole in her heart.

That had been fate, an unavoidable coincidence that rewrote her world. But Clayton ghosting her? She could have avoided that pain. Could have made it so the absence didn't blindside her.

"We should talk," she blurted as she peered around

the room and saw that she'd successfully spoken to every person in it for at least a couple of minutes. She could afford to simply let her guests enjoy themselves for a little while. "Do you have a minute?"

He frowned down at her. "Now?"

"Yes, please." Her body vibrated with the emotions of the conversation to come. The unhappiness she would willfully bring herself. But still, better this way than to wait for him to break her heart. "I think the party will be self-sufficient for a few minutes. Besides, Cassandra is in unofficial secondary hostess mode, so she'll find me if I'm needed for anything."

Taking Clay's arm, she didn't wait for an answer before steering him toward the back office. The same place where they'd had incredible sex that made her realize she was developing feelings for him. The office she'd used as her gala headquarters all day long.

"Fair enough," Clayton agreed, hand at her waist to guide her protectively through a throng of partygoers waiting for their turn to stand under the mistletoe for a photograph. "I've been wanting to talk to you tonight too."

Anxiety doubled, pitting into a cold ball in her stomach. Would he beat her to it and try to write her off again before she even found a chance to take control of the relationship situation?

She couldn't allow that to happen. Not when she was on the precipice of what should be a new start for her. An expanding vet practice, supported by her community, bringing significant new care to animals who needed the services. Before Clayton Reynolds had returned to Silent Spring, that would have been enough to make Hope happy and fulfilled. Thrilled, even. Now?

She feared tonight's victory would feel hollow without him by her side. Her heart ached more as they stepped into the office and closed the door behind them.

"That's fine," she said distractedly, more nervous than she could ever recall being. Since when was she an anxious person? Damn it, this wasn't like her at all. None of it. The drama, the nerves, the unwillingness to do what needed to be done.

She just needed to grit her teeth and get through it.

Before she could say more, however, Clayton's eyebrows furrowed in a dark slash as he closed the gap between them and gently wrapped his hands around her upper arms. "Something's wrong. What is it?"

And that made it so much worse. Why did he have to unveil his sweetest side now when she needed to end this facsimile of a real relationship?

"I just wanted to, um—clear the air," she began, scrambling for words she hadn't really thought through. "About you leaving."

His expression eased, a sigh of relief shuddering through him. "In that case, maybe it's best I share my news first."

"What news?" Confused, she stood very still, afraid if she wasn't very careful, she would sink into the comfort of his strong arms. His broad chest. His warmth.

"I had a good talk with my brothers tonight, and it made me wonder if I need to leave Silent Spring so soon." His green eyes studied hers. "I could stay a little longer, and we could—" he brushed a caress over her cheek "—enjoy this thing between us."

Hope felt like the floor fell out from under her feet as she tried to make sense of what he was saying. Stay in Silent Spring? But only for the physical connection, since they'd never talked about anything more than that?

"Wh-what do you mean by this *thing*?" She couldn't help the ice in her voice. She needed clarity from him, not some wiggly "seize the moment" plan.

He must have heard the edge in her words because his hand fell away from her face. "The chemistry. The connection."

But she was already shaking her head, hearing everything that wasn't said. Knowing that agreeing to this would only defer her broken heart. Possibly, it would be even worse if she let herself get more and more attached to him.

If she allowed herself to love him.

In the silence that followed his words, the sound of another holiday tune full of sad longing drifted through the closed door. Why was this season always so full of hurt for her? She'd hoped planning a gala at this time of year would help fix some of those old griefs, but she seemed to find new ones.

"I can't do that." She pushed the words over dry lips, knowing what she had to do. "I can't keep allowing myself to—" Her voice cracked and she halted. Cleared her throat and began again. "I don't want to see you anymore, Clayton."

She forced herself to look him directly in the eye. And it pained her to see a flash of hurt there. But she reminded herself that the toll on him was nothing compared to the cost to her since only one of them was in love.

"I don't understand." His gaze narrowed, as if he could solve the puzzle if he studied it hard enough. "We just started seeing each other again—"

"That was a mistake, the same way it was a mistake three years ago." She hadn't wanted to bring up the past, but there it was, still tied to the hurt she felt today since there had never been any real closure for her. "And this time I want to be sure there's no misunderstanding between us in the goodbye."

She paced farther away from the closed door to the office, as if she could escape the holiday music. Pausing in front of a bookshelf full of framed photos, her eyes fell on one of Duke Kingsley with his four sons. A rare photo, she would bet, and not one Duke would have ever placed in his office. But then, this place was new and the mementos here reflected the new Kingsley family. In the photo, Clayton stood apart from the others, his cowboy hat low over his eyes. Even as a teen, he'd been a loner.

It made her want to reach back in time to the young man in the photo. Tell him he was worthy.

"I know I'm not the right person for you, Hope,"

he began quietly, taking the conversation in an un-expected direction. "But in the short term at least, you can't deny we make each other happy."

Turning from the photograph, she thought about what he'd just said. "What do you mean, 'not the right person'?"

"Just what I said. I know that I tend to disappear when people need me, that I take strength from being alone. And you deserve someone that will be there for you twenty-four seven."

She blinked through her confusion, hating that he felt that way even if it didn't change anything about her need to break things off with him. If anything, hearing the way he admitted something so personal made her love him all the more.

If only he felt the same.

"Clay." She crossed the office floor, skirting around the cocktail table to stand in front of him again be-cause she wanted him to hear the message. "You are worthy in every way. The strongest man I know. I don't care if you take your strength from the Alas-kan tundra or from a can of spinach like Popeye. You cope with life in a way that works for you, and that's a whole lot more than most people can say."

Clayton shoved a hand through his hair. Frus-trated. "You've always seen the best in me. Yet when I tell you that I can stay longer, that I want to keep seeing each other, you push me away with both hands. I don't understand that."

Hope ached from her head to her toes, wishing

she could make him see how much he hurt her. How much power he had to hurt her again. She didn't like the idea of revealing her deepest pain to him, but how else could she make him see that they couldn't go on in a relationship of half measures?

"When you left last time, Clay, it wasn't that you needed to leave that devastated me. It was that you *never talked to me*. You cut all contact." Just thinking about those first weeks after his departure renewed her commitment to breaking things off. To ending this before he could hurt her again. "And after the way I lost others in my past, that was about the cruelest thing you could have done."

For a beat after her announcement, his lips moved but no words came out. He scrubbed a hand along his chest, rumpling his tie. "I had no idea."

"I know that now." Hope took a deep breath and exhaled it slowly, steadying herself. Screwing up her courage no matter how much it hurt, she told herself this needed to be done. "And the past is over. But I can't have a repeat of that, Clay. So I think it's better if we end things now. Clean breaks heal faster."

She allowed herself one last look at the man she loved in all his gorgeous tuxedo-wearing glory. But then, she would have felt every bit as much pain right now if he'd been dressed in jeans and boots. It was the man inside those clothes that she loved. That she craved.

A man who didn't understand her and had never loved her back.

So, lifting her chin, she walked toward the office exit and slipped through the door to return to the Christmas gala. Her heart, however, she left behind.

Thirteen

Clayton needed air.

The close atmosphere of the party, the high spirits and Christmas cheer were all too much for him when he felt like Hope had just cleaved him apart. She didn't want to see him anymore. She preferred a clean break to the messy possibilities of exploring a relationship.

And that hurt like hell.

But what pained him even more? Knowing that he had wounded her so badly in the past that she felt she needed to take this drastic step. He'd been selfish. Embroiled in his own frustrations with his father. And he'd failed her completely.

Leaving the back office of the Thoroughbred show arena, Clayton stepped out of a side exit to the building, one where he didn't have to pass any people. He needed the solitude that had soothed his soul in his tundra home. The frigid air was bracing since he wore no coat over his tuxedo, but his time in Alaska had given him a high tolerance for the cold. He stuffed his hands in his pockets as he walked a recently cleared path, his way visible thanks to the motion lights on the side of the arena. The snowfall had slowed, but white flakes still floated down from the sky, blanketing the Kingsland Ranch acreage in white.

You are worthy in every way.

Hope's earlier comment circled his mind as he walked, every exhale huffing a cloud in front of him. The words were the one good part of an otherwise painful talk. Because it was news to him that she wasn't bothered by his need to step away from people and drama sometimes. Or at least, she acted like that was a character quirk she could live with. If anything, she'd been supportive about that when she'd said she didn't care where he took his strength from—just that she needed him to communicate with her. That had been revelatory. Encouraging.

For Clayton, that simple revelation cleared the path for a connection he'd never dared to dream possible before. But he'd hardly had time to savor the moment before she slammed the door closed on any relationship between them. This was the source of the uneasiness that had dogged him all week. The impending doom.

Had a part of him known all along that Hope would dump him?

Behind Clayton, music blasted out of the show arena as a door was opened. Footsteps padded lightly down the path, muffled by the snowfall. Turning as the steps grew closer, Clayton came face-to-face with his youngest half brother, Gavin.

"Everything all right?" Gavin asked, his hands shoved in his pockets. He'd been smart enough to grab a jacket on his way out, the long wool peacoat covering much of his tux. A black Stetson rested on his head. "I noticed you were gone when Hope was set to take the stage to announce how much was raised tonight."

Clay blew out a frustrated breath as he looked up to the sky still showering down snowflakes. Not that there were any answers up there either.

"She just gave me my walking papers," he explained, confiding in the brother who understood best how it felt to be an outsider. Gavin had run as hard and fast as Clayton had from the Kingsley name, and yet here he was, in the thick of the fold again.

Maybe Gavin understood something about carving out a life here, apart from the past.

"That sucks, and I'm sorry to hear it." Gavin skimmed his black dress shoe through the snow, clearing a path to reveal the dark stone of the walkway beneath. "Hope is not only a well-liked woman around here, she's also a force to be reckoned with." Gavin cut a glance Clayton's way. "A good counterpart for you."

The assessment brought a sad grin to Clay's face. Because what did it matter if anyone else thought they were a favorable match if Hope didn't see it?

"She figures I'm only going to leave again," Clayton continued, talking it through for himself as much as for Gavin. Because he still didn't understand why she was so quick to shut him down. "Even though I told her I was looking at extending my stay here."

From inside the show arena, the holiday music halted. Applause followed. And then there was a feminine voice at the microphone, the words too soft to be heard outdoors, but Clayton knew the speaker must be Hope announcing the total raised by the gala.

He'd thought he would be in there right now, somewhere close by, to celebrate her success with her. But she hadn't wanted him there. Not tonight. Not ever.

Pivoting on his heel, Gavin faced him head-on. He tipped up the brim of his hat to take in Clay. "Can I ask you something that might offer you clarity on the situation?"

Clayton quit straining to hear the words being spoken into the microphone indoors to focus on Gavin.

"I'd welcome that," Clay told him honestly, even as he recognized how rarely in his life he'd had this sort of exchange with anyone. Even his mom, whom he'd been close with. For his whole life, Clayton had worked out his problems alone. Slowly.

But after the toast at Levi's house, Clayton had come away with the feeling that he didn't have to operate in a vacuum anymore. That this new, more mature version of his family might be a landing place for him in tough times.

"Do you love Hope?"

Gavin's simple, straightforward question reverberated through Clayton like a gong had been struck. The vibrations kept resonating. Not just in his chest where he felt it most deeply. But everywhere in his body.

Did he love Hope?

He'd never framed the question for himself—even though he should have. And yet the moment Gavin asked it, the answer was right there, front and center. Obvious. True. Maybe his avoidance of the subject spoke volumes in and of itself. He'd been hiding from his feelings out of fear of being hurt again.

"I love her with my whole being." It was as simple as that. And the answer shuffled pieces inside him, making him see the last few weeks with Hope in a whole new way.

Made him realize the depth of his mistake in how he'd handled their conversation in the office.

"In that case, your way forward should be clear," Gavin explained, shoving his hat more firmly on his head again. "Speaking as a former expert at cutting and running on relationships, I can tell you that my feelings for Lauryn made no sense to me until I realized she was The One. As soon as I understood that I didn't need the old MO anymore—that I didn't want to ever be without her—everything else fell into place."

Could it really be that easy? Clayton didn't think so, not after how much he'd hurt Hope in the past. But the way Gavin put it sure made Clay want to try his luck with Hope again. Because he absolutely loved her. He'd walked out on her before, but he didn't intend to make that mistake again. Whatever it took, he would show her his love was constant. The idea warmed him, chasing away the chill of the night air.

"I'm going to try talking to her," Clayton decided, knowing he couldn't leave Silent Spring without a concerted effort to be heard. Scratch that. He wasn't leaving at all until she understood how much he loved her. Then, if she needed him to stay, that's a sacrifice he was willing to make because any life he built somewhere else would be worthless without her in it.

She'd said he was the strongest man she knew. It was time he started acting like it. Because even if her answer was still no, Hope deserved to know she was—and would always be—loved.

As the Thoroughbred show arena emptied after the gala, Hope waited for a sense of victory. The Christmas event had raised more than she'd dared to dream, with everyone giving generously at a silent auction. Plus, with the funds matched by the Kingsley family, she could afford the state-of-the-art facility this corner of western Montana deserved in addition to upgraded equipment for her work in the field.

Between that success and forging ahead with her decision to make a clean break with Clay, she ought to feel victorious. Empowered, at least, that she'd been the one to put an end to things this time instead of waiting for the boom to fall.

Yet as she watched the band members pack up their equipment for the night now that the arena had emptied of guests, Hope only felt hollow and empty inside. If anything, the emotional fallout was worse now than three years ago. At least then, she hadn't acknowledged the fact that she loved Clayton, so it had been marginally easier to let go.

Now, she understood exactly what they were giving up. Or rather, what she was giving up, since the love portion of the equation was all on her side. The weight of that loss threatened to drive her to her knees right beside the towering fir she'd decorated with Clay and McKenna. Hope trailed her fingers along the fragrant needles toward a glittery glass ball she'd made in grade school. She'd used her personal decorations for the tree this year since she'd never bothered trimming her own tree after her mom's death. It had been too hard to remember the last time she'd packed away the ornaments, so they'd remained in their cases until this year.

Hanging the things with McKenna and Clay had been easier as they'd talked about other matters. McKenna had regaled her with stories of her fishing expeditions in the Bering Sea, and Clayton had distracted her even more with his tales of the exotic birds found only on the Aleutian Island chain where McKenna and Quinton would spend most of their year.

At the time, Hope had been grateful for the diverting stories to get through a difficult "first" for her. The first tree trimming since her mom had died on Christmas Eve. But now, when the night had conspired to deliver one emotional blow after another, she allowed herself to remember the joys of the holidays before her mother's passing. Those years had made Hope who she was today, and they deserved to be remembered.

Much like her time with Clay deserved to be remembered, considering the kindnesses he'd shown her over the last weeks. She'd been so focused on not getting hurt, she hadn't allowed herself to truly enjoy the way he'd helped with the gala, securing the space for her when her original plan crapped out on her. Or how he'd relocated the wolves after calming down the McMasterses on the night Petal was injured.

Fingers going still on a hand-painted globe depicting a childishly drawn cat, Hope remembered the year she'd made that one, her mom at her side. Her eyes burned with emotion by the time a footstep sounded nearby.

"Congratulations on a successful evening," a familiar masculine voice rumbled in the octave guaranteed to send a shiver through her.

Surprise chased after the shiver. Because she had figured once she put an end to things with Clayton, he would be on the first plane back to Alaska. What had delayed his departure?

"Clay." His name tripped from her tongue before she could stop it, the word infused with too much longing. She straightened from the Christmas tree to face him. Schooling her features to remain neutral, she held her head high. "I'm surprised to see you here. When you weren't around for the announcement of the Kingsley donation match at the party, I assumed you'd left for the night."

Not that she would have blamed him for taking off after the way she'd sprung a breakup on him in the middle of the event. She hadn't planned to talk to him then, but she'd been keyed up and nervous, wanting to get it over with.

Now, seeing him in his tux, his tie gone and the top button of his shirt unfastened, she craved him so much she ached. Why had she thought splitting up would make the parting any easier? There was no easy way to lose the love of someone's life.

"I took off briefly to think through the things you said to me. But now that I've had some time to reassess, I knew I needed to see you just once more." He moved closer to her across the space that had so recently been filled with dancing couples. His dress shoes made a soft clack against the planked temporary flooring before he stopped inches in front of her.

Just once?

She swallowed hard, bracing herself for whatever he had to say.

"I'm listening." To escape his piercing gaze, Hope busied herself with rolling up an extension cord that led to the podium, needing something to do with her hands.

Gently, Clayton took the electrical cord from her hands and laid it aside on a speaker, his fingers brushing lightly along hers. "I can help you wind that up in a minute. First, I'd like your full attention."

Her eyes darted to his. Wary. Her gut clenched. She could still feel the place where he'd touched her, the skin tingling pleasantly.

"All right, you've got it," she assured him, breathing in the scent of pine from the tree.

Overhead on the skylight built at the center of the rafters, snow accumulated. White lights still burned on the strands over the dance floor.

"I had a useful conversation with Gavin after you and I spoke earlier," he began, his green eyes never leaving hers. "And he helped me see the most basic truth that I hadn't come to terms with before."

She lifted her brows. Waiting. Curious in spite of the insistent voice inside her that said this conversation went against her resolution to make a clean break.

"I love you, Hope."

The world around her went utterly quiet and still as Clayton spoke words she had never anticipated hearing from him. Those simple words narrowed her focus to just the two of them and crumbled her every last defense. She opened her mouth to speak and couldn't quite find her voice. Could she dare to trust he really meant it?

"I don't understand," she finally managed, shaking her head. Unwilling to believe something that didn't make sense to her, no matter how much she wished it were true. "I thought you were ready to move on when I suggested we break things off. You never said—"

"Because I'm a fool. I didn't say it because I didn't realize it myself. Not until Gavin asked me one simple question—did I love you?" Clayton's expression was serious. Intense. "And everything I'd been struggling with suddenly fell into place. Because that's exactly where I'm at, Hope. I love you. That's why going back to Alaska without you holds no appeal. It's why I keep wondering if you would enjoy the Arctic life, even though I know you've carved out a meaningful career here. And if you can't find your way to love Alaska, then I'm all in staying here with you—"

"Wait a second." Hope's mind raced to keep up with Clayton's words. A problem she'd never imagined facing with this quiet man who kept his feelings to himself. "Go back to the love part. Do you really believe that?"

She could understand Gavin's point about that. Because everything else got simpler if that first part was true. Her heart was already racing with anticipation. Tenderness. Affection. Need.

Then, Clay's hands settled on her shoulders,

strong and warm through the lace of her black evening gown.

"Hope Alvarez, I love you deeply," he vowed, the gravity of the sentiment evident in the way he spoke. The way he touched her. "And even if you don't want me in your life again, you deserve to know how much love I have for you. How committed I am to building a future with you."

Happiness surged through her in a wave so strong she wavered on her feet. She clutched at his arms to steady herself even as she clung tight to the words in her heart.

"Clayton, I love you too. So much that the thought of losing you again terrified me into breaking things off with you." She swayed closer to him, wanting the comfort of his arms around her. The reassurance of his love. "But that was foolish of me since it didn't save me a single ounce of pain once I walked out that door tonight. The same hurt was right there, because what I craved more than anything was to have your love in return."

Clayton's strong arms folded her into him as he held her tight. He kissed the top of her head over and over, speaking softly between kisses. "Never doubt that you have it, Hope. Not for a second."

Her knees felt like liquid as she sank fully into him, her arms banding around his waist while they held one another. A hundred details needed to be worked out. Where to go from here? How would they negotiate their different lifestyles? Could she find time away from her career to enjoy Alaska with him if only on a part-time basis? Could he really be happy here if she couldn't make a go of it in the far north?

But those things felt easy with that one certainty underneath it all. Clayton loved her. And she wasn't going to allow her old fear of loss to hold her back from loving him the way he deserved to be loved. They'd both made mistakes, but they could right them. Grow from them.

Still, she levered back to peer up at him, the glow of white Christmas lights outlining his head as he stared down at her. "I'm going to build this state-of-the-art veterinary center," she informed him, conscious of the implied promises she'd made when she'd held her fundraising event.

"You wouldn't be the woman I love if you didn't finish what you set out to accomplish." He kissed her lips briefly before stroking her hair away from her face, looking into her eyes like she was the most precious thing on earth.

At least, that's how she felt when he looked at her that way. The joy of knowing his heart filled her with a contentment that went to her toes. Anchored her. Strengthened her.

Dragging in a breath, she explained a possible direction for their future. An idea they could tweak as needed. "But once it's built, there's nothing saying I have to be the only doc on staff. I can hire on a partner. Take some time to go see a few Arctic wolves and polar bears in the north or boat around the Aleutians to check out the birdlife."

She could already imagine the joint research projects they could do to help native species thrive. Mostly, she could imagine day after day at this man's side, making a life together that would fulfill and challenge them both.

The corners of Clay's mouth turned up. "You would do that for me?"

"I would do that for both of us. Knowing how much you've enjoyed your life there, I want to experience it for myself." She framed his jaw between her hands, wanting his lips on hers.

Not just now, but all night long. And maybe for days afterward.

"In that case, we'll travel there whenever you're ready." He lifted her up so they were at eye level. Mouth level. Then, very deliberately, he steered her under a ball of mistletoe that hung over the dance floor. There, he kissed her long and deep, until they were both breathless. "As long as it's not tonight."

She couldn't suppress a grin, the happiness inside her so light she thought she might float away if he didn't hold her down.

"And why not tonight exactly?" She kissed her way along his jaw. Arched her back just enough to press her breasts to his chest.

"Because tonight," he growled at her in the low voice that thrilled her to her toes, "I'm going to show my love for you in graphic detail. Repeatedly."

Ribbons of pleasure cascaded through her, every inch of her tingling in anticipation.

"Then for pity's sake, Clay, take me home so we can get started."

She didn't need to tell him twice.

* * * * *

Tanya Michaels is the award-winning author of nearly fifty books and novellas. She lives outside Atlanta, Georgia, with a small dog and two rescue cats who have an ongoing competition to see who can trip Tanya the most times in one day.

Books by Tanya Michaels

Harlequin Western Romance

Cupid's Bow, Texas

Falling for the Sheriff
Falling for the Rancher
The Christmas Triplets
The Cowboy Upstairs
The Cowboy's Texas Twins

Harlequin Desire

One Night with a Cowboy

Visit the Author Profile page
at Harlequin.com for more titles.

You can also find Tanya Michaels on Facebook, along with other Harlequin Desire authors, at Facebook.com/HarlequinDesireAuthors!

Dear Reader,

I don't know about you, but I always feel better when I have a plan. Of course, my life rarely goes according to those plans, but still...

After her former business partner's embezzlement, veterinarian Mia Zane has a plan to save her clinic. It includes working lots of extra hours and assisting with a Colorado cattle drive for a bonus payday. It does *not* include romance, but ranch hand Jace Malone is irresistibly sexy. Mia reasons that one night with the cowboy is an indulgence she's earned, a few steamy stolen hours before resuming her single-minded focus on work.

Except after their one night together, Mia finds herself pregnant. And learns that "ranch hand" Jace Malone is from one of Colorado's wealthiest families.

Jace Malone has suffered great loss in his past, and he doesn't want to lose his unexpected chance at a future with Mia. He's convinced that they belong together, even though Mia worries that they're from different worlds, and he's determined to woo her into seeing things his way.

Does their courtship go as planned? Definitely not. But their chemistry is undeniable, and they both learn a lot about love—and themselves—along the way.

Tanya Michaels

ONE NIGHT WITH
A COWBOY

Tanya Michaels

Thank you, Sally Kilpatrick.
I am more grateful than I could ever express.

One

"Whoa." Shari's admiring tone was the one she normally reserved for perfectly crisped risotto balls or exquisitely seasoned red stew. "This is the guest cottage? I'm officially jealous." She dropped the duffel bag she'd offered to carry and darted past Mia to explore.

Setting down her backpack and medical bag, Mia Zane looked around. She'd known the Climbing W dude ranch was one of the most popular in the state, but the cabin was far more luxurious than she'd expected—gleaming hardwood floor, vaulted ceiling, stone fireplace, fully stocked wine rack and a massive four-poster bed draped in an unmistakably expensive duvet. She wondered if they had to special-order custom sheets. The bed was beyond king; it was a whole kingdom.

"There's a whirlpool tub!" Shari called from the bathroom. "I can't believe you're getting paid to stay here."

"Just for tonight." Starting tomorrow, Mia would be staying in a tent, living the slightly less glamorous sleeping bag life. This week she was trading her scrubs for blue jeans as consulting veterinarian on a cattle drive that was equal parts ranch work and tourist attraction. She wondered if the trail boss, Alonzo Boone, would have offered a night in the posh cottage to any vet who took the job, or if she'd benefited from his being an old poker buddy of her dad's.

Shari emerged from the bathroom with a handful of green bottles. "These toiletries are spa quality!"

"Take anything you want to try—unless one of them's sunscreen." Mia had packed some, ever diligent about protecting her pale skin from freckling and burning, but it never hurt to have extra. "You should take my complimentary bottle of wine, too. It's the least I can do after you gave me a ride. And agreed to house-sit."

"*And* finished your packing when you got called into surgery this morning." Shari grinned. "I'm the best."

"You really are." Growing up with three older brothers, Mia had often daydreamed about learning she had a long-lost sister. Meeting Shari Freeman at a luncheon for local business owners had been the next best thing. There might not be much family re-semblance between the full-figured redhead and the petite Black executive chef, but they were sisters at heart. "Speaking of the surgery, I should call Dr. Kline and follow up."

A vet in the next county had phoned Mia about an emergency laryngeal paralysis case because she had more experience with the corrective procedure. He'd been grateful for her surgical acumen; Mia was grateful for the extra income. She was determined to rescue her mixed-practice clinic, which treated both large and small animals. Although patient re-ferrals and the cattle drive bonus were steps in the right direction, they couldn't undo all the damage of Drew's embezzlement.

"Hold up, Zane—I recognize that stress scowl. Do not spiral," Shari admonished. "And don't waste any mental energy thinking about your rat bastard ex."

"I'm over Drew. But I'll never be over what he did to the clinic." Ironic that her father and brothers had been so relieved by her engagement, glad she had a man to "look out for her."

"Your practice is going to be okay—not just okay, better than ever. How many vets under thirty already have a reputation as solid as yours? Trust me, you've got this." Her eyes narrowed. "Still, if that SOB ever shows his face in Colorado again…"

"My brothers will pummel him."

"Not if I get to him first."

Mia chuckled. Shari might stand five foot two in

her bare feet, but only a fool would underestimate her. "What would I do without you?"

"Overwork, forget to eat and waste away. Your life would definitely be less fun without me. That's F-U-N. You remember the word, right?"

Mia ignored the recurring suggestion that her life had become all work and no play. "We both know I've never been in danger of wasting away. After your last batch of test recipes, I'm lucky my jeans still zip." They weren't as forgiving as her elasticized scrubs.

"Pfft. You are rocking those jeans, and I could find a dozen guys on this ranch who would enthusiastically agree with me. In fact..."

The sudden gleam in her friend's gaze made Mia uneasy, and she quickly changed the subject. "Thanks again for the ride. I should head down to the barn, talk to Alonzo, check on the pregnant heifers."

"Sure, sure, but while you're doing all that, appreciate the time away from the clinic. Take the opportunity to meet new people." She jabbed her index finger toward Mia, her tone emphatic. "Have fun."

"I'm not one of the vacationing tourists, Shar. I'm here in a professional capacity." Even as she said the words, Mia heard how uptight she sounded. Maybe Shari was right. While the clinic and its employees had to be her priority, it might be healthy to relax every once in a while, reenergizing herself to work even harder.

Shari typed on her smartphone, then read from

the screen. "*Fun*. Noun, meaning enjoyment or merriment. Also an adjec—"

"Okay, okay! Point taken. I promise to enjoy myself this week." After all, she'd be in the June sunshine and fresh air, doing her dream job. Even with the stress of catching up on the commercial mortgage and rebuilding her finances, she'd never for one second regretted opening the clinic. She loved animals, whether they were beagles, bovines or bearded dragons.

Shari nodded her approval. "All right, then. I'm headed back to your place to snuggle that trio of foster cats. The no-pet policy is the only thing I hate about my otherwise perfect condo. Good thing you always have animals around."

"Try not to spoil them too much."

"I make no promises." With a wink and a wave, Shari turned to open the door. "See you in a week."

Once she was alone, Mia pulled out her phone to call Dr. Kline. But first, she sent a quick reminder to her friend. Text me when you get there so I know you made it safely. Mia was still a little jumpy after last month's car accident during a rainstorm. This trip had given her the perfect opportunity to leave her vehicle at a garage for the remaining bodywork it needed. She'd debated whether cosmetic repairs were worth the expense, but at least her brothers and father would stop commenting on the dents.

A moment after Mia hit Send, Shari texted back a thumbs-up emoji. And a screenshot of the online dictionary entry for *fun*.

* * *

"Please don't take it personally. You're great—this just isn't where I'm supposed to be at this point in my life." Jace Malone flashed an apologetic smile and reached out to pat Yenefer's shoulder.

The young quarter horse nickered softly, assuring him that his complaints hadn't caused any hard feelings.

"I'll say this, Yen. You may be the best listener I've ever met." Definitely better than either of Jace's older brothers, who'd adamantly rejected his input since his return to Colorado. A few weeks ago, getting hired on here at the Climbing W had seemed like a smart first step to earning his brothers' forgiveness. But now Jace questioned whether he was wasting his time.

It's not a waste if it proves to Grandpa Harry that I've changed.

He owed his grandfather everything. Harrison Malone was the only one who'd doggedly believed in Jace after—

No. Jace couldn't change anything that had happened, so there was no sense dwelling on the past. What he *could* do was focus on the future, make amends with his family and take his rightful place at Malone Energy. During his exile in Texas, he'd learned a lot, and he'd come home with ideas for modernizing the family business. His brothers, however, didn't want his help. Heath, the middle brother and Malone Energy's chief financial officer, had called his suggestions "naive meddling" that could negatively affect hundreds of employees.

"We have to worry about those people's livelihoods," Reed had added. "But why should you care about consequences? You've had everything handed to you."

As if Jace hadn't suffered the consequences of his actions every damn day for eleven years? "You were born just as rich and privileged as I was."

"Heath and I worked grueling summer jobs. *We* earned straight A's. Harry's donations got you into college, and when you couldn't hack that, he called in a favor to land you a job. Which you quit."

Only because of ethical concerns after years with the oil company.

Jace was no longer a grieving teenager or a hard-drinking frat boy, but his brothers refused to give him a fresh start. Even their grandfather was skeptical. Despite enthusiastically welcoming Jace back to the Triple Pine, the Malones' sprawling luxury ranch, Harry had sheepishly agreed that it was probably best if Jace didn't have a role in the boardroom. Jace was determined to prove himself, though. If he gave up his hopes of joining Malone Energy, it would only reinforce their view of him as a quitter.

His long-term goal remained the same, but he'd taken a strategic detour to the Climbing W, getting hired as a ranch hand without using any Malone connections, to demonstrate he wasn't afraid of long days and hard labor.

"So here I am, Yen. I should be helping steer the family business into a new era, but instead I'm talking to a horse." He gave her an alfalfa pellet, partly because she'd done well during this afternoon's farrier training and partly because he appreciated her nonjudgmental company.

"You about done, Mr. Malone?" A lanky ranch hand who looked younger than his twenty years approached from the other side of the fence. "Boone wants your help with orientation and going over pack weights."

"Yeah, just finishing up here." Jace untied Yen's lead. "But, Levi, I've told you—don't call me Mr. Malone."

"Sorry, Mr. Mal... Er, sorry."

Jace sighed. Only two men on the spread knew his identity. Too bad one of them was Levi. The ranch hands frequently played poker in the bunkhouse, and the kid's attempts at bluffing were tragic to behold. "Just call me JT."

He wasn't even going by Jace, using his initials to help distance himself from the regionally famous Malone family. Alonzo Boone knew who he was, but the seasoned trail boss was too gruff to suck up to anyone, even a billionaire. Unfortunately, Levi had been a Malone Scholarship recipient and had recognized Jace from family photos. Although puzzled by Jace's desire to remain incognito, the kid had promised to keep his secret.

"Tell Boone I'll be along in a minute. Just let me get Yen back to the barn."

"Yessir, Mr. Mal—JT."

Well, that was progress. Sort of.

Jace turned in the direction of the barn. He wasn't expecting to see anyone there since most hands were currently working to get the busload of tourists checked in. However, a lone woman leaned against the fence adjacent to the barn. Her long red hair glinted gold and auburn in the sunlight. It was pulled back in a ponytail, but the wind swirled strands around her face, momentarily obscuring her features.

As Jace got closer, he saw she was talking on her cell phone. And she was stunning.

About five-and-a-half feet tall, she had lush curves and bold features. Strong cheekbones, full lips. One denim-clad leg was bent and propped on the lower rung of the fence, emphasizing her shapely hip. He itched to be the one who helped her onto her horse tomorrow just for the excuse to touch her.

Who was she traveling with? Guests rarely came on these cattle drive vacations alone. Was she here with friends who had "authentic Western experience" on their bucket lists? Or perhaps coworkers who saw this week as a team-building exercise? Or would she be sleeping under the stars with a lover? Jace gritted his teeth at the possibility even as he acknowledged that, single or not, she was off-limits to him.

Seduce a paying customer? *Hell, no.* Boone had

fired hands for less than that. It would be unprofessional and impulsive and would only confirm his brothers' low expectations of him.

Next to him, Yen nickered and rubbed her head against his shoulder.

Jace knew she was just angling for another treat, but the timing felt like commiseration. "Thanks for the sympathy, sweetheart. Keeping my distance from her is gonna be…" *Hard* was an understatement.

Still, he couldn't undermine his goals and his family standing for an ill-advised fling. Even with a woman who looked like she would be worth it.

The breeze gusting around Mia made it harder to hear the other end of the phone call, but Shari's unrepentant laugh was unmistakable.

"Fine, you caught me. I added a few things to your bag. You were mid-surgery, so I made some judgment calls. You're welcome."

Mia sighed. "I don't mean to sound ungrateful for the help, but I was trying to pack light, and—"

"A lacy red bra does not add noticeable weight."

It wasn't *just* a bra, but the same logic also applied to the silky nightshirt and the sleeveless knee-length wrap dress Mia had been surprised to find in her duffel.

"You don't even have to take the extra things on the trail," Shari said. "Leave them in the guest cottage if you want. I was just giving you options—and a reminder that there's more to life than vaccinations and surgeries."

"But—"

"I get it. The clinic is as important to you as my restaurant is to me. But sometimes you need to stop and smell the wildflowers."

There was, in fact, a field of riotous yellow and purple blooms to the left of the paddock. How sad was it that Mia hadn't even noticed them until now? Few people were lucky enough to work in an "office" like this, with puffy white clouds dotting an endless blue sky and the backdrop of breathtaking mountains and the sexiest cowboy she'd ever seen staring right at her.

Wait, what?

Where had he come from?

Mia blinked. For a split second, she wondered if the broad-shouldered cowboy leading a chestnut horse was a hallucination brought on by sleep deprivation and stress. *Nope, definitely not a hallucination.* Instead of disappearing, he was getting closer.

"You've gotta learn how phone conversations work," Shari teased as the silence stretched on. "See, first *I* say something, and then *you*—"

"Sorry." Belatedly, Mia realized she was openly staring at the man.

He tipped his hat in greeting, and his lips curved in a slow smile.

Her mouth went dry. "I have to go. I…" She wanted to tell her friend about the cowboy, but the only thing more embarrassing than being caught ogling would be if he overheard her describing him.

That didn't stop her from a mental assessment, though. Her gaze swept from his hat to his boots, lingering appreciatively on the areas in between. He was deliciously scruffy with a shadowed hint of beard and well-worn jeans. The sleeves of his checkered shirt were rolled up, exposing sinful forearms. From what she could see, his hair was even darker than the black hat he wore, and though she couldn't tell his eye color from this distance, the way he looked at her was hotter than the summer sun.

Resisting the urge to fan herself, she averted her gaze to the field of flowers and dropped her voice to a whisper. "There's a man coming toward me."

"Okay. Why do you sound weird? Are you in danger or something?"

"What? No. He's just, um…"

"Oh."

Damn. There were drawbacks to having a friend who knew you so well.

"This is exciting," Shari said. "Text me a pic!"

"We both know that's not gonna happen."

"Well, give me details, then. What does he look like?"

He looked… Mia risked glancing his way again, and their gazes collided. His grin deepened. An answering smile tugged at her lips.

He looked like fun.

Two

As soon as she disconnected, Mia regretted ending the call. Talking to Shari had given her something to do besides breathlessly wait for the man to reach her. She felt exposed now that she was off the phone. Her stomach fluttered with nerves.

The cowboy spoke first. "I've never complained about the company of a beautiful woman, but tourists aren't supposed to be here."

"I'm not."

"You're not here?" His deep voice was rich with humor. His eyes, as it turned out, were a sparkling blue so distracting that she struggled to find words.

Get a grip, Mia. She'd grown up in a houseful of men; it wasn't like her to be tongue-tied in front of one. "I meant, I'm not a tourist. Dr. Mia Zane, veterinarian." Normally, she would have extended a hand to shake, but he was occupied with the horse nudging at him. "Alonzo Boone hired me to join the cattle drive."

"Ah. Then you must be a fantastic vet. Boone isn't easily impressed. I'm JT, and this pushy young lady is Yen." He patted the filly's neck, then glanced back at Mia, his expression unreadable. "So you aren't a paying customer?"

"No." Didn't he believe her?

"I'm one of the hands on the drive. What do you think that makes us?" he mused. "Coworkers?"

"I'm not sure it makes us anything."

"Well." His grin was mischievous. "Not yet, anyway."

"Are…are you flirting with me?" It was an awkward question, but Mia believed in forthrightness, more than ever since Drew's betrayal.

"When I'm flirting, you won't have to ask. But if you'd rather I don't, now's a good time to say so."

Did she want him to flirt with her? *Yes.*

No, you're here as a professional. She opened her mouth to politely remind him of that, but instead heard herself say, "Too soon to tell. I reserve the right to say no later."

"Noted. But fair warning—I'll do my best to make you want to say yes."

This time, the flutter low in her abdomen wasn't nerves. It was heat. And giddy elation that she'd been the one to put that gleam in his eyes. "Noted," she echoed back at him.

He chuckled, but then his expression shifted. "Last thing I wanna do is cut this conversation short, but orientation is supposed to start soon. And I'm leading it. See you there?"

She nodded. Alonzo had told her it wasn't necessary for her to attend, but she was suddenly feeling very motivated to make sure she understood all the safety guidelines. "I'll be in the front row, taking notes." Or ogling the instructor and doodling erotic sketches.

"I have a better idea. It could be helpful for demonstration purposes if I had an assistant. Feel like volunteering, Dr. Zane? If Boone hired you, your equestrian skills must be solid."

"They are. But I'm a little out of practice. It's been a while since I've been in the saddle."

"It'll come back to you. Most of it's instinct. And, even if you're a little rusty, you're in good hands."

Anticipation shivered through her. She bet JT was great with his hands. The question was, would she be bold enough to find out? A little harmless flirting was one thing, but sneaking into a stranger's tent? It was a pleasurable fantasy, but she'd never done anything like that in real life.

JT grinned, his expression so wickedly irresistible that she could imagine he'd read her thoughts.

His earlier statement echoed in her mind, and

what had seemed like a playful challenge now felt like a thrilling promise. *I'll do my best to make you want to say yes.*

The man was as good as his word.

Normally, Mia had unshakable focus, but she struggled to concentrate on the routine orientation because she was so distracted by JT. His tone had been strictly professional when he introduced her to the assembled crowd, but the tourists seated on the rustic wooden benches couldn't see the way his thumb idly grazed the inside of her wrist as he handed Mia the reins. No one watching knew the electric sizzle caused by the slow back-and-forth slide of his skin against hers. And they certainly didn't know how good he smelled. When he'd helped her onto the bay mare, it had taken every ounce of Mia's willpower not to close her eyes, lean closer and inhale deeply. His scent was rich and earthy, almost sandalwood but less definable.

JT was igniting all her senses, reawakening dormant hormones and desires. She focused more on the low, drawling timbre of his voice than what he was actually saying and missed her cue at one point. Fortunately, he covered the brief gap. The man was charisma personified and obviously not shy about addressing a crowd.

Of course, he was far from timid in one-on-one situations, too. *When I'm flirting, you won't have to ask.* His tone had been playful but self-assured. A man who was confident in his skills. A flutter of appreciation twisted low inside her as she imagined—

The horse shifted beneath her, jarring Mia back to reality. This was hardly the time to be fantasizing. With effort, she tamped down her uncharacteristic lust and gave the rest of the demonstration her undivided attention.

More or less.

Finally, JT dismissed the crowd with the reminder that there was a free hour before cocktails were served if anyone wanted to explore or change for dinner. Then he started to help Mia dismount. He covered her hand with his. "You're probably expert enough not to need the assist, but we're a full-service operation at the Climbing W."

"No complaints here," she murmured, pivoting toward him to drop down from the saddle. As she touched the ground, the tips of her boots brushed his. She was enveloped in his warmth and his almost-sandalwood scent, close enough to see the ring of darker blue around his light eyes.

They were standing close enough to kiss.

The errant thought caught her off guard. Mia didn't kiss men she'd just met. *Well, why not?* At the moment, it seemed like a fantastic idea. Her gaze dipped to his mouth, and her pulse thudded with exhilaration.

"Speaking of full service," JT began.

She swayed closer. "Yes?"

"If you're not otherwise engaged, may I join you

for dinner? I couldn't possibly let a visitor to the Climbing W dine alone."

Mia smiled at the request, warmth spreading through her at the promise of more time with him. "It's a date." The word danced in her mind, full of possibility. She might not be reckless enough to kiss a stranger, but a date?

That was a different story.

I owe Shari an apology. Mia stepped inside the spacious refurbished barn, smoothing the hem of her skirt. She'd swapped her jeans for the short dress Shari had packed and replaced the earlier ponytail with loose curls that framed her face.

"Champagne, ma'am?" A waiter effortlessly balancing a tray of drinks approached. "Or perhaps the Climbing W's signature rum cocktail?"

Mia thanked him but opted for a sparkling water instead. No alcohol buzz could match her pleasant rush of expectation. At the moment, JT was in a corner talking to a pair of newlyweds who'd chosen the cattle drive as their rustic honeymoon, but Mia knew he'd noticed the moment she stepped inside. She *felt* his awareness of her, an electricity across her skin, like a thunderstorm rolling in.

Resisting the urge to go straight to him, Mia let herself get caught up in conversation with tourists who wanted a vet's opinion. A woman from Denver showed Mia pictures of her tortoiseshell kitten on her phone. A couple from New Mexico asked her opinions on which dog breeds did best with children. In a way, Mia relished the interruptions that delayed her from reaching JT. It was like how she used to binge a TV show, in her pre-clinic days, but postpone watching the epic finale, reveling in the anticipation.

The guests around her, however, proved too adept at supplying delays. Before she knew it, Alonzo Boone was clanging a small metal wand against an iron triangle, the dinner bell long used by cowboys and chuck wagon cooks.

"If I could have everyone's attention, please." Boone was a barrel-chested man with a silver mustache and a voice that did not need a microphone to fill the space. "I wanna thank you all for joining us. Starting tomorrow, everyone will have rotating chores assigned to them, but tonight, we wanted to treat you to some five-star luxury. You'll be enjoying an alfresco dinner prepared by an award-winning chef, followed by s'mores and a campfire song. Just remember we have an early morning."

There was one joking groan in the crowd, but given that every tourist in attendance had paid handsomely to take this trip, Mia doubted anyone was genuinely annoyed by the mention of chores or getting up at dawn. As she made her way outside with everyone else, she was surrounded by happy murmurs and lively conversation.

Long wooden tables were decorated with fresh flowers. Fairy lights twinkled in the overhead branches of towering aspen trees. It was an enchanting setting, worlds removed from the bustle of her clinic and the stress that had become her too-constant companion. She felt light and liberated. The only thing that would make the night even more enjoyable was her dinner partner.

"Mia!"

She blinked, shifting her focus to the trail boss in front of her. "Oh. Mr. Boone. Hi."

He snorted. "I remember when you were yea tall and called me Uncle 'Lonzo. Let's split the difference. Just call me Boone. Sorry I haven't had a chance to catch up with you until now. Day before a drive is always hectic."

"I totally understand. Don't worry about me. I'm here to work."

"Yeah, I heard you helped lead orientation." He lowered his voice. "I didn't realize you and Jace were already acquainted?"

Mia frowned, not quite following. "Sorry? Who?"

"JT." Boone rocked back on his heels. "You two know each other?"

The *J* stood for Jace? She smiled inwardly, charmed to have discovered more about him. "We met earlier today, and I, uh…" *Managed not to jump him down by the barn.* "Volunteered my assistance. I hope that's all right."

"Of course. Sure. I just thought maybe— Oh, Levi is waving me over. Better see what he needs." He was already striding away when he added over his shoulder, "Enjoy dinner!"

She scanned the small crowd gathering at the tables in search of JT. When she finally spotted him, it wasn't amid the diners but along the perimeter, deep in conversation with two other ranch employees. Their eyes met briefly, his expression apologetic. She understood immediately. *Duty calls.* How many lunch dates had she canceled or dinners had she been late for because of her clinic work? Drew's typically churlish responses had bewildered her, since she'd considered the clinic a partnership, something he was as invested in as she was.

Despite a mild disappointment as JT and the other men retreated in the opposite direction, she accepted that he had a job to do. She resolved to enjoy the beautiful night anyway. The fresh air had given her a real appetite, further bolstered by the tantalizing food smells. Her dinner companions engaged her in conversation as a grilled shrimp appetizer was served. Mia shared lighthearted anecdotes about the kittens she was fostering while enjoying chilled white wine. A lovely, unfamiliar calm washed through her.

This must be what "relaxed" feels like. No wonder people recommended it.

After dinner, some of the tourists headed for their bunks while others paired off around the crackling campfire. Still mellow from a wonderful meal, Mia sat alone on a log, trying to remember the last time she'd roasted marshmallows.

"Is this seat taken?"

She glanced over her shoulder to see the welcome sight of JT—Jace—behind her, his jawline etched in the glow of firelight. "Hey." Her greeting sounded breathless, but she didn't care. She was unabashedly happy to see him.

Although she scooted over on the log bench to give him room, the seating was still cozy. His denim jeans brushed against her thigh, and his arm grazed her shoulder as he reached across her to get a skewer and the bag of marshmallows.

Hyperawareness jolted through her body, and she nearly lost her grip on her skewer. It dipped toward the fire.

"Oops." She pulled up three flaming marshmallows and blew them out.

He laughed. "Want to trade with me?" He handed her his skewer and took the trio of blackened marshmallows. "I actually like them this way."

She cast a skeptical glance at the marshmallows, which were puckered and bubbling. "You do?"

"When I was five, I burned some marshmallows on a campout with my dad and older brothers. Reed was so snotty when he told me I was doing it wrong that I made a point of always setting my marshmallows on fire thereafter, just to irk him."

"Older brothers, huh? How many? I survived three."

"Yeesh. You have my condolences. Two was more than enough."

She laughed, bumping her shoulder lightly against his. "It wasn't *all* bad."

"Bet it wasn't all good, either." He slid the first charred marshmallow off the stick and into his mouth. "Mmm. Once you get past the cinder crunch, it's gooey perfection. Maybe it's an acquired taste, but I always got to skip the wait and enjoy my s'mores before my brothers."

"So you're an instant gratification kind of guy?"

"Sometimes." He turned his head to meet her gaze. "But I can slow down and take my time, too."

Good to know. She swallowed, unable to look away from him. But then, why would she want to?

"Careful, Doc." With a grin, he nodded toward the skewer she held. "You don't want to burn a second batch."

Probably not. But she couldn't resist the idea of playing with fire tonight.

"Sorry I missed dinner," he said. "Got called down to the stables to help with a high-strung mare."

"That's okay. Dinner was delicious, but I was more looking forward to…"

"Marshmallows?" His words held a note of friendly challenge, daring her to come right out and say what she wanted.

"No." She could do better than words. "This." Mia leaned forward, bracing herself with one arm as her lips met his.

He went still for a millisecond. But then he cupped the nape of her neck and deepened the kiss. His

mouth slanted over hers in a slow, smoky-sweet seduction. Mia's head spun. She would never again
taste a toasted marshmallow without remembering
this moment.

"Damn." He sucked in a breath, pressing his forehead to hers. "I'm *really* sorry I wasn't available until
now. But I am at your disposal—anything you need
from now until tomorrow morning."

An entire night with him? *Hell, yes.* She wanted
this stolen, spontaneous night with a fierceness that
surprised her. Her heart pounded. "Walk me to my
cabin?"

"Yes, ma'am."

It wasn't until they stood that Mia remembered
they weren't alone, not really. Other couples were
silhouetted in the firelight. This was his job—and
hers, too, for the week. She shouldn't have kissed
him in front of potential witnesses, but she couldn't
bring herself to regret it. Fortunately, no one seemed
to be paying them any attention. They were just another couple enjoying the crackling fire and the starry
night.

Still, in the name of discretion, she didn't reach for
his hand as they walked toward the path. She didn't
allow herself to touch him at all. The space between
them took on a life of its own. Instead of contact
and sensation, she was awash with anticipation and
yearning.

Mia barely registered the journey up the subtly lit
trail to the guest cottage; she was preoccupied with

the luxurious bed awaiting them. Earlier today, it had seemed comically large. But it was exactly the right size for sharing with the cowboy next to her. She quickened her steps, picturing him there with her. Imagining how good it would feel once they were free to explore each other.

Maybe there was something to his marshmallow philosophy. Sometimes patience was overrated.

Despite her enthusiasm, or likely because of it, her fingers shook as she tried to unlock the cabin door. It was a relief when his hand covered hers.

"Let me."

With one deft click, they were inside. Neither of them bothered turning on a light. The moonlight through the window bathed them in silver, more than enough illumination for her to appreciate the lines of his body and planes of his face. Although his blue eyes were shadowed, the hunger in them was unmistakable.

His gaze slid down her in a nearly tangible caress, making her ache. "You are one sexy woman, Doc."

"Thank you." *And thanks* to *you.* She was often a stress-ridden workaholic, but not tonight, not in his eyes. His appreciation made her a temptress, a voluptuous goddess. A siren who took what she wanted.

She stepped forward, skimming her fingers past the collar of his shirt, over the vee of exposed skin. "I want to see you." She began unbuttoning her way down. "Want to touch you."

He inhaled sharply. "Feeling's mutual." After

shrugging out of his shirt, he helped her with his jeans. His body was like a sculpture, lean muscle and taut abs shaped by physical labor. He tugged playfully at the neckline of her dress. "Your turn."

She shimmied free of the fabric, letting it slide down her body and pool at her feet. He took his time drinking in the sight of her. Mia wasn't much of an exhibitionist, but the sheer lust in his expression made her feel proud and powerful. And very grateful that her duffel bag had included lacy lingerie.

It had not, however, included any birth control. "Oh." She bit her bottom lip. "I don't suppose you have condoms with you?"

He nodded, picking up his discarded jeans and reaching into a pocket. "Not that I was assuming—"

"I like a man who's prepared," she interrupted with a grin.

Grinning back, he pulled her close for another deep, hungry kiss that obliterated all thought. She swayed on her feet, clinging to him. Pleasure sizzled through her, sparking a need she hadn't felt in a long time. Or maybe ever. She felt completely out of control, and it was *glorious*.

A small sound of protest escaped her when he ended their kiss. But then his mouth was at the hollow of her throat, grazing her sensitive skin and working his way toward her cleavage. He palmed her breast through the lace, and she moaned. She arched her back to give him better access, struggling to maintain her balance, and he solved the problem by tumbling them across the king-size mattress.

Mia landed atop him. She rocked against his erection, and Jace gasped. His hands dropped to her ass, urging her to do it again. She moved with abandon, shifting her weight and swiveling her hips in wanton eagerness. He sat up to unclasp her bra, then rolled them over so that he was braced above her. On another mattress, they would have fallen off.

"This bed is definitely Texas-sized." His tone was amused, but arousal made his voice lower, rougher.

"Right?" She lightly bit his collarbone.

"Let's make good use of it." He brushed the backs of his fingertips over the curve of her breast, tracing light, teasing patterns that made her nipples tighten and left her breathless for more.

"Jace."

He stilled, eyebrows drawn.

It took her a moment to realize how she'd caught him off guard. "I heard that's what the *J* stood for. I—"

"Say it again." Maybe it was a trick of the moonlight, but for a moment he looked surprisingly vulnerable.

She cupped his face between her hands. "Jace."

With a low hum of satisfaction, he bent his head to her breast and sucked hard, his stubbled jaw a tantalizing friction against her skin. There was no featherlight teasing this time; it was a sensual onslaught. He shifted from one breast to the other, wringing cries from her with his lips and tongue and teeth. Heat flooded her, and her hips bucked of their own accord.

When he brushed his fingertips over her inner thigh, she trembled. The warm tingles of desire she'd felt when he first kissed her had become something far more primal. She needed to get closer, needed him inside her. He moved his thumb over her clit, and her back bowed off the mattress.

"Oh, God." Her voice was broken, desperate, but she didn't care, not while he was touching her like that. She was frantic, on the edge of bliss and raw craving. He pressed harder, rotating his thumb as he speared a finger inside her. Uncensored words spilled from her, and she was only distantly aware of them, hearing "yes," and "please," and his name.

Jace hadn't been able to imagine a bigger turn-on than seeing Mia naked, but *hearing* her was downright addictive. His name on her lips, her uninhibited moans, her unabashed pleasure in his touch. He couldn't get enough. He wanted more of her gasps ringing in his ears.

Part of him wanted to do this all night, lavish her with touches and kisses until the sun rose. But he wanted to be inside her when she came, wanted to feel her shatter around him. He reached blindly for the condom he'd dropped on the mattress, sheathing himself in record time.

Even as wet as she was, she was tight. She felt so fucking good. He kissed her, using all his self-control to move slowly at first, then faster when she curled her nails into his back. He rolled his hips, and Mia wrapped her legs around his waist, taking him deeper. He lost himself in the rapturous sensation. Her body clenched around him as she gasped his name, shuddering against him. Pleasure erupted, starting at the base of his spine and coursing through him. With a guttural yell, he fell forward, balancing the brunt of his weight on his arms so he didn't squash her.

For long moments, the only sounds in the room were their mingled panting breaths. He wasn't sure how much time passed before he finally managed an admiring, "Wow."

She sighed contentedly. "Now I know how your marshmallows feel."

Jace pushed up on one arm. "Excuse me?"

"Like I just went up in flames." She grinned. "And now I'm sticky."

He laughed.

"I could use a shower." She wiggled out from underneath him, her progress slowed when he pulled her back for a kiss.

Eventually he let her go, hungrily watching as she sauntered across the room, moonlight hugging all of the curves he had just explored.

"Want to join me?" she asked over her shoulder.

"Right behind you...and loving the view."

She blew him a kiss and gave an extra swish of her hips as she disappeared around the corner. Jace scrambled after her. Had it only been hours ago that he'd been complaining to a horse about his life? Because right at this moment, he felt like the luckiest man on the planet.

Three

Despite not getting much rest, Jace woke feeling refreshed and more content than he had since returning to Colorado. The beautiful woman nestled against him was responsible for that. She had one leg thrown over his, and her head was resting on his bare chest, her hair a riotous red-gold tangle. He wanted to run his fingers through it, but touching her was why he hadn't gotten more than two hours of sleep. The sun was starting to rise, and he had work to do. If he touched her now, how would he find the self-discipline to get out of bed?

He hadn't even left her yet and was already looking forward to seeing her later today. Of course, once the drive started this morning, he'd have to share her company with the tourists and other ranch hands. At yesterday's orientation, watching her interact with others had only improved his already high opinion of her. She was kind and answered questions thoughtfully, and she liked horses as much as he did. She spoke about her vet practice passionately but cracked jokes, too. Unlike his brothers, she seemed capable of balancing both a work ethic and a sense of humor.

There was a lot to enjoy about being with her, but Jace particularly appreciated that she *saw* him—not as an eligible billionaire or a family screwup, merely as a man she desired. Too many people in his life had preconceived or outdated notions about him. Or ulterior motives for wanting to get close. It was a relief to spend time with someone who didn't.

Well, spending more time together will have to wait until you're on the trail. He'd lingered here too long.

He moved away from her as gingerly as possible, trying not to disturb her.

"Oh, no." She mumbled her protest facedown into the mattress. "Morning already?"

"Afraid so. You can probably grab another hour, but I need to head out. The last thing we want is for Boone to come looking for me." Jace hoped none of the ranch hands had noticed his absence from the bunkhouse last night. It wasn't uncommon for a hand to spend an evening in town with a sweetheart or even camp out in nice weather, but the night before a drive, everyone was usually accounted for. "Need anything before I go?"

"I have some syringes in my medical bag. Any chance you could inject some coffee straight into my veins?"

Chuckling, he brushed a kiss against her temple. "See you later, Doc."

She muttered a drowsy response and fell back asleep as he finished dressing. He carried his boots out to the front porch and pulled them on. He was just fastening his belt when his cell phone vibrated. Someone was calling him at this hour? It was barely dawn. Shit. Maybe Boone *had* noticed he was missing.

Jace strode away from the cottage before answering, hurrying in case his presence was required at the stable or main house. But once he had his phone in hand, it wasn't Boone's number he saw on the screen.

Heath? When was the last time the middle Malone brother had placed a call to him? If Reed's preferred method of communication was disapproving lectures, Heath's was terse text messages.

"Hello?"

"Jace." The shaky voice on the other end of the phone certainly didn't sound like stoic, number-crunching Heath. The last time Jace had seen him upset was…

Fear coiled in his gut, and Jace went cold all over. "What happened?"

"It's Grandpa Harry. Heart attack. Reed's asking

questions, but we'll know more when he's out of surgery. You should be here. Just in case—"

"On my way." Jace cut him off before he could say anything more. The possibility was too awful to contemplate, much less hear out loud.

To hell with the cattle drive.

The whole reason he'd been here instead of at home on the Triple Pine was that he'd wanted to prove himself to his grandfather. But if being here had robbed Jace of the chance to say goodbye? A horrible déjà vu churned in his gut, his mouth sour with the long-familiar cocktail of guilt and loss.

Jace broke into a run, praying that the universe wasn't going to take another loved one.

The beautiful morning matched Mia's sunny mood. But her stroll to the rustic picnic tables for breakfast came with a few muscle twinges. After last night, she would definitely be a little tender in the saddle. *Worth it.* She was grateful she and Jace made the most of the opportunity while they could—repeat occurrences on the cattle drive would be unprofessional and awkward.

Yet despite her mature resolution to maintain a friendly distance, she found herself already glancing around for him. *To say good-morning, not to seduce him on a picnic bench.* That was just common courtesy.

"Excuse me? Dr. Zane?"

Mia turned to find a gangly young man, his freckled face anxious. "Morning, Levi." They'd met last night when he came by the dinner table to introduce himself to the group. At first, she'd mistaken him for a teenager vacationing with his family, but it turned out he was an agriculture major who worked summers on the dude ranch. Had Boone sent him to find her? "Is there an issue with one of the heifers?"

"No, ma'am. Leastwise, not as far as I know. I was supposed to keep an eye out for you so I could give you a message from Mr. Mal—from JT."

"Oh?"

"He 'bout ran me over on his way off the ranch this morning. Family emergency, so he won't be making the cattle drive after all. He asked me to tell you goodbye."

Oh. She wouldn't see him again this week? Disappointment stabbed through her, far more intense than she would have expected.

If Levi found anything strange about the fact Jace had singled her out, he didn't comment on it. He frowned. "I hope everything turns out okay with his family. His brothers and grandpa are real nice."

So Levi knew Jace personally? A half-dozen questions flitted through her mind, but she didn't allow herself to ask them. It would be wrong to use a crisis as an excuse to pry. "I hope everything's all right, too. Thanks for passing along the message."

Levi nodded, then tipped his cowboy hat and ambled away. Mia lined up with the tourists at a long trestle table laden with pastries and bacon, but she wasn't really hungry.

Maybe this is for the best. Not the emergency part, of course—she hoped whatever it was could be easily dealt with—but perhaps a clean break was an unexpected blessing. If she was this bummed now to see Jace go, how would she have felt after a week on the trail with him?

Last night had been unforgettable. Perfect. She'd never been so uninhibited with a man, so insatiable. From the second he'd opened the door to her cabin to the moment she'd finally drifted to sleep in his arms, she hadn't cared about the outside world.

Including her clinic.

But this was a new day, and she had responsibilities. His departure spared her further distraction and any resulting awkwardness that came from a one-night stand. It was best not to see him again—except in the occasional, inevitable fantasy. Sighing wistfully, she said a silent farewell.

See you in my dreams, cowboy.

Six weeks later

TRUCK! The word roared in Jace's head but caught in his throat. He opened his mouth to shout a warning to his dad, but no sound emitted. Then, impact. Their car spun out of control. Metal scraped metal, and glass shattered. Jace heard his mom scream, and the world flipped upside down as darkness pressed in around him. Sirens shrieked in the distance, grow-ing louder as—

Jace struggled awake, his heart and head both pounding.

The specific details of the nightmare sometimes shifted, not always accurate. Sometimes he dreamed he'd been in the front seat instead of his mom or that the color of the truck speeding through the in-tersection had been different. But the suffocating dread never changed. He swallowed roughly, his mouth dry. Before returning home to Colorado, it had been months, maybe years, since he'd had the too-familiar dream, but ever since Grandpa Harry's heart attack…

That's not a siren.

Although he was awake now, the shrieking noise from his nightmare hadn't stopped. He belatedly re-alized it was a baby crying. *Brooke.* His niece might only be four months old, but her volume was impres-sive as hell.

Relieved to focus on something besides bad dreams and his grandfather's health, Jace grabbed the T-shirt balled up on his nightstand and followed the sound of his wailing niece. The house was dark, but he'd gone up and down the main staircase plenty of times without light, often when sneaking out or returning after curfew.

The main house was a sprawling three-story home with an indoor pool and two apartment suites added during renovations. Jace was willing to bet Brooke's cries could be heard through every square inch. Hell, they could probably hear her in Grover, where he'd spent most of the week working in one of the Malone field offices.

The main kitchen, with its multiple ovens and four-thousand-dollar refrigerator, was the province of the cook, the housekeeper and occasional catering staff. There was a smaller offshoot that was little more than a microwave and a long oval table that had hosted a lot of family game nights…and game-related arguments. It was in that room where Jace found his brother Reed, barefoot and uncharacteristically disheveled, pacing laps across the tile floor with Brooke in his arms.

From what Jace could hear, his brother was attempting to reason with the red-faced infant. "If you're not wet and you don't want a bottle, maybe you're just tired. Sleep would fix that. Please, *please* go to sleep."

"Maybe," Jace drawled, "she can't sleep because someone is making an unholy racket."

Halting mid-lap, Reed glared. "Really? I hadn't noticed."

Jace almost chuckled. Normally, Reed was above sarcasm. Of course, normally his hair wasn't standing on end, either. Was it weird that Jace preferred 2:00 a.m. Reed to the competent older brother who ran the company and was trying to run the family while Grandpa Harry was in cardiac rehab?

"Here, let me take a turn," Jace offered. "You look like you need a break."

Reed clutched his daughter tighter. "What do you know about babies?"

This is the thanks I get for trying to help? "Just that you're supposed to give them light beer instead of the regular stuff and you have to change their diapers once a week." He gritted his teeth. Why had he thought his brother would welcome his assistance? "Enjoy your screaming bundle."

"Wait…"

Jace paused.

"I do need a break." Reed slowly passed over the baby. "Be careful with her! Sorry—that wasn't personal. Just reflex."

Being a divorced single parent couldn't be easy, but it had to be easier for billionaires. "Don't you have a nanny?" Jace resumed Reed's path around the kitchen, adding a tiny bounce to his step.

"For during work hours, yeah. But if I leave her to someone else at night, too, when would I see my daughter?" Reed shoved a hand through his dark hair. No wonder it was on end. "That's not how we were raised. Mom and Dad were hands-on. Down-to-earth."

Reed's uncharacteristic mention of their parents vividly conjured the images of Jace's nightmare. In the first year after the accident, the arguments and accusations had been so brutal the brothers had almost come to blows. It had taken many talks from Grandpa Harry and some grudging family therapy before an uneasy truce had been reached.

Jace swallowed. "You don't talk about Mom and Dad."

"Well, I think about them all the time. And I owe it to them to be the best dad I can. I owe it to Brooke." He looked away, composing himself. "Sorry she woke you."

"I'm not."

Reed raised an eyebrow.

"Bad dreams," Jace mumbled, embarrassed to sound like he was still six and needed their father to check under his bed.

Reed didn't ask for details, and Jace didn't offer any. When the pause grew uncomfortable, they both turned their attention back to Brooke and her intermittent cries. Though she was clearly winding down, she still stubbornly fought sleep. *Hardheaded.* Definitely a Malone.

"You're good with her." Reed's compliment would have carried more weight if he didn't sound so shocked.

"What can I say? Ladies love me."

His brother rolled his eyes.

"I picked up some practice around the office in Dallas. We offered an employee day care for infants and toddlers." It was one of the few company policies Jace had been proud of. He sighed. "I understand why you think I'm a quitter, but I didn't leave Dallas because I was bored or because the job was too hard. Clint's cutthroat tactics and our corporate disregard for long-term environmental impact were making it impossible for me to live with myself."

His employer had shot down his appeals for change. Jace had come home hoping he would have better luck with his own family. *Ha.*

Frustration tinged his voice. "Energy companies should be a positive force in their communities."

"Are you saying Malone Energy *isn't*?"

Jace opened his mouth, closed it again and remembered that he was trying to soothe a baby, not pick a fight with his brother. "No. But I am saying that we could take something already good and make it even better. For everyone, including future generations." He glanced meaningfully at his now-sleeping niece.

Reed looked thoughtful.

"I'm not the selfish kid you remember," Jace added. There was so much more to him than the shoplifting teen or flippant college dropout who'd charmed pretty classmates into writing his papers. He just needed the chance to prove it.

In his darker moments, though, he agreed with his brothers. Maybe he didn't deserve that chance. After all, if it weren't for him—

"Alonzo Boone did say you were a hard worker when he called to check on Harry. And I probably shouldn't take the recommendation of a four-month-old, but my daughter seems to like you."

She was peacefully snuggled against Jace's chest. He'd overheard moms in the office say babies could sense stress. She might have been feeding off of Reed's exasperation that he couldn't do more to help her. Jace refrained from pointing that out, however. His sleep-deprived brother might take it as criticism. This was the closest they'd come to mutual respect in over a decade, and Jace didn't want to disrupt the peace.

Reed exhaled heavily. "I hope, for Grandpa Harry's sake, you're right about having changed. He wants to believe in you. And he has enough heart problems without you breaking it."

Again. Jace knew how many times he'd let their grandfather down.

Well, no more. He renewed his determination to stick to his goals and not get derailed by anything, including past loss. Or more recent, pleasant distractions, like decadent nights with breathtaking red-heads. In the weeks since he'd seen Mia, he'd thought of her frequently and even considered reaching out to her through her clinic. He'd told himself that the least he could do was say goodbye properly.

But he'd ultimately talked himself out of it. Explaining that he was no longer JT the ranch hand would be complicated, and he wasn't looking for complications right now. *Focus.* He needed to make his family proud and help assure that their legacy was a positive one. Chasing after a woman he barely knew was something the old Jace would do.

He passed Brooke back to his brother. "You can trust me."

Reed studied him for a long moment, and Jace

hoped his brother would find whatever it was he was looking for. But all he said was, "Good night."

Jace sat alone in the kitchen after Reed left, in no hurry to fall back asleep and risk more nightmares. But the truth lingered, haunting him even now that he was awake. While the accident was technically the fault of the trucker who'd nodded off and run through a red light, Jace's parents being at that intersection was his fault. They would have been at a city hall event if Jace hadn't been nabbed by security on his way out of a novelty gift store.

The memory was so vivid. The muggy air of the warm night, the familiar smell of his mom's perfume, the disappointment etched on his dad's face.

"Do you know how mortifying it is that my son was stealing?" his father demanded as they climbed into the car. *"You could have paid for everything in that store—we have money! And, damn it, we have values. Haven't we taught you better than this?"*

Jace leaned sullenly against the back window, staring out at dusk. It was pointless to explain. How could his parents understand when they were beloved in the community? He was not. They didn't know what every day was like for him at school. Teachers expected him to live up to his straight-A brothers, but he wasn't as disciplined as Reed or as smart as Heath. Classmates either resented his family's riches or jockeyed for favors and gifts.

His mom turned around in her seat. "It's those

new friends of yours. Why are you so determined to hang out with troublemakers?"

Because he'd finally found a few people who didn't treat him like a Malone, but merely a fellow delinquent. He stayed silent, unable to meet his mother's concerned gaze.

And in refusing to apologize or justify his actions, Jace had unknowingly squandered the chance for one final conversation with his parents. He'd give anything to undo that, to undo all of it. He missed them every day.

I'm so sorry.

He couldn't bring them back. But, even though it was too little, too late, he would work his ass off to become the son they'd deserved.

Four

Being a doctor took more than skill. Mia's patients and their owners counted on her confidence, precision and attention to detail…which made it all the more concerning that she was blanking on the name of the vet tech who had worked with her for three years.

"Dr. Z? Are you all right?"

"Um, sorry…" Anna? Abby? "I overslept this morning and it's like I've been running at the wrong speed ever since." Mia picked up the file the tech had set on the desk. *Anita?* "Guess this is what happens if I don't have time to get caffeine before I come in."

"I totally understand. One time," Amanda began, "during finals—"

"Amanda!" Amanda Rockwell. Mia couldn't believe it had taken her so long to come up with the right name.

The blonde drew back, looking startled. "Yes?"

"What?" Oh, right. Because Mia had just shrieked the tech's name. "Nothing. Never mind. Thanks for the file. You'll, um, call Mr. Lee and follow up on how Roscoe is doing?"

"On my way to do that now." Amanda peered at her. "You sure you don't need anything else?"

"Nope, I'm good." Mia pasted a smile on her face, struggling to look convincing.

Amanda still looked skeptical when she turned to go. *Like last night.* Mia had tried to assure an adoptive cat family that she was all right, but they'd been alarmed by her tears. So had she. Mia certainly hadn't expected to bawl her eyes out when the last of the foster kittens was picked up. After all, finding them forever homes had been the goal! She'd fostered cats and dogs dozens of times in the past and never sobbed when they left her place. So why the embarrassing crying jag?

She'd eventually exhausted herself to the point of sleeping straight through her alarm this morning.

What the hell is wrong with me? She slumped back in her chair. Whatever it was, it had caused her to reread the same sentence three times.

"Dr. Z?"

She glanced up from the file to see Amanda hovering in the doorway. "Yes?"

"I thought this might help." With a sympathetic smile, the tech handed her a mug of coffee.

"Thank—" An unexpected wave of nausea caused Mia to tightly clamp her mouth shut. She normally loved the smell of coffee. She owned coffee-scented candles. At the moment, however, her body violently protested the aroma. She couldn't have been more repulsed if it was week-old fish. Pushing past a wide-eyed Amanda, she hurried to the restroom, her stomach roiling.

Moodiness.

Fatigue.

Vomiting.

A person didn't need a medical degree to recognize those symptoms. Dizziness swamped her, and Mia gripped the edge of the sink counter to steady herself. *No, no, no.* It wasn't possible! She didn't even have a sex life. Well, except for that single night with Jace, and they'd used condoms.

She eyed her reflection critically, looking for any visible hints that she might be...

It was hard to even think the word. *Pregnant.* But she was letting her imagination run away with her. It was more likely she was coming down with something. Yet even as she repeated this reassurance to herself, she scrolled through the contacts on her phone. Her budding panic eased the tiniest bit when Shari answered.

"What's up?" Shari asked around a yawn. "Aren't you at work?" They rarely spoke this early in the day.

"I am, but I'm not staying. I hate to ask you this, given how late you were probably at the restaurant, but can you meet me at my house?" Mia couldn't keep her voice from trembling.

"Of course." Shari's tone was fully alert. "Give me five minutes to change."

"Take ten," Mia said. "I have to make a stop on the way."

"Thank you. Again." Sitting with her back against the bedroom wall, Mia turned to face Shari so that her friend could see how much she appreciated her being here. "I'm sorry for probably overreacting and wasting your time."

Shari, seated on the floor right next to her, patted her hand. "Hey, you'd do the same for me. Besides, you timed your emergency well. The restaurant's not even open. If you'd called me during a lunch or dinner rush, I would have told you tough luck."

Mia started to laugh, but her stomach cramped. "It's probably food poisoning. Or rotavirus, and now I've exposed you. I can't possibly be pregnant!" She glanced to the clock on her dresser. In another minute, they'd know for sure. She felt like she could literally hear the seconds ticking, but the clock was digital.

"It is *technically* possible. But unlikely," Shari hurried to add. "And it would be cosmically unfair. You've only had sex once in the past year."

"Well, one night. Three times." Her memory reeled

with images of Jace, braced above her on those sculpted arms. Smiling down at her, his grin becoming endearingly lopsided as he grew sleepy. Even now, scared that there might be life-changing consequences from that night, she didn't regret any of it.

Would Jace? How would he feel if it turned out she was carrying his child? Would he be sorry for what they'd shared or supportive? Or would he dismiss pregnancy as her issue alone to deal with?

Her instincts told her he wouldn't do that, but she didn't really know him, did she? For all Mia knew, he found a "special assistant" to help with orientation every cattle drive. Tears pricked her eyes again, and she groaned in frustration. Now she was crying over random imagined liaisons?

Maybe she was just overworked and overtired, and the stress was making her queasy. It was exactly the kind of emotional and physical burnout Shari always cautioned her to avoid. *There's only one way to know for sure.*

Time to look at the test. All she had to do was glance at it, and she could quit spinning wild worst-case scenarios. Her life would return to normal.

Or never be the same again.

"I don't think I can," she whispered. "Can you look for me? I know it's stupid. I know it's probably just stomach flu, but…"

"Of course. I got you." Shari bounced to her feet and disappeared through the bathroom doorway.

Mia heard a sharp intake of breath.

Her friend reemerged a second later. The apologetic worry in her dark eyes confirmed Mia's suspicions even before she spoke. "Oh, honey. Your flu has two pink lines."

A dozen infant faces smiled up at her, and Mia gulped. "That's a lot of pressure. I feel like I'm being judged by a baby jury."

"The waiting room magazines are not judging you." Nonetheless, Shari reached out and flipped over the closest one; the cover baby was replaced by a stroller ad. "You're projecting. What do you feel guilty about?"

"I still haven't figured out how to tell my family." Her overprotective father and three brothers? Yeah, that should be fun. Maybe she would start with Nolan, the only one who lived out of state. But even as stressful as the idea of telling them was, it didn't compare to… "Or Jace," she added softly.

It was the biggest irony of her life that she was sharing something so profound with a man whose phone number and last name she didn't even know. At least the Climbing W gave her a way to find him. Jace deserved to know he was a father. And, for the baby's sake, she had questions about his family's medical background.

Still, even knowing she had to get in touch with him, she'd stalled by scheduling today's OB appointment, reasoning that until she heard it from Dr. Bakshi, her pregnancy wasn't Official. Never mind the three over-the-counter tests and persistent morning sickness.

"Of *course* you don't have it all figured out yet. You've only known for a few days. Give yourself a minute to breathe. And don't let this crowd of cherubs overwhelm you." Shari waved at the babies on the magazines. "You'll only have to deal with one."

"Right." She wasn't having a litter; she didn't even know of any twins in her family. "Thank you."

"Plus, your kid will have Auntie Shari, so Baby Zane is already winning at life."

Mia was smiling at that when a nurse called her name.

The visit itself was perfunctory but conclusive. Dr. Bakshi said it was too soon to hear the heartbeat and that the first sonogram would come later.

"I'd say I'm surprised you're having morning sickness already, but every pregnancy is different," the doctor told her. "I was nauseous constantly with my daughter but never with my son. I advise starting your day with a banana or a few crackers, and call us if it gets too bad."

One prescription for prenatal vitamins later, Mia was shown out to make her next appointment, as if her life hadn't just been permanently altered.

I am officially going to be a mom. She swallowed hard. Would she be good at it? Mia had been ten months old when her mom got sick, but over the years, her dad and brothers had regaled her with stories about the woman she barely remembered.

She was accepting a reminder card from the receptionist when Shari joined her at the counter.

"You okay?" Shari asked.

Yes. No. Maybe? She took a deep breath. "Can we pick up a prescription on the way back to my place?"

"Anything you need, hon."

"What I need is to talk to Jace."

An hour later, she and Shari were seated on Mia's sofa as she dialed Alonzo Boone's number.

"Mia!" He greeted her with his usual hearty cheer. "Thanks again for joining us on the drive. We have another event in August if you—"

"Um, my summer schedule has become a little bit complicated, but I can recommend some vets if you need one." She hated to lose the potential income, especially now. Her head spun at the new costs she'd need to start budgeting for. "I'm actually calling because I need to get some contact info. Did JT—um, Jace—did he ever come back to the ranch after our week out?"

"No, as a matter of fact. I heard his grandfather's doing better, but… Any particular reason you're looking for him?"

She faltered, trying to find an innocuous answer that sounded plausible.

"Mia?" The longer she went without responding, the more agitated he sounded. "He didn't do anything inappropriate, did he? Because I don't give a damn how rich he is, I'll—"

"Rich?"

At that, Shari's head jerked up, eyes wide. Mia was sure her own expression was equally surprised.

"I wasn't supposed to tell anyone," Boone grumbled. "But your old man and I go back a long way, and I don't owe Jace Malone a damn thing. You say the word, and—"

"He didn't do anything wrong, Boone. I just needed to talk to him about something." After a few more reassurances that she was okay, Boone gave her Jace's phone number. She tried to sound casual when she said goodbye, but she was reeling.

"Already on it," Shari said, typing into the browser on her phone. "That's Jace Malone?"

Along with his number, Mia had written down his name, surrounded by scribbled question marks and exclamation points.

"Of Malone Energy?" Shari asked. "The Malone family of Triple Pine?" She whistled under her breath and turned her phone toward Mia. "*This* is your cattle drive fling?"

Mia stared in shock at the well-dressed man on the screen. Smiling back at her was an extremely familiar-looking stranger. The man on the internet wore an expensive suit and a million-dollar smile. Or billion-dollar, according to the article's headline.

"I slept with a billionaire?"

"I can see why. He is hotter than a Scotch bonnet pepper."

"I thought he was a ranch hand, Shar." Her rising disbelief brought to mind how she'd felt the day she learned of Drew's embezzlement. Was there something fundamentally wrong with her that caused her to be attracted to liars? "I thought he was charred marshmallows and scuffed boots! Turns out he's caviar and…and—"

"Really expensive boots?"

On the bright side, at least Jace was unlikely to steal from her. *Since he's freaking loaded.*

Groaning, she dropped her face into her palms. "Millions of men in Colorado, and I picked the dimpled billionaire who looks good in dusty jeans. What am I going to do?"

"The same thing you were already planning to do. Tell him the news, and take each day as it comes."

Shari made it sound almost manageable. *I can do this.* Tell Jace the news. Take one day at a time.

And fervently hope for no more surprises. Having the billionaire's baby was more than enough surprise for one lifetime.

Before Mia knew it, her one-at-a-time days had stretched into another week with Jace none the wiser about their baby. Even though she had his phone number, she couldn't bring herself to use it. News of this magnitude should be delivered in person. Calling him to set up a meeting would require a reason, and what could she say after two months that wasn't painfully awkward?

Even worse than the potential awkwardness was

the possibility that he wouldn't want to meet. Had he thought of her at all since their night together?

She knew where he lived—the Triple Pine Ranch was hardly subtle—but she couldn't show up at the family home like a stalker. By default, she decided that visiting the Malone Energy headquarters was the best course of action. Neutral ground, less of an ambush than the ranch.

At least, that's what she'd told herself during the hour-long drive to his office. Once the building was in sight, however, she began to second-guess her decision.

The office complex wasn't a towering monolith like Denver's Republic Plaza, but it was unmistakably elegant, even down to the parking deck. Instead of a utilitarian concrete structure, the four-story lot boasted color and landscaping. Impeccably manicured flowering bushes erupted from openings on each level. The skywalk connecting the deck to the main building was painted with a lively mural, and the elevators were glass, allowing her a peek at each carefully decorated floor. According to her research, Malone Energy owned the top two floors, one of which was accessible to the public. The other was sectioned into mini-suites for visiting VIPs.

When the elevator doors opened into a receptionist area, Mia had half a dozen colliding thoughts at once. What if he was in a meeting? Or out of town? Had she subconsciously chosen coming here with no warning as a form of self-sabotage?

"Welcome to Malone Energy." The polished blonde receptionist could have starred in a biopic about Grace Kelly. "How may I help you?"

"I, uh… I'm not sure you can. I don't have an appointment," Mia admitted. "But I was hoping to meet with Jace Malone. Can you tell him Mia Zane is here? I don't mind waiting."

The receptionist's expression remained pleasantly neutral. "He's on a call at the moment, but if you'll have a seat, I'll see what I can do."

Leather chairs framed a coffee table large enough for a Thanksgiving dinner. Mercifully, none of the magazines fanned out on the table's surface featured smiling babies.

"Doc?"

Mia's head jerked up. The devastatingly handsome man walking toward her matched the pictures she'd seen online, but not the cowboy in her memory. Despite everything she'd learned about his identity, it was still startling to see Jace in this sleekly luxurious environment. She met him halfway despite a brief urge to bolt in the opposite direction.

"I couldn't believe it when Carol told me you were here! I had to see for myself." He sounded bewildered but genuinely happy to see her. Would he still be smiling once she'd told him the news? "Come with me, and we'll catch up. Do you want any coffee? We have an espresso maker, or—"

"No. Thank you. Just a, uh, place where we can speak privately?"

"Of course." He dropped a hand to the small of her back as he steered her through the lobby. The touch was casual but distracting as hell.

And why did he have to smell so good? For a change, her pregnancy super senses weren't turning her stomach. Quite the opposite. She had to actively resist leaning closer and breathing him in.

Jace led her through a doorway into a posh conference room. As he shut the door behind them, his smile faltered for the first time. "If you're here, at Malone, you've obviously figured out who I am. I just want you to know, I wasn't trying to hide that. I mean, I *was*, but not from you specifically. You must feel like I owe you an explanation."

Mia hesitated, unsure how to respond. She hated feeling deceived, hated how off-balance she'd been since learning who he was, but it was important they didn't start this conversation with Jace thinking she felt entitled to anything.

He scowled. "Oh, hell, did you see that article describing me as 'practically engaged'? Is that how you…" Gone was the slow drawl he'd used on tourists at orientation. He spoke so quickly Mia would have thought him nervous if he weren't a rich, gorgeous man from a powerful family. It was more likely he'd had one too many of the aforementioned espressos. "Valencia and I have known each other since elementary school."

She shook her head, frustration bubbling up inside

her. His rapid-fire delivery was making it difficult to get her thoughts straight. "That's—"

"We're not involved romantically."

"Jace, wait. I didn't—"

"We've just been working closely on this gala fundraiser, and—"

"I am not here because of tabloid headlines! Or your net worth. Could you get over yourself for a minute?"

His jaw dropped, but he recovered quickly. "My apologies."

"No, I apologize. That was bitchy, and I shouldn't have snapped at you." She sagged into a chair, her thoughts jumbled and her stomach now queasy. "God, I wish we could just erase all this and start over."

He sat next to her and held out his hand. "Hi, I'm Jace."

"I'm pregnant."

Five

Pregnant? Jace cocked his head, convinced he'd heard her wrong. "But…"

"Sorry to blurt it out like that. I practiced a speech in the car—well, a bunch of them, really. Guess this is what I get for never settling on one."

His gaze dropped to her stomach as if he expected to see evidence of the pregnancy, which was dumb. Women didn't start showing until…well, he didn't know. But not this soon. He'd have to ask Reed about stuff like that. About pregnancy and about being a fath—

"Oh, no." Reed was *just* starting to come around, to view Jace as something more than a reckless screwup! Having a one-night stand and accidentally getting a woman pregnant? "This is terrible."

"Hey!" Mia's hazel eyes flashed with hurt.

"I did not mean that the way it sounded." He pushed away the worry about his family. Mia deserved all his attention right now. "How are you feeling? Can I get you anything? You must have been stunned."

"To learn that I was having a baby," she said wryly, "or to learn that the father was one of the famous Malone brothers?"

She didn't sound accusatory, just overwhelmed.

Jace had been so surprised to learn she was in the building, as if he'd somehow conjured her with his stubbornly persistent thoughts, that he'd been functioning on autopilot. Now he stopped to truly study her, noting the subtle changes he'd overlooked. Although she was as beautiful as he remembered, there were shadows beneath her formerly sparkling eyes. And she'd lost weight.

He remembered her kissing him by firelight. Smiling over her bare shoulder at him as she invited him to join her in the shower. She'd been bold and carefree. At the moment, she looked fragile.

Because of me. Guilt slammed into him. It was all of his brothers' worst opinions of him—leaving someone else to shoulder the consequences of his actions while he was blithely unaffected.

"I will make this right," he swore. "You are not alone. My family will clamor for a prenup, especially after Reed's divorce, but—"

"What in the blue hell are you talking about?"

"Taking care of you and our baby." *Our baby.* The words filled him with unexpected longing. All those years feeling like an outsider exiled to Texas, and now he had the chance not just to be a member of a family but to create one of his own. "I'm not going to abandon you."

Her eyebrows shot up so far they were in a different zip code. "Jace, you can't 'abandon' me because we were never in a relationship in the first place. I didn't come here looking for a proposal. Why would I marry a man I don't know anything about? Except that I slept with him under false pretenses."

"But…" There'd been nothing "false" about the chemistry between them or the way she'd made him feel. He cleared his throat, trying to find the words to explain his impulsive reaction to her news. "I lost my parents a long time ago. They were killed in a car accident."

"I read that," she said softly. "And I'm sorry. I was so young when my mom died that I barely remember her, but there are still times when not having her in my life is a tangible ache. I can't imagine how hard it was for you."

He took her hand. Even that simple touch was like an electric current between them. "You've lost family, too, so you know it's not something to take for granted."

"Agreed." She slowly slid her fingers from his, as if reluctant to lose the connection. "But I'd like to think that if Mom were here and could give me advice, she'd tell me it was a terrible idea to marry a stranger. I'm sure your brothers will tell you the same thing."

"My brothers…" That was such a complicated subject that he didn't know where to begin. He rolled the office chair back away from the table, then forward again, four-wheeled pacing.

"Oh, God." Mia's voice sounded hollow. "They're going to think I'm some kind of gold digger, aren't they? The woman with the struggling vet clinic who conveniently turns up pregnant."

"Struggling?" He frowned. Everything he'd seen and heard on the ranch led him to believe she was skilled at what she did, and she was certainly good with people. It was difficult to imagine she wasn't highly successful.

She waved her hand. "Not the point."

"Right. No one can brand you a gold digger," he assured her. "After all, you just turned down being engaged to a billionaire."

"I did, didn't I?" Her laugh had a slightly manic edge to it. "It's so ludicrous out loud. No one knows *billionaires* in real life."

Well. He knew several, but he doubted pointing that out would put her at ease.

"I don't know how I'm going to explain this to my family," she said.

They had that in common. "Telling my brothers…" How could he convey his trepidation without sounding as if he were ashamed of her or the baby? "Lord knows you don't owe me any favors, Doc, but I have to ask one. Maybe I reacted rashly by bringing up marriage—"

"Maybe?" Her lips curved in a teasing smile, a real one this time.

He grinned back. "A debate for another day. But I do want to be involved with our child, and I want you to meet my family. The favor part is, can we hold off on sharing our news? Not that we did anything wrong or that it's any of their business, frankly, but I'd like them to have the chance to know you without making it overly complicated. I hope that doesn't sound—"

"No, I get it. My family will want to meet you, too, once they know. And it would be nice if we could make it past first impressions before my brothers try to beat you to a pulp."

Well that was something to look forward to. "So, we're on the same page? Casual introductions now, life-altering announcements later?"

"How casual were you thinking? Like arranging a coincidental run-in on the elevator down to the parking deck?" She frowned. "Do you even drive to work, or is there a limo?"

"And sit in traffic like peasants? We use the helipad on the roof."

Her face went slack.

"Kidding! Mia, it was a joke." There *was*, however, a small private jet the family used for field visits and occasional recreation. Perhaps he'd save mention of that for later. "Malone Energy is cosponsoring a gala to raise money for capping abandoned oil wells." Helping with Colorado's orphaned wells was one of the initiatives he'd convinced his brothers to let him pursue; it helped the state and was good PR. "Would you be my date?"

"To a gala your family is throwing?" She bit her bottom lip.

"Please, Doc. You've already turned me down once today." He pressed a hand over his heart, his expression dramatic. "I don't think I can take another rejection."

Despite his playful cajoling, he felt surprisingly anxious as he waited for her answer. He really wanted this opportunity for his brothers and Grandpa Harry to meet the smart, beautiful woman carrying his child. And it would be gratifying to have Mia with him on a night that was important to him, to show her who he was beyond the ranch hand she'd believed him to be.

"Okay," she said after a moment's thought. "I'll be your date." She stumbled over the word, but smiled shyly. "And you can do the same for me, with my family. I mean, we don't have any black-tie events coming up, but sometimes my friend Shari sends me with a fancy dessert to our monthly cookouts. You can come to one of those, and sometime down the road, I'll just tell them things didn't work out between us, that our lifestyles were too different."

"Wow, we haven't even had our first date, and you've already decided why we break up." It was definitely for the best that he hadn't mentioned the plane.

"At least it lets me tell them a version of the truth. I don't like lying. I hate it," she emphasized. "But you and I are from completely dissimilar backgrounds. They'll understand that."

Completely dissimilar? They were each the youngest child in a family of older brothers, and they'd both lost parents. They had more in common than Mia was admitting, but he could only imagine how disorienting it had been to learn his identity. The billionaire label was probably still a shock. Given time, though, could he coax her to see past it?

He hoped so.

Jace regretted rashly suggesting marriage. It was a decision that deserved consideration, and she deserved something far more romantic than a knee-jerk conference room proposal. Still, matrimony aside, why should they rule out a relationship? For weeks, he'd tried unsuccessfully not to think about her. He'd spent more than one night lying in bed, imagining her there with him. Now that she'd unexpectedly come back into his life, maybe he could persuade her to give them a chance.

Trying to carve out a place for himself in the family business took persistence, strategy and more diplomacy than he'd ever demonstrated before. Those traits might help him win over Mia. And if a romantic evening at a ball where people had good things to say about him gave him a home-field advantage...

Well, that wasn't cheating; it was just playing smart.

* * *

"We'll miss you so much," Mrs. Patterson said, scooping her five-year-old Maine coon into a soft-sided cat carrier with one hand while holding the leashes of two small dogs in the other. "You and the staff are practically family to us."

"We'll miss you, too," Mia said. *In more ways than one.* The Pattersons were some of Mia's favorite clients, and their six pets were definitely a factor in the clinic's quarterly budget. "But we wish you the best in Colorado Springs. If you need any vet recommendations for the area, I can ask around for you."

"That would be great, thanks. I'll be swamped getting started at the new job and making sure the paperwork's done for the kids to start school in the fall."

At the mention of kids, Mia's hand went to her stomach. That was happening more and more, as if she could somehow check in with the baby growing inside her, even though it was too early to discern any movement. Feeling conspicuous, she dropped her hand to her side. She didn't want to tell anyone at work until she was past the first trimester, but if she kept taking so many bathroom breaks, someone was bound to catch on.

Mia walked Mrs. Patterson out to the reception area, where Amanda approached with phone messages in hand. "Naomi says these are the most urgent ones you might want to return before lunch. Also, your 1:15 called to say she's running late, *and...*"

After a dramatic pause, the tech gestured to the side cabinets, where samples were stocked. "You got flowers! Aren't they gorgeous?"

Mia did a double take at the pink-and-blue glass vase with its vivid profusion of violets, orchids and multicolor roses. "Was there a card?"

Amanda nodded. "Still in the vase."

Sure enough, a small rectangle of paper was peeking up through the blooms, held in place by a painted clothespin on a wooden stick. The note was handwritten.

Thinking of you, Jace. P.S. The florist assured me these were all non-toxic to cats and dogs.

She smiled at that, charmed by his thoughtfulness.

"So," Amanda prompted, "feel like telling me who sent them? Fletcher and I have been racking our brains."

"A friend."

"Huh. Wonder why none of my friends ever send me extravagant bouquets like that."

Still smiling, Mia made her way to the back office and dialed Jace's number. With the gala the day after tomorrow, she knew how busy he was and suspected she'd get his voice mail, but she still wanted—

"Did the flowers arrive?"

"Hello to you, too," she teased. "They did, and they're beautiful. But you didn't have to do that."

"Of course I didn't. Floral arrangements are not necessity items. But I wanted to send something to show how much I'm looking forward to our date Friday. It was either the flowers or a bag of marshmallows."

She chuckled at that, remembering the marshmallows she'd set on fire when he sat down next to her at the Climbing W, but the laugh faded as she also recalled kissing him moments later. The sweetness of it, the mutual eagerness that had led to a long, memorable night.

His voice lowered, as if he somehow knew what she was thinking. "Maybe I should have gone with the marshmallows. Next time, then."

"No 'next time.' I'm already fielding curious questions from staff. Marshmallows would definitely lead to speculation."

"I don't know. I kind of like the thought of being your mystery man."

He was joking around. There was no logical reason for the thrilling shivery sensation that went down her spine. But logic couldn't change the effect he had on her.

"How are you feeling today?" he asked.

Again with the thoughtfulness. For the last couple of nights, he'd texted her to ask if her day had been all right and how she was feeling. It was considerate without being intrusive—but it left her thinking about him as she tried to fall asleep, with mixed results. Pregnancy was giving her some very vivid dreams.

"I'm okay. I get tired faster than normal, but the

stuff I've read said that the second trimester will probably be better."

"I hate that I can't pick you up before the gala, but I'd like to send a car for you. That way, I can drive you home afterward." He planned to be on-site in the hours leading up to the event to make sure everything went smoothly and to get the silent auction started.

"No need. I'll drive myself."

If he took her home, how would she resist inviting him in? Even though Friday might be a date in the most literal sense, sleeping with him again would be a bad idea. Her emotions were all over the map, which made her unusually vulnerable. Once their child was born, Mia's life would forever be entangled with Jace's. She should make practical short-term decisions so that they could all have a harmonious future.

"But you said yourself that you get fatigued faster than normal. Why risk driving home late from an unfamiliar venue?"

The genuine worry in his voice tugged at her heart. "I can take a car service both ways then. You may be fatigued yourself once the event is finally over."

"Nah. I've got pretty good stamina."

Don't I know it. Erotic recollections of his endurance and thoroughness rolled through her memory.

Heat stung her cheeks, and she was relieved he couldn't see her blush over the phone. "I, uh… My next appointment will be here in a minute. I should let you go."

"Until Friday, then."

"Friday," she echoed. By then she might have her libido under control. Or at least have figured out how to lie to herself more convincingly.

The knock came promptly at six thirty, and Mia opened the front door to find a well-groomed middle-aged man in a blue suit.

"Dr. Zane?" he asked.

She nodded.

"I'm Liam. I work for the Malone family. Right this way, ma'am." He led her to a luxury sedan with dark-tinted windows and opened the door for her. "There's chilled water available. Please let me know if there's any specific music you'd like to listen to or if you'd like me to adjust the temperature."

Climbing into the car, she should have felt like a modern-day Cinderella. *Your all-wheel-drive carriage awaits.* But she did not feel like a fairy-tale princess. Was there a version of the story where Cindy gained ten pounds the week before the ball, and the mice broke two zippers and their collective spirit trying to get her into a dress?

She wasn't technically showing yet, but even if her body wasn't unmistakably pregnant to the casual observer, her figure was rapidly changing. For starters, her bra felt two sizes too tight. She'd nixed the first dress she planned to wear because the cleavage was strained to the breaking point; she'd had horrific images of a boob popping free and injuring an innocent bystander. She'd finally settled on a gown with billowy sleeves and an empire silhouette that helped camouflage her fuller stomach. The gold base and shimmering green overlay were both good colors for her, but she fretted that she might be underdressed for the occasion. *Boho chic is a thing, right?* She'd done the best she could with makeup and a curly updo that left tendrils around her face. She really wanted to make a good impression tonight.

She didn't have much practice "meeting the family." Drew had claimed his parents lived in the UK and that he'd take her to visit someday. For all she knew, that had been another lie. Maybe he was an orphan. Or maybe his parents were con artists from Hoboken. The point was, she'd skipped over the normal version and gone straight to a formal gala surrounded by rich strangers. Plus there was the added stress of being secretly pregnant and knowing Jace's family could be in her life forever, so she'd better win them over while she had the chance.

"Liam? Could you, uh, boost the AC a little?"

"Of course." He obligingly bumped the climate controls to near arctic temperatures, and she breathed a sigh of relief.

At least she wouldn't have to worry about sweating her makeup off.

As the car wound up the mountain, the magnificent view began to eclipse her stress. The event tonight was being held at what Jace had jokingly called the area's "most famous failure." A millionaire in the 1940s had wanted to build the most impressive mansion Colorado had ever seen, complete with gold-leaf light fixtures, a castle facade and a formal courtyard. Unsurprisingly, he'd run out of money. The would-be palatial home was left unfinished and never lived in.

Eventually the property was purchased for commercial use and completed by investors in an appropriately lavish style. Mia had seen pictures of extravagant events held there and was pretty sure the exterior had been used in a movie or two. She'd never expected to get her very own engraved invitation to visit.

She spotted the lights twinkling through distant trees well before the stone-and-iron gate came into view. Maybe this *was* what Cinderella felt as her coach rolled up outside the royal ball—mild intimidation and the ardent hope that she didn't embarrass herself. The spacious drive split into two lanes approaching the front of the castle, one for valet services and one for being dropped off. Kind of like the airport, but with designer evening gowns.

They waited for the two cars ahead of them to roll away, and then it was their turn. Liam walked around to open her car door. "I texted Mr. Malone that you've arrived. He'll meet you just inside."

Someone must have alerted the security guard at the front as well, because he cheerfully ushered her inside without checking her invite. The "foyer" was so dazzling it almost hurt her eyes—not just the gold-veined wallpaper or twin chandeliers that were bigger than her car, but also the jewel-bedecked guests. *Cuff links and chokers and bracelets, oh my.*

"Mia."

She'd been so agog over her surroundings that she hadn't noticed Jace approaching. But now she did a double take at the sight of him in a perfectly tailored tuxedo. "Damn." How did the man get sexier every time she saw him? She'd done coursework on immunity; scientifically speaking, shouldn't her pulse-pounding response to him fade with time and exposure?

"Back at you, Doc." Jace twirled his finger in one of the curly strands framing her face. "You are a goddess tonight. I was sorry I couldn't drive you myself, but maybe it was for the best." He leaned close, his voice husky. "The way you look, we might not have left the house. For sure, your lipstick would have been smudged."

It was far too easy to picture that happening, especially since she was already fighting the urge to kiss him hello. Her gaze dropped to his mouth, lingered there.

"Mia." He growled her name, his tone hotly possessive. She wasn't sure whether it was meant to be a warning or a promise.

Taking her hand, he bent down to brush a quick, civilized kiss across her knuckles. And then he turned her hand palm upward, scraping his teeth over the delicate flesh of her wrist. Need shuddered through her, accompanied by searing memories of how wickedly he could use his mouth.

"There you are," a man interrupted. "Valencia is looking for you."

Jace straightened, and Mia got a better look at the speaker. She recognized him from online pictures as Heath Malone. If Jace weren't present, Heath would probably have been the best-looking man in the building. Despite slight differences in their builds and in the shades of their dark hair, the family resemblance was strong. She still had no idea if Heath had a dimple like Jace's, though, because he wasn't fully smiling in any of the photos she'd seen or in person.

"Thanks for letting me know. But while you're here, there's someone I want you to meet." Jace drew his arm around Mia's shoulders, gently pulling her closer. "This is Mia Zane. She owns a veterinary practice outside of Lakewood."

Heath nodded cordially. "Nice to meet you."

"Can you take Mia to our table while I find out what Val needs?"

"Certainly." Heath extended an elbow toward her, and she took his arm, grateful for the help navigating the glittering throng.

"Jace must be pleased with the turnout," she said. "This is…a *lot* of people." Thank God tables were reserved. It would be daunting to go through the ballroom looking for an empty seat.

"You sound unnerved. Not a fan of crowds?"

"I'm more accustomed to herds of cattle than people."

Heath made a soft noise that almost qualified as a chuckle. But then he sighed as he looked around the packed room. "I wonder how many of the esteemed guests are here because they care about the cause. Some just care about being seen."

She was surprised by his cynicism. Wasn't Malone Energy a major sponsor of the event? She rephrased his earlier question. "Not a fan of charity galas?"

"They're inefficient." He steered her toward a large round table at the front of the room, just left of the stage. "All the money spent on fashion and caterers and musicians. Wouldn't it be better spent—"

"Oh, no." Another male voice interjected, this one laced with humor. "Heath, what did I tell you about talking to the guests? You'll scare them all away."

Mia turned to find the third Malone brother. "You must be Reed."

"If a beautiful woman says I must be, then who am I to argue?"

"Don't flirt," Heath reprimanded him. "This is Mia. She's with Jace."

"Ah. We've been curious to meet you." Reed pulled out a chair for her.

They were both looking at her with such unabashed scrutiny that she squirmed in her seat. "Am I not what you were expecting?"

Heath shrugged. "We didn't know what to expect. We haven't met any women in his life since he's been back, but when he told us this week he'd met a vet on a ranch, it just seemed so...remarkably down-to-earth."

"A sign that he's maturing." Reed nodded approvingly. "I was skeptical he'd changed, but it makes sense now. He's working to impress the beautiful doctor. You're a good influence on him, Mia."

She blinked, caught off guard by his leap in logic. "I don't know about that."

"Don't be so modest." Reed sat in the chair next to her. "It's nice to see him buckling down at work, taking an interest in the community. Are you heavily involved in charitable foundations?"

"I do what I can," she stammered. "Pet adoptions, donating time to animal shelters, assisting my friend Shari with her summer program to get food to kids. I've never done anything on a scale like this." She gestured broadly around the ballroom. "Truly, you shouldn't give me credit for Jace's accomplishments. He's self-motivated."

The brothers exchanged a look, clearly unconvinced.

She found herself mildly exasperated at their underestimating Jace. Although it had been disorienting to see him shift from stubbled ranch hand to tuxedoed philanthropist, his work ethic had been evident on the ranch, too. He'd moved from one task to the next, displaying competent cheer with humans and horses alike. He'd worked at the stable until well after dark and left her bed at dawn to start another day. Did his siblings not know him at all?

"Maybe you've made more of an impact than you realize," Reed suggested. "There was a time I wouldn't have trusted him to be responsible for a hamster, but you should see him with my daughter..." He scrolled through his phone and held it up so she could see the photo. "Cute, right?"

Jace was beaming at an infant in a onesie and tiny denim jacket with the Triple Pine logo as she laughed in pure delight and reached for him with chubby hands. Mia sucked in her breath, a pang in her chest. *That could be him and our daughter a year from now. Or our son.* Mia knew he planned to be an active dad, but to see actual photographic evidence of the doting father he would be... Her eyes stung.

Oh, hell. The last thing she wanted was to cry in front of Jace's brothers. *My eye makeup!*

"Please excuse me. Ladies' room," she mumbled. She scraped her chair back and popped to her feet, almost knocking over a statuesque brunette, the most gorgeous woman Mia had ever seen in real life.

"Whoa." Jace reached out, steadying a mortified Mia with his hands on her hips.

"I am *so* sorry," Mia told the other woman. "I wasn't looking where I was going. Obviously." It was pretty hard to miss a six-foot woman in a bright yellow strapless evening gown. *And yet I managed.* "Please forgive the blunt question, but are you by any chance a supermodel?"

The woman laughed. "Oh, I like her, Jace. Sorry

to disappoint, but I'm afraid I'm a boring lawyer. Not as boring as Heath the accountant, of course…"

Jace snorted at that. "Mia, this is Valencia Blanco. Her family's law firm has represented Malone Energy for decades, and she was my coconspirator on making tonight happen. We made a good team negotiating with vendors. If the situation required charming finesse, I called Valencia. And if the situation needed someone to stand tough—"

"He called me twice as fast."

"Damn right." Jace winked at Mia. "Anyway, I just wanted to introduce you two before we officially kick off this shindig. Have you met Grandpa Harry yet?" He glanced around in search of his grandfather.

Reed shook his head. "His blood pressure was a little high earlier. His aide thought he could use a moment of peace and quiet before dinner."

The merriment in Jace's gaze faded to a more somber expression. It was clear in that moment just how much his grandfather meant to him and how worried he was about Harry. Wishing there was something she could do or say to ease Jace's concerns, Mia impulsively reached down to squeeze his hand.

He looked surprised for a split second, then squeezed back.

Valencia sighed in the direction of the stage. "I'm afraid we can't stall forever. Time for the dreaded one-two punch of public speaking and asking for money."

"Right behind you," Jace told her. He turned to

follow his partner but glanced back at Mia, mouthing *thank you*.

For the second time since she'd reached the table, her heart ached with bittersweet poignancy. When she'd arrived here tonight, she'd thought the biggest risk in spending time with Jace was their overpowering physical attraction. There were moments she wanted him with such reckless intensity that she almost didn't recognize herself. But she was starting to realize how wrong she'd been.

The *real* risk was that whatever they shared between them was far more than physical.

Six

Despite Mia's initial exasperation with Jace's brothers, they turned out to be good company throughout dinner. By the time plates were cleared away after the main course, she had discovered that Heath *did* possess a sense of humor, albeit a very dry one. And Reed was endearingly earnest when he talked about his daughter.

People had been coming by the table throughout the evening to network with the Malone family, and now all three brothers were circulating the ballroom. While most guests formed lines at the decadent dessert buffets on either side of the room, Mia stayed at the empty table with Harry, discreetly slipping off her shoes under the tablecloth and wiggling her toes. *Bliss*.

Harry smiled at her. "You're kind, but you don't have to stay and babysit me if you'd rather go socialize. I remember what it was like to be young. Vaguely."

"Actually, this is all a bit much for me. I'm thrilled for Jace, though." The auction had raised thousands of dollars, and she could only imagine what Val and Jace were coaxing from key donors. "You must be very proud."

Harry's blue eyes, so like his grandson's, were bright with affection. "Always knew the boy had it in him." He didn't seem to harbor any of the misgivings Jace's brothers had expressed.

"Here you are, sir." Harry's aide returned to the table, setting down an artfully arranged berry parfait.

"What in the hell is this, Kevin? I sent you to get chocolate turtle cheesecake."

The young man sighed. "We've talked about this. The parfait is heart-healthy."

"Fine. You can let the driver know we'll be headed out as soon as I'm finished with this fruit salad."

"Yes, sir."

Harry took a bite, then pursed his lips grumpily.

"No good?" Mia asked.

"It's delicious. Damn it. But it's not what I wanted. Family patriarch, captain of industry, and I don't even get to pick my own desserts." His expression softened. "But I suppose it's a small price to pay for more time to watch Brooke grow up. Who knows? If I stick around long enough, might even have other great-grandkids someday."

Someday was a lot sooner than he expected. Mia's hand went to her stomach. It would mean so much to Jace for Harry to meet their baby. *And to me.* Even after only a few hours, she'd grown fond of Jace's grandfather.

Once he finished dessert, Harry rose slowly. Mia wanted to help him but didn't want to hurt his pride. She moved in to hug him good-night, subtly offering support.

"It was an honor to meet you," she told him. "Jace thinks so highly of you."

"Make him bring you around for a Sunday supper or a family game night," Harry told her. "Something where we don't have to dress up fancy and spend all night trying to remember people's names."

She laughed. "Sounds perfect."

Kevin returned and escorted Harry toward the exit. They were stopped twice along the way. When a third guest approached, Mia watched the aide maneuver Harry to freedom and silently cheered them on. She envied their ability to go. It had been a lovely evening, but her feet hurt and her face ached from the strain of politely smiling at everyone she'd met.

"Cocktail, ma'am?" A waiter paused with a tray of the evening's signature beverages. Mia had been told they were delicious.

"Oh, no, thank you." But maybe she should go to the bar and get a glass of water. It would give her the opportunity to make some small talk with people. She was the host's date. Sitting barefoot at an empty table while stifling yawns was bad form. Getting her feet back into her shoes was a lot more difficult than removing them, but she persevered.

As Mia made her way to the bar, an elegant silver-haired woman stepped into her path with a bright smile. "Dana! Marvelous to see you again."

"Um, sorry," Mia said. "You must have me confused with someone else."

The woman frowned. "Didn't we meet at the PCF Charity Golf Tournament?"

"Afraid not."

"Which foundations are you a member of? I'm sure our paths have crossed."

"Actually, I'm just here tonight as Jace's date."

"Jace Malone?" The woman's eyes widened. "Oh, but I thought he and Va— Never mind. Lovely to have met you, dear." She turned in the opposite direction, departing at an impressive speed given her high heels.

"I'm sorry, did you say you were here with Jace Malone?"

Mia turned to find a slender brunette, dripping in diamonds. Her statement necklace would probably pay off Mia's mortgage. "Y-yes."

"I'll bet you and I could swap some wild stories," the woman said in a confidential tone. "I dated him in college. Not for long, of course—he wasn't there long. But our time together was certainly memorable."

"I'm sure." Mia worked to conjure a smile. "I was on my way to the ladies' room, though, so..."

"Another time, then. You tell him Bex said hi."

"Absolutely." Were rich, thin women his usual type? No wonder his brothers had scrutinized Mia earlier tonight as if she were a confounding specimen.

Plenty of people seemed to think he and Valencia were a couple, and Mia had no trouble picturing it. The likable lawyer would fit into Jace's world so easily. She was glamorous and funny and probably didn't have any anecdotes that involved sticking her arm inside a cow.

Leaving behind the buzz of party chatter, Mia made her way down thickly carpeted stairs. The anterior lounge leading to the women's restroom was a study in old-school opulence. Heavy velvet curtains hung on either side of the archway; two mahogany-stemmed fainting couches and a leather love seat formed a triangle around a marble-topped table. There was a fireplace framed in matching marble. She was amused by the over-the-top golden phone booth in the corner.

Was the love seat as comfortable as it looked? She sat down, giving a contented sigh at the softness of the leather. It would be so nice to rest here for a few minutes. Jace was busy enough that he wouldn't miss her.

Her eyes slid shut. *Just a few minutes.*

Jace was relieved when his brothers found him to say good-night, extricating him from a conversation with an ex who'd been hinting that her marriage was unhappy. Heath had removed his jacket and loosened his tie.

Reed, on the other hand, remained perfectly pressed and buttoned-up. He gestured broadly at the ballroom. "Not too shabby, little brother."

Jace laughed. From Reed, the casual words were high praise. "Thanks. But you don't get to use 'little' when I'm an inch taller than you."

"Half an inch, tops."

Heath rolled his eyes at them. "I settled up with the caterers. Make sure you and Valencia get me any receipts I don't have already. Oh, and tell Mia we said goodbye."

Reed nodded. "Sorry we didn't get a chance to say it ourselves."

As his brothers walked away, Jace tried to remember the last time he'd seen Mia. He could understand if she'd decided to leave early, but she wouldn't have gone without telling him. She'd been amazingly supportive tonight, gracious about all the strangers she'd been introduced to and understanding at the constant interruptions whenever he actually found a moment to be with her. When she'd praised his efforts, was it Jace's imagination, or had her compliments been rather pointed? She'd seemed to go out of her way to call him successful in front of his brothers.

He pulled out his phone and sent a quick text. Can't find you. Everything ok?

No response.

"Hey! You're supposed to be charming people,

not scowling at your phone," Val chided. "We're almost done. Don't give out on me now."

"Sorry." He slid his phone back into his pocket. "I can't find Mia." Guilt gnawed at him. Inviting her here tonight had been arrogant. He'd wanted to impress her, had wanted to show her off to his brothers, but she'd worked on her feet all day before coming here. She was probably exhausted. Or sick.

"Maybe she's in the ladies' room?" Val suggested.

"Yeah. I think I'm gonna go check."

She arched an eyebrow. "*You're* going to check the ladies' room?"

He just needed to know she was all right. "I can knock on the door."

"Or I could go downstairs for you."

"It looks like an opportunity to talk to the mayor just opened up." He nodded over Val's shoulder. "Didn't you want to chat with her about some city business?"

"Oh! Yes, I did."

While Valencia seized her opportunity, he went down the hall to the grand staircase. The floor below was hushed, dimly lit with wall sconces that were electric but designed to flicker like candlelight. This part of the building was enough like an ancient castle that one could forget the place had state-of-the-art Wi-Fi. The corridor led to a huge arch, and he passed through the draperies to a sitting area.

Mia wasn't exactly sitting, though. She was slumped sideways on a love seat, her hair tumbling free of its updo, one foot dangling bare, her lips slightly parted as she slept. His chest tightened at the vulnerable picture she made. She looked adorable, but he experienced a fresh rush of guilt that he'd insisted on taking her home instead of sending her with Liam.

Resisting the urge to kiss her, he gently brushed her hair away from her face. "Hey, Sleeping Beauty."

"Nuh-uh. Cinderella," she mumbled without opening her eyes. "But I turned into a pumpkin."

He laughed. "I'm not sure that's how the story goes. You did lose a shoe, though." He picked up her fallen sandal.

"Jace?" She blinked, sounding surprised to see him. "Thought I was dreaming."

He liked the idea that he appeared in her dreams. She'd sure as hell starred in some of his.

"I can't believe I fell asleep!" Now that she was fully awake, embarrassment colored her expression. She covered her face with her hands. "I'm so sorry."

"My fault." He sat next to her. "You warned me how easily you wear out right now, because of the baby." *Our baby.* It still gave him chills. Even though he'd requested they wait to tell his family, part of him wanted to shout from the rooftops that Mia was pregnant with his child. He hadn't expected it, hadn't even known he wanted it, but the idea of their baby filled him with indescribable satisfaction and fierce protectiveness. "Inviting you tonight was selfish, but I wanted to impress you."

A short laugh escaped her. "Impress *me*? That's ironic."

"How so?"

"Everyone I met tonight is so glamorous. I spend my days in scrubs. And with the pregnancy changes..." She frowned down at herself. "I know they're normal, healthy changes, but I feel puffy. Ungainly."

He shook his head. "Lush and voluptuous and sexy as hell. You're the most beautiful woman here."

"That's nice of you to say."

"Doc." He waited until she met his gaze. "When I look at you, my thoughts aren't 'nice.'"

A rosy blush stained her cheeks. "No?" Her breathing quickened, drawing his eyes to the square neckline of her dress, to the rise and fall of her full breasts.

"I've wanted you since you walked through the door tonight." His voice was ragged, gruffer than he'd intended. He'd thought about their night together so often, and now, with her this close, he felt like his edges were fraying. "No, I've wanted you since I walked out of your cabin that morning."

Her eyes widened. "I thought... I thought it would be simpler if we kept things platonic."

A brutal sense of loss gutted him, robbing him of words. His jaw clenched, but he nodded to show that he respected her decision.

"But I want you, too," she admitted.

His gaze jerked to hers. Jace held himself still, not reaching for her until he knew they were in agreement.

"And I'm already having your baby," she added. Her

lips curved in a slow smile. "So we passed 'simple' a few exits ago."

"You sure?"

She leaned toward him, and Jace gave in to temptation, tunneling his fingers through her hair and capturing her mouth in a long, thorough kiss meant to demonstrate exactly how much he craved her. When he pulled her into his lap, she purred a low *mmm* of encouragement. Damn, he'd missed her sexy sounds.

He only stopped kissing her because he needed to look at her, to memorize her passion-glazed expression and generous curves. He traced his index finger from her collarbone to her cleavage, outlining the swell of one breast. "Your skin is so soft. I could touch you for hours." Even as he said it, he knew he should be back upstairs already. He had to say goodnight to donors and volunteers—not to mention he and Mia could be interrupted at any moment.

But he needed his hands on her like he needed his next breath. He bunched up her skirt, which felt like miles of fabric, until he was caressing her thigh. She shifted, planting one foot on the ground and angling her leg to give him better access. The erotic contrast of touching her so intimately while they were both fully dressed had him rock-hard. He wasn't alone in his desire. Even through the silky material of her panties, he could feel how wet she was.

Under other circumstances, he'd go to his knees in front of her and taste her earthy sweetness, taking his time to bring her closer and closer to the edge of pleasure until she shook and shuddered. Instead, he slid aside the narrow band of fabric separating her from his touch, and she gasped, melting against him. Jace held her, his chest muffling her cries, as he strummed his fingers over her, ruthlessly chasing her orgasm until she stiffened, going up on her toes as her body bowed. Then she relaxed against him with a sigh, her hair tumbling in waves around them.

He pressed a kiss to her forehead. "I can't leave yet, but I'll have Liam take you home."

She bit her lip, obviously conflicted.

"Mia, go. You're resting for two now. I'm sorry tonight was tedious."

Her laugh rumbled through her. "Yes, earth-shattering climaxes in castles are *so* tiresome."

He stole another kiss, grinning against her mouth. "Smart-ass."

She stood, smoothing her dress into place, then fussing with her hair. He didn't have the heart to tell her it was a lost cause. She looked thoroughly, hopelessly debauched. He couldn't stop smiling.

"Will you call me when you get home?" she asked.

"That defeats the purpose of my sending you off so you can get to bed."

"Jace." She looked up at him with wide hazel eyes, gently imploring. "I want yours to be the last voice I hear before I go to sleep."

It was like a sucker punch to his heart. He barely

refrained from rubbing his chest. He would give her anything she wanted. "Then I'll talk to you soon."

The boomerang of pregnancy hormones took a lot of getting used to. Mia had gone from so worn-out that she'd fallen asleep in a public place to buzzing with energy. As Liam walked her safely to her front door, she felt supercharged enough to repaint the house. The drive had given her time to question whether she'd made a mistake throwing herself at Jace, but it was hard to argue with how good she felt.

And when he called her an hour later, she couldn't deny her giddy eagerness to hear his voice. She snuggled under her comforter with a smile. "Hey."

"Did I wake you?" he asked.

"Nope, Buster and I were just getting ready for bed. He's a Lab mix who's temporarily staying with me." Hearing his name, Buster looked up from the dog bed in the corner of her room and thumped his tail. "With any luck, we're gonna find him a fur-ever home this weekend."

"I'm sure you will. If not, we have plenty of space for a dog here on the Triple Pine."

"Your heart's in the right place, but a dog is a life-time companion, not an impulse buy. Besides, you haven't completed adoption screening." It was jarring to realize she knew more about the families who took home the animals she fostered than she did about the man who would co-raise their child.

The baby's not coming for months. She took a

steadying breath and reached over to turn off the bedside lamp. There was time for her and Jace to get to know each other.

"Fair enough," he said. "I suppose I am impulsive sometimes."

Her cheeks heated at the memory of coming against his hand in a semipublic place. That had been pure, lust-fueled spontaneity. "Well. We all have our moments."

"Val asked me to tell you she was sorry she missed saying good-night. She liked you a lot. She said…"

"Yeah?"

"She's glad I didn't meet you in Texas. She joked that if I had, I never would have come home."

Mia didn't know how to reply to that. It was equal parts flattering and unnerving. Did his friend really think his feelings for Mia were that strong? *It was a joke. He just said that.*

"So now that you've spent an evening with my friends and family, what about yours?" he asked. "When do you want me to meet your dad and brothers?"

Our kid's high school graduation. She grimaced in the dark, knowing that sooner was better than later. If she waited too long, her baby bump would be unmistakable. "I don't know. They've always been overprotective. I was the youngest of the family."

Jace snorted. "So was I. I think my siblings took a different approach, though."

"Mom got sick not long after I was born, and it's

like they took all their love for her and their frustration that they couldn't make her well and turned it to me, constantly worried about my well-being. When I got engaged—"

"You were engaged?" Obviously that possibility had never occurred to him.

"There really is a lot we don't know about each other."

"I guess so."

"His name was Andrew, and we met in vet school, although he didn't finish. He pushed to get engaged but was in no hurry to set a wedding date." He'd been in a hurry for access to joint banking and clinic passwords. He'd called them the perfect team—she was a brilliant doctor and he was going to handle the business end of things. Even now, Mia was still discovering new ways he'd shortchanged her in office and equipment purchases. "As much as my brothers like to scare off my dates, everyone was relieved when I accepted the proposal, like they didn't have to worry about me so much with someone else on the job. But after... Well, it didn't work out, and now they're more fiercely protective than ever."

"Didn't work out? What happened?"

She squirmed. The truth that she'd been engaged to a crook was embarrassing and made her sound like a terrible judge of character. "He turned out to be a liar."

"Tell me he cheated on you, and I will find the man."

She laughed wryly. The police hadn't had much

luck, but Jace could probably afford to hire elite private investigators. "It wasn't like that. And I don't need anyone beating the guy up. If I did, Shari has offered."

"I think I'd like Shari. Maybe I could start by meeting her."

"That idea has appeal." *You're stalling because you don't feel like dealing with your family.* Yep. That was part of the appeal.

"Let me make up for tonight," Jace pressed. "In retrospect, asking you to stand around while I hobnob with donors was a terrible first date. We should do something fun and low-key."

"Your grandfather said something along the same lines. He mentioned a family game night."

"Oh, hell no." Jace sounded horrified. "Our game nights are *not* low-key. His aide has banned them because of his blood pressure. Harry's only allowed to play chess right now, but occasionally we sneak in a rogue Scrabble match. Don't tell Kevin."

She laughed. "Your secret is safe with me."

There was a pause before he asked tentatively, "How do you feel about bowling?"

"Bowling?" Whatever she'd expected him to suggest, it hadn't been that. "I'll check with the doctor's office to make sure it's okay, but bowling could be fun."

"If Shari's seeing anyone, maybe we could make it a double date."

"Hmm. Maybe." Shari periodically dated a dashing but opinionated food critic. They argued passionately over seasoning and culinary preparations and whether pineapple had any place on pizza; Shari had confided they were just as impassioned when they weren't fighting. "She normally takes Thursday night off before the weekend crowds."

"Thursday works for me if she's interested," Jace said. "Just let me know. And good luck with the pet adoptions this weekend."

"Thanks."

"Sweet dreams, Doc."

"You, too."

"Count on it." His tone was pure seduction. "I know exactly what I'll be dreaming about."

Her toes curled. "Good night, Jace."

After setting her phone on the nightstand, she stared up at the ceiling and blew out a puff of air. "Buster, I may be in over my head here."

Thump thump thump was the sympathetic reply.

What was she getting herself into? She'd never responded to a man on such a visceral level. Drew had been her most serious relationship, and even that had been because it seemed sensible. *Nothing* between her and Jace had been sensible.

To quell her fears, she channeled Shari. She knew her best friend well enough to imagine what she would say if she were here. *Don't spiral, Zane.* Yes, everything with Jace felt unexpected and different. But given how badly her engagement had ended, different was bound to be an improvement.

Plus, Jace was obviously working to meet her in her comfort zone, which she appreciated. Tonight's billionaires in black tie had been daunting. But a nice, normal bowling date? She could work with that.

"A private bowling alley at your house is not normal." Mia gaped as neon lights came on around them. When Jace had texted her that he had a bowling lane, she supposed she'd pictured something more along the lines of the yard set her brothers had when they were kids. This looked like a professional establishment, albeit one with only a single lane.

"This isn't the house," Jace said. "It's a converted three-car garage. Does that help?"

Actually, three-car garages weren't most people's norm, either. She appreciated the normalcy of his jeans and black T-shirt, though. The man had great arms.

He walked to the center of the room, looking around as if he were seeing it for the first time, too. "The staff keeps it up, but I haven't been here in years." His voice was low, reverent—the kind of tone one might use in a museum or church.

"You don't like bowling?" She knew he'd lived in Texas after college, but he'd been back plenty long enough to bowl a few frames.

"It's not that." He hesitated, looking suddenly… vulnerable?

She had the unfathomable urge to hug him. "Jace?"

"When I was in middle school, my parents decided they needed a fun date night and joined a bowling league." His mouth curved in a half smile, his gaze distant. "Mom was terrible. I mean, truly awful—the gutterball queen. One time she threw the ball into someone else's lane. Dad had this installed so she could practice. We used to play in here as a family, but after they were gone…"

He shook his head. "Sorry, I didn't mean to get maudlin. I don't talk about them often."

Which made it all the more touching that he'd shared that with her. "I'm here to listen." She walked closer. "Anytime."

He reached for her hand. "Thanks, Doc. It's hard, though."

"Because of how much you miss them?" She'd had more and more melancholy moments now that she was pregnant, wishing she could ask her mom for advice. It must be so much harder for Jace, knowing the people who'd raised him would never get to hold their grandchild.

"Yes. But also…" A storm of emotions passed over his face.

She'd never seen him look so tortured. She held her breath, wishing she knew how to help.

The door behind them opened. "Mr. Jace, your guests have arrived."

Mia turned to see a bearded man usher in Shari and her favorite food critic, Adwin Morris, a tall man with green eyes and killer cheekbones.

Jace stepped forward to welcome them. "Shari,

Adwin, I'm so glad you could make it. I'm Jace Malone. I hope you won't judge me too harshly on our rather basic snacks of chips, dip and a veggie tray."

"Not at all." Shari gave him a sunny smile. "I'll only judge you based on how you treat Mia. And remember, I own a restaurant...lots of access to professional-grade knives."

Mia choked back a laugh. Shari's unapologetic words were good practice for when he met Mia's brothers and father.

Jace nodded sagely. "I understand."

Shari beamed. "Then it's nice to meet you."

While the two men exchanged pleasantries that didn't involve cutlery, Shari sidled closer to Mia. "He's even better-looking in person. How is that possible?"

"Unnerving, right?"

"Okay, I have shoes for everyone," Jace announced. He'd asked Mia to text him sizes; that had been when she realized this would not be the standard bowling alley experience. He went to a counter that ran the length of the back wall, bracing his arm on it to swing his legs up and over in a fluid, athletic motion that made her mouth go dry. "Hope everyone's okay with '70s rock—the sound system hasn't been updated from Dad's favorites." He flipped a switch, and a Rolling Stones song came on overhead. Then he returned with a stack of shoeboxes. "Should we play guys versus girls or couple against couple?"

A couple. It seemed like such an official term for

something Mia was still trying to emotionally navigate, but she liked how easily he said it.

Shari took the box he handed her. "Women versus men works for me. Oooh, these are surprisingly cute."

"Full disclosure," Mia murmured to her friend, "I am very out of practice."

"Eh, if it's anything like my nephew's virtual bowling game, I'm good enough for both of us."

Everyone laced up, and Shari volunteered to go first. As Jace typed their names into the computerized scoreboard, the rest of them selected balls from a rack on the side. Mia's obstetric nurse had assured her that bowling should be perfectly safe as long as she was careful not to cross the foul line onto the slicker part of the lane and used a lightweight ball. Standing in front of the rack, Mia found herself wondering if Jace's brothers ever used this alley or if they, like Jace, avoided it. She hoped they reestablished their family tradition of bowling nights. She imagined Brooke here in a few years' time and smiled at the idea of preschool-sized bowling balls. *What traditions will we establish with our own little one?*

"Hey."

She turned to find Jace at her side, looking concerned, and realized that she'd lost track of time while daydreaming.

"You okay?" he asked. "You seem a little out of it."

"I was, but in a good way. Thank you for inviting

us all here tonight." Cupping his face in her hands, she reached up to kiss him. She traced his lips with her tongue, and his mouth parted beneath hers. He pulled her tight against him for a brief, tantalizing moment before releasing her.

His eyes sparkled with heat and humor. "Is this your way of distracting me to throw off my game?"

"Oh, like those jeans you're wearing aren't a major distraction?"

He laughed. "Good to know."

Her gaze lingered as he walked away. Then, with a happy sigh, she turned to pick up the lightest ball available. She would have apologized to the others for the delay, but from the way Shari was sitting sideways across Adwin's lap, snuggled against him as they spoke in low voices, they were enjoying themselves just fine even without the game.

When Jace asked if everyone was ready, Shari bounced up and came over to Mia's side of the ball return. She blew a kiss to Adwin. "Sorry, but you're the enemy now."

Shari knocked down an admirable eight pins but was unable to pick up the split. Jace ended his turn with a spare. Mia finished with a total of seven, and Adwin knocked down a single pin on the far right before rolling a gutterball.

"He may be lousy at bowling," Shari whispered, "but he has other wonderful talents."

On his second turn, Adwin knocked down only the pin on the end.

"No worries," Jace told his partner. "We're still warming up."

The other man shrugged. "Anyone can hurl a ball with brute force and knock down pins," he joked, "but it takes sniper-like precision to consistently pick off one."

Shari laughed. "Keep telling yourself that, boo."

They all improved as the game went on and finished with a fairly close score, the men edging out the women with Jace's final strike.

Jace went to the refrigerator in the corner and brought back sodas for everyone. Watching him drink out of an aluminum can made Mia giggle to herself. *Billionaires—they're just like us.*

Truthfully, the evening had given her a chance to see him with new eyes. From the night she'd met him on the ranch, everything that had happened between them had felt separate from her day-to-day reality. A fling with a handsome stranger at a secluded location. The shock of learning she was pregnant. A grand ball ending with a hotly illicit encounter. It had all been exciting, but it had been surreal, too. Here, tonight, flirting with Jace and laughing with her friends and singing along off-key to songs she only knew the choruses of, she felt connected to him in a completely new way.

"Rematch?" Jace asked. "Or do we switch up teams?"

Shari took Adwin's hand. "I pick you. This is where we show them your first few rounds were a clever ploy to get your opponents to underestimate you."

Adwin kissed the side of her neck. "I like your optimism." She whispered something, and his eyes widened. "You really know how to motivate your team, Coach."

Whatever she said must have been effective, because they did indeed win the second match. Mia had to admit that she stopped following the game at some point. She kept getting distracted watching her teammate. Had she ever realized how mesmerizing a man's hands could be? Watching Jace roll the ball between his fingers until he had it positioned just right was riveting.

While there was none of the rumored hostility of the Malone family game nights, Jace struck her as innately competitive. It wasn't that he cared about their losing score, but he clearly challenged himself to do his best and exceed previous results. As soon as he stepped up to the lane, his easy, confident body language subtly shifted. His jaw would tighten in determination, a new tension in his muscles. It was sexy, but it also reminded her that he could be hard on himself.

"This was fun," Shari said after the second game, "but we're going to scoot."

Mia bit the inside of her cheek to keep from laughing. It was clear from the looks Shari and her date were exchanging that they couldn't wait to be alone. Mia knew how they felt.

"It was great to meet you both." Jace walked them to the door. "Shari, I'll definitely be making a dinner reservation for next week. The summer tasting menu sounds incredible."

"It is," Shari said matter-of-factly. "Bring Mia with you, and I'll even give you the friends-and-family discount."

Jace glanced at Mia. "Think you can find a night free for dinner?"

"At Shari's place? Always."

The two couples waved goodbye. Then Jace and Mia were alone. Without the scrape of the balls down the lane or the crash of falling pins, the music suddenly seemed unnaturally loud. Jace went to the back to turn off the sound system.

Mia propped her elbows on the counter and flashed him a contrite smile from the other side. "I owe you an apology."

"What? No, you don't."

"I let you down as my teammate." Her smile widened. "Because I was too busy undressing you with my eyes to care about the game."

His lips twitched. "Well, I forgive you for costing us the victory. Just this once." He reached across the counter, kissing her as deeply as he could with the barrier between them.

She pulled back with a chuckle. Joy and desire were a fizzy, potent combination in her system. "Either I need to go back there, or you have to come over here."

"I don't think so, Doc." His blue eyes glinted. "I want you in a bed this time."

Hell, yes. "I don't suppose you have one stashed around here somewhere?" she asked hopefully.

"Good enthusiasm, but no." He vaulted over the counter and stole another kiss, sucking at her bottom lip. "It's been a very long time since I snuck a girl up to my room. Years."

"We should fix that," Mia suggested.

"You're as brilliant as you are beautiful."

The distance between the bowling garage and the house was about half the length of a football field. They alternately hurried and paradoxically made the trip longer because they couldn't keep their hands off each other. They stopped several times to kiss in the dark, including against the side of a garden shed, where Jace lifted her up so she could wrap her legs around him.

He caught her earlobe between his teeth, and molten need pooled inside her. "My least favorite thing about being pregnant," she said, "has been that everything just feels so *swollen*. But you..." She rocked her hips. He was so hard against her. "You make swollen a good thing."

The sound he made was half chuckle, half groan. His grip on her tightened as he raised his head to lock eyes with her. "Do that again."

She moved in a slow, deliberate grind, feeling erotically anchored by his gaze as much as his body. *"Jace."* Were they even going to make it to a bed?

As if he'd heard the question out loud, he lowered her to her feet and took her hand. They ducked into the house. The sound of a TV came from somewhere, but all the rooms they passed through were dark. She stayed close to Jace to navigate the unfamiliar surroundings. It wasn't until they were upstairs, with his bedroom door closed and locked, that he turned on a light, angling the desktop lamp toward the center of the room.

If any part of her felt self-conscious about that, it was outvoted by her strong desire to see him, too, to revel in him and the way he made her feel when he looked at her. She had vague impressions of her surroundings—a matching desk and bookshelf and a bed with a turquoise-and-brown comforter—but all she cared about in the room was the man in front of her.

He reached behind his head and pulled off his shirt with one hand. "I have thought about you being here so many times."

"I'll try to live up to the expectations." Leaving on the blouse that fell to the tops of her thighs, she unbuttoned her shorts and let them drop. Then she lowered the pair of black lacy panties.

He followed their slow descent down her thighs and over her calves, swallowing hard. "More."

She started to unbutton the blouse, but he was no longer content to be a bystander. He removed the top before they even made it halfway through the buttons, and he reached for the front clasp of her bra. When his hand grazed her nipple, she jolted.

He stilled suddenly. "Did I hurt you?"

"No." Quite the opposite. "My breasts are just, um, really sensitive."

"Oh." His lips curled in a devious smile as he led her to the bed. "Just to be safe, I'll be extra gentle."

He kissed his way across the slope of one breast, stopping before he reached the tip and then switching to the other side. A brief lick of his tongue across the aching peak had her squirming beneath him, desperate for more. The trade-off for waiting was sweet, sharp anticipation that heightened everything. Even his breath on her skin made her quiver. She allowed him to tease her for long minutes until she felt nearly crazed. Then she threaded her hand through his thick hair and tugged. He chuckled darkly as he finally closed his mouth over her, sucking deep. When he grazed her with his teeth, she thought she might come from that alone, but then he positioned himself against her and surged forward, filling her.

He closed his eyes, his expression beautifully stark with arousal. "You feel so good around me."

She couldn't catch her breath to answer. Sensation coiled through her body, winding tighter and tighter as he slid against her in slow, smooth strokes. Ecstasy loomed closer with every shared movement of their bodies, but neither of them rushed, letting it build. Just as the line between anticipation and frustration began to thin and Mia thought she might sob with need, he rubbed his thumb over her nipple and thrusted. The building tension inside her snapped, erupting into waves of pure pleasure. Jace muffled her cries with a kiss, his body stiffening as he followed her over the edge.

While she waited for her racing pulse to slow, he rolled to his side without letting go of her. He cradled her against him as if she were precious, his deep sigh one of utter contentment.

She propped herself up on her elbow, greedy for the sight of him even though they'd been together all evening. "So?" she asked impishly. "Did that live up to your expectations?"

He took a moment to think it over carefully. "It was all right," he deadpanned, "but there's room for improvement if you want to try again."

Laughing too hard to snark a comeback, she instead grabbed a pillow and lightly smacked him with it.

"Hey, no pillow fights!" he chastised in a mock whisper. He wrapped his arms around her. "Are you trying to wake everyone up? Lesson number one of sneaking into a boy's room is to keep a low profile. Sheesh. You must've been busted constantly as a teenager."

She snuggled closer, breathing in his familiar, addictive scent. "No sneaking in my teen years." Between her brothers scaring off would-be dates and her bookish focus on grades, she hadn't had the opportunity. "I was the quintessential good girl."

"Then you wouldn't have liked me," he said rue-fully.

"Don't bet on it. Good girls can be corrupted." She was joking, but he didn't laugh. She poked his side. "You're pretty hard on yourself about your past. And your brothers certainly have some judgmental moments."

"I was not a good student. Or a particularly good grandson or brother. Or son." His voice was gruff with emotion, the same pain she'd witnessed earlier when he mentioned his parents.

"Whatever you've done or been through, it's shaped who you are now. And you'll be a better father because of it," she said. "Empathetic. When our kid screws up, you'll be able to relate, to share the benefit of your wisdom, to love them despite their mistakes."

Jace stared. "You're pretty amazing, you know that?"

Mia blushed, ducking her gaze because the expression in his eyes felt even more intimate than the sex they'd just shared. "Um, speaking of our kid... I have a sonogram appointment next Thursday. I don't know if you'd be interested in joining me or not, but—"

"That's where they take pictures of the baby and tell you if it's a boy or a girl?" The excitement in his tone warmed her.

"No, that's still down the line. This one will show the fetal heartbeat. Sorry."

"Don't be. I'm glad to be included." He stroked her hair. "Do you have a preference? Boy or girl, I mean?"

"Not really. The answer you're supposed to give is that you just want a healthy, happy baby, which *is* true. But I've wondered… Growing up with no mom and surrounded by brothers, my childhood was all camping and horseback riding. There were no ballet recitals or princess tiaras. I didn't learn how to apply makeup until my college roommate taught me."

"Not all girls like ballet," Jace pointed out. "Or makeup."

"Obviously not, but my niece Kimber, for instance, has always loved dance. She's at cheerleading camp right now. What if my kid wants to be a cheerleader? I don't even know how to French-braid hair!"

Jace didn't laugh outright, but his eyes danced with amusement. "Um, is there any chance Kimber could help with that? Or her mom? Or an online tutorial?"

She sighed. "I'm being ridiculous, aren't I?"

"I would never tell a beautiful woman naked in my bed that she's ridiculous."

"That's not a no."

He tried unsuccessfully to hide his grin. "What you are is understandably worried about being a good parent. I worry, too. I mean, this kid's gonna have my genes." He paused, pressing a hand to his chest. "What if he or she is *too* good-looking and charming? The world may not be ready for Jace Junior."

Laughing, Mia looked around for another pillow to smack him with.

Later, though, as she drifted into sleep, she thought that perhaps there was a grain of truth to his outrageous teasing. After all, she sure as hell hadn't been ready for Jace Malone. He was an unexpected roller coaster of a man who'd turned her life upside down. Now she was mid loop-the-loop, screaming in exhilaration and hanging on for the ride. Mia didn't know what was around the next curve, but she was glad they were in it together.

Seven

With one eye on the clock, Mia patiently but firmly explained to Mrs. Kasinoff—again—that feeding her pug so many treats was going to cause long-term health problems. "I know how much you love Astaire, but nutritionally speaking, a belly rub is a much better way to show him that."

Mrs. Kasinoff's lips twisted. She obviously resented being scolded, but she promised to try to do better. When she led the pug out to the lobby so that the receptionist could process payment, it was already ten minutes past the time Mia had planned to leave for the OB's office. Mia hung her lab coat and washed her hands. She'd just grabbed her keys and purse out of the locker when Amanda came around the corner.

"I know you're headed to the dentist," the tech said apologetically, "but I thought you should know we lost the internet again."

Mia squeezed her eyes shut. Their phone system went through the computer, so that meant the phones were down, too. Hopefully it was a brief glitch. "Did you try resetting the router?"

"Fletcher tried that twice. No luck."

"I'll call the IT guy on my cell," Mia said. "Can you work on the medication stock order without the internet?" There were prescriptions that they sent clients to pharmacies for and others, like heartworm preventative, that they tried to keep on hand.

"Yeah. I'll finish that, and Naomi's going to catch up on some filing. But we'll lose any incoming calls."

Which meant potentially losing business. Mia sighed. She was already late; she couldn't worry about that now. "Do the best you can. Text me when we're back online?"

Amanda nodded. "Will do, Boss."

On the drive across town, she haggled with the IT provider via speakerphone, exchanging some free office visits for his German shepherd for a discounted rate. She belatedly realized she'd taken a wrong turn. She ended the call, refocusing on her route and trying to shove away the work stress. It was difficult, though. Her long-term plan for the clinic was to bring in another vet and expand the business, thus making a profit and increasing job security for her staff. But expansions were costly, and Mia's ability to work overtime or take shifts at the emergency hospital had been diminished by the pregnancy.

"Not that I hold it against you," she said aloud as she parked. She put a hand over her stomach for a quick second, then grabbed her purse and hurried to the automatic doors.

Jace, already in the waiting room, was visibly relieved to see her. It wasn't out of the ordinary for expectant fathers to be in the office, but they were usually with their partners. He sat alone, looking even more masculine than usual among the pastel furniture and half-dozen women in the waiting room.

"Sorry I'm late," she greeted him. "Be back as soon as I check in."

The receptionist let her know that they'd already admitted the person after her because she'd missed her appointment time. Mia nodded; she'd occasionally had to do the same thing at the clinic. She knew they'd circle back to her. She just regretted causing a delay in Jace's day.

"Thanks for taking time from work to be here," she told him as she sat down. "Hopefully it won't be too much longer."

"Hey, right now, this is my priority. But there are some exciting things going on at Malone."

"Like what?"

"I don't want to bore you," he said sheepishly.

"It's not boring to learn more about the work you do. Besides, it's only fair. I talk about my job plenty."

She hadn't discussed her financial woes with him, but she'd vented plenty about other issues.

"Okay. If you're sure." He explained to her a new corporate rating system that examined not only profit and productivity but also employee care and environmental impact. He was working to make Malone Energy one of the first fully certified companies in the state. The legwork involved some travel, including a weeklong course in California, and he was clearly passionate about the project. His eyes were bright with enthusiasm as he spoke, matching his tone, and she got so caught up in listening to him that she stopped checking her phone every five seconds for updates on the clinic's internet.

But apparently the brief distraction was not enough to lower her blood pressure after a stressful morning.

When Dr. Bakshi came into the exam room, she was tutting over the reading the nurse had done. "Mia, this is even higher than last time," the doctor chided.

Jace looked alarmed. "Is she okay? Are you okay?" he asked Mia.

"Dr. Bakshi, this is Jace, the father. And I know my reading was a little high last time. I was caught off guard by the pregnancy and a bit freaked out." She darted a guilty glance in Jace's direction, hoping that didn't make her sound bad, like she wasn't happy about their baby.

But he was hyper-focused on the doctor, still looking worried about Mia's vitals.

"I know, which is why I wasn't too concerned,"

Dr. Bakshi said after shaking Jace's hand. "But now it is even higher, which is a trend. And not the one we want."

"Well, I had a hectic morning, and—"

"Exactly. I know how hard you work, but as you prepare for the baby, you should ease up a little for both your sakes, okay?"

Mia suddenly knew how poor Mrs. Kasinoff felt when Mia had scolded her about Astaire's weight. "It'll be lower next time."

"I hope so. Have you told your staff yet? It's important to delegate."

"Not yet." Mia sighed. She couldn't use the dentist excuse forever. *Might as well get it over with.* They had a meeting every Friday morning to wrap up the week. "I'll tell them tomorrow."

"Good. Now, are you ready for the fun part?"

A few minutes later, Mia and Jace held hands and looked at a computer screen where a grainy flutter showed their baby's heartbeat.

Jace was grinning from ear to ear but, after watching for a moment, noted, "It doesn't seem steady."

Dr. Bakshi gave him a reassuring smile. "That is not abnormal this early on. Don't worry. The beats fall into the healthy range and tend to become more regular as the baby grows."

At the end of the visit, Dr. Bakshi had the tech take Mia's blood pressure one last time while she checked in with another patient, but she still declared the systolic too high for her liking. "Manage your salt intake, but more importantly, manage your stress level. Consider meditation, take naps. There's a prenatal yoga class that meets at the center across the street. If your BP keeps escalating, we'll discuss other measures at the next appointment.

"In the meantime, you two enjoy the rest of your day. It was nice to meet you," she told Jace.

Mia signed up for her next appointment with the receptionist, and then Jace held the door open for her as they walked into the summer sunshine. Both of them were quiet. Seeing the heartbeat together had been a lovely moment, but she kind of wished he hadn't been there for the rest of it. At least he had been noble enough to walk away while the admitting nurse weighed her.

"I feel like the time I brought home a report card with a bad grade on it," she finally said.

He raised an eyebrow. "*The* time? Let's never talk about my grades."

"Seriously, I don't want you to think I'm not taking care of the baby."

"And here I was feeling guilty because after our dinner at Shari's restaurant the other night, the rest of our evening was, um, not restful."

Mia couldn't help laughing at his shamefaced expression. "I got the doctor's okay on that kind of activity. We'd have to be much more deviant for it to pose any danger to the baby."

"Well, that's a relief." He put on his sunglasses. "She's right, though. You work *really* hard. Even when you aren't at the clinic, you're doing stuff like the cattle drive or this weekend's adoption fair."

"I promise, I haven't driven any cattle in weeks," she teased. "And since you volunteered to help me at the fair Saturday, I'll have a minion to fetch me water and bring me case files and assemble care packets."

"I'm honored to be your minion. But, speaking of Saturday, I've done something that maybe I should have discussed with you first."

"How serious are we talking?" She unlocked her car door. "Should I be sitting down for this?"

"There's a local reporter who likes to cover my family. A little too much," he grumbled, and Mia wondered if this reporter was the one who'd once hinted he and Valencia were "practically engaged."

"I tipped her off that I'll be volunteering at the pet adoptions in case she wants to do a feel-good piece with cute pictures and animal anecdotes. I thought it would get some exposure for the shelter animals and a little name recognition for your clinic."

Her heart melted. "That's so… Thank you, Jace."

"Are you sure it's all right?" He shifted his weight from foot to foot. "Now I'm worried that this is the wrong time to be drumming up more patients for you."

"It's the *perfect* time. Extra business would be re-assuring, thus less stress. I just need to hire another vet to help juggle it and to run the place when I go on maternity leave." Finding the right fit and negotiating terms would come with its own set of problems, but at least it would be moving in the right direction.

"Okay. I'll see you Saturday, then. In the meantime, take breaks and think calming thoughts."

"Easy for you to say." Her thoughts would be a lot calmer if her clinic wasn't losing longtime customers and Wi-Fi.

"You're right." He frowned. "I'm giving out advice while my life is relatively unchanged. Meanwhile, you're the one making all the adjustments. Is there more I could be doing? Should I—"

"Jace." She put her hand on his arm, moved by his thoughtfulness. "You came with me to the OB. You're volunteering at the adoption. You're *meeting my family* next week. Trust me, that's way worse than morning sickness."

"Maybe meeting them won't be as bad as you think."

"No, it definitely will. But that wasn't my point. You're not getting your blood pressure checked every month, or your weight—lucky bastard—but you are in this with me. We're…" Her eyes watered, and she ducked her head, embarrassed to find herself on the verge of tears. How had this man come to mean so much to her in such a brief time? She swallowed hard. "We're a team."

He enveloped her in his arms and pulled her into a long, silent hug. Then he kissed the top of her head. "Go, team."

Sunday brunch was a staple of Shari's workweek, but Saturday mornings were usually slow enough that she could sit down and enjoy breakfast with Mia, as was the case today. The food had been characteristically fabulous, but Mia was morose over denying herself the stuffed French toast in favor of the healthier veggie omelet.

She pushed away her empty plate. "After the baby is born, I am coming in one weekend for an appalling amount of French toast and mimosas."

"Well." Shari leaned back in her chair, her eyes sparkling. "By that time, you'll have more parking options."

"The permits went through? That's fantastic!" Expanding the parking lot had been one of Shari's major goals this year. Even with the growth in the takeout market, most of her business still came from sit-down diners, and the current lot was too small to meet demand. "I can't believe you waited until now to tell me."

"I was saving it, kind of like looking forward to dessert."

"No wonder you're in such a great mood. I figured your date with Adwin last night went really well."

Shari heaved a dramatic sigh.

"Uh-oh."

"I was telling him about a killer plate of shrimp and grits I once had in Littleton, and conversation turned to grits in general."

"Oh, no." Mia shook her head, knowing her friend's strong personal opinion about putting sugar on grits. "Don't tell me."

"Yep. Sugar."

"So is he dead to you, or have you decided to overlook this deep character flaw?"

The corner of Shari's mouth twitched. "The things I tolerate for that man…"

"I'm sure he'll find a way to make it up to you."

"Mmm." Shari sipped her orange juice with a smile.

"In the meantime, you and I should do something to celebrate your parking lot success! Are you free Thursday?"

"Sadly, no. I've got two servers who needed the night off, so we'll be short-staffed. What about Tuesday evening?"

Mia grimaced. "I don't even want to think about Tuesday."

"Oh, I forgot! Taking Jace to meet the family. How do you think it will go?"

"I don't know." She wanted to keep her expectations realistic. "Ian mellowed a lot after he got married, but now that his daughter's old enough to have her first boyfriend, his protective instincts are back on high alert. And I'm not sure Dad has ever liked *anyone* I dated, not even Drew, which is weird, because he really wanted us to get married."

Shari cocked her head, considering. "I kind of get that. The 'I don't want my daughter to be alone' but 'no one's good enough for my little girl' catch. Parents have high standards. Can you imagine if I told my folks about Adwin's depraved grits behavior?"

Mia snickered. "Heaven forbid."

"You and I are both attending the businesswomen's forum Wednesday, right?" At Mia's nod, Shari suggested, "Why don't you come over afterward? We'll toast sparkling grape juice and binge-watch a few episodes of something."

"Sounds great."

"That actually reminds me. Grace Yu came in to pick up dinner last night, and she said Nina's salon dropped out of the Heritage Festival. So they have a last-minute opening for a sponsor booth."

"You're kidding!" The annual Heritage Festival, held each August, was a popular event with locals and tourists. It was made up of vendor booths with unique wares to sell, and sponsor booths that provided free activities or goodies for the attendees in return for the exposure. Slots went fast and booked out nearly a year in advance. "If it's still available, you should see if you can take it. A booth would be great promotion for the restaurant."

"Trust me, the thought crossed my mind, but the entry fee is steep. I have that new parking lot to bankroll."

"Good point."

"What if *we* take it?" Shari mused. "The committee doesn't normally allow sharing, but they might make an exception to get someone signed up this late."

"Seriously?" Mia's mind raced. Even if she scraped together the money for her half of the fee, the opportunity was as overwhelming as it was exciting. People usually put months into planning; she and Shari would have only a few weeks.

"Think about it," Shari encouraged her. "We split the fee, decorate one side with the restaurant logo and the other side with cute pet photos. People could submit pictures via email and vote on a winner at the festival. I can make mini-cakes decorated like, I don't know, doghouses."

Mia raised her eyebrows.

"Okay, probably not doghouse cakes. But we'll figure something out. My nephew can help us set up, carry anything heavy. You definitely will not be doing that."

The more Shari talked, the more excited Mia got. "I could ask if any of the techs would be willing to pitch in for a shift or two. Amanda's outgoing and loves talking to people. We could actually do this."

"Of course we can! We're badasses, remember?"

"It was a rough week. I was feeling low on badassery," Mia said. "Thanks for the reminder."

Shari raised her glass of juice in salute. "What are friends for?"

There were few things in the world better than Shari's stuffed French toast, but friendship was definitely one of them.

"Ohmigosh is that *him*?" The blonde woman standing next to Mia spoke in an enthusiastic and highly unsuccessful whisper.

Jace tried to bite back a grin as he approached the folding table with the animal shelter banner across the front of it. "Morning, ladies."

"Hey." Mia's smile was rueful as her eyes met his,

acknowledging that he'd overheard her colleague. "Jace, this is Amanda Rockwell, one of the techs from the clinic. And that's Scott and Fiona, from the shelter." She gestured to a man and woman who were transferring dogs from individual crates into a large, open-topped pen that allowed them to romp and play on the grass.

"It is so nice to meet you." Amanda reached for his hand and pumped it heartily. "I've heard a lot about you. Well, no, actually, I haven't. But I've *wondered* a lot about you. Are you—"

"Hey, Amanda," Mia cut in. "I think I left my clipboard in the car. Would you mind grabbing it for me?"

"No problem, Boss." Finally releasing Jace's hand, the blonde bounded off toward the nearby parking lot.

Left alone with Mia, Jace seized the opportunity for a quick kiss, then pointed at some paperwork in her chair. "Would that be the clipboard in question?"

Her eyes danced with unrepentant humor. "Yes. Yes, it would." She moved the clipboard and sat down. "I'll wave her back over in a second. Amanda's energy makes her a very effective employee, but sometimes it's a lot. Especially since she found out about the baby. It's only been twenty-four hours, and I think she's already suggested about two hundred names."

"Huh." Jace blinked. Aside from the occasional "Jace Junior" joke, he hadn't really thought that far ahead. "I guess we should talk about names at some point." Even though he'd seen the baby's heartbeat for himself, the idea of giving their child a name—imagining the actual person they'd be bringing into the world—made everything more real.

Mia's answering smile was almost shy. "I guess we should."

"I didn't see a clipboard," Amanda said, her sudden reappearance making Jace wonder just how long he'd been staring into Mia's eyes. "But I grabbed this notebook just in case that's what you meant. Oh, you found it!"

"Yeah, but thanks for looking," Mia said sheepishly.

"You know me," Amanda said. "Here to help!"

"Same," Jace agreed. "Let me know how I can be useful and put me to work."

Two hours later, Jace leaned against a tree outside the dog pen and told Mia, "I don't know how you do it. How do you resist taking them all home with you?" He watched an adorable chocolate-brown puppy wag its tail so hard that it toppled sideways—only to spring back up and repeat its actions. A shy terrier with a sweet expression was peeking out from beneath an old towel, and a curly-haired mutt with a relaxed attitude seemed blissfully content to enjoy the fresh air and people-watching. Jace swore the dog was actually grinning.

Mia patted his arm sympathetically. "It's tempting, I'll admit. But hoarding animals wouldn't be fair to them or to me. They deserve love and attention to help them transition into their new homes. And with the hours I work? Plus a baby on the way?"

Her hand dropped absently to her abdomen, and Jace smiled at the unconscious display of maternal instinct. Impending motherhood suited her. She was even more beautiful than when they'd met, something he wouldn't have guessed possible.

"Dr. Zane?" Amanda called from the table. "This gentleman has some questions about Bandit's medical records."

"I'll be right there," Mia replied. Then she asked Jace, "Are you okay on your own for a few minutes?"

"Yep." With Scott and Fiona on a lunch break, Jace had taken over letting potential adoptive pet owners in and out of the pen to interact with the pups. He'd just closed the gate behind a couple who said they'd moved into a home with "the perfect backyard for a dog" when an amused voice behind him drawled, "I wouldn't have believed it if I hadn't seen it with my own eyes."

Reed? Jace spun around to find both his older brother and his grandfather, with Brooke sleeping in a covered stroller between them. "What are you doing here?" The cobblestone shopping center featuring two department stores, an upscale deli, and a grassy area with benches and a picturesque fountain was a high-traffic area but outside of his brother's usual orbit.

Reed gave him a too-innocent smile. "Well, when your assistant mentioned to my assistant that you had 'volunteering' on your calendar for the day, I thought I should stop by and see if it was something Malone Energy should be involved in. You're always telling us how important community outreach is."

"Pffft." Grandpa Harry shook his head. "I'm here because I heard that cute Dr. Mia would be around. Ah, and here she is now!" He waved at Mia, who stutter-stepped, her obvious surprise mirroring Jace's.

He met her halfway, putting his arm around her waist for moral support. "We've been ambushed," he said under his breath. In a regular tone, he added, "Mia, you remember my grandfather and brother."

"Nice to see you again," Reed said.

Mia blushed a rosy pink, and Jace recalled that the last time she'd encountered his brother had been outside Jace's bedroom just after sunrise. "H-hi."

Harry wagged a finger at her. "Young lady, you haven't taken me up on my invitation for a game night."

Reed cleared his throat. "Or maybe something more low-key might be better for all our sakes? Don't want to traumatize our guest or wake Brooke with the inevitable arguing."

"Fine," Harry grumbled. "I suppose I'm still allowed to do a movie night without getting a doctor's permission? What's your pleasure, Mia? Thrillers? Westerns? Musicals?" He glanced from her to Jace and back again. "Romance?"

With a groan, Jace pressed the heel of his hand to his forehead. "Subtle, Grandpa."

"Old people don't have time to be subtle. So it's settled? We'll see you soon for movie night?" Harry pressed.

Mia laughed. "I promise."

"Good, good." Harry smiled fondly, then looked past her to where a man was trying to coax the shy terrier into playing with a ball. "Had a dog that looked like that when I was a boy. Best friend a kid could ask for."

He sounded so wistful that Jace wondered if Harry would benefit from some four-legged companionship. Maybe a senior dog or even a cat. Jace made a mental note to broach the subject with his brothers later since Harry would need some assistance caring for it.

"Well, if you'll excuse us," Jace said, "Mia and I have work to do. Besides, Brenna should be here any minute." He smirked at his brother. Brenna Hodge had come to Malone Energy to do a follow-up interview after the gala fundraiser and had flirted rather aggressively with a discomfited Reed.

"Brenna the journalist? The one who kept asking to see pictures of Brooke and hinting that she's great with children?" Reed's gaze shifted as if he expected the reporter to suddenly pounce from either direction. "Why? How did she even know I'd be here?"

"I invited her." Jace tried to keep the smugness out of his tone; it was rare to see Reed unnerved. "She's doing a write-up about the shelter and some of the animals that still need homes." To Mia he added, "She seemed quite taken with my brother."

"A good-looking billionaire?" Mia grinned. "Go figure."

Reed smiled weakly. "Well, we don't want to get in the way, so we'll just be on our... Grandpa?"

Harry had wandered closer to the dog pen and was chatting with the man now playing fetch with the terrier.

"Don't worry." Jace lightly socked his brother's shoulder. "I don't think she's hiding in the trees—we should see her coming."

"Honestly, if she thinks I have the energy to date, she's giving me more credit than I deserve. Eventually, sure. But with an infant?" Reed glanced down at his sleeping daughter. "I love her, but I have my hands full figuring out parenthood. Why would I add trying to figure out a relationship on top of that?"

Mia's brows drew together in a frown, and Jace wished he had shooed his brother away sooner. *Our situation is different.* For starters, neither of them had gone through a bitter divorce. Having a child wasn't the only reason Reed steered clear of romance. Besides, Jace and Mia still had months to figure things out before the baby came. They hadn't discussed where they stood romantically—mainly because he didn't want to add any emotional stress—but he was optimistic. He believed they had a future together.

At least, he hoped so. Because with each passing day, it was harder to imagine a future without Mia in his life and in his bed.

Eight

"Are you sure you don't mind driving?" Jace asked as he climbed back into the car. "Traffic can be stressful."

"We're pretty much past the traffic part," Mia told him. "That's why I wanted to stop here—it's the last gas station before Dad's place. When he retired, his goal was to move 'off the beaten path.' Trust me, he succeeded. GPS is no match for Martin Zane."

What Mia didn't add was that driving gave her something to focus on besides her raging nerves. There was no telling how tonight would go, but the stakes felt much higher than when she'd first proposed it. Meeting each other's families before telling them about the pregnancy had been a deceptively simple agreement.

She'd expected to see his grandfather and brothers once, maybe twice. Instead, they'd popped up at a pet adoption, and she was answering texts from Harry's aide about best canine temperaments for a senior citizen. She had looming plans for a cozy Malone movie night and was still trying to repress the memory of stumbling into Reed early one morning, with her hair disheveled and her shirt misbuttoned. The story of that encounter had earned a fit of laughter from Shari but still made Mia's cheeks tingle with embarrassment.

"You're awfully quiet," Jace noted as she drove. "Crisp fifty for your thoughts? That's billionaire humor."

She rolled her eyes. "Very droll. But I was thinking about your family."

"Really?"

"They're…unexpectedly sweet."

He chuckled. "I can't wait to tell them you said so—and find out which brother is more chagrined by the description."

The corner of her mouth twitched as she pictured the exchange. "Seriously, though. They were so careful to make sure I didn't feel excluded at the gala, where I didn't know anyone. And when I ran into Reed that one morning, he was very chivalrous about it." He hadn't even pointed out that she'd missed a button. She'd discovered that in the car later. "Not to mention Harry inviting me over for movie night. They've been very welcoming."

"It's not because they're 'sweet' by nature. Well, Harry, maybe. But you won my brothers over on your own merits. Hardly surprising that they like you." His playful tone faded, his voice soft and serious. "There's a lot to like, Doc."

She cast him a sidelong glance, and when their eyes met, her skin tingled with something far different than embarrassment. The air between them crackled, the growing silence charged with something more profound than words. Reminding herself to watch the road, she tore her gaze away from him. Breaking that connection was both a loss and a relief. In another second, she might have babbled a confession of all the things she liked about *him* and all the ways this was new to her. She'd never felt like she did when she was with Jace.

He cleared his throat. "Anyway, now it's my turn. Time to repay the favor and win over your family."

"Don't get your hopes up. I mean, Leigh will like you, but—"

"Leigh is your sister-in-law, the teacher who met your brother when Ian started coaching high school football. And their daughter, an only child, is at cheer camp."

Mia's eyebrows shot up. "What did you do, make flash cards?"

He ignored that. "Dylan, the younger brother, is a ski instructor who works retail during the off-season, and your other brother lives out of state."

"Yeah, but you didn't list anyone's birthdays or middle names, so I have to deduct points."

"Make all the jokes you want, but I've learned the best way to shut my brothers up in meetings is to be hyper-prepared. I am ready for this."

"I'm not worried about you being prepared. *You* aren't going to be the problem." Mia turned on her blinker out of habit—there were no other cars around— and made a left onto an unmarked dirt road. "Historically speaking, my brothers and father haven't warmed up to anyone I've brought home. Don't take it personally."

"I won't. But it isn't going to be an issue," he said confidently. "You'll see. Your family will love me so much that when they find out about the baby, they'll throw us a parade."

Doubtful.

But since they had arrived, there was no use in worrying any more about it. They rolled into the driveway past the familiar Akebia-covered mailbox. She'd teased her dad once that she was going to stop using the obscured house number when she addressed his birthday cards and just send mail to "care of the climbing purple flowers."

"You should carry in Shari's desserts," she suggested. "At least it starts you off with a positive association."

He snorted. "Like I was going to let you carry anything bigger than your purse."

She shifted the car into Park, about to retort when the dashboard caught her attention. "Hell."

"What's wrong?"

"The check engine light. It's probably no big deal." At least she prayed it wasn't. She was barely scraping together funds to invest in the festival booth; the idea of car repairs on top of that was dizzying. "It came on a while back and turned out to be just a loose fuse they had to reset. No big deal," she repeated emphatically. Maybe if she said it convincingly enough, she could manifest it as true.

"I can give you the name of a top-notch mechanic if you want," he offered.

She made a noncommittal sound. Though she appreciated the thought, she suspected "top-notch" was synonymous with "expensive." She had no doubt Jace would offer to pay for it, but she was still reeling from the last time she'd mixed romance and finances. She wouldn't make that mistake again anytime soon.

They walked toward the front porch, which boasted a fresh coat of blue paint and numerous planters. It was picturesque, but the bottom stair was still cracked. It had been at the top of her dad's to-do list since he moved in.

"Watch your step," she said over her shoulder. "And remember, if things go sideways tonight, you can always stand behind me."

"You almost sound serious."

She shrugged. "Dad's ex-military, and they all

played football. I don't like your chances in a three-to-one."

"Mia! There's no chance in hell I would ever use you as a human shield."

"I was joking." Mostly. "But they can be unbearable."

"I grew up with Reed," he reminded her as she reached for the doorknob. "I've been training for 'unbearable' my whole life. Quit being paranoid."

"Paranoia is my version of preparing."

Her hand was on the doorknob, but before she had a chance to turn it, the front door swung open.

Dylan wore a Rockies jersey and an ear-to-ear grin. "Sis! And friend. Welcome." He eyed the large paper bag Jace carried. "Please tell me that's from Shari."

"Rum cake for Dad," Mia confirmed, "and cayenne brownies for you."

Dylan nearly swooned. "I would marry that woman if she'd have me." He turned to take the bag. "I'm Dylan, Mia's favorite brother."

Jace laughed. "Nice to meet you."

"Everyone's in the living room watching the ball game, except Leigh," Dylan told him. "She's making her famous margaritas."

Perhaps Dylan had already enjoyed a margarita or two, Mia speculated. It would explain his boisterous greeting. Among family, he was known for his sense of humor, but he didn't normally reveal it to strangers. *Or maybe he's mellowed with age, and you really* are *paranoid.*

Maybe. But Jace still had to contend with Ian and her father.

Dylan led them down the short hallway to the living room. Mia fidgeted when she noticed Jace studying framed family pictures. Her middle school years had not been photogenic. It was really a shame that when her dad bought this house, the movers hadn't lost the box with those particular portraits.

"Dinner should be ready in another ten or fifteen minutes," Dylan said. "Are you a beer man or a tequila guy?" he asked Jace. "Or we've got sodas, too. Water?"

Mia did a double take. Her brother's politeness was a welcome surprise, but his tone surpassed basic courtesy. He sounded eager to please in a way she found suspicious—like when he'd switched the salt and sugar as a kid and offered to sweeten his siblings' cereal for them. She stared at him hard, both assessing his motives and attempting to send a silent warning.

Jace, on the other hand, looked perfectly at ease. "A cold beer sounds great, thanks."

"I'll take one, too." The gruff voice came from the center of the room, where Martin Zane presided from his battered recliner. When any of his children had challenged house rules growing up, Martin habitually declared that he was the king of his castle, with a throne built by La-Z-Boy.

"Hi, Dad." Mia went toward him to hug him hello, and he met her halfway.

"And this must be Jace," Martin said.

She nodded. When she'd told her dad on the phone that she was bringing Jace, he hadn't asked for a last name, and she hadn't volunteered it. They could get into the complications of who Jace's family was another time.

Not only did her dad shake Jace's hand, he gave him a hearty thump on the back. "Pleasure to meet you." Martin nodded toward the baseball game on TV. "Do you have a favorite team?"

"To be honest, I'm more of a football fan."

Her dad grinned approvingly, and Ian rose from the couch to also shake Jace's hand.

Mia blinked. *What is happening?* After the Andrew fiasco, she'd expected them to scrutinize her choice of men even more critically than before. Was this their attempt to get him to lower his guard? Or had they decided that anyone she brought home had to be an improvement over a thieving con artist?

Maybe she could steal a moment with her sister-in-law to get Leigh's take on the situation. "Where's your better half?" she asked Ian.

"Right behind you, Red." Leigh squeezed by Mia, handing her a margarita glass as she passed. "This is for you. And hi," she greeted Jace, passing him a chilled bottle. "I hear you requested a beer. Dylan says he's checking on the brisket, but it was probably a mistake to leave him alone with the desserts."

"Uh…" Mia looked at the margarita in her hand, wondering where to set it down. Ian was blocking the bookshelf, and if she abandoned it on the coffee table in the middle of the room, it would become obvious to everyone. "I could use a glass of water, actually. I'll go safeguard the brownies."

But as soon as she'd walked out of the room, she hesitated, wondering if her dad and brother would seize the opportunity to interrogate Jace. Obviously, he could take care of himself. That wasn't the problem. She was worried about her family making a lousy first impression because she genuinely wanted Jace to like them. She was only just now realizing how important that was to her. Even though her family had no way of knowing, Jace would be in her life for years, probably decades, to come.

In what capacity? They'd only spoken vaguely about the future. Would Jace be spending Christmas Eves exchanging gifts with her brothers and sipping Leigh's famous eggnog? Or, once this initial bright blaze of passion burned out, would he and Mia settle into a more limited partnership, where she had their child for some holidays and Jace did for others? That thought was oddly depressing.

"Uh, Mia?" Dylan brought her out of her reverie as he tried to pass through the narrow hall. "You *drink* the margarita, not just stand with it and stare at the wall."

"Actually, here. I'm on some allergy medication, so…" She gave him the glass. "Look, Dylan, you guys be nice to Jace, okay? For real. I'm hoping he's gonna be around for a long time."

"Don't worry." He ruffled her hair. "We plan to give him the royal treatment."

There was a time she would have taken that as a veiled threat, but over the next hour, she had to concede that her family was living up to Dylan's promise. They asked Jace's opinion on sports, on gardening, on local government and movies. When they asked about his job, he gave a simplified answer, telling them truthfully that he worked for an energy company and was part of an interdepartmental commission on sustainability.

The tension Mia had been carrying all day began to ease. It may have taken until she was almost thirty, but her family had finally stopped being ridiculously overprotective. Either that, or this was one of those science fiction scenarios where the citizens had been replaced by alien clones. Regardless, it seemed that Jace had been right. This evening was going smoothly, and her paranoia was unfounded.

More or less. When Martin turned to say something to Dylan, he scowled past his son's shoulder at Mia's car parked outside the window. "You're still driving that bucket of bolts?"

"You still haven't fixed the bottom porch step?" she countered.

"Sass at my own table," Martin muttered with a shake of his head. "I worry that car's not safe."

"I've only had one accident," she reminded him, "and it was due to the weather conditions. The car's fine."

Jace opened his mouth, and she shot a look across the table to communicate that the words *engine light* would have dire consequences. He took a sudden avid interest in his garlic mashed potatoes.

Leigh diplomatically changed the subject. "So how did you and Jace meet?"

"On one of those tourism trail rides," Mia said. "Jace was doing some summer work there, and I was consulting."

"Wait, the drive from Alonzo's place?" her dad clarified.

Mia sighed. "Yep." She knew that the minute she left, Martin would call his old buddy for any and all information on Jace.

That was fine, inevitable really. She wasn't trying to keep Jace's identity a secret; she'd just wanted her family to meet him without the billionaire label attached, so they wouldn't be weird about it. *And now you've accomplished that.*

Once it looked like everyone was finished, Leigh stood, picking up both her and Ian's plates. "Who wants dessert? *Besides* you," she said as Dylan's hand shot up.

Jace rose, too. "I'll help you clear."

The two of them carried out the dishes, and Martin patted Mia's hand. "Sorry I gave you grief about your car," he told her. "Hope I didn't make you look bad in front of your beau. I just worry about you."

"Thanks, Dad." It was hard to be annoyed given

the affection in his tone. "But I'm a grown woman. You don't have to worry about me so much."

"I suppose that's true now, circumstances being what they are."

"I don't think twenty-eight is a 'circumstance,' but—"

"Gotta hand it to you," Ian said with an admiring smile. "When you trade up, you *really* trade up."

She didn't have time to reply before Jace returned with a Bundt cake in one hand and a knife in the other, Leigh at his heels with brownies and a carafe of coffee.

"None for me, thanks," Mia said. "Trying to cut back on caffeine."

While dessert was being served, she excused herself to use the restroom. She washed her hands and leaned against the vanity, taking her first deep breath since they'd arrived. Introducing Jace to her family had gone far better than she could have anticipated, and she was relieved to have this milestone behind them. When she told her family later that she was pregnant, she'd be working forward from a positive.

But for now, cake. And hand soap. She'd used the last of it but knew she could replenish it from the upstairs supply closet. Her dad bought most of his toiletries and groceries in bulk, a lingering habit from raising four kids on one salary.

"Mia!" her sister-in-law called up the stairs. "If you don't come back soon, I'm not sure we can keep Dylan from eating your piece of cake."

Mia chuckled. "Coming!" She rounded the corner but stopped in her tracks at the sight of a local newspaper on the hall table.

Familiar faces smiled up at her—including her own. She and Jace were standing on either side of a cheerful three-legged golden retriever, just above a headline. "Billionaire Boosts Awareness for Animals in Need." Suddenly Dylan's promise that they would give Jace "the royal treatment" felt less like brotherly assurance and more like happiness that she'd landed a rich date. And what had Ian said? *When you trade up, you* really *trade up.*

Dropping the soap on the table next to the paper, she stalked back down to the dining room.

Jace did a double take at her expression. "Are you okay? You look pale."

"I'm a redhead. I'm always pale." She'd meant it as a joke, but her delivery was too sharp. The annoyance she felt at her family had spilled out at the wrong target.

Martin raised his eyebrows. "We don't get snippy with guests in this house, Mia Jean."

"You've been snippy to literally every guy I've ever brought home until today!"

Martin waved a hand. "What's done is done. The past doesn't matter. What matters is the bright future between you and this dear boy."

Good Lord. After only a couple of hours, Martin was basically inviting Jace to call him Dad—a warm welcome that turned out to be financially motivated.

"Unbelievable!" Did her father still not think she could take care of herself?

"Mia, your blood pressure." Jace's whisper was low but intense. "You know what Dr. Bakshi said."

"Dr. B?" Leigh's eyes went wide. "Oh my God!"

Ian frowned. "Isn't Dr. Bakshi the one who delivered Kimber?"

Yeah. Mia had first visited the ob-gyn after the recommendation of her sister-in-law, a former patient.

"You didn't have a margarita or coffee," Ian said slowly. He shot to his feet, his gaze swinging to Jace. "You son of a bitch. You two barely know each other! Did you pounce on her the second you met her?"

"What are you talking about?" Dylan asked. "Mia, what is he talking about?"

But their father had pieced it together, based on his enraged expression. He stood and leaned closer, studying Mia's hands. "Why don't I see an engagement ring?" he demanded.

"I don't see how that's any of your business," Mia retorted. "And Ian, *I* pounced on *him*, so shut up."

"Ahem." Jace cleared his throat. "I understand this is a shock to everyone, but arguing can't be good for Mia or the baby. Maybe if we all sit back down…"

Leigh nodded her support, leveling stern looks at all three Zane men. "Take a breath or take a lap if you need to cool off, but pipe down." She came around the table to hug Mia. "Congratulations, Red. I am so sorry about all this."

Mia sighed. "You're not the one who blurted out Dr. Bakshi's name." It hadn't occurred to her to mention to Jace that her family knew the OB. Maybe she *had* underprepared him.

"Weeks or months from now," Leigh pledged, "I will throw you an epic baby shower to make up for this." She skewered her husband with a glare. "You will send an expensive present. You will not send unsolicited opinions."

Ian scowled. "Look, he—"

"No." She turned to her father-in-law. "Marty, I'm sorry to overrule you under your own roof, but us moms have to stick together. Mia is old enough to make her own life decisions without your approval."

Mia swallowed, struggling not to cry. This was basically the nightmare version of how she thought dinner might play out. At least she had her sister-in-law in her corner. For long moments, no one spoke. Mia wasn't sure if it was because they feared Leigh's wrath or just because they didn't know what to say.

Jace ventured into the conversational void. "I'm going to take Mia home now. Thank you for the, um, hospitality. Want me to grab your purse from the living room?" he asked her.

She nodded wordlessly.

"Mia Jean."

It was difficult to meet her father's eyes. They were full of conflicting emotions, and she had her own myriad of emotions she was trying to sort through.

"You know I love you," he said gruffly. It sounded

like the beginning of a sentence, not a completed statement. *You know I love you. But.*

You know I love you, but I'm disappointed. You know I love you, but this isn't what I want for you.

She sighed. "I love you, too." But they both needed time to calm down before they attempted this conversation. "I'll call you this week, Dad."

He nodded, saying nothing else as she walked past. Leigh gave her a reassuring pat on the arm. Mia tried to look on the bright side—at least she'd solved the problem of trying to decide how to tell her family about the baby. That was one check on the to-do list.

She met Jace at the front door and took her purse with a mirthless laugh. "Still think I'm paranoid?"

As concerned as Jace had been seeing Mia distraught, her withdrawn silence as they pulled up to her house was even more troubling. He parked in her driveway next to his own car and turned to face her.

"Mia, I—"

"You really don't need to apologize again. That fiasco was a group effort."

Maybe, but only one person there had indicated that she had a medical condition or mentioned the name of her obstetrician. He'd panicked in the moment. The only thing worse than his regret was the idea of leaving her alone like this.

"Do you maybe want to watch a movie?" he ventured. "I could come in for a little while." Or maybe she preferred that he drive away and never come back.

"Thanks for the offer, but I'm going straight to bed."

Although it wasn't that late, she did look exhausted. Guilt churned in his gut. He wished he knew what to say, but as he walked her to her door, the only words that came to mind were *I'm sorry*. He'd already apologized dozens of times, but what was the point? No apology could erase what had happened.

How could he have messed up so royally? He'd known how nervous she'd been about today. His ride home was plagued with self-castigation, thinking too late of all the ways he could have changed the subject or de-escalated the situation.

When he came through the front gates of the Triple Pine, Jace didn't want to talk to anyone—he'd said more than enough for one day. So, naturally, his entire family was gathered on the front porch, enjoying the summer evening. Brooke was asleep in her baby swing, and Harry looked half asleep in his rocking chair. Heath had his ever-present laptop open on the glass tabletop between him and Reed, their faces illuminated by its glow.

Whatever they were discussing, Jace hoped it was enough to keep them occupied. He gave a quick nod of greeting as he took the stairs two at a time.

"Have you been following this proposed animal husbandry statute?" Heath asked. "If it passes—"

"Not now." Unfortunately, Jace's voice sounded exactly as aggravated as he felt.

Reed arched an eyebrow. "What's with you?"

Jace ground his teeth.

"Don't say 'nothing,'" Grandpa Harry admonished, looking over the top of his glasses. "I let you get away with that too much when you were a kid. Shoulda pushed you to talk about things. Maybe you wouldn't have acted out so much."

Jace's temper cooled slightly. "You did the best you could. And in spite of myself, I turned out okay." *Dinner with the Zanes notwithstanding.* He sighed. "I fuc—"

"Ahem." Reed shot a glance in his sleeping daughter's direction. He'd said that if they didn't train themselves to stop swearing before she started talking, they'd never manage it later.

"I screwed things up with Mia."

"Damn." Reed pinched the bridge of his nose, seemingly oblivious to his own double standard. "I was afraid of this."

"Whatever you did wrong," Heath said, "fix it. Make a romantic gesture."

Easy for you to say. "I'm not taking advice from a guy who gave his first crush a rock from our yard as a Valentine's Day present."

"She was allergic to chocolate, and rocks don't wilt."

"Quit squabbling," Harry said mildly. "Jace, what happened?"

"I... It's complicated." He supposed an impromptu family meeting on the front porch was as good a place as any to tell them the truth. It wasn't as if Mia had been given her dream scenario for the Zanes finding out. "There's something I haven't told you. Mia's expecting. A baby," he clarified haltingly. "My baby."

"Shit." Reed violated his own rule twice in one conversation.

"Has there been a prenatal paternity test?" Heath asked.

Jace's fists clenched as he took a step forward.

"Heath!" Harry shot a disappointed look at the family accountant and leaned forward in his chair, putting himself in Jace's direct line of sight. "How does she feel about this?"

"The idea took a little getting used to, but we're both happy. We just saw the heartbeat last week at an ultrasound appointment."

"And you kept this all to yourself?" Surprisingly, Reed sounded more hurt than accusatory.

"She hadn't told her family yet, either." He dragged a hand through his hair. "I met them tonight. And accidentally broke the news."

"Good God." Heath looked appalled. "I don't think there's a romantic gesture big enough to fix that. Just give her your shares in the company."

"Would it help if I offered your grandmother's wedding ring?" Harry asked.

It was for the best that Reed's ex-wife had wanted to design her own jewelry; Jace doubted she would have returned the family heirloom. "Thanks, Grandpa, but no. I already asked Mia to marry me, and she rejected me on the grounds that it was way too sudden."

"She's right!" Heath and Reed both agreed.

She'd also been adamantly opposed to the idea of marriage when her father brought it up, so Heath needn't worry that she was after the family assets.

He plopped down on the top step, head in his hands. "This must all sound reckless to you. I wanted so much to show you I've changed..."

"Of course you have." It was surprising to hear how quickly Heath agreed with him. "I could name four or five different metrics we could measure your behavior on, and they all indicate the same thing. The last few weeks at the office, you've been energetic and resourceful. It's obvious that you care and that you're open to feedback."

"And you met a woman worthy of this new Jace," Reed put in. "Mia's smart and compassionate and beautiful. We'd be lucky to have her in the family, but if that's not what she wants, I'm sure you'll work out a parenting arrangement. We support whatever the two of you decide."

"You do?" An unfamiliar warmth spread through Jace's chest.

Grandpa Harry harrumphed. "Of course we do. What did you expect?"

"I don't know," he admitted. "But you definitely took it better than her family."

Reed winced. "Yeah, that's a mess you need to clean up. As soon as possible."

How? As much as he wished otherwise, he couldn't undo what had happened. Maybe he could visit Martin Zane again sometime and apologize man-to-man for breaking the news in such a chaotic, unpleasant way. But Mia's family was a secondary issue.

Making things right with her was priority number one.

Mia's alarm going off Wednesday morning was adding insult to injury—a reminder as she lay there, already awake, of the hours she'd spent tossing and turning. *Maybe I should just take a sick day.* She dismissed the idea as soon as she had it. Even if she could afford to cancel her appointments, the last thing she wanted was to stay home with her thoughts and relive yesterday's disaster ad nauseam.

Instead, she tossed away her comforter and dragged herself to the shower. Once she was dressed, she found that she'd missed several texts from Jace, checking to ask if she was okay. She sat on the edge of the bed, trying to decide how to reply. Some things were too complicated for text message, but she didn't want him to worry.

All good. Just gearing up for a busy day.

After a moment, she added, Plans with Shari tonight. Talk to you tomorrow? She wasn't angry with Jace. But she wasn't ready to rehash what had happened, either. She was too drained.

Apparently, her physical appearance wasn't any better than her emotional state. As soon as Mia walked into the office, Amanda gasped audibly before offering a sympathetic, "Oh, dear."

Mia grimaced. "That bad?"

"If I didn't already know you were pregnant, I would have guessed monster hangover."

Well. That should instill confidence in the pet owners who came in today.

"Are you all good for surgery?" Amanda looked at her watch. "You have the Wilsons' collie in an hour."

Mia nodded. It was a routine spay, and when she operated, she gave her patient all her focus, which would be a relief.

As she prepped for her first appointment, she lost herself in the comforting rhythm of her work, doing her best not to think about Jace or her family or that newspaper article or how badly she reacted. She retreated into her professional demeanor, letting it numb the harsh emotions of the night before. The day went by surprisingly fast, and she was grateful for the many distractions the clinic provided. Almost before she knew it, it was time to leave and meet Shari at the forum.

She gathered her belongings and headed to the front to tell her staff goodbye.

Amanda signaled her with an index finger as she finished with a customer on the phone. Then she said, "Your father's holding on line two. Do you want me to tell him to call your cell instead?"

Her dad had called the clinic? Was he afraid she wouldn't have answered if he called her directly? "N-no. I'll talk to him before I go. I'll pick it up in my office, thanks."

She didn't bother turning the light back on in the office—enough spilled through from the hallway—but the dim interior highlighted the red blinking flash on the phone. Her hands shook as she reached for the receiver. *Low stress, calming thoughts.* She took a breath and pictured the ocean. "Hi, Dad."

"Mia Jean." He didn't sound like his usual blustery self. He sounded…timid. "I'm gonna have a grand-baby."

"Yep." Tears stung her eyes. She hadn't gotten to share the momentous part of that with her loved ones amid the yelling and mortification.

"How are you feeling? Are you and the baby doing okay?"

"A little tired, but yeah, we're okay."

"All I ever wanted for my children is for them to be happy and healthy. If you're happy, I'm happy."

"Thank you."

"But you can't blame me for thinking you'd be happier with a billionaire."

"Dad."

"Think about all the things you wouldn't have to worry about anymore!"

"What I worry about is my family believing in me and trusting that I can take care of myself."

"I believe in you. I always have. But I know that

bastard ex left you with more struggles than you admit to." He sighed. "It's not just about the money. I've raised kids with a partner by my side, and I've raised them alone. I know which is easier and which is harder."

"Just because we aren't getting married doesn't mean he won't be helping. There's more than one family model, Dad." She changed the subject. "Why didn't you tell me you already knew who he was?"

"Maybe because I figured you would tell us yourself. Guess we both had our poker faces on. Your brothers and I are sorry we didn't handle your news better," he added. "You caught us off guard."

They were caught off guard? She'd watched it avalanche on her and hadn't been able to stop it.

"Come back soon for dinner," her dad said. "Whether you bring your friend or not is up to you."

"I'm sure he's eager to repeat the experience."

Her father grunted. "Sass. Always with the sass."

She laughed, feeling something close to human again by the time she hung up the phone. Still, the sleepless night had taken its toll. By the time she reached the community center, she was stifling yawns and wondering if Shari would mind if they took a rain check on their girls' night.

Her best friend's sharp gaze clocked the shadows under her eyes immediately. "I take it meeting the family did not go well?" Shari said as they signed in at the welcome table.

"That would be accurate. But everyone knows about the baby now, so at least that's out of the way."

Shari's eyebrows shot up.

"Long story," Mia said. "Definitely too much to cram into the five minutes we have before the forum starts."

"Well, then it's lucky you're coming over after and that I'm a good listener. Or we can sit in silence and stare at the TV if you just need to zone out for a while. Whatever you need."

Mia bit her lip. "Those both sound like great options, but honestly, it'll be a miracle if I don't fall asleep during the meeting. I'm beat."

"So, another night. No problem."

"You're the best."

Shari grinned. "I really am."

When Jace texted Mia midmorning on Thursday to ask if he could take her to lunch, she was feeling recharged enough to accept. They agreed to meet at a bistro not far from the clinic. Before leaving to meet him, she brushed on some extra lipstick and mascara. She no longer looked like an extra for a zombie movie, but there was still room for improvement.

She didn't see his car in the parking lot when she arrived but spotted him immediately, already seated at a booth, once she walked inside.

He stood as she approached, earnestly scanning her expression. "Mia."

His obvious concern was touching. "It was a disaster of major proportions," she said as she slid into the booth, "but it wasn't all your fault."

"I still feel terrible."

"I talked to Dad yesterday. It was awkward, but not—"

"Hi, I'm Daisy. Can I get y'all started with something to drink?"

Since Mia didn't have long for lunch before she had to get back to the clinic, she asked if she could go ahead and order her entrée as well. She requested her favorite steak salad, minus the blue cheese, and Jace said he'd take the same.

Once they were alone again, he flashed her a surprisingly mischievous smile, apparently bouncing back to his usual self now that he knew she wasn't angry. "I have a surprise for you."

"Like introducing me to the reporter?" She still appreciated that but couldn't help wishing her family hadn't seen the article.

"No, much better than that. I was planning to do this after lunch, but I can't wait. Can you come outside with me for just a sec?"

"I guess so." If the surprise was gift-wrapped, she was glad he hadn't brought it in. The last thing she needed was a room full of waitstaff mistakenly serenading her with "Happy Birthday." In her opinion, no one needed that even *on* their birthday.

She followed him outside, glancing around. "Where are you parked?"

He pulled the keys from his pocket and hit a button on the car remote. A nearby blue sedan chirped in response.

"Pretty color," she commented.

"Glad you like it." He beamed at her like a kid on Christmas morning. "It's yours."

"What?"

"Come here." He took her hand and tugged her toward it, and she was too stunned to do anything other than follow along. As he pressed another button, one of the back doors slid open. "See, perfect for when you're carrying a car seat and don't have a hand free. And the trunk space when you lay the seat down is plenty big enough for a dog kennel. The safety ratings are—"

"Jace!" She pulled her hand back.

"Yeah?" He was practically vibrating with glee.

"I…" She stared, wondering where to begin. "I'm sure the safety ratings are great. But you can't buy me a car."

"I already did."

Because he wanted to make up for an unpleasant evening? "A car is not an apology." *Low stress, calming thoughts.* Mental image of the ocean…dunking Jace under the waves… "Apology gifts are, I don't know, a candy bar or a funny mug. Or a funny mug full of candy bars. How could you think I would accept this?"

"Why wouldn't you?"

"It's a *car*. A major life purchase."

"Okay, I know it's an expense, but proportionally, for me—"

"Right, because you're rich."

He looked hurt. "You don't have to say it like it's a character failing. I mean, it's not a virtue, either. It's just a fact. And sometimes it allows me to do good things for people. For instance…" He swept his arm toward the car. "It has more space than yours, more safety features, and the check engine light isn't blinking. But if it were, it would be covered under warranty."

He was trying his best to sound reasonable, and she paused, trying to match his tone. She didn't want to lash out, but her irritation that he wasn't hearing her was growing.

"Maybe it would even score me some points with your dad," he tried to joke.

"Oh, that's all I need! The men in my life deciding what I drive without my input."

A couple heading into the restaurant stopped to stare, and Mia realized how shrill she sounded. She took a deep breath and lowered her voice. "I know dinner with my family ended badly, but throwing money at uncomfortable situations isn't the solution. What happens when you become a dad yourself?"

He folded his arms over his chest. "What does that have to do with anything?"

"No matter how good a parent you are, there will be times your kid feels let down. Or gets mad. What then? You buy the kid a pony?"

"I live on a ranch. You're a large animal vet. Pretty sure our kid will have a pony."

"Oh my God!"

"You act like I got you a Corvette or I'm trying to buy your affections. Yes, I wanted to make a grand gesture, but this car is sensible."

Sensible was taking a sweater in case you got cold! "The gesture was too grand. And it makes me feel…" She didn't know how to articulate the pit in her stomach.

When Shari had seen she was upset, her friend had offered "whatever you need." Jace had decided on her behalf what she needed, then went out and splurged on it.

The last time she'd let a man insist on what would be best, she'd ended up filling out police reports and insurance claims. This was obviously different. Jace meant well. But at least Drew had given her the illusion of consulting with her.

"I'm sorry about lunch," she said, "but I don't have much of an appetite."

"Mia, wait." The frustration in his expression faded to chagrin. "You need to eat. I'll go if you want me to, but the baby—"

"It's okay. I have fruit in the fridge at the clinic." The last thing she wanted was to argue with him, but she wasn't sure how to politely sit across from him for the next twenty minutes and pretend this big blue mistake wasn't parked in the lot outside their window.

His shoulders slumped. He looked so crestfallen that she almost hugged him, but her own emotions were all over the map. Instead, she gave him a small wave. "Call me later, okay?"

On the way to the clinic, she consciously drove with a light foot, careful not to mash the brake or accelerator in her aggravation.

Amanda looked startled to see her back so soon. "I thought you had a lunch date."

"I did, but he tried to give me a free car, so I screamed at him in the parking lot and bolted."

Amanda tittered nervously, like she thought it was a joke but was confused about the punch line.

Join the club. Mia was confused by everything that had just transpired. Was Jace really deluded enough to think buying her a car was appropriate?

Maybe. After all, he had his own bowling alley in his garage. The mayor, a retired NBA player and an actress had all been present on their first date. Perhaps when your family owned a plane, cars started to seem like less of a big deal.

In his mind, maybe he'd bought her a bicycle, but with a better sound system and windshield wipers. She sighed, absolutely certain that she wasn't in the wrong but less certain that he *was*.

Leigh and Ian had once gone on a marriage retreat, and Leigh told her later it was all about learning to communicate with your partner in the same "language." Mia and Jace did not speak the same language. Could they successfully learn to?

And, bigger question, was it worth the time, effort and emotional energy to find out?

Nine

When Mia pulled up to her house Thursday evening, she was surprised to see Jace's car in the driveway—his actual car, not the Blue Mistake. He was sitting on her top porch step, ruggedly handsome in the sunlight, and even after all the missteps of the past few days, her heart leaped at the sight of him.

"Hey." She greeted him shyly, not sure where to start after her earlier outburst.

"Don't worry." He held his hands up in a placating gesture. "I returned the car."

"Thank you."

"And I thought very hard about what constitutes an appropriate apology gift. Will you give me another shot at it?"

"Sure, but I think you're missing the point," she said gently. For the first time, she wondered about the expectations of previous women in his life. Had they presumed expensive gifts and posh vacation getaways because of who he was? She'd been ill at ease with his wealth, but she hadn't realized that it probably also complicated relationships for him. "You don't need to buy me things."

"That's why you're going to like this better," Jace said enthusiastically. "I took a brand-new approach. Full disclosure, I also went by Shari's restaurant, threw myself on her mercy and begged for help. She let me into your house—under her supervision— with the spare key. I hope that's okay, but if not, please don't be mad at her."

"I'm not mad." Mia trusted her friend's judgment. Plus, her curiosity was piqued. "But I reserve the right to change my mind later."

"Noted."

He opened the front door for her, and Mia stepped into her living room, which currently evoked the waiting room of a spa. Electric candles had been placed along the coffee table and mantel, and classical music accompanied by nature sounds played through a wireless speaker. A handful of rose petals were scattered on the end tables, but not enough to create an overwhelming scent.

"Wow," she said. "This is nice."

"I picked up food from Shari's," he told her. "It's in the kitchen with heating instructions. If you're in agreement, I thought I could make you dinner and give you a foot rub. Or a back rub. Or both."

After standing all day and performing multiple surgeries this week? She almost moaned. "Congratulations, you've done it! This *is* the perfect gift."

"I'm glad you think so." He reached past her to retrieve something from the bookcase. "This was my plan B in case you didn't want my company."

When she saw the mug full of chocolate bars, laughter burbled out of her. How could she resist chocolate and a massage? *And how could I possibly resist those blue eyes?*

She wrapped her arms around him. "Thank you, Jace." She kissed him, and the strain of the last few days evaporated.

His mouth on hers caused the usual zing of pleasure, but it was even sharper, sweeter, than before. They'd argued, but instead of holding a grudge, he'd redoubled his efforts and reached out to her again, careful to meet her on her terms. *Learning to speak my language.* That was sexy in its own right.

Rising on tiptoe, she deepened their kiss, thanking him without words for his thoughtfulness. He buried his hands in her hair, nipping gently at her lower lip.

She angled her head back just long enough to ask, "Do we have time for a shower before dinner?"

"We?" he echoed, his eyes gleaming. "Oh, hell yes."

They stumbled, tangled in kisses, toward her bathroom. Watching him discard his clothes reminded her of the night they'd shared in the Climbing W's guest cabin, when they'd showered together after making love. He was stunning. And right now he was all hers.

She nearly purred. "I don't think I'll ever get used to how sexy you are."

"Back at you, Doc."

Unabashedly naked, he stepped forward to help her out of her clothes, taking his time and heightening the anticipation. His hand brushed the side of her breast as he lifted her shirt over her head, and her breath caught at the teasing contact. He crooked one finger in the band of her underwear, slowly drawing them down over her thighs. She was almost shuddering with longing by the time they stepped under the warm spray of the water.

Jace grabbed a bottle from the shower caddy. "Want that massage I promised?"

She quirked an eyebrow. "Why do I think this isn't going to be a relaxing experience?"

His smile was a wicked promise as he squeezed coconut bodywash into his palm. He worked the suds into a lather and cupped her nape with both hands, his fingers doing magical things to the muscles in her neck.

Her sigh was a sound of pure bliss. "Damn, you are good with your hands."

He kneaded his way to the front of her throat, sweeping his thumbs over her collarbone, following the tropical-scented rivulets to the swell of her breasts, his touch achingly gentle. He captured a handful of silky suds, drawing them across her nipple, then ducked his head to blow them away. The flirty, ethereal caress of his breath against her had her dissolving faster than the bubbles.

"You make me feel like soapsuds," she heard herself say. "Fizzy. Iridescent." The words were nonsensical, silly, and she would have understood if he laughed.

But his eyes darkened, and he leaned forward to kiss her. There was nothing silly about his touch as his soapy hands slid down her body, slicked over her curves and tugged her tight against him. She moaned into his mouth, raising one leg to hook around his hip, trying to close the distance between their bodies. All she accomplished was a delicious friction as she tried to keep her balance.

She was surprised when he turned her away from him, toward the water, his hands sluicing the suds from her shoulders before palming her breasts and slowly trailing down her torso. Once all the bodywash had been rinsed away, he reached to turn off the faucet.

"Are we done here?" she asked eagerly. As much as she'd been enjoying the shower, it provided certain logistical challenges, and her bed was just a few feet beyond the bathroom door.

"In here, yes. But I'm definitely not done with you." He leaned in to lick a bead of water from the side of her neck, and Mia trembled in response. "God, you smell delicious."

He wrapped a towel around her, not bothering with one for himself, and carried her into the bedroom, laying her sideways across the comforter before falling on her with hungry, avid kisses that made her toes curl. The towel fell open, and he worked his way down her body until his lips brushed her inner thigh. Mia was quaking with need, her legs wantonly splayed to give him better access, her pulse racing. Even though she knew what was coming, the heat of his mouth on her was still an erotic shock to the system.

He shifted, his grin devilish. "I was right. You are delicious." Then he repositioned them so that her knees rested over his muscular shoulders, the sight of his dark head between her legs decadently carnal. Mia's body arched, taut with pleasure and heat and thrumming energy that built with every flick of his tongue. Her fingers bunched the comforter on either side of her, and she offered herself up to Jace with an abandon more powerful than she'd ever known. She could feel a cry in the back of her throat, but when he sucked hard at her clit, the orgasm that overtook her was so powerful that for a moment, she couldn't make sound. With a gasp, she went up on her elbows, her head thrown back as wave after wave of satisfaction rippled through her.

"Jace."

Lightning-quick, he was there with her, kissing her deeply as he thrust into her still trembling body, drawing out her own climax as he found his. They didn't speak afterward, but clung to each other, damp and replete.

It felt like the room was spinning, but in a good way, rocking her to sleep. Mia couldn't keep her eyes open. Languid darkness closed in around her. She gave in to it, drifting off before she had a chance to tell Jace that what he'd just done was a far more luxurious gift than a car.

"NO!"

Mia shot awake, confused. It took her a second to remember that she wasn't alone in her bed and to realize that Jace was the source of anguish she'd heard. "Jace?"

His eyes were open but staring forward, past her, unseeing.

She poked him in the side with her finger. "Hey, Jace. Are you okay?"

He slowly focused on her, his face more pale than she'd ever seen it. Maybe it was partly because of the moonlight washing out the room, but she didn't think so.

"Bad dream?" she asked.

He sat up, swinging his legs over the side of the bed. "Sorry."

"Nightmares are involuntary, nothing you need to apologize for." She put an arm around him, resting her chin lightly on his shoulder. "Do you want to talk about it?"

"No." His voice was raw. "But I might as well warn

you. It's bound to happen again." He pulled away from her and began to pace alongside her bed. "It's always the same nightmare. Reliving my parents' accident."

Reliving? "You were in the car with them?" It was too horrible to imagine.

Although he didn't answer her question directly, his grim expression was reply enough. *He must have been terrified.* She recalled his trying to tell her yesterday about the new car's safety ratings. She regretted rejecting the gift so harshly. Her own minor accident last spring had left her more worried about crashes. What he had endured...

"You should go back to bed," he told her.

"What about you?" Whenever she'd had a nightmare as a kid, her dad would reassure her that it had only been a dream, that whatever scary image she'd conjured wasn't real. But she couldn't offer Jace the same comfort. His nightmare was all too real. "Can I get you a glass of water? A shot of whiskey?"

After a second, the corner of his mouth quirked. It wasn't quite a smile, but it was a vast improvement over his earlier frozen expression. "Is that what you'll offer our kid when he or she has bad dreams?"

"Of course not—whiskey's much too strong for a kid. Vodka, obviously."

He did smile then, and the knot of tension inside her loosened. "You're going to be a great mom." The compliment was tinged with sadness, and she knew he was still thinking about his own parents.

"I'm going to try," she promised. There were still

moments when the fact that she would be a mother didn't seem quite real. She got out of the bed. "Come with me."

They went down the hall to the guest room, which was so seldom used that it had become easy storage for everything from off-season clothes to her Christmas tree. It wasn't messy, but it was cluttered.

Jace raised an eyebrow. "I've heard pregnant women go through a 'nesting' phase, but this is an odd time to decide you want to organize a room."

"The nursery," she said. "Eventually. What do you think—crib along that wall?"

"If you move the treadmill, sure."

She laughed. "Maybe a garage sale before the baby comes would be prudent. Or hauling some stuff down to the basement. Not me personally," she quickly added when he scowled at her. "I do have brothers, remember?"

"How could I forget?" Jace put his arms around her, resting his hands protectively over her abdomen. "Have you talked to them yet?"

"Only through awkward texts. I think they're embarrassed, but they'll come around. Or Leigh will kick their asses."

"I told my family, too. About the baby."

She craned her head to look up at him. "You did? How'd that go?"

"They were happy for me." He sounded bemused. "And weirdly supportive. Harry offered…"

"Offered what?" she asked when he fell silent.

"To babysit if we ever need it," he finally said.

"Oh. Well, that's nice of him, but still a long ways off. What I really need is a nursery theme. Got any ideas?"

After a second, he grinned. "Cowboys and ponies? Maybe a pastel mural of cattle along the far wall."

"Mint-green and yellow cows? Never mind, I'll ask Shari. She has good taste."

"Shari!" He clapped a hand to his forehead. "I never cooked you that dinner I promised."

"We got a little sidetracked." Now that she thought about it, she *was* hungry. "But if you're offering now…"

So they walked to the kitchen, hand in hand, discussing baby furniture and laughing about paint colors, the lingering hurt of past tragedy fading in the light of future joy.

"Mr. Malone?" Carol's voice came through the intercom on Jace's desk. "There are two men here to see you."

Jace straightened his tie. "From the certification commission?" They were early, but he was excited to take this meeting.

"Um, no, sir. Ian and Dylan Zane?"

Ah. Mia's brothers had come to toss him out a window. He supposed that had been inevitable. "Please show them back, Carol." He found himself anxious to face them. For Mia's sake, he wanted to establish a good rapport—if that were still possible.

Carol ushered in Mia's unsmiling brothers and offered to bring them and Jace coffee. All three men declined, then stood silently, taking each other's measure like gunslingers in the Old West.

"Please, sit down," Jace invited them.

They did so, exchanging glances, as if silently debating which one of them should speak.

Ian sighed. "It was good of you to agree to see us, especially after how we acted."

"Leigh called us idiotic jackasses," Dylan put in. "Repeatedly."

Ian scrubbed a hand over his face. "It might not seem like it, given how much we upset her, but we adore Mia. I remember the day she came home from the hospital, her tiny pink face. She was the most fragile thing I'd ever seen. It's hard to remember she's not fragile now. When I realized you…that she…"

"We know she's a grown woman," Dylan said. "But she's barely over Drew. The last thing we want is to see her get hurt again."

"I would never intentionally hurt her," Jace promised them. Even if his and Mia's relationship hadn't started in the most traditional of ways, it was important they knew she was a priority. "I care about her a lot."

"So do we. And she deserved better from us than what she got," Ian said. "We reacted poorly."

"We should have kept our noses out of your business," Dylan said. "At least we don't have to worry that *you're* going to steal from her, so that's something."

"Steal from her?"

Once again, the two brothers exchanged glances. Jace put the pieces together. "Like Andrew did?"

"Right." Ian looked woeful. "She asked me, you know, if I thought it was a good idea for spouses to be business partners or if that would put too much strain on the relationship. I ride to work every day with Leigh and have lunch with her on the quad. I thought it would make their foundation even stronger. I didn't know he was going to embezzle from the practice and jeopardize her loan!"

Jace saw red. Her ex was the reason Mia worked until she dropped? That she pushed herself until her blood pressure was too high and still drove a car with a blinking check engine light?

"How could you have known?" Dylan tried to reassure his brother. "She doesn't blame you."

"Anyway." Ian cleared his throat. "You're a busy man, and we shouldn't take up more of your time. We just thought we owed you a face-to-face apology."

"I appreciate that. And please know that, busy or not, I'll always be here for Mia and the baby."

Ian stood. "For your sake, I hope the first one's a girl. If she's older than her brothers, maybe they won't grow up to be overprotective clods."

"Or just have all girls," Dylan said as he followed his brother out.

Jace was still trying to determine how to be the best father he could to *one* child, much less future children. So why was it so easy to imagine a pair of little girls who looked like their beautiful mother?

When Grandpa Harry had offered the family ring, Jace would have taken it if he thought Mia would accept. Did that mean that he loved her, or was he simply being too impulsive? *Like I was with the car.* He had a track record of careless actions and hasty decisions. But, as Mia had pointed out, mistakes were how people grew. He was proud of everything he was accomplishing at Malone Energy and proud of his closer relationship with his family. It gave him hope that he could truly be a great dad.

Maybe even a man worthy of Mia's love.

Ten

Ever since Mia had told her staff that she was pregnant, there was a new buzz of curiosity at their Friday morning meetings, as if they couldn't wait to see what other bombshells she dropped. So everyone was avidly listening when Mia told her techs she was officially looking for another veterinarian. "Let me know if you're friends with anyone who wants to switch practices," she encouraged them. "I'm not trying to poach, but I definitely want someone in place before my third trimester. There are a lot of changes coming, and I thank you all in advance for your patience. One change is, starting today, we close an hour earlier on Fridays."

A cheer went up, but it was bittersweet in Mia's

ears. She knew she had to cut back her hours, but it felt like backwards progress.

She palmed her stomach. *You're worth it, kiddo.*

"On to new business," she said, trying to sound enthusiastic. "I appreciate everyone who's already chipped in to help us get ready for the Heritage Festival, but we still have room for anyone who wants to volunteer for a shift at the booth. And if any of our clients ask about submitting a picture for the Pet Wall of Fame, please direct them to Amanda, who is putting the display together."

Once the meeting ended, she retreated to her office to put her feet up for a few minutes before her first appointment. Having taken Dr. Bakshi's warnings to heart, she closed her eyes and did some deep breathing exercises, doing her best to think calming, oceanic thoughts. The clinic had been her number one priority for so long, but she had to accept that she would be facing a few limitations as a brand-new mom. *Temporarily.* Yes, it would take her longer than she'd planned to pay off the building, and the expansion she'd dreamed of would have to wait. But there would still be cats and dogs and horses and pigs who needed her after her maternity leave.

As long as my competitors don't grow so fast that my little clinic becomes obsolete.

Crap, that was not a calming thought.

Determined to shake off her funk, she pulled out her phone and texted Jace. We still on for movie night?

His response was almost immediate. Absolutely. The private theater is the big building behind the barn. I'll send the ushers to help you find it.

Ha ha.

It was funny how quickly a person's *normal* could shift. Most of her Friday nights over the past year had been spent at the nearby animal hospital or eating takeout from Shari's restaurant, and tonight she would be hanging out with a few billionaires on a ranch that had been featured in numerous magazines and apparently even an HGTV segment.

Still, while that thought might have once intimidated her, she was becoming more and more comfortable at the Triple Pine. When she crossed through the black iron front gate that evening, she found herself humming, the happiest she'd been all day.

One of the house staff let her in, and Reed greeted her in the foyer, Brooke on his hip. "Jace had to take a call, but he'll make it quick. Come on in."

She nodded to the baby. It was the first time she'd seen her awake. "She's beautiful. Do you mind if I hold her, or is she shy with strangers?"

"Not shy, but you might want to lose the earrings. She's in an extremely grabby phase."

Mia laughed. "Thanks for the warning." She slipped the earrings into her pocket and took the infant, inhaling the sweet scent of lavender shampoo and baby powder. Her stomach gave an odd little flip-flop, and she swallowed back a lump of emotion. "The only baby I was really ever around was my niece, but she's thirteen now, so it's been a while."

"Well, if it makes you feel any better," Reed said, "Jace has never been around a baby until Brooke, so you're on even footing. But between you and me, I think he's going to be a great dad. I recently realized I don't give him enough credit."

She arched an eyebrow. "I could have told you that."

"Mia!" Jace came over to hug her, including baby Brooke in the embrace. "Sorry, I had to talk to the pilot about next week's trip."

Most people making travel plans would talk to an airline's customer service team, but no, he was chatting with the actual pilot. Of their private jet. Would that, too, eventually seem normal?

She poked him lightly in the ribs. "We can have popcorn with the movie, right? Not, like, foie gras?"

He laughed. "Air-popped, and no butter or salt, per Kevin's orders. Harry is fit to be tied."

"Actually, the lack of salt would make my OB happy, too. You can tell him he's making the sacrifice for me." She handed Brooke back to her dad.

"We'll be there in a minute," Jace told Reed. "But can I show Mia Brooke's nursery? Maybe get some ideas for the baby registry?"

"Of course. I think I still have the decorator's card if you want it," Reed offered.

An interior decorator? Mia had been thinking more in terms of a long afternoon of assembling a crib with

Shari and asking Jace to paint the walls. Shaking her head, she followed Jace up the stairs.

"I wanted to mention a few things before we start the movie," he told her. "First, my trip next week is going to be a little longer than I realized. Feel free to send me indecent texts while I'm gone." He wagged his eyebrows at her. "Secondly, your brothers came to my office."

She almost missed a step. "Oh, God. I'm so sorry. Did you have security boot them from the building?"

He laughed. "It wasn't like that. They apologized. We bonded."

"Really?"

At the top of the landing, he turned to study her. "How come you never told me about Andrew? I mean, you did, but not everything. He stole from you?"

She bit her lip, briefly envying only children who didn't have siblings to give up their secrets.

"Dylan might have let a few details slip," Jace said. "I'm pretty sure he thought I already knew."

"Please don't take it personally that I didn't tell you. It's not really relevant to us." She sighed. "And, if I'm being honest, it's embarrassing as hell. Trusting the wrong person made me feel like a fool. That's not how I want you to see me."

"Never," he said softly. He tipped up her chin, and she saw the sincerity in his eyes. "You're a smart, capable, *very* sexy woman. And your ex is a conniving rat bastard. That's not on you."

"I appreciate that. But I don't want to focus on

what he did. I want to look ahead, keep moving forward."

"Good. Because that's the other thing I wanted to talk about." Jace led her into the nursery and switched on the light. The room was weather-themed, with a puffy rainbow mobile over a crib with sunny yellow bedding. The walls were painted sky blue, and one was stenciled with smiling raindrops. "I was tucking her in recently and looking at the nursery, thinking about our baby. And it raised some questions."

"Like what kind of monitors are the best?"

"Like whether I should move out. And I decided the answer is yes."

She blinked. He was leaving the Triple Pine? He'd talked about his years away and how important reconciliation with his family was. And it wasn't as if they were cramped here—he practically had his own wing. "Are you sure?"

"I am. And I wanted you to be the first to know."

"Before Harry and your brothers?" Poor Harry. "Your grandfather will be sorry to see you go."

"Maybe, but he'll support the decision. It's the right thing for us, Doc. I don't know exactly what our co-parenting is going to look like, but finding my own space allows me to make all the accommodations that I—that we—might need."

"You're doing this for me?" It was as unnerving as it was flattering. "The timing is ironic. Because on the drive in, I realized how at home I'm starting to feel."

"At the Triple Pine?"

Yes. But also, with him. "Have you ever been on a bad vacation?"

He frowned, but she wasn't sure whether his confusion was at her non sequitur or at the idea of a subpar holiday. Billionaires probably didn't stay in motels with lumpy beds and tepid swimming pools.

"The whole point of a vacation is to get away," she said, "but sometimes they lose your luggage and the resort doesn't look at all like it did in the brochure and the people in the next room are too loud and you realize all you want is to be home, sleeping in your own bed. Motherhood, a relationship—they weren't things I wanted for myself right now. At least, I didn't think they were. But I'm more excited about this baby every day, and being with you... Being with you feels like coming home."

His eyes shone. "That's one of the nicest things anyone's ever said to me."

She swallowed. "Well, I mean it."

"Mia, I—"

"Are you two joining us anytime soon?" Reed hollered from the bottom of the stairs. "At this rate, they'll have a sequel made before we get the movie started."

"There in a second," Jace called back.

"Slowpokes!"

"Slow?" Mia couldn't help laughing at the irony. "Hardly. Everything's changing so fast."

"Isn't it great?" Jace beamed at her.

"Um…" Parts of it were. But just because change was exhilarating didn't mean it was easy. Jace, however, seemed downright giddy.

"I moved back to Colorado actively seeking change," he reminded her. "And I got even more than I could have hoped. Moving out is an extension of that. It's celebrating the possibility of the future, celebrating all the changes still to come."

"It sounds more exciting when you describe it. I wish you'd been at our staff meeting this morning. I could have used you as a hype man. My view of change wasn't quite as enthusiastic. I did announce that we were cutting back hours. That went over well," she said sourly.

His gaze turned sympathetic. "It's only temporary."

"Right, I know." There was no reason for it to feel like she was failing. She tried to shake it off. "I was promised a movie and some flavorless popcorn?"

He laughed. "Coming right up." But he paused at the doorway, sliding his hands down over her baby bump. "Mia, just think. This time next year we'll be having conversations like these in the middle of *our* kid's nursery."

Their gazes locked, and the sweetness of the moment washed over her. Jace was right. Some changes were beautiful.

If anyone had told Mia that she could listen to the procedural details of a corporate certification process as raptly as she could a symposium on equine theriogenology, she wouldn't have believed them. But Jace was so passionate in his nightly updates that she looked forward to their phone calls all day.

Plus, it probably helped that she was wild about him.

As if to prove that point, her phone chirped, and her heart leaped. "Hi."

"Sorry I couldn't call sooner," he said. "Dinner ran late. You weren't asleep yet, were you?"

"Nope. Just got into bed."

"Wish I were there."

She chuckled. "No, you don't. This is too important to you. It's a major factor in why you came back to Colorado."

"True. But when I came back, I didn't know you yet. You are also major."

"Aw. You should write greeting cards."

"Smart-ass. How was work?"

"Good. Everyone's excited for the festival tomorrow."

He made a noise. She knew that he was caught between wanting to be supportive and worrying that she was overextending herself.

"I'll be sitting most of the day," she assured him. "I have plenty of help, and I'm not doing any of the heavy lifting."

"I know, I know. But I'd still feel better if I was there to lend a hand. When I get home Sunday, I plan to pamper you. You won't need to lift a finger."

She sighed happily, not because she particularly needed pampering but just because she was eager to see him. She hadn't expected to miss him so much this week. It had really brought into focus how big a part of her life Jace had become. When he got back, she wanted to discuss their relationship, their future. Childbirth classes started in a month and a half. When everyone went around and introduced themselves, it would be nice if she had a better response than, "And this is Jace, my uh…? I don't really know."

They chatted about how his day had gone and the steps Malone Energy was taking to meet the certification criteria. There were a number of positives in what Jace was attempting to do, but one of them was that it seemed to be bringing him and his brothers closer together. She was glad. As irksome as her own brothers could occasionally be, family was important.

"I should let you get some sleep," he said as he wound down. "I keep forgetting it's an hour later there, and you have a big day tomorrow."

"I hope I *can* sleep. We're having a heat wave, and it's miserable." Last night she'd been restless and prickly, kicking away her sheets and getting up several times throughout the night to splash water on her face.

"Now I'm really sorry I'm not there. I bet I could help you unwind."

She smiled, a different kind of warmth suffusing

her. "That was certainly the case the last time you spent the night."

"I miss the way you taste. The way you move against my mouth."

Damn. No wonder she was wild about him. "And if I wanted to return the favor?" The thought of taking him in her mouth, being able to wring the same kind of shattering bliss he'd given her, had powerful appeal.

On the other end of the phone, there was a sharp intake of breath. "I'll wake the pilot. We can be there in an hour."

She laughed. "I'll see you Sunday."

"Well, thank you for the sweet dreams I know I'll be having."

She hoped he was right. If it were within her power, she would definitely replace his periodic nightmares with pleasurable fantasies. "Good night, Jace." *I love you.* The words were on the tip of her tongue, a surprise and yet not a surprise. She repeated it in her head, giving herself a moment to process. It was true. She did love him. "I…"

"Doc?" he prompted. "Did I lose you?"

Quite the opposite. But she wanted the first time she told him to be in person. "Sorry, forgot what I was going to say. Pregnancy brain. See you in a couple of days," she reiterated.

"Counting the minutes."

Laughter and the sounds of varying midway games surrounded the booth. It was clear that festival attendees were enjoying themselves despite nearly record-setting heat. Mia was grateful for the ever-present misting fans posted throughout the fairground, but she was still sweating copiously.

Shari fanned herself with one of the sample restaurant menus on display. "Think condo management would let me fill the swimming pool with ice cubes when I get home?"

"Sounds entirely reasonable to me," Mia said. They'd talked to a lot of people today, and she thought that their promotional efforts had been worth the time, but she would also be glad when the day was over. "I'm surprised Amanda isn't back with our drinks yet." They'd started the day with a small cooler of beverages, but the three of them had finished those before lunch, and Mia's refillable water bottle had been empty for the last hour.

Shari snorted. "I'm not. She has a huge crush on that cutie volunteering with concessions. Brad? Brent? Haven't you noticed her trips have been getting longer and longer?"

Mia laughed. "I hadn't realized. Far be it from me to begrudge her a happy love life."

"You mean like the one you have?" Shari asked slyly. "You're *glowing.* And I don't think it's because you're pregnant."

"I…love him, Shar. I haven't told him yet, but I do."

Her friend smiled. "Lucky for you, he feels exactly the same way."

Mia's toes curled. "I hope so. I think so."

"Pfft. I've seen how that man looks at you."

Mia wondered what the next step was for them. She knew he wanted to move out of the Triple Pine. Would it be folly to suggest they try living together? She didn't know if it was too soon, but it would certainly make co-parenting easier. More than that, though, she wanted to be around him. Pure and simple. She wanted to start her mornings and end her days with him.

"Speaking of love lives…" Mia nudged her friend in the side, tilting her head toward the handsome man approaching their booth.

"Hello, beautiful." Adwin grinned at Shari. "Is it hot out here, or is it just you?"

Shari groaned. "Hacky lines like that will be why I block your number."

He leaned on the table. "Nah, you aren't petty enough to ghost a guy over terrible lines. You care about the big issues. Like crunchy peanut butter versus smooth."

"So true." She popped out of her seat long enough to give him a quick kiss hello.

He looked from her to Mia. "Seriously, it is hot out here. Are you ladies surviving okay? I can get you a couple of sodas or ice-cream bars if you want. It will take a few minutes, though. The lines for drinks are long."

"Thanks," Shari said, "but our assistant should be back any minute with some. What I really need is intel. What are the best restaurant booths you've visited? I like to keep tabs on my competition."

As they discussed a nearby barbecue vendor—and whether sauced barbecue was equal to dry rub—a little girl with pigtails and a superhero cape pinned to her T-shirt approached Mia. "Are you the vet lady?"

Mia nodded. "I am indeed."

The girl held up a photo of a guinea pig. "This is Freckles. Mommy said he could go on the Famous Wall."

Mia chuckled. "I'd be happy to put him on our Wall of Fame, and if you'd like, my friend Shari here has some mini cupcakes." Mia stood to add Freckles to the display, and an unpleasant *whoosh* went through her, as if she were trying to stand on a rocking boat.

Her vision dimmed, and her pulse pounded so hard that it blocked out the noise of the festival. Then she heard Shari call her name, although it sounded really far away, and Adwin had his arms around her, trying to help her up.

Mia hadn't even realized she was on the ground. But when she tried to stand, the pounding got worse. Everything went gray and silent.

As Jace thanked the driver who'd brought him to the private airport, he thought about the lectures Reed used to give him on work ethic. His brother just hadn't used the right motivation. There had never been a beautiful redhead involved. Since Jace had finished all of the training modules early, there was no reason for him to stay for additional sessions tomorrow, which meant he could get home early and surprise Mia.

If that didn't motivate a man to work faster, he didn't know what would.

As he boarded the plane, he wondered if Dr. Bakshi would okay Mia taking a short flight. He'd love to sweep her away somewhere for a long weekend. Lord knew the woman could use a vacation. Maybe once she'd finished the interview process and had another vet established at the clinic, she'd agree to going away. And after the baby was born, it would be amazing to travel together. For the three of them to visit new places, for Jace to see the world through his son's or daughter's eyes.

Although…making plans to travel the globe as a family might be skipping ahead a few steps. Jace should figure out where he was going to live before he started making plans to travel the globe.

He was settling in his seat when his phone vibrated. He pulled it out of his pocket, surprised to see Shari's number. "Hello?"

"Jace, I'm so glad I caught you. I didn't want to leave a voice mail."

"Is everything okay? Is Mia okay?"

"I think so. But she collapsed at the festival. It was sweltering out there, so it's probably nothing more serious than heat exhaustion. The on-scene paramedics were concerned about her heart rate, though, so they took her to the hospital."

Hospital. The word reverberated in his ears. Mia was in the hospital? Adrenaline surged through him, the need to reach her clawing at him.

"I'm headed there now," Shari said. "I'll call you as soon as I have an update. I debated whether I should wait until later to let you know, but you care about her as much as I do, and if our positions were reversed…"

"You did the right thing. We're about to be wheels up. I'll be there in two hours." And he already knew they'd be some of the longest, most grueling minutes of his life.

The ER nurse had suggested Mia rest, but with the beep of machines monitoring both her heart and the baby's, not to mention the IV in her arm, Mia hadn't thought she would be able to fall asleep. She must have been wrong, though, because when she opened her eyes, it was dark outside, and Shari was sitting on a nearby chair.

"You're awake!" The unexpected male voice was thick with relief.

Mia whipped her head around and found Jace standing on the other side of the bed. "Shari, do you see him too, or did I hit my head when I fell?"

Jace tried to laugh, but it sounded strangled. "I'm here."

"Is it tomorrow already? How long was I out?"

"Still festival day." Shari joined them on the side of Mia's hospital bed. "You scared the hell out of me, hon. If your plan was a big dramatic moment to draw a crowd to our booth, I wish you'd clued me in first."

"How are you feeling?" Jace asked. "The doctor said you're okay, that the baby's fine, but your pulse was so fast they're keeping you for observation."

Mia had been told the palpitations were probably due to dehydration, but she was going to Dr. Bakshi's office to follow up on Monday. "It was scary— it was just so *sudden*—but I'm okay." The concern in Jace's eyes melted her heart. "Really."

He squeezed her hand, his eyes overbright, and then blinked hard, looking away.

Following Shari's lead, Mia tried to make a joke of it. "If I'd known it would get you back sooner, I would have fainted two days ago. Missed you."

"You say that now, but wait until I don't leave your side for the rest of the pregnancy. You'll get pretty sick of me."

"Your dad wanted to be here, too," Shari said, "but he and Dylan were camping, and it took me a while to reach them. He said they could come in the morning, but you'll probably be discharged by then. And Amanda sent those." She pointed across the room to a ludicrously large flower arrangement that Mia had somehow not yet noticed.

"Good Lord." Mia stared incredulously. "She could have brought me an entire rosebush, and it would have been smaller."

"When she heard 'dehydration,' she freaked out that it took her so long to bring drinks back."

"Oh, no. Please make sure she knows it wasn't her fault. It was a combination of things. Pregnant bodies don't regulate temperature well."

"Knock knock." The nurse said it out loud instead of actually knocking against the partially opened door. "I'm afraid visiting hours are technically over, although for our pregnant patients, we do allow the father to stay if you'd like."

"You don't have to," Mia told Jace. "I'll probably be asleep again as soon as she's done, and that bench thing in the corner makes my college futon look like the height of luxury."

"Nice try, but I already warned you. You won't be getting rid of me anytime soon."

She exhaled in relief. It had been a harrowing day, and what she really wanted was to scoot over in the narrow bed and let him hold her. For now, she'd settle for knowing he was close by as she slept. "Good. When I said you didn't have to stay, I was just being polite."

He kissed her forehead. "I'm not going anywhere, Doc."

Headlights sliced through the windshield at the wrong angle, and Jace knew impact was inevitable. He spun the wheel, but there was no response. In the passenger seat, Mia screamed as metal scraped metal, and glass shattered.

"Mia!"

Jace was already upright before he realized he was in a dim hospital room and not a car spinning out of control. His breath came in ragged pants, and he reached for the nearest wall to steady himself, adrenaline pounding through his veins. The nightmare about his parents. He'd never had it about anyone else before.

Miraculously, he hadn't woken Mia. She was still, her breathing reassuringly deep and even, the beep of her monitors reminding him that it had only been a dream. Still, he needed to see her face, needed to reach out and touch her warm skin and know that she was alive and well and here with him.

He tiptoed closer to her bedside, taking in her familiar features and the graceful sweep of her lashes above her cheeks. *I love her.* As terrified as he'd been for both her and the baby earlier today, this was no longer just about the fact that he and Mia were having a child together. Mia challenged him and made him laugh and listened to him. She turned him on so much he could barely remember his own name, but hers would be engraved on his heart for the rest of his life.

The flip side of love, though, was loss. He was vulnerable now in a way he hadn't thought possible again. If anything happened to her, it would be like having a hole punched through him.

She's worth the risk. He wouldn't willingly give up what they shared. Hell, no. He'd fight for it, doing everything in his power to protect their relationship. To protect her.

He stared at the clock on the wall. It was only about an hour before sunset, and he definitely wouldn't be going back to sleep, so he began to plan, mapping out what needed to be done. Heath was an early riser, and there was no one Jace trusted more for financial advice. He'd call his brother soon.

Later, he'd talk to Grandpa Harry. He needed to share his plans to move out. And it was time to ask for that wedding ring.

"Morning!" the nurse chirped. She rolled the cart with the blood pressure cuff toward Mia. "And how are we feeling?"

"We" are feeling like "we" could have used a lot more sleep before someone came to check vitals. But with a thermometer in her mouth, Mia limited her response to a thin smile. Had Jace managed any sleep? She glanced around the room.

"That tall drink of water who was with you said he'd be right back," the nurse said. "He hated to leave your side. So romantic."

Nothing about hospitals was romantic, but Mia's heart warmed anyway.

Sure enough, Jace returned a few minutes later, just missing the nurse, who assured Mia all her vitals were strong and within healthy ranges. Even her blood pressure.

"Did you bring me a file baked into a cake?" she asked him. "I need you to spring me from this joint."

He laughed. "I saw some plastic spoons in the cafeteria. Maybe we can tunnel our way out."

Blessedly, they didn't have to wait long for the doctor on rounds to come by and confirm her discharge. In under two hours, she was climbing into Jace's car, ready to put this entire misadventure behind her.

"When was the last time you ate anything besides hospital food?" Jace asked as she buckled her seat belt. "Want me to pick up somewhere along the way?"

She shook her head. "I'd rather get straight home and take a bath as soon as possible."

"All right. I can cook for us while you do that."

"Deal."

Once she'd had a bath and "the Jace specialty" (scrambled eggs and mildly burned toast), she felt completely restored. But she was unsurprised that Jace still insisted she take it easy.

He put his arm around her, snuggling her close on the couch. "We can binge that fashion competition you pretend you're not addicted to."

She laughed. "If you had to wear scrubs all the time, you'd get excited about alternate wardrobes, too."

"Speaking of things to wear…" He scooted away from her and slid off the sofa, kneeling in front of her. "I know I didn't come through on the cake with a file. But what I do have to offer you is my heart. And this." He held up a blue box. "I love you, Mia."

"I love you, too." The words practically leaped out of her, and she was surprised she'd been able to keep them in this long.

"Will you marry me?" He opened the box to reveal a diamond ring that twinkled at her, dazzling through the blur of her sudden tears.

"Oh my God." Happiness flooded her, but she was almost too overwhelmed to process what was happening. Here she'd been wondering if moving in together was too big a leap, and he'd upped the ante. It was a big step, but it felt strangely right. Far more so than the previous time she'd gotten engaged, to a man she'd known far longer. *I've never loved anyone like this before.* And Jace loved her. She closed her eyes, savoring the moment.

He must have read her silence as uncertainty because he shifted, an undertone of nervousness beneath his bravado. "If you need me to sweeten the deal, I have the perfect engagement gift."

She opened her eyes, taking in the sight of the man she loved, eager to share a future with her. "It doesn't get much more perfect than this."

Rejoining her on the couch, he pulled her close for a sweet, searching kiss full of promise and possibility. Their kisses became deeper, fervent, and she was practically in his lap before they came up for air.

"I don't suppose," she asked hopefully, "that the gift you mentioned is spending the day in bed together?"

"You're supposed to be taking it easy." His tone

was heavy with regret. He kissed her once more, chastely this time, and then angled away from her as if trying to remove himself from temptation. "But we could sit in bed and discuss plans for the nursery. Or plans for the clinic." He paused, then grinned at her with endearingly boyish enthusiasm. "It's yours."

"You mean it's my choice?"

"No, I mean the clinic is yours. That's the gift. I paid off the loan."

"You did what?" *No no no no no.* Was that even legal? She'd heard of anonymous donors paying off student loans and residential mortgages. Hell, maybe he'd bought the bank. "I can't believe you."

"You aren't happy." He was staring at her as if she'd sprouted a second head. Like *she* was the odd-ity in the room.

"No shit." Had he learned *nothing* from the car incident? This was so much worse.

"But now you can stop worrying about it. You can take the time off for your maternity leave without stressing over—"

"It's my stress!" She shot to her feet. "My life. Not yours to play god with."

"That isn't fair," he objected. "I'm not trying to control anything. I was only trying to help."

"Then you should have asked me what kind of help I needed." After all the extra hours she'd worked, after all the contingency plans she'd lain awake at night devising… "You've busted your ass trying to get Malone Energy certified. How would you feel if you walked into work one morning and found that Reed or Heath had taken over the project without talking to you, completed it without your input?"

He flinched. "It's not the same, though. Your health's on the line. I was in a position to look after you."

"Goddamn it. As I have told my father and brothers repeatedly, I *do not need* a man to look out for me."

"Mia." His placating tone set her teeth on edge. If his next words were to tell her to calm down, she feared for his safety.

"What I want in life is a partner," she told him. "Not someone who thinks throwing money at everything magically solves problems." If that was Jace's approach to all of their conflicts, she would always be at a disadvantage in their relationship. They'd never be equal.

"I know better than anyone that money's not magic." His expression darkened. "Being rich didn't stop my parents from dying. I can't buy back their lives, which will haunt me for the rest of mine. They're dead because of me."

She blinked, still pissed off, but responding on some level to the pain in his voice. "That's not true."

He waved a hand. "I didn't cause the accident, but I'm why we were in the car. At that intersection. They'd come to clean up one of my messes because I was a selfish fuckup. But I'm not anymore. So I won't apologize for doing everything in my power to protect the ones I love. I genuinely thought you'd be happy about the loan, but I'd do it again anyway."

His bald statement knocked the wind out of her. "You had no right."

"I disagree."

She sat back down. The diamond ring winked up at her from the floor, where it had been dropped while they were kissing. With Jace's mouth on hers, their bodies and desires in sync, she'd felt in total harmony with him. But that bubble had popped, nothing more than a fragile illusion. "You should go. And you should take this with you." She scooped up the ring and held it out to him.

He jerked away from her, stricken. "Wait, no. I understand you're upset, but—"

"You understand *that* I'm upset, but not why. Which means you don't understand me." Worse, he'd already said he would do the same thing over again, in spite of her express wishes. It was a violation, and she didn't know how to make him see that.

"Keep the ring for now." He refused to take it. "You don't have to make a decision right this minute."

"That's rich, coming from you." He could have talked to her about the loan before taking decisive action, offered to help without taking the choice away from her.

He clenched his jaw but didn't respond. Finally he said, "Are you sure you're okay to be alone?"

Frankly, she was more worried about her state of mind if he *didn't* leave. "I'm sure."

He nodded stiffly and was gone a moment later, his absence echoing through the house. And in the sudden emptiness in her chest.

She set the ring on the table, wishing Jace had taken it. She didn't want to touch it. She could barely bring herself to look at it. So she grabbed the quilt she kept folded on the back of the couch and covered up the reminder of that brief, shining second when she'd truly thought she'd found the man of her dreams.

Well, that's the thing about dreams. Sooner or later, you always had to wake up.

Eleven

Jace stood in the tastefully appointed employee lounge, waiting for the coffee to finish brewing. He could have asked Carol to bring him some, but she'd taken to regarding him with such naked sympathy that he was currently avoiding her.

"You look like refried hell." Reed made this observation from the doorway.

Jace flipped his brother the bird without looking up.

"Fair enough," Reed said. "But you're starting to bring down office morale. What do you think about taking a few days off?"

That suggestion caused a hot stab of panic. Work at least gave Jace something to distract him from the fact that Mia hadn't called and wouldn't answer his calls. Without his job… "No."

"Okay, but it's been two weeks. If this keeps up, the family will have to hold an intervention, and you know how Heath feels about 'people' and 'feelings.'"

Maybe Heath was onto something. At the moment, Jace wished he had considerably fewer feelings. Being numb would hurt a hell of a lot less.

"You can remind Heath that I'll be in the field next week, anyway, so no one here will have to deal with my feelings."

Reed sighed. "Maybe the change of scenery will help."

No, what would help would be Mia changing her mind. He knew she loved him, and he didn't think one fight should keep them apart. Couples compromised and found ways to move forward, didn't they? He glanced at his brother, thinking about Reed's acrimonious divorce. *Maybe not.*

"There's actually one other order of business, but I don't think you're going to like it. Someone's here to see you," Reed said cautiously.

"Who?" It couldn't be Mia because his brother would have told him that immediately. Yet, even knowing that, part of him still hoped Reed would say it was her.

"Shari Freeman."

"Mia's best friend."

Reed nodded, having heard about her from both Mia and Jace.

Once before, Jace had enlisted Shari's help at winning Mia's forgiveness. Was there any chance of doing so again? He rejected the idea almost instantly. Mia had said she wanted a partnership. Well, so did he. But that came from two people meeting in the middle, not one person constantly begging the pardon of the other.

"I had Carol show her to the Opal Room."

"Thanks." Jace walked there with the halting resignation of a condemned man. Shari coming all this way was not a good sign.

She was seated at the small conference table, her expression unreadable.

Instead of a polite greeting, he blurted, "How is she?"

"Better than you look. Marginally." Shari slid a small blue jewelry box across the surface of the table. "I told you not to hurt her."

"That wasn't my intention. I love her." He sank into the chair opposite her. "You know that."

Sympathy shone in her brown eyes. "Yeah, I do."

"Just between you and me, do you really think what I did was so wrong?"

Her eyes narrowed, the sympathy gone. "Ah, but it's not between you and me. It's *her* feelings you have to take into consideration, and you didn't. You treated her feelings like they were unimportant."

Not unimportant. But not more important than keeping her healthy and safe, keeping her clinic secure and her pregnancy stable.

"Anyway. The ring was too valuable to send in

the mail, and she wanted to make sure you received it in person."

But didn't want to bring it herself. He swallowed. "She and I were supposed to attend childbirth classes together."

"That's still the plan, as far as I know. You're still the baby's father, and Mia still wants you in your child's life. Just not in hers, not like that."

His throat tightened, and he couldn't find his voice.

Shari rolled her chair back and stood. "See you around," she said gently.

She'd reached the doorway when he asked, "Do you think there's any chance she'll change her mind?"

Regarding him over her shoulder, she sighed. "Do you think you'll change yours?"

Shari picked up the remote control and paused the movie they were watching—well, the movie *she* was watching. Mia hadn't heard any of the dialogue in the past ten minutes. "I've been patient," Shari said, "but now I'm starting to worry that your head will explode. Just ask about it already."

Mia considered feigning confusion, but that would be an insult to Shari's intelligence. "I don't want to."

"Yes, you do."

"I don't *want* to want to," she amended in a small voice. She wished she could curl up in a protective ball, but that wasn't feasible since her stomach currently was a protective ball.

"Oh, honey. I know." Shari rubbed Mia's shoulder. "If it helps, he looked rough."

"Yeah?"

"I mean, as rough as a really hot rich guy can."

"Hey!" Mia managed a bark of outraged laughter. "Whose side are you on, anyway?"

"Yours, obviously. Which I made clear to him. But being on your side means wanting to see you happy. He made you *very* happy."

Yes, he did. When he wasn't making major life decisions for her and ignoring her wishes "If Adwin decided to surprise you with, say, a new parking lot without talking to you or renovated your kitchen, what would you do?"

Shari's mouth thinned into a hard line.

"So you understand where I'm coming from," Mia said.

"Of course I do. But in the bozo's defense, you were lying in a hospital bed. I'm sure he felt powerless. He wasn't in his right mind, and he doesn't have a medical degree, so he latched on to something he actually could do."

"And now that I'm not in a hospital bed and he's had time to come around?" Mia prodded. "When you talked to him, did he say he was sorry? Did he seem like he regretted it?"

Shari opened her mouth, closed it, then punched the play button on the remote control.

Yeah. That's what I was afraid of. The movie resumed, and Mia did her best to watch it through watery eyes, her friend's silence confirming her fears. Nothing had changed.

Including how much she loved him. And how hard it was to fall asleep at night without telling him about her day. And how much she wanted to tell him about the tiny, bubbly sensation in her abdomen that might be indigestion but might also be their baby moving around, beginning to make his or her presence known.

This constant ache sucked.

The only thing worse than not being with him was the fear that if she forgave him, she'd be condoning this pattern of behavior for their future.

She could never be happy with a man who made her feel like a bystander in her own life—not even one who was charming, rich and unbelievably sexy.

"Oh my God, you're pregnant." Somehow, despite everything that had happened, Dylan sounded genuinely surprised.

Scowling, Mia pushed past her brother. "You knew that, dummy."

"I know. But this is the first time I've seen you that you're actually starting to look it." His tone turned awestruck. "I'm going to be an uncle again. I miss when Kimber was little and thought I was cool."

"You mean before she grew up enough to realize the truth?"

"Exactly." Dylan was slow to close the front door, peering outside as if hoping to see someone else.

Mia sighed in exasperation. "I told Dad it was just going to be me."

"Yeah, I know. But things could have changed."

"Nope. As I told our father and Leigh and now you, Jace and I aren't seeing each other anymore. Not romantically, anyway."

"That's a real shame, sis." Dylan looked genuinely saddened. "Ian and I like him."

"You mean you liked his net worth," she grumbled.

"Hey. We really bonded when we talked to him in his office. He's a decent guy."

"You have got to be kidding me!" Leigh marched into the foyer, wagging her finger at her brother-in-law. "What was our *one rule* for tonight? No discussing the *J* word. She's barely in the house, and you've already screwed up. Ian! Can you come have a word with your lunkhead brother?"

Ian poked his head around the corner. "What did you do, lunkhead? Hey, Mia. Wow, look at you. My kid sister's gonna be a mom," he said affectionately.

In a stage whisper, Leigh told her husband, "Dylan's already brought up the *J* word."

Ian stepped forward to smack his brother on the back of the head. "Dude. We had one rule."

Mia laughed in spite of herself. She loved her family, even if her brothers were a couple of lunkheads. They were overprotective and often misguided, but bighearted and fiercely loyal. *Is Jace really so different?* She could imagine either of her brothers doing what he'd done, if they'd had access to the same kind of funds.

Her brothers had overstepped many times in her life, yet she'd always forgiven them. Was she being too hard on Jace? The thought unsettled her.

"Are you going to hurl?" Dylan asked, taking a step back. "That's a thing with pregnant women, right? You look queasy."

She rolled her eyes. "I'm not queasy. Just second-guessing whether I should have stayed home tonight."

"And miss quality time with your favorite brother?" Dylan dropped an arm around her shoulders. "Don't be silly."

Allowing her brother to draw her into the kitchen, she pushed thoughts of Jace aside. Or at least, as far to the sides of her consciousness as she could manage, which was about two degrees left of dead center. It was sweet of Leigh to coach everyone not to bring up Jace, but it was ultimately pointless. He was with Mia either way.

"All done with the dinner crowd." Jace held out the checklist Fiona had given him. Most of the dogs at the shelter had the same food regimen, to make mealtimes easier, but some had special dietary or medical needs, so volunteers had to carefully read over instructions.

Fiona had been brushing a large rust-colored dog who would be very regal-looking once he was less tangled. She rose and took the clipboard from Jace. "Thanks. I'll put this in the office. You heading out?"

Was it pathetic that he stalled at the shelter most evenings because it kept him from getting home too soon? The hours after work and before bedtime were lonely and left way too much time to wonder what Mia was doing and whether he should call her. And then there was bedtime, which was excruciating. The nights Brooke was too fussy to sleep were turning out to be the easiest since he welcomed the distraction of either staying up with her or keeping Reed company.

"I don't have to go yet, if there's anything else you need," he offered. In addition to keeping him busy, volunteering made him feel somehow more connected to Mia, even though she had no idea he was here. He stayed away from the weekend adoption fairs, though, imagining her reaction if she felt cornered.

"If you want to finish brushing out Bear, I need to go through Chewy's training exercises." Her face twisted. "Such a sweet baby, but he's been returned to the shelter by two different families."

"That's awful." Jace knew how excited everyone was when a pet was adopted, hopeful they'd found their "fur-ever" home. The thought of one being rejected afterward was crushing. "Does that happen a lot?"

"More than we'd like. Chewy gets excited and jumps on people, not realizing his own size. He knocked the owner's kid down twice. He means well, but he wasn't trained as a puppy, and he has no impulse control. He acts on what he wants and leaves wreckage in his wake, most recently including a broken chair, an entire roast and a scraped-up six-year-old."

"So what happens now?" Jace was almost afraid to ask.

"We're working with him in the hopes that the third time will be the charm. It's harder to train dogs once they're adults, but not impossible. He's smart and loyal and affectionate. If I can just teach him to listen, he'll make the perfect family pet."

She handed Jace the dog brush and disappeared back to the kennels. A few minutes later, she emerged with a shaggy leashed dog, who was trying to bound into the courtyard. Fiona wouldn't let him drag her along, but it was obviously a struggle, given Chewy's size. Jace watched as she walked the dog around in a slow, deliberate circle, stopping whenever he tried to exuberantly pull ahead. Then she practiced setting a treat in front of him and making him wait before he gobbled it down.

It would never have occurred to Jace to compare himself to an untrained mutt, but was this how Mia saw him? Someone with no impulse control who didn't know how to listen? It was not a flattering view of himself. *You're projecting.* Not everything was about his relationship with Mia. Or lack thereof.

"Mr. Malone, is that you?" A young blonde

woman had entered the restricted section of the shelter, her face nearly obstructed by a box of blankets and toys.

"Amanda?"

The vet tech peeked around the edge of the box. "Yep, it's me. Just making a delivery. Sometimes when one of our patients crosses the rainbow bridge, the families give us the like-new items that still have a lot of use in them. So…"

"Here." He took the box from her. "I'll let Fiona know."

"Thanks! It's funny running into you because I had this whole plan worked out where I was going to stop by Shari's restaurant and sneakily get your number from her."

"Uh, my number?"

She nodded enthusiastically. "The clinic staff is throwing a surprise baby shower for Dr. Z. We wanted to invite you."

He froze, not sure how to respond. His first instinct was to say he would absolutely be there, followed a millisecond later by an equally strong instinct to say he would absolutely not be there because he didn't want to upset Mia. Ideally, he would ask her whether it was okay with her, but that would spoil the surprise. He really wished he could discuss it with her.

It was a barbed realization—that he would readily seek her opinion over something as simple as a party invite but that he'd conveniently disregarded it when meddling with her livelihood. He could have asked, could have pleaded his case without catching her off guard. He could have offered her a no-interest loan with a formal contract that respected her boundaries. He could have suggested some kind of silent partnership, even though he was quite sure that after what happened with Drew, she would have said no.

However, if she'd demurred, he could have used his tact and negotiating experience to persuade her that the financial assist was just him doing his part for the pregnancy. Honestly, she was doing all the hard stuff. He still believed that paying off her loan and giving her less to worry about for the remainder of the pregnancy had been the right thing to do, but she was a reasonable woman. So he probably could have convinced her of that, given enough time and compromise.

I handled this badly.

"Mr. Malone?"

"I'll definitely be there," he told Amanda. "Just give me the day and time."

"I know it looks bad because of the swelling," Mia consoled the tearful woman, "but the fact that he was bitten on the face is actually a good thing."

The panicked dog owner had come in with a husky mix who'd been bitten on the nose by a poisonous snake. Luckily, the fangs had hit bone. If the bite had been elsewhere, or it had been a smaller dog...

"He's already showing a little improvement with

the antihistamines, and we've given him antibiotics." Mia petted the dog between the ears. "You need to keep him under close observation, but it's probable the meds we're giving him now will be all he needs. The only additional course of treatment I could suggest is antivenom, but truthfully, it's very expensive. I hesitate to recommend it in a case like this, where we got lucky with the bite location."

The woman took a steadying breath. "Ranger is family. If his chances of recovery are better with the antivenom, it's worth the cost."

"I know what you mean," Mia said. "In your place, I would make the same decision." She recalled telling Jace that throwing money at problems didn't solve them. That was true. But being able to afford solutions was nothing to take for granted.

Jace had been in a unique position to help the woman he loved. Maybe part of her anger had stemmed from knowing she couldn't have done the same for him. She simply didn't have the resources, but the clinic took in donations all the time for local shelters and pet foster homes. It wasn't a failing to need help.

"Thanks again for staying open to see us." Ranger's owner sniffled, but she'd stopped crying. "It was so late in the day, and the nearest animal hospital would have taken me another twenty minutes. I was really scared."

Mia gave her a sympathetic smile. "I'm sure. Ranger's lucky to be so loved."

"Maybe." She hugged the dog. "But I'm just as lucky to have him."

Mia surreptitiously wiped at her own eyes. Crying on the job would be highly unprofessional.

Once she was finished with Ranger, it was time to lock up the clinic. She went into the lobby, where Amanda was doing some filing behind the counter.

"You didn't have to stay late," Mia told the tech. She hoped Amanda wasn't still feeling unnecessarily guilty about that day at the festival.

"It was no problem. Just finishing up a few tasks." Amanda stood. "But before I leave, there is one thing I wanted to get your opinion on."

"Sure." The way the woman had phrased it, Mia wasn't sure if this was animal-related or a personal issue.

She still wasn't sure a moment later, when Amanda walked away, toward one of the extra exam rooms that would be seeing a lot more use once Mia hired another vet. Dr. Kline had recommended a friend who'd recently moved from Nevada, and Mia had an interview set with the man next week.

"Amanda? Is something wrong with the equipment?" At least equipment could be replaced. If it was something structural, like a leak in the roof or—

"No, no. Nothing's wrong," Amanda was quick to assure her. "Just kind of odd. So I thought you should probably see it." She swung the door open.

"Surprise!" People spilled out of the room like it was a clown car, and Mia blinked, startled to see not only the staff members she'd thought had left for the day but also Shari and Leigh and Fiona from the local shelter. Some people were holding balloons; others had gift bags and wrapped boxes in their hands.

"What is going on?" Mia asked.

"Happy baby shower!" Amanda said, looking pleased with herself.

"You guys…" Mia was speechless. Her eyes welled up again. At least this time, there were no clients to witness it.

As Leigh hugged her, she whispered, "I'll still be throwing you a shower at a later date, but when Amanda called me, I thought you could use a cheery event. And extra diapers. You can never, never have too many diapers."

Mia laughed. "Noted."

Shari was next to hug her. "I wasn't sure Amanda would be able to keep the secret, but I guess she did, because you should see your face. I brought snacks, by the way."

"Of course you did," Mia said affectionately.

Everyone made their way to the lobby, where there was more room, and her staff began producing cups and plates and party favors from various hiding spots that amused and impressed her. A centerpiece that looked like a two-tiered cake, but was actually made of folded diapers, appeared from somewhere. Leigh caught Mia's eye and gave her a thumbs-up sign.

There was a knock on the locked glass door at the end of the lobby, and Mia tried to remember if she'd turned the sign to "Closed." As long as it wasn't another emergency on par with the snake-bite, one of her staff could turn whoever it was away. Amanda opened the door, and Mia expected to hear the woman say they weren't seeing any more patients today. Instead, the tech ushered in Jace Malone.

"Our other guest has arrived," Amanda said happily. "Better late than never."

Leigh and Shari exchanged glances, both of them stepping forward to flank Mia.

"J-Jace." God, he looked good. He hadn't shaved in a few days, and the faint beard covering his jaw was ruggedly sexy. Now that it was autumn, he was paler than when they'd met, making his blue eyes appear brighter than ever.

"Hi, everyone." He smiled, but his tone was wary. He held a large gift bag in front of him. "Is there a place I can put this?"

Amanda gestured to a folding table where Fletcher was arranging gifts and what looked like mildly embarrassing party games.

"I had no idea she invited him," Shari whispered. "I'm so sorry."

"Don't be." Mia took a deep breath. "We're starting birthing class soon, anyway. It's not like I can avoid him forever."

"Very mature of you," Leigh said approvingly. "But if you don't want to talk to him, we'll run interference."

Mia turned her head from side to side, grateful for

the moral support. "I love you both." And she loved Jace, despite her best efforts not to. She swallowed back a lump of emotion, trying her best to look composed as she walked toward him.

His gaze on her was so hungry that she shivered. He didn't have to tell her he'd missed her. She could feel it, a powerful, palpable draw that sent liquid heat through her veins. She half suspected that if she turned around, Shari and Leigh would be fanning themselves.

"Mia." He drank in the sight of her, as if cataloging every minute change since he'd seen her last, and it made her feel simultaneously self-conscious and powerful. "Can I talk to you alone for a moment?"

Gulp. If he got her alone, would they be able to stick to just talking? "Okay." She glanced over her shoulder, considering the very private exam rooms. "Um. How about we step outside? I could use some air."

Following him out onto the sidewalk, she shoved her hands in her pockets—not because she was cold, but because that made it easier for her to keep her hands to herself.

"First of all," he began, "I wasn't sure if you would want me here. Say the word, and I'll go. I've already put in an appearance and left a gift, so if you want to make my excuses to Amanda, tell her I had a work emergency or—"

"No, I'm glad you're here. I really am," she said slowly, feeling the truth of the words. She was nervous but not angry. If he'd walked into her clinic a couple of weeks ago, she might have resented it. It was different now. "I've been doing a lot of thinking."

"About me being a high-handed jackass?"

"Yes. At first. But recently, it's just been about how much I miss you."

He took a step closer. "I've missed you. We got our certification."

"Jace, that's fantastic! You must be so excited."

"You would think. But while we were popping champagne at the office, I kept staring at my phone, wanting to call you, wanting to share the victory with the person who knows how much it means to me. Just like I should have understood exactly what your clinic means to you." His tone was regretful.

Her heart leaped with hope. "Does that mean that if you had it to do over again…?"

"I'd wait until I had your permission."

"And if I didn't give it?"

He took another step closer, his voice low. "I'd convince you."

Her knees went weak. *Hell, yes, he would.*

"I've made myself a better person than I used to be," he told her, "but I'll never be perfect. I'm still going to act on instinct and do impulsive things without always remembering to check with others."

She recalled going to bed with a cowboy she'd just met. "Spontaneity isn't all bad."

"I'm relieved to hear you say that, because I recently adopted a large, badly behaved dog."

"Jace!"

"Don't worry. I know it's a lifetime commitment, and I'm ready for it. You're going to love him," he said fondly. "In addition to having Fiona out to the Triple Pine to work with him, I've enrolled Chewy and me in formal training classes. I believe in him, and by the time the baby is born, Chewy is going to be a model family pet. But even if he's not, I will love him anyway. Just like I hope you'll love me anyway. Despite my screwups."

Her heart melted. "I think I can do that," she murmured, "if you can love me despite my being stubborn and fiercely independent and occasionally irritable."

"You?" He looked skyward. "I hadn't noticed."

She laughingly jabbed him in the side, and the second they came into contact, her world shifted. Like those half-cast days when she didn't even realize it was cloudy until the sun suddenly broke through, nearly blinding in its brightness. She stared up at him, wondering if he'd felt it, too.

His eyes were ablaze with the same love and lust and light rushing through her. "You gotta quit looking at me like that, Doc. Or we're not going to make it back inside."

She closed the distance between them. "My car's parked in the back." Out of view from the street or the lobby.

When they rejoined the party ten minutes later, Shari did a double take at Mia's flushed cheeks and rumpled hair.

"And where have you been?" Shari asked.

"Just following your advice."

Shari raised an eyebrow.

Mia grinned. "Having fun."

* * * * *

PATERNITY PAYBACK & THE TEXAN'S SECRETS

PATERNITY PAYBACK
Texas Cattleman's Club: Diamonds and Dating Apps
by Sophia Singh Sasson

Journalist Willa St. Germaine's interview with her ex, rancher Jack Chowdhry, is the perfect chance to settle the score. But their "professional" reunion reveals untamed desires—and Willa's secret daughter...

THE TEXAN'S SECRETS
Texas Cattleman's Club: Diamonds and Dating Apps
by Barbara Dunlop

Computer hacker Emilia Scott just scored her best hack yet—matching herself with handsome, enigmatic "Nick" on the K!smet dating app. She doesn't know he's successful CEO Nico Law, a man with secrets as complex as her own...

MIAMI MARRIAGE PACT & OVERNIGHT INHERITANCE

MIAMI MARRIAGE PACT
Miami Famous • by Nadine Gonzalez

Gigi Garcia will do anything to save her struggling film production—even marry to ensure her inheritance. Restaurateur Myles Paris is the perfect fictional fiancé, if she can seduce the sexy, stubborn chef into agreeing with her plan.

OVERNIGHT INHERITANCE
Marriages and Mergers • by Rachel Bailey

An unexpected inheritance thrusts Australian schoolteacher Mae Dunstan into the world of single father Sebastian Newport, her business rival...and now her secret lover. Will sharing his New York City office, and his bed, end in heartache?

FALLING FOR THE ENEMY & STRANDED WITH THE RUNAWAY BRIDE

FALLING FOR THE ENEMY
The Gilbert Curse • by Katherine Garbera

After losing years to a coma, Rory Gilbert wants all life has to offer, including a steamy romp with Kitt Orr Palmer. Little does Rory know, she's the sister of Kitt's enemy—forcing him to choose between his desire for Rory and revenge.

STRANDED WITH THE RUNAWAY BRIDE
by Yvonne Lindsey

When wedding planner turned runaway bride Georgia O'Connor is stranded with loner Sawyer Roberts, they never expected attraction to turn into a heated affair. But when reality intrudes, can he let her go?

HARLEQUIN
PLUS

Try the best multimedia subscription service for romance readers like you!

Read, Watch and Play.

Experience the easiest way to get the romance content you crave.

Start your **FREE TRIAL** at
<u>www.harlequinplus.com/freetrial</u>.